Gibson Guitars

Ted McCarty's Golden Era
1948-1966

by Gil Hembree

ISBN-13: 978-1-4234-1813-9
ISBN-10: 1-4234-1813-1

Published by GH Books, Austin, TX
Publisher's Contact: Hal Leonard Corporation
                             7777 W. Bluemound Rd.
                             P.O. Box 13819
                             Milwaukee, WI 53213

Printed in the United States of America

First Edition

Library of Congress Cataloging-in-Publication Data applied for.

10 9 8 7 6 5 4 3 2 1

BISAC code: MUS023060
Subject category: Musical Instruments / Guitar

Front cover photos: The 1955 Gibson Les Paul Humbucking Pickup Test Guitar by Ward Meeker and Doug Yellow Bird, guitar courtesy Gil Hembree; Ted McCarty in 1953 from the GH archives. Back cover photos: Ted McCarty, Julius Bellson, Rollo Werner, John Huis, and PPG officials in 1953 from GH archives; buffers in 1953 from GH archives.

Cover Designs: Penny Meeker

To Wilbur Fuller and all of his
former co-workers at
Gibson's 225 Parsons Street,
Kalamazoo, Michigan

TABLE OF CONTENTS

SECTION III   The World's Greatest Guitar Factory

SECTION IV   The People of Gibson / People Make the Company

SECTION V The McCarty Legacy and Second Golden Era

FOREWORD

Growing up in southern New Jersey, I was very fortunate to meet and talk with Les Paul and Mary Ford during a show at the Steel Pier, in Atlantic City. I was just starting to learn how to play guitar, and was introduced to Les by my uncle, Bid Furness, who was a local musician and worked for several big bands. Backstage, he told me about his guitar and how the pickups worked, and how a gadget attached behind the bridge, called the "Paulverizer," allowed him to control his recording and playback system, which sat backstage. As a 13-year-old, this experience inspired me to work on guitars, study how pickups worked and how they were constructed.

I also remember going into Klayman's Music in Woodbury, New Jersey, in 1963, and playing a new Gibson Les Paul SG Custom. The neck felt so long, and it had three gold-plated humbucking pickups. It was the first time I heard a Les Paul through a Gibson GA-79 RVT stereo amplifier. The store gave me a new Gibson catalog with photos of instruments, amplifiers, and artist endorsers. I took the catalog to school with me every day, studying all the guitars and pickup configurations. I was excited to learn to play guitar, and for Christmas that year, I got my first amplifier and electric guitar. It was a Sears Silvertone Model 1482 and Jupiter 1423L guitar shaped like a Les Paul Standard with two pickups, black finish with gold metalflake, and white binding. A few years later, I bought a black '56 Les Paul Custom with a bridge P-90 pickup and Staple pickup in the neck position, from Hughes Music in Norwood, Ohio. It was called the "Fretless Wonder" because of the ebony fingerboard and low-profile frets.

In '68, I drove to the Gibson Factory at 225 Parsons Street in Kalamazoo, Michigan, and was given a tour of the factory. There, I met Walt Fuller, and made lists of each guitar and bass and noted which pickups and assemblies were used. The Gibson service department gave me schematics for each guitar and amplifier.

One of the employees suggested I visit Ted McCarty, who was then working with the Bigsby company. I met with Ted, who gave me an outline of Gibson models, including the years they were introduced. We also talked about the pickups designed by Fuller along with Seth Lover. I was especially interested in how pickups were wound, which wire gauges they used, magnet polarity, and how they were wired. Ted knew I lived in Cincinnati at the time, and he talked about his time at The University of Cincinnati.

I visited Gibson again in 1978 to undergo two weeks of repair-certification training. I again visited with the talented guitar builders and repairmen, and was put in charge of removing and repairing a neck from Les Paul's personal instrument, which needed a new fingerboard. I also worked with Deloris Shilts in the service center. She had long, thin fingers that could fit into the F hole of an ES-335, or hold potentiometers in place while the washer and hex nut were tightened. We removed parts from instruments that were broken or needed restoration and put them in a 55-gallon drum that was emptied into a dumpster at the end of the day. Hundreds of old parts were just thrown away, so I asked if I could get some of the parts for my research. Deloris had the service department send me five boxes! I was interested mostly in pickup parts, so Deloris was sure to include a box full of cream humbucker mounting rings from the 1950s, as well as truss rod covers, bobbins, and decals that were no longer used. I often display these items at guitar shows.

Also in 1978, I met Seth Lover. He lived in Garden Grove, California, at the time, and showed me his prototype pickups and drawings. I held the first humbucking pickup – the one used on the patent application, and his Staple P-90, Firebird, Deluxe Humbucking, EB-0 Bass, as well as various pickups he designed for Fender. We sat for hours talking about his designs and experiences with Gibson and Ted McCarty. In the late 1990s, I took Seth to the PRS Guitars booth at a National Association of Music Merchandisers (NAMM) show, where Ted was a guest. They hadn't seen each other in almost 33 years, and it was good to see them tell stories about their Gibson days.

The Gibson humbucking pickup is such an important design for its tone, and has been copied or used by just about every guitar company in the world. For me as a young guitar player, looking at early Gibson catalogs was truly an inspiration. Meeting Gibson artists, and asking questions about their playing style and technique, was always a thrill. Over the years, I've collected some great-playing and great-sounding instruments, and still enjoy meeting players and collectors at shows.

When Seth Lover passed away, his family gave me his original P.A.F. humbucking pickup, along with his other prototype and production Gibson pickups. Over the years, I've had a lot of help from pickup designers and manufacturers, and I love to share what I've learned. At the January, 2005, NAMM show in Los Angeles, my company had a display celebrating the 50th Anniversary of the humbucking pickup. It included various stages of humbucking pickup construction, with various components and bobbin combinations. The highlight of the display was a Gibson Les Paul Standard with some of the first humbucking pickups. The guitar was the hit of the show, and its present owner, Gil Hembree heard many stories about this historic guitar.

Over the years, I've kept in touch with several former Gibson employees who still live in Kalamazoo, including Deloris Shilts, Marv Lamb, J.P. Moats, Jim Deurloo, Rem Wall, and the folks at the Heritage Guitar Company, who continue to make quality instruments. 225 Parsons Street has such a great history, and I hope many more books will be written about it.

Ted McCarty had a vision, and made a tremendous impact on the guitar industry. During the McCarty era, Gibson made many models that today are the most sought-after instruments in the world. I'm glad to have grown up in an era of electric guitars and for the experience working with the folks in Kalamazoo. This book is long overdue, and Gil deserves our gratitude for gathering so much great Gibson history, and uncovering the stories from (and about!) Ted McCarty. In these pages you will learn much about this great period of modern-music history while you read stories that will make you feel as if you were there, working side by side with these great employees and master builders.

Seymour W. Duncan

"The Future of Music Depends Upon The Echo of The Past" – Seymour W. Duncan

INTRODUCTION

Dozens of books have been written about Les Paul, Leo Fender, Gibson Guitars, Fender Musical Instruments and dozens of lesser-known brands. But nothing has been written about Ted McCarty, save for a handful of magazine articles and a few paragraphs in a couple of books. But until this book, there has not been an in-depth look at the man or his employees, the factory where he oversaw the construction of legendary musical instruments, or his legacy.

McCarty distinguished himself while serving as C.E.O. of Gibson Guitars from 1948 to 1966. The period is acknowledged in the industry as the Golden Era of electric guitars and McCarty-era Gibson electrics are considered the finest fretted instruments ever made. Market acceptance suggests they eclipse any from Fender or Martin, and McCarty's best models even eclipse the two other prestigious Gibson eras – the Lloyd Loar era of the 1920s, and the 1930s, known for its flat-top guitars and flathead tone-ring banjos.

Gibson Guitars: Ted McCarty's Golden Era contains information obtained in conversations with McCarty, whose wish it was for it to be published as a complete book. Section I acts as the foundation, telling about McCarty's life from cradle to grave. Section II deals with the instruments that made McCarty an industry legend. No doubt they are the stars of the Golden Era, and thus have received most of the attention in prior books. But here you'll find more insider information about the instruments, and while other books have been dedicated to guitars built in the 1950s and early '60s, this book offers mostly new facts that concern "Golden Era" instruments. This is not intended to be a comprehensive review of vintage Gibson guitars, but will instead provide new details about McCarty's contributions.

Section III discusses the world's greatest guitar factory, the Gibson plant at 225 Parsons Street, and Section IV is about the people who worked in the Gibson factory. McCarty didn't want this book to stop with his biography; he also wanted it to lend a voice to the employees at Gibson. He said, "People make the company," and was loyal to them. While interviewing former employees, I found out as much as I could about the world's greatest guitar factory. I discovered where specific tasks were performed, and reconstructed the plant layout as it was in the 1950s. Section IV deals with the people who built the Golden Era instruments, and this book is dedicated to them.

Anecdotally, my Gibson experience began in 1962 when I purchased my first new guitar, a Gibson Southern Jumbo flat-top. I wanted a professional-grade folk guitar, but as a teen I could not afford to pay too much. In 1963, I went electric, buying a new Gibson SG Special with short-arm Maestro vibrato. The Cherry-finish SG was the only cool solidbody that fit my budget while providing name-brand prestige. I was a self-financed (in other words, poor!) young person who soon discovered first-hand that Gibson provided excellent value for the money.

As a college student attending American University in 1966, I took a job as counter salesman at Kitt's Music in Washington, D.C. Kitt's was the city's Gibson dealer, and hidden behind the counter were old Gibson catalogs that caught my attention. I read them, learned a lot, and soon purchased an old Gibson Les Paul model that I found in a newspaper classified ad. With that purchase, I discovered that I could buy a much better guitar for a lot less than the cost of a new one. This encouraged me to search for old guitars, and I began collecting guitars in '66.

While later raising a family in Michigan, I continued to look for old guitars in cities like Flint, Saginaw, Port Huron, and Kalamazoo. On November 21, 1998, I purchased a very interesting '55 Gibson Les Paul in Kalamazoo. Research led to a May 5, 1999, phone conversation with Mr. McCarty, who immediately said, "Call me Ted" as we struck up a friendship. During a second interview on August 12, he invited me and my wife, Jane, to Kalamazoo. On August 21, he introduced us to dozens of former employees and gave me permission to record our conversations about his life and career. McCarty confirmed that the '55 Les Paul goldtop I'd found in Kalamazoo was the first guitar to receive Gibson's humbucking pickups. He said it was the guitar used to test the new design. I taped further interviews with him on October 23, 1999, November 13, 1999, and May 6, 2000. During one of our talks, McCarty gave me another tape he'd recorded at his home in Maui, Hawaii, on November 6, 1995. These interviews contain a significant amount of never-before-published information. Following McCarty's suggestion, this book also contains a significant amount of new information taken from conversations with the employees who worked alongside McCarty at Gibson.

During my research, I often visited Kalamazoo. It was only a couple of hours away from Flint, Michigan, my home at the time. Almost every visit included a trip to 225 Parsons Street, home of Gibson Guitars from 1917 to 1984. After 30 years of walking through equally ancient General Motors Corporation plants as Corporate Audit Supervisor, I gained a great deal of insight and respect for the old facilities. While touring Parsons Street, my goal was to reconstruct the mid-'50s plant layout. With the help of people who worked there in the 1940s, '50s, and '60s, I was able to do that!

Section V deals with Ted McCarty's legacy, which extends beyond Gibson's "Golden Age" and includes more than just the 1959 Gibson Les Paul Standard, '58 Gibson ES-335, '64 Gibson SG Standard, and the rest of the McCarty "Golden Era" instruments.

Gibson Guitars: Ted McCarty's Golden Era is a compilation of new information about Gibson's Ted McCarty era, its employees, its manufacturing facilities, its products, and its influences.

Wilbur Fuller and Jane Hembree prepare for an October 1, 2001 tour of 225 Parsons Street

The Ted McCarty Biography

The Gibson Story: 1894-1948

There would be no need for a book on Ted McCarty had it not been for the Gibson Guitar Company. When McCarty became General Manager and CEO of Gibson in 1948, he inherited a great guitar-building tradition. He knew Gibson was a great name.

Orville Gibson founded the company in the mid 1890s in Kalamazoo, Michigan, as a one-man workshop dedicated to new-instrument design and manufacture. His everlasting contribution to lutherie was the development of a graduated carved-top body style. This revolutionary design represented a radical change and was suited for use on both guitar and mandolin. And it was particularly well-timed.

The late 1800s saw a boom in interest in the mandolin, and players found the Gibson archtop/flat-back mandolin had more volume, and more musical sensitivity and articulation than the standard Italian-style bowlback mandos. When Orville went into business, co-incidentally, mandolin bands toured the country and the mandolin took the spotlight away from other stringed instruments. As the word spread about Gibson mandolins, professional players converted to the louder, more pronounced-sounding Gibson instrument.

Orville was an old-fashioned craftsman and perfectionist. He used no power tools, instead employing hammer, saw, chisel, gouge, file, screwdriver, etc. He also used varnish, like 16th-century violin makers, which itself was an art form. By 1897, his mandolins were recognized by music dealers and professional musicians, but had not yet obtained a national reputation. Nonetheless, music teachers and dealers could easily sell every Gibson mandolin they obtained. There was tremendous demand, but precious little supply.

1902 was arguably the most important year in the history of the Gibson Company. It went from sole proprietorship to a corporate format, and the key figure at the time was Lewis A. Williams, a music teacher and dealer from New York who found he could sell every Gibson mandolin they could ship to him. But obtaining them was a problem. So he journeyed from New York to Kalamazoo, with the intention of ordering as many mandolins as he could. While he was unsuccessful in obtaining a large order from Orville, he also teamed up with four other Kalamazoo businessmen and bought the Gibson Company.

Williams' ally was Sylvo Reams, who was also in the music business and realized the growing power of the Gibson name. The three other partners – John W. Adams, Samuel A. Van Horn, and Leroy Hornbeck – were all lawyers, businessmen, and friends of Reams.

The Gibson Mandolin-Guitar Manufacturing Company, Ltd. was created October 10, 1902, and a division of labor was immediately put into place. The music men, Reams and Williams, were given guitar-related assignments. Reams, with the moral support of his brothers (who were also in the music business), would run the factory as corporate secretary and General Manager. Williams would be the corporate Sales Manager. Adams, a prominent citizen and judge, would be President. Van Horn, the lawyer and businessman, would be Treasurer. Hornbeck, the lawyer, would be a Director. The Gibson Company incorporated in 1904, and issued stock to raise money for expansion. In '06, more stock was issued for expansion, and the corporation became the Gibson Mandolin-Guitar Company.

On the factory floor, Gibson of the early 1900s was nothing like a modern corporation. Everything was done by hand. As employees were hired to do the work that had previously been done by Orville, they were given specific instruction and supervision. The task of passing Orville's skill sets on to employees was assigned to Reams, who had a mission to nurture and improve Orville's ideas. Under Reams, playing actions were made easier, necks were streamlined to facilitate fingering, raw material quality was improved, and new finishes replaced the Gibson violin varnish.

The upgrades annoyed Orville, and seven months after the partners organized, Orville's contribution to the company became limited. His plight – inventing and building, but being unable to deliver economic quantities and thus being taken over – was normal in business. Who remembers David Buick or Ransom Olds?

Reams is probably the second-most-important figure in Gibson history, behind Orville. He established the factory assembly methods, initially with the help of Orville. Plus, he benefited from the experience of his two brothers; Arthur owned the brothers' music store in Kalamazoo and provided market feedback about Gibson products, while Andrew Jay was a professional musician who tested product. Sylvo and his four partners were committed to keeping quality in the Gibson name.

When asked to become General Manager of the company in 1948, Ted McCarty knew Gibson was one of the most prestigious names in the music industry. He knew it was a corporation, and he knew its leaders. McCarty owed a debt of thanks to Lewis Williams and Sylvo Reams, and their partners, who were enlightened enough to know that Gibson products could prosper if they continued to be made by hand, with quality materials, under the financial security of a corporation. If not for Williams and Reams, Gibson would not have been what it was when McCarty arrived.

Although Gibson had good years and not-so-good years, overall it prospered from 1902 through '48. As a successful company, it occasionally fell into the corporate trap of being too conservative, often being late to the market, as when mandolins lost favor and were replaced by mandolin-like tenor banjos. But in true corporate fashion, it bounced back by introducing what would become the world's most valuable banjo model, the 1930s Master-tone.

When he took over, McCarty inherited a corporation that had a history of strong operational and financial management, good work rules, loyal employees, and a tradition of passing along the building techniques first used by Orville. Decade after decade, the secret to Gibson's success was on the factory floor, where old-timers taught new hires how a job should be done and instilled a sense of pride in the motto, "If you build it, your name is on it and your reputation is on the line with every instrument."

This was the strength of the Gibson system; its employees weren't born great woodworkers, but they learned to be great woodworkers under a system passed down from generation to generation.

Theodore Milson McCarty circa 1912

Ted McCarty: The School Years, 1909-1928

Born October 10, 1909, Theodore Milson McCarty was born in Somerset, Kentucky, to Raymond Andrew McCarty and Jenny Milson Carr McCarty. Ted was the couple's second child, his brother Raymond, Jr., was born two years earlier. Raymond, Sr. had a penchant for changing jobs, so the family frequently had to move from one house to another.

When Ted was three years old, his mother died suddenly and Ray, Jr. was taken in by his grandmother, Stella McManama McCarty, while Ted went to live with his grandmother's sister, Nora McManama Wrampelmeier, and her husband, Frederick, in Cincinnati. The Wrampelmeiers had no children of their own, and accepted Ted like a son. Ted and

Fred 'Pop' Wrampelmeier with Ted

his great uncle developed a very close relationship. Frederick, who Ted affectionately called "Pop," was a civil engineer. The family was well-off, but not wealthy. "Pop" was recognized within his trade for being lead engineer on the Southern Bridge project for Cincinnati Southern Railroad over the Kentucky River, in addition to building 27 railroad tunnels for the railroad's 350 miles from Cincinnati to Chattanooga, Tennessee.

In 1915, Pop, Nora, and Ted moved from their Cincinnati apartment to a newly constructed home at 2616 Madison Road, in Hyde Park.

"It was a nice suburb with lots of other families around. It was built in what had once been a big orchard," Ted recalls. "As boys, we played in the cherry trees and peach trees. I had a lot of fun growing up."

Pop and Nora demonstrated their affluence by being the first in their family to purchase an automobile, a 1915 Ford touring car. Like almost everyone of the age, Pop had no idea how to drive the car when he went to pick it up, but after a quick introduction he was off and running. Pop, the ever-vigilant engineer, had a battery compartment and electric starter put on the car, something relatively unheard of at the time.

When Ted was five years old, Nora felt he was too delicate in size and health to start school, so he was not enrolled. The next year, though, she introduced him to the Hyde Park Public School kindergarten teacher. "She took me off and talked to me for a little bit and came back and told my aunt, 'This boy is too advanced for kindergarten, put him in the first grade,'" said Ted. "So that's how I happened to skip kindergarten. It's been a family joke for years."

The Hyde Park public school system was strong, and all 25 of Ted's first-grade class-mates could read by the end of the school year. In second grade, Ted demonstrated an interest in leadership and scholarship when he and a classmate named Jane started a school newspaper, *The Hyde Park Herald*. One day in third grade, his teacher told her class that the student who achieved the most perfect scores on their papers would win a box of candy at the end of the school year. "I saved all of my papers with 100s on them," Ted said. "And I had the most, which was a great deal to me because we were not wealthy people."

In the sixth grade, Ted joined a school athletic club called The Midgets, which allowed only boys who weighed less than 80 pounds. In eighth grade, he became interested in crystal radios.

"My brother, my friends, and I all made crystal sets," he said. "We would listen to KDKA in Pittsburgh, and WLW in Cincinnati."

Ted mixed his interest in crystal radios with his interest in baseball. Unfortunately, when designing and building a micro-mini crystal set, he cut his finger severely, putting an end to his early baseball aspirations.

Withrow High School was only three years old when Ted entered ninth grade in 1924. The school, at 2488 Madison Road, was about five blocks from his home, so he could easily walk back and forth, which gave him the opportunity to participate in many extracurricular activities. He took the high school's college career enrollment path in the industrial section, which included a specialization in mechanical drawing. He pursued mechanical drawing throughout high school, earning good grades, and was a member of the tumbling team.

A number of Ted's friends were from wealthier families, and many attended exclusive summer camps in Maine. Ted, meanwhile, enrolled in a military-training summer camp in Kentucky, where he enjoyed training in marching and gunmanship. One evening, he and some other campers were hanging out after chow, when a military officer showed them a set of boxing gloves and asked if anyone would like to have some fun. Ted had sparred with his older brother for years, so he put on the gloves and started to spar with another camper. When the other camper got mad and started swinging wildly, the Captain yelled, "Take the gloves off!" Seeing that he had some ability, the Captain invited Ted to take boxing lessons from a professional boxer at the camp.

In high school, Ted tried out for a role in a play being presented by the school's Acting Club. The director was pleased, and one teacher asked Ted if he was interested in an acting career. But the unintended consequence from acting came in his senior year when Ted met an attractive blue-eyed blond named Francis, who also had a part in the play. They became boyfriend and girlfriend.

In celebration of his high school graduation in 1928, Ted's family (who vacationed regularly beginning when he was eight years old) traveled to Key West, Florida, and rented a boat for a two-week trip to Havana, Cuba. Ted later went to college, but Francis, whose father had died when she was a child and was raised by her mother, did not have the means to attend college. So, Ted and Francis drifted apart.

"Good things happen to good people." It could certainly be said of Ted McCarty's life.

During his school years, he excelled academically, athletically, artistically, and socially. He wasn't a musician – his introduction to music came from hiring into the nation's greatest music-industry business, Wurlitzer, where he learned about instruments, and the guitar business.

As a child, he was happy, intelligent, and industrious. He was likeable and talented, interested in sports, interested in academics, and had a penchant for art. But he wasn't particularly musical, and was somewhat co-dependent on friends and family. McCarty was also a natural leader. And while his ancestors had their share of financial ups and downs, they were relatively well-off. His family tree included William Arnold, who served as a Captain during the Revolutionary War. Ted's grandfather was a successful businessman who had once owned a mansion in Somerset, Kentucky, but lost his fortune during an economic depression in 1893.

Ted McCarty: The University of Cincinnati, 1928-1933

On September 17, 1928, Ted enrolled as a freshman in the co-op engineering program of the University of Cincinnati, which meant he attended school year-round, one month in school, then one month on an assigned job, then back to school, etc. Pop paid for Ted's basic tuition, but Ted covered all other college expenses by working a co-op job.

Leslie J. Schwallie was the Assistant Professor of Coordination in the College of Engineering and Commerce. One day early on, Schwallie called Ted out of chemistry class to tell him about his first co-op assignment, in the warehouse at Gibson Greeting Card Company. The job paid $16 a week for 5½ days of work. Ted wasn't impressed with the pay, and told Schwallie, "No, thank you," explaining that he clerked for Kroger Grocery during his summers in high school, and made $22 per week. Kroger also offered Ted a job after high school with the intention of making him a store manager. Ted turned down Kroger's offer so he could attend college, and simply could not see himself going back to work for $16 a week.

Ted returned to chemistry class, but within 15 minutes was called back to Schwallie's office, where he was promptly advised on the facts of life and that he would take the job if he intended to graduate from the University. Ted had never been talked to in such a manner, and immediately decided he better take the job!

Part of the co-op program included writing a complete survey of the month's work, including what the company did and a job description, all in engineering style. The coordinator would grade the report and send it to the English department for another grading.

The greeting card business was seasonal, so Ted's co-op job didn't last long and Schwallie assigned Ted to the college bookstore, where he would serve as a clerk. Ted had worked in retail since he was 15, so the bookstore seemed to be a perfect match. But Ted was disappointed because he'd hoped to get an engineering job. Schwallie explained to Ted that he

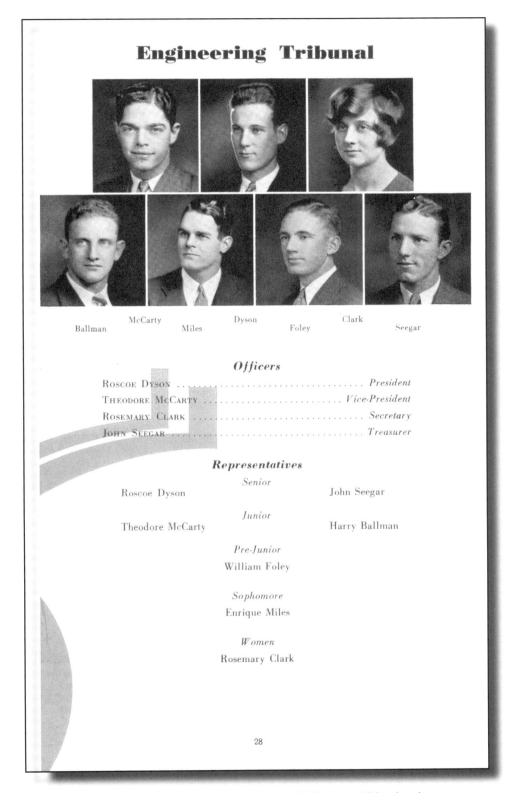

Engineering Tribunal

Ballman   McCarty   Miles   Dyson   Foley   Clark   Seegar

Officers

ROSCOE DYSON . . . . *President*
THEODORE McCARTY . . . . *Vice-President*
ROSEMARY CLARK . . . . *Secretary*
JOHN SEEGAR . . . . *Treasurer*

Representatives

Senior
Roscoe Dyson   John Seegar

Junior
Theodore McCarty   Harry Ballman

Pre-Junior
William Foley

Sophomore
Enrique Miles

Women
Rosemary Clark

28

The 1932 Cincinnatian - University of Cincinnati Yearbook

7

Ted McCarty (left) learned to box at military summer camp, then went on to become a college boxing champion at the University of Cincinnati. Here he is shown with his instuctor.

was in the Commercial Engineering section, which was a five-year course that included three years of basic business engineering and two years of business administration. From the business administration standpoint, the University thought the job was perfect, plus it paid a little more than the warehouse job.

Ted argued a bit, but knew all too well that the stock market had crashed and a job was hard to come by. Everybody seemed poor in Ted's eyes, so he planned to do everything he could to protect the job. He reported to work as a clerk, but soon advanced to bookkeeper, which meant he operated the Burroughs bookkeeping machine. The college bookstore became Ted's co-op home. When the manager of the store graduated, Ted was given the job. He went to class in the morning and ran the bookstore in the afternoon. By this time, there were three bookstores – a main store, one in Engineering, and one in Liberal Arts. Ted supervised four employees, and earned additional income grading papers for night classes. A professor hired him for $.20 an hour, and he treasured the extra income, especially in a time when every nickel counted!

Ted joined the Alpha Tau Omega social fraternity and as an upperclassman was elected Worthy Master (fraternity president) of the Ohio Delta Lambda ATO Chapter, a post he held for three terms. In its May '33 edition, the ATO magazine *The Palms* recognized Ted's contribution as three-term Worthy Master, which had never been done before. The ATO house was a top-rated academic house on campus, and during Ted McCarty's tenure the Pan-Hellenic association awarded ATO with the scholarship award for three consecutive terms. Pan-Hell also ranked it fifth among all campus organizations.

Ted also served as Chapter President of the Engineering Tribunal, a student governance body. If an engineering student was accused of cheating, the case went before the Engineering Tribunal, whose decisions could trump the University. Thus, the Tribunal was

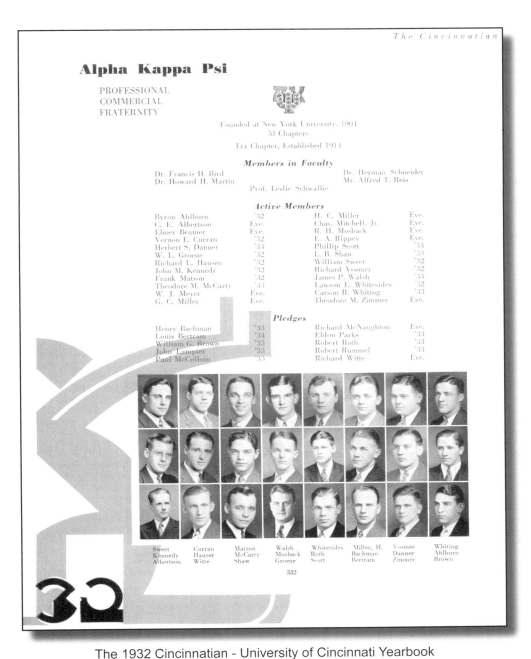

The Cincinnatian

Alpha Kappa Psi

PROFESSIONAL
COMMERCIAL
FRATERNITY

Founded at New York University, 1904
51 Chapters
Eta Chapter, Established 1914

Members in Faculty

Dr. Francis H. Bird   Dr. Herman Schneider
Dr. Howard H. Martin   Mr. Alfred T. Reis
                Prof. Leslie Schwallie

Active Members

Byron Ahlburn	'32	H. C. Miller	Eve.
C. E. Albertson	Eve.	Chas. Mitchell, Jr.	Eve.
Elmer Beamer	Eve.	R. H. Mosback	Eve.
Vernon E. Curran	'32	E. A. Rippey	Eve.
Herbert S. Danner	'33	Phillip Scott	'33
W. L. Groene	'32	L. B. Shaw	'33
Richard L. Hausen	'32	William Sweet	'32
John M. Kennedy	'32	Richard Vosmer	'32
Frank Matson	'32	James P. Walsh	'33
Theodore M. McCarty	'33	Lawson E. Whitesides	'32
W. J. Meyer	Eve.	Carson R. Whiting	'33
G. C. Miller	Eve.	Theodore M. Zimmer	Eve.

Pledges

Henry Bachman	'33	Richard McNaughton	Eve.
Louis Bertram	'34	Eldon Parks	'33
William G. Brown	'33	Robert Roth	'33
John Lampier	'33	Robert Rummel	'33
Paul McCollum	'33	Richard Witte	Eve.

Sweet   Curran   Matson   Walsh   Whitesides   Miller, H.   Vosmer   Whiting
Kennedy   Hauser   McCarty   Mosback   Roth   Bachman   Danner   Ahlburn
Albertson   Witte   Shaw   Groene   Scott   Bertram   Zimmer   Brown

332

The 1932 Cincinnatian - University of Cincinnati Yearbook

very important to student life.

In addition to being a leader in the University's engineering community, Ted also was a member of Alpha Kappa Psi, a professional business fraternity. Ted pledged AKP on December 22, 1930, and was initiated on January 31, 1931.

Ted also was a member of the Omicron Delta Kappa (ODK), a highly exclusive fraternity that recognized rare individuals who demonstrated the highest level of efficiency. Ted called it, "A dean's list," but it was much more; ODK was founded in 1914 at Washington and Lee University and established at the University of Cincinnati in '31. Ted was initiated in '32. Ted was very proud of his membership in Omicron Delta Kappa.

He also was a member of one of the University's two Reserve Officer Training Corps (ROTC) groups. The University ROTC system required athletic endeavor, and Ted weighed 126 pounds! So, he got back into something he knew – boxing. He joined the boxing club during his junior year and began training in the featherweight division. He made many friends and won five matches to become Featherweight Champion of the University. The athletic department honored Ted with an artistic caricature labeled "Ted McCarty Champ." With that success, Ted decided to rest on his laurels. He did not box during his senior year, much to the relief of his family.

Prior to his June, 1933, graduation from the University, the ATO fraternity wrote of Ted in its April edition, "At this time of year, pleasure and sorrow intermingle as we turn our attention to our seniors. In June, we will lose Ted McCarty, our Worthy Master for three terms. Ted is a dynamic little fellow; handsome, energetic, and likeable; with the making of a good politician. For several years, he has been the hub of U.C. politics. When Ted takes his degree of commercial engineer, he may look back on a successful course interspersed with varied activities which range from junior prom chairman and Omicron Delta Kappa to featherweight boxing champion. It will take a good man to fill his place."

On June 10, 1933, Ted graduated from the University of Cincinnati with a degree in Commercial Engineering.

Ted McCarty 4 and Elinor Bauer

Upon graduation, Ted was made Graduate Manager of the bookstores, put under contract, and managed 24 employees. One contract stipulation stated that 'the manager should not get married.' Marriage meant loss of the job. Ted had no intention of getting married, so this suited him fine. In 1935, he was offered a new contract, this time without the marriage clause. The bookstore was doing well in '35, and a new one was being planned.

While in college, Ted seldom saw his high school sweetheart, Francis, but he did meet other girls, including Elinor Bauer. When they met at a dance, Elinor was seven years Ted's junior and attractive to Ted in every way. They eventually became friends as the years went along, and after finishing high school, Elinor attended the University. Ted, of course, had a good job and the two married on Flag Day, Friday, June 14, 1935. Ted was 27 and Elinor turned 20 the day after their wedding.

Ted McCarty: Wurlitzer, 1936-'47

While things were going well at the bookstores, Ted did not see a long-term future for him working as district manager of the bookstores. He wanted to get away from academics and pursue a career as an engineer. He happened upon an advertisement announcing a job opening at Cincinnati's renowned Wurlitzer Company. He went to Wurlitzer and talked with Mr. Hillsman, company Treasurer and the man responsible for hiring. While Ted really wanted an engineering job, it was the business aspect of his commercial engineering degree that landed him the job. When Hillsman discovered that Ted was the district manager for the University bookstores, he hired him. Wurlitzer matched the bookstore's salary, so for Ted it was more about upward potential than a pay increase, and he joined Wurlitzer in January, 1936.

Ted expected to be assigned to the accounting department, but Hillsman wanted him to enter the company's new management training program. Wurlitzer needed managers, and Ted would be one of the first to enter the new program.

Regardless of what he was told in the interview, Wurlitzer had a problem "sequencing" him, perhaps wanting to evaluate him. He ended up at the company's Cincinnati store, writing dunning letters to people who had not paid their bills. His first job was talking into a dictation machine. Later, in the Wurlitzer accounting department, he was assigned to audit and coordinate insurance records for all 21 retail stores. This was perfect for Ted, because in college he had studied the mathematics of accounting and insurance.

After about six months, Ted was transferred to Rochester, New York, to work as an assistant manager, making him one of the youngest employees to hold this title. Elinor was expecting their first child, had never been away from her home town, and was very upset about the move. But she told Ted, "We're married, and I will go." Still, they moved, and their first child, Theodore Frederick McCarty, was born March 6, 1937, in Rochester.

Rochester, like all Wurlitzer stores, was focused on teaching. They had studios, and people would come into the store, but Wurlitzer also had salesmen on the streets, going to homes, trying to sell accordions. Piano-accordions were a big business in the late 1930s. Wurlitzer made its own accordions in its DeKalb, Illinois, piano factory. In '39, it sold more accordions than any instrument except pianos.

As part of the management training, Ted had to learn the system. The store had a man in charge of teachers, and salesmen offered the "55-Lesson Plan" for $6.25 per lesson. The student started out with a small bass accordion for $6.25, then paid $6.25 for 55 weeks. Most of the students were children, and after a handful of lessons, students learned to play several pieces on the 12 bass accordion, then move to a more advanced piece that was impossible to play because there weren't enough keys on the instrument. The teacher would say, "Oh, you have a 12 bass, don't you? I'll tell you what. You have your mother and father come to your next lesson, and we'll see whether you can go any further than the 12 bass."

So the parents would come down. The instructor had phonograph records in his office to play while "testing" the parents on their musicality. Then they'd have the child come in, and the youngster would obviously play better than the parent. The instructor would say, "I don't have anything to do with sales, but Mr. So and So probably would like to talk with

A 1941 photo of the McCarty family (Ted, Sue, Ted, and Elly) in Cincinnati

you. Maybe he could show you some bigger accordions."

So the teacher would introduce the parents to the salesman and tell the salesman how well the child was doing on the accordion. The salesman would show the family a 120 bass accordion and explain how they allowed credit in trade equal to the amount paid for the 12 bass. In most cases, customers would buy the bigger instrument. Keep in mind, this was during the depression, and the large 120 bass cost $800. The Wurlitzer sales system worked very well. And the Rochester area was replete with Holland-Dutch descendant farmers whose farms were also doing well.

The Wurlitzer sales system also included C-melody saxophone, which, like the 12 bass accordion, was very limited and couldn't readily play along with other instruments except to accompany a piano. The salesmen would push C-melody saxes along with the 55-Lesson Plan. As the student advanced, a larger, more standard saxophone was required, so again the student and parents had to trade up to the more expensive instrument. As the kid progressed, it was time for a clarinet, which sold for $250 during the Depression! But everything was sold on a time-payment plan that was extended with each purchase, and each customer was happy as a lark as they left for home.

Ted's hours were long. The store was open until 9 p.m. and Ted had to stay until closing. As store credit manager, he would be introduced to the customer by the salesmen, and would work out the payment plan. One of Wurlitzer's secrets was to stretch the payments over long periods, reducing the customer's monthly payment, but increasing the store's interest (and overall) income.

Eventually, Ted moved from Assistant Store Manager to Sales Manager. He learned first-hand the art of selling instruments. Violins and guitars were not sold under 55-Lesson Plan and were not limited, like the 12 bass and C saxophone. Violins came in $1/4$, $1/2$, $3/4$, and full-size, but there wasn't enough demand in Rochester to develop a sales strategy. The guitar was not a limited instrument; you could play any guitar forever, so the 55-Lesson Plan was not suitable for the guitar. Wurlitzer's selling guitars provided Ted's introduction to the retail aspect of the guitar business.

Rochester was a full-line music store with plenty of walk-in traffic that included professional musicians. Business was good from 1937 to '39, the years Ted was there.

After 2½ years, though, Hillsman called and asked Ted to move back to Cincinnati. Ted called Elinor, asking, "How soon can you be ready to move back to Cincinnati?" Elinor, lonely for her family exclaimed, "How soon can you get a truck here!" So Ted and Elinor got a truck, and on Saturday they packed their belongings. Elinor and the baby hopped on a train to Cinci. Ted, with Elinor's parents and the family dog, drove back. The McCartys stayed with the Bauers until they could secure their own home.

Ted reported to work on Monday, as he had promised, and discovered he was being put in charge of accounting for all 21 retail stores, including inventory control. As the Retail Store Accounting Manager, he reported to the Assistant Treasurer, and was assigned to standardize all systems and write the company's accounting practice and procedures manual (AP&P). There were about 100 people in the accounting department, with a good portion of them in accounts payable, accounts receivable & credit, the cost department, and the allied department. There were two top managers – Ted and the General Credit Manager.

Besides writing the AP&P, Ted was given many other catch-all assignments. For example, the Assistant Treasurer asked Ted to analyze the 55-Lesson Plan and come up with a new 20-Lesson Plan. Ted wrote a proposal and gave it the AT, who looked at it, tore it up, threw it in the trash, and told Ted, "You can do better."

Ted did two more before the AT was satisfied. Still, though, things were going well. Ted was still a relatively young up and comer. His family was happy to be back home, and Ted and Elinor's second child, Susan, was born March 14, 1940.

Ted's reward for the good work was *more* work. This time, as General Credit Manager. Because so much of the Wurlitzer system revolved around the 55-Lesson Plan, which was based on payments over time. Credit information was kept on ledger cards, and the credit department was a large and critical part of the operation.

The position presented Ted with a new challenge. The outgoing credit manager was fired because he had a drinking problem, so the joke around the office was, "Do you drink, or do you work for Wurlitzer?" You never did both! Wurlitzer was the biggest music retailer of the day, and bosses knew that good internal control meant sober employees, so drinking, even casually after hours, was not acceptable. There were also rumors that the credit manager was guilty of what would now be called sexual harassment issues, and such conduct was also taboo at Wurlitzer.

The firing of the Credit Manager left a hole that needed to be filled. Ted was the only person in administrative headquarters that had strong credit experience. As assistant manager in Rochester, he doubled as store credit manager and accountant. Credit managers were required to have repossessions below a certain level, while maintaining a level of sales on the company credit plan. One thing Ted liked about the credit manager's job was that he could earn a $25-per-month bonus, plus points towards a diamond ring, if he made his numbers each month. Ted did so each month, and was so successful the company had to keep increasing the size of the diamond.

Taking on the General Credit Manager's job was something different. Ted, in effect, had to work two huge jobs. Wurlitzer named him interim General Credit Manager, which required that Ted visit all 21 of the retail stores on a regular basis – three stores each week. He would take the midnight train Sunday evening, and return home the following Saturday. A typical week might entail jumping on the train to Buffalo, then mid-week to Cleveland, and finishing the week in Detroit.

The job was very lonely. The GCM was not allowed to fraternize with store employees. And not only was it tiring, but it created problems at home. Elinor had always told Ted, "I don't want to get married to a husband who's not there." Suddenly, Ted was conflicted. Elinor did not like it, but she put up with it and Ted filled the position for about one year.

Ted's friend and mentor, Hillsman, tried to talk Ted into taking the job permanently, but Ted told him, "It's not the type of thing I want to do." So Hillman promised to protect Ted, who made plans to leave Wurlitzer if something didn't give. Then, to make matters worse, Hillsman left Wurlitzer to work in a bank in Detroit.

With the departure of Hillsman, Wurlitzer President R.C. Rolfing called Ted into his office. He said, "Ted, I'm disappointed. I've been expecting you to walk in that door and ask for that General Credit Manager job, because you are doing a fine job!" Ted replied, "Well, I've been doing two jobs and not getting any more money." Rolfing replied, "You didn't ask for more money." But Ted knew Rolfing was aware he didn't want the General Credit Manager job.

Nonetheless, Rolfing told Ted to be standing at the door the next time a promotion became available. He had hired a new General Credit Manager and told Ted, "For the next six months, I want you to keep doing what you're doing, *and* I want you to introduce the new man to every store, and explain the system."

Ted recalled, "I spent six months traveling with the new man. By this time, Elinor was getting fed up with Wurlitzer." Finally, Ted went back to managing the accounting department, and the treasurer position was vacant. Would it be Ted's? It was a Division Head assignment, which answered only to the President. Ted wanted the job. But the Treasurer position was not to be Ted's.

Rolfing had another idea. He'd discovered that each store manager was handling insurance policies, and from store to store, coverage wasn't consistent. Rolfing called Ted into his office and asked him, "Ted, what do you know about insurance?"

"Well, I did my post-graduate work on the mathematics of insurance," Ted replied. "When I started here, I set up all the accounting records and insurance records for all the 21 stores."

Rolfing then said, "What do you know about real estate?" When Ted replied, "I don't know anything about real estate," Rolfing said, "Good! You're the man I'm looking for."

Ted's new assignment was Division Head of Real Estate, Insurance, and Plant Accounting. Within that discipline, he was responsible for the two large manufacturing facilities, the piano factory in Illinois, the Wurlitzer juke box factory in North Tonawanda, New York, and all 21 retail stores. He was given the office formerly occupied by Hillsman, and the best secretary at Wurlitzer.

Ted became friendly with Rudolph Wurlitzer, who was Chairman of the Board. Wurlitzer took a liking to Ted and frequently visited his office. Over lunch on day, Wurlitzer told Ted about the old days of Wurlitzer, how the company was made, and all of the interesting business that was otherwise kept quiet.

The Wurlitzer company was built on one clarinet. Rudolph Wurlitzer's father emigrated from Germany and took a job in a Cincinnati bank. The young man was frugal, but managed to purchase a clarinet from Germany. When he got the invoice, he though that he could triple his money if he sold it to a Cincinnati music store. But when Wurlitzer quoted a price the store owner, he shouted, "Get out!"

Wurlitzer went home and sat down to re-figure the price – he was only 21 years old at the time and was not very familiar with the money system. He recalculated, and this time multiplied the cost by five, then he went back to see the man to quoted him his new price. The fellow said, "I'll buy it, can you get me any more?" Mr. Wurlitzer said, "I'll try; I'll talk with my people in Germany."

That was the beginning of the U.S.A. Wurlitzer Company, which eventually became the largest music chain in the United States.

During his luncheons with Rudolph Wurlitzer, Ted noticed something odd. After lunch, Wurlitzer would say, "You got any money, Ted? I haven't got any. Pay the bill would you?" So Ted paid the bill, but as soon as the men got back to the office, Wurlitzer would pay Ted back. Ted never knew whether he was being tested or teased.

Rolfing, who recognized Ted as a competent young executive, was brought in to help straighten out Wurlitzer. But somehow, with all of their success, the company had gotten itself in trouble during the Depression and lost $6 million. Originally, the bank brought Rolfing in so he could get the bank's money, pay off the loan, and close the business. But Rolfing discovered nothing wrong with the company.

Now in control, Rolfing wanted to move back to his home town. So he called Ted into his office and said, "Ted, I want you to go to Chicago and find a place to move the office. And I don't want the bank to be in on it. Our bank wants me there, but I don't believe in getting too close with your company bank."

Ted found a place on the 45th floor of the Bankers Building.

"One of the Wurlitzer brothers was running the factory in North Tonawanda, which from the insurance angle, came under me," said Ted. So the Wurlitzer office staff – and the McCarty family – moved to Chicago.

At the time, there were rumblings that the U.S. was going to get involved in the ongoing war in Europe. Rolfing called his staff into the conference room and outlined new orders from the government – Wurlitzer was going to pursue "war work." Rolfing was excited, and wanted everyone to get into it. His attitude suggested that the war work would be good for Wurlitzer.

Rolfing said, "Ted, I want you to go to DeKalb. We have a contract with the Navy, we're going to build robot bombers there in the piano factory."

Wurlitzer was about to join other American companies in what would become the biggest military buildup the world had ever seen.

The DeKalb assignment was an import mission for Ted, and Rolfing was counting on Ted's experience to get the job done, telling him, "We need your experience and training out there. You're going to be the Purchasing Agent. You're going to contact other companies who are going to make things for us, because we can't make everything."

At the time, DeKalb had a population of 9,000 people. The plant was a significant operation, with about 1,200 employees. Ted was assigned to oversee Wurlitzer's top retail salesmen – at least those who hadn't enlisted or been drafted into the military. These salesmen became Ted's buyers, and called on suppliers such as Schwinn Bicycles to purchase the components needed to make robot bombers. Ted coordinated the effort and used his engineering background when designing some of the parts.

All quotes had to be accompanied by blueprints and technical drawings, which meant Ted rediscovered his engineering skills. This would later prove helpful when he was engineering Gibson products in the late 1940s. But DeKalb meant another move for Ted and Elinor's family. And this one was different because it was war-time.

In a town of 9,000 people, finding a house in DeKalb was difficult. Ted stayed in a hotel for three months, commuting on train to Chicago on weekends, while working and trying to find a house in DeKalb. Elinor was alone again with the kids in Chicago. Ted recalled, "There was a house with five bedrooms, and the lady who owned it rented it to students because this was right next to a college campus. But the boys that had been living there were off in the army and there weren't many young men around. So she didn't have anybody to rent to. So we got lucky, and my family had a place to stay."

One day, while having lunch in Chicago with Mr. Rolfing, Ted was told, "We have to have a good car to make trips back and forth from DeKalb to Chicago." It was 65 miles, and Ted knew that Rolfing had asked one of the VPs at DeKalb to get him a car, but that the guy couldn't get it. Ted's next-door neighbor managed a Ford dealership in Chicago that had an opposite problem – they couldn't sell this car because most customers didn't have enough war-time government points to buy it. But Ted had all the government points needed, so he told Mr. Rolfing, "Getting a car doesn't seem such a difficult thing. All you have to do is to appoint somebody who knows the ropes."

Ted picked up a Chrysler at the dealership, and Rolfing told him to get a Wurlitzer decal on the door and drive the car until everything was settled in DeKalb. But, gas was so scarce that most of the travel between DeKalb and Chicago was by train.

World War II turned out to be the beginning of the end for the great Wurlitzer Retail Store Division. Although it remained in business for two decades afterward, the war proved a major hindrance because Wurlitzer couldn't get brass instruments from Germany or Czechoslovakia. No non-essential items could be made with more than 10 percent metal. Wurlitzer was founded on importing band instruments from skilled manufacturers in Germany. During and after the war, that source no longer existed. In fact, very few sources of musical instruments existed *anywhere*.

In the mid 1940s, there was much disarray in the musical instruments industry, and Wurlitzer was no exception. Many employees had left for war, never to return, while other, older employees passed away, old job positions were deleted, and people took new jobs created by war work. Everything was up in the air. In the mix, Ted found himself returning as the Wurlitzer Corporate Purchasing Agent. It was a key position, and any successful retailer relies most heavily on it because it's where a company draws profit. McCarty's staff was responsible for purchasing all merchandise for everybody at Wurlitzer. But in the post World

War II environment, nothing of value was for sale, including musical instruments.

By the end of 1944, Ted and his family moved back to Chicago and he split his time between Chicago and DeKalb. Though the Purchasing Agent assignment was difficult, Ted remembers, "I was doing very well; I got a nice pay increase, finally. I got to stay at home, and the family bought a real nice home in Winnetka. Everything was going great."

As usual, Ted had to wear many hats, several of which were assigned because of his deep experience. In 1945, Wurlitzer's retail operations were unprofitable, not only because of the lack of inventory, but because of an earlier tactical miscalculation; years before, when the stores were first put into place, the company would not buy the land upon which the stores were built. During the war, many of the leases ran out and the new leases were unbelievably expensive compared to the initial lease price. Wurlitzer, faced with severely diminished revenue, faced a double jeopardy situation with the higher lease costs.

These losses prompted Rolfing to once again call on Ted. "I want you to go upstate and get rid of the Dayton store," Rolfing told him. "You have to get rid of that building." Ted complained, "Mr. Rolfing, I'm not in charge of that department anymore." His boss said (in an angry tone of voice), "Oh, nonsense! Just get over there and get it done!" Ted said (in a pleasant voice), "Okay. Yes, sir." And set out to sell Dayton and six other Wurlitzer retail stores, sometimes accompanied by Elinor. It was just another year at Wurlitzer; Ted was again handling two jobs at once.

In another shake-up, Wurlitzer's Vice President for Retail resigned. His replacement was one of Ted's former bosses, the man who had been store manager at Rochester. Ted thought he himself should have been offered the Vice President position and was upset about being passed over. But he was happy as Corporate Purchasing Agent. Life was good with his wife, son, and daughter, living in a lovely home just a few blocks from Lake Michigan.

But it didn't last. Wurlitzer retail store managers had an annual sales quota. The new V.P. of Retail set the targets, and the Purchasing Agent was responsible for stocking stores with merchandise. The V.P. set new sales goals that required $3 million worth of inventory, which Ted considered insane – there was no way in the post-war environment that he could buy that amount of merchandise.

Ted talked with the V.P. and was told, "That's ridiculous." Ted replied, "But that's the number you set for store managers. They aren't dumb, they'll know that they can't possibly make the quotas. If they haven't got the merchandise to do it, they're not going to try." But Ted was rebuked and told, "That's my business. Ted. You take care of your business."

Though Ted personally thought the V.P. was a nice guy, he also considered him a "knucklehead," especially given his reputation with store managers, who called him "the best store closer in the business." Ted thought him incompetent, and just couldn't get in sync with him.

Given everything – being passed over for the V.P. spot, being continually asked to do two jobs at once, working for a company that was experiencing financial trouble, and being asked to work for an incompetent V.P. – Ted decided to quit, and gave his resignation to the President.

"The war was over and nobody knew what the hell was going on," said Ted. "It was time to get out, and I wasn't going to put up with this guy anymore. So in October, 1947, I gave Mr. Rolfing my signature in resignation effective January 1, 1948.

"Mr. Rolfing wouldn't accept it. He just threw it in his drawer and said, 'Ted, you don't want to do that. You have a nice bonus coming for the work you did in Rochester. Now that the war is over, we can pay you for that.'" Ted said, "I think I want to make a change and I think the best time to do it is the first of the year." Rolfing responded, "We'll talk about this later."

Ted's decision to quit was not impulsive, and when he decided to tell Rolfing, he had a few of the proverbial irons in the fire. After the war, companies needed managers and Ted had been contacted by a few.

His boss would still not accept his resignation, but after Christmas, his resignation was accepted. He did not receive the bonus from Wurlitzer.

Ted McCarty: Wurlitzer to Gibson, 1948

Within three months, Ted was on his way to Kalamazoo, Michigan. He had a couple of wishes in pursuing a career change; first, he didn't want to stay in the musical instrument business; and second, he loved his home in Winnetka – he and his family enjoyed their time on the beaches along Lake Michigan. After everything he'd been through, it seemed he might finally be able to settle in. So it would be hard to pry him and his family away from Chicago.

Ted's best lead in Chicago was with the Brach Candy Company, which was looking to hire an assistant treasurer. When he interviewed with Brach management, he was told the treasurer was near retirement and Brach's plan was to put the new assistant in line for the position. Brach eliminated all but two candidates, and Ted had an inside track because he and the treasurer were alumni of Alpha Tau Omega fraternity. Unfortunately, the company president was on winter vacation in the Bahamas and no one knew when he was going to return – and they weren't about to bother him on holiday.

"I waited a couple of months," Ted said. "And finally, Maurice Berlin talked me into helping him." Berlin was Chairman of the Board of Chicago Musical Instruments

"It was fortunate that I left Wurlitzer," Ted added. "Because Mr. Berlin would not have talked with me about a job if I were still working there. Berlin had worked for Wurlitzer; he knew the people, and they knew him.

"Mr. Brach was still in the Bahamas, while I was typing resumes at night and passing them out in the daytime. I was in Bill Gretsch's office – we were friends in Chicago – and I told him I was retiring from Wurlitzer. Bill said, 'What are you doing!?' and I said, 'I'm waiting for Brach to get back, I'm waiting for him.' And Bill said, 'Hey, Berlin is back!' And I said, 'So what? Gretsch said, 'He's home from vacation. Why don't you go over and see him?' I said, 'I don't want to go see him! I'm getting out of the business.' Gretsch said, 'Ted, you're too well-known in this business.' I said, 'I've been working in eight different cities. It was too much.' Gretsch said, 'Go over and see him – he has a lot of contacts in Chicago.' I said, 'I know. But I really don't care about getting back into the music business. I'm burned out.' But he said, 'I don't want to see you get out of this business, we need you.'

"So what does he do? He calls Berlin and says, 'Maurie, I've got a friend of yours sitting across the table from me here, Ted McCarty, and right now he's not doing anything.' So he hangs up and tells me, 'Maurie is looking for you to come over, and he's going to take you out to lunch.' So I went to Mr. Berlin's club for lunch, and he wanted to know what I was doing. I told him I was typing resumes. He said, 'Would you happen to have one?' I gave him one, and he said, 'If you happen to be around at about 5 o'clock, stop in.'

"I was living in Winnetka, and he lived in the next town. I thought, 'What he wants is to have me drive him home, his Cadillac is right across the street.'

But he read the resume and called me two or three days later. I went down and had lunch with him, and he said, "I didn't know you had an commercial engineer's degree.' I said, 'I guess it just never came up.' And he said, 'Well, I don't have anything that I know of, but I've got a lot of friends, a lot of people with businesses. I might run into somebody. If I do, I'll recommend you.' I didn't tell him that I wanted to get out of the music business – you never do that with someone like Mr. Berlin. And after three or four meetings he said, 'What is with you?' Are you still waiting on the candy store?' I said, 'Yeah,' And he said, 'Why don't you go over to Kalamazoo and see if you can figure out why I'm losing $100,000 a month.'"

Ted had dealt with Berlin and CMI as the purchasing agent for Wurlitzer, so they were familiar with each other. And on subsequent trips home, Berlin pressed on. "Gibson is having a terrible time. I'll arrange for you to meet the president in Kalamazoo, to tell you what the problems are that they may need help with. You'll be given any and all information you need."

Berlin knew what he was doing. He'd owned Gibson for three years and was confident in it. But his two top men in Kalamazoo were getting old, were in ill health, and were losing control of the plant.

In Kalamazoo, Ted met with Gibson president Guy Hart and was given carte blanche to find problems. Berlin wanted Ted to examine Gibson's books, so he met with George Comee, the finance man, to understand the monthly losses. Ted's education and experience provided the perfect background – his engineering training helped as he toured the manufacturing facilities, where he also met a foreman named John Huis, who filled him in on the plant's problems.

After 10 days in Kalamazoo, Ted had a clear picture. He returned to Chicago, wrote a report, and met Berlin. After reading the report, Berlin offered Ted a job as General Manager. Ted declined, but Berlin persisted.

"Mr. Berlin would take me out to lunch at his club, and we finally decided it wasn't going to work," said Ted. "Until one day he said, 'Look, if you'll take that job, and you turn the company around, within a year, you'll be President.'

"So this was a whole new ball game! The very idea that somebody my age – 38 – could be a company president, and at *Gibson*, which was one of the number one companies in the musical instrument business. I'd become President within a year, but in the meantime I would be CEO, and the President would have no authority over me. So I talked it over with my wife and she said, 'Well, if you want to go, I'll go with you.'"

So, just three months from his resignation from Wurlitzer, Ted had landed a great opportunity. He was proud of the fact that he'd be one of the youngest corporate presidents in the U.S., and he'd be *the youngest* corporate president in the music industry. It was also important to him that he'd be the Chief Executive Office at Gibson, reporting only to Berlin, the President and Chairman of the Board of Chicago Musical Instruments.

The Gibson Years: The Turnaround, 1948

Ted started at Gibson on March, 15, 1948. At CMI, there was a friendly bet as to how long it would take Ted to straighten things out and get the place to make a profit. Clarence Havenga, the General Sales Manager, said, 'Well, if Ted does it in six months, he'll be doing very well. But I believe it will take at least a year.' Berlin told him, 'I think it'll work out much quicker than that.' Berlin was right. Gibson lost money in March and April, but the Kalamazoo plant turned a profit in May. Berlin was delighted.

When Ted was sent to Kalamazoo to get the place organized, Guy Hart had served as general manager of Gibson since 1924. Some historians feel that Hart was fortunate to follow Harry L. Ferris as GM. Ferris was a short-timer who lasted just long enough to reorganize Gibson into a modern business. Ferris battled with Gibson President Adams, and after only one year was asked to resign. During the 24-year Hart era, the L-5 guitar, Mastertone banjo, Super 400, SJ-200, Advanced Jumbo, and electric ES-150 guitar models were introduced. While Hart may have had a disputable career, Gibson Company historian Julius Bellson considered the Hart era 'remarkable.'

By 1948, Hart was in

Ted with his children Sue and Ted at their 2311 Glenwood Drive home in Kalamazoo, September 1948.

declining health. Coincidentally, his longtime assistant, Neil Abrams, died of a heart attack, leaving a hole in management. Gibson historian Julius Bellson gives Abrams considerable credit for keeping Gibson on top for so many years. The turnaround initiated by Ted was a straightforward exercise that was no more difficult than his assignments at Wurlitzer. His leadership abilities, honed at Wurlitzer, made him perfectly equipped for the challenge.

"Gibson was an independent corporation," said Ted. "All of its stock was held by Chicago Musical Instruments, which was owned by Mr. Berlin. Other CMI businesses were subsidiaries. Berlin had purchased Gibson during the war, but it, like most other companies, was doing mostly war work under government contract. When the war ended and it was time to return to making musical instruments, all the tools, dies, and fixtures were stored away. When they tried to get into production, they had to find the stuff. A lot of old timers were gone – either killed or had other jobs. Gibson's outside vendors also had to find their tooling. The support companies had to be re-started. Because of the tooling, Gibson was losing money."

Ted discovered that in addition to the tooling mish-mash, there were people problems. His first priority was to get into the plant, and during his initial fact-finding trip, Ted discovered a very able and business-like supervisor named John Huis, who had started at Gibson in 1926, fresh out of high school. Huis and Ted were about the same age, and after working for 18 years at Gibson, Huis served in the war before returning to the company in 1947. He was skillful with tools and equipment, and he was a serious Dutchman. Those traits caught the eye of the new boss, who recruited Huis to advise him during the rebuilding. Ted and Huis walked the plant and found many people with bad attitudes toward Hart. Ted developed the impression that Hart did not treat employees like people, but like *workers*, and found areas where nobody would claim responsibility for certain operations.

Under Hart, the foreman reported directly to the General Manager. Gibson was still a small operation with a flat management hierarchy, and Hart made a practice of holding meetings with foremen at his home. Ted tried the same, but found nobody would talk. Huis, himself a foreman, told Ted, "They won't talk because under Hart, the guy who talked the most wouldn't be at the next meeting."

"Huis grew into his position," said Ted. "He was a very fine person and fine factory man. He wasn't an accountant, but we had other people who did that type of work. John and I went through the factory every morning, seeing how things were done, and if we could improve the method. We talked with the men and women about what was wrong and what could be done to improve it. We found slight changes that resulted in slight improvement, and became friends with employees. We asked for their ideas, and tried to build them up. Many of them were old-timers."

These walk-throughs were perhaps Ted's most important strategy. It was perfectly natural for him, because he was confident in his own knowledge, he was likeable, and he enjoyed interacting with his workforce. He practiced the most useful management technique – management by walking around. He also practiced the other important management technique – "1,000 things 1 percent better." Evolution, not revolution, was the McCarty way.

As Ted was getting Gibson on its feet, Berlin told the CMI salesmen, "Don't sell anything except organs. Don't sell guitars, but take a Gibson order if the dealer wants one." Still, dealers ordered plenty of guitars – drawn by the power of the Gibson name.

The Kalamazoo plant did its best to keep up. The factory banked inventory – it took three months to make a guitar, and inventory needed to be in-process when an order came in, and dealers generally understood when something was backordered. "There was never a time guitars piled up – they sold quickly," said Ted. "We tried to keep the instruments in the white wood and wait for orders."

Ted reestablished accountability in the manufacturing system, and building a competent staff. "One of the things I'm most proud of was developing a cadre of capable executives," he said. "Together, we did some impressive things. Not only did we modernize factory methods, but John Huis, who had been a foreman until he became superintendent in charge of manufacturing, did a fine job, as did Julius Bellson, George Comee, Larry Allers, Walter Fuller, and quite a few woodworkers who were in charge of the various sections of the factory."

There was no one thing that led to the turnaround. Tooling, equipment, and personnel issues were important, but Gibson, unlike other CMI companies, was a profit center, which meant it recorded sales to CMI rather than just transferring costs. The Parsons Street plant operated on a standard budget with standard volume expectations. When production volumes were not met, plant costs were underabsorbed, leaving a loss at the plant level. Parsons Street would generate consistent fixed and semi-variable costs that needed to be absorbed by producing a standard number of units. When Ted arrived, that wasn't happening. Something was causing budget under-absorption, and that something was low output to finished-goods inventory. Too much product wasn't passing inspection, so it became scrap that created a double loss. Lost cost-absorption and increased material-scrap expense were part of the problem.

Gibson had a tradition of strong inspection, and in 1947/'48, there were seven inspection points in its system. The first was the craftsman doing the work, followed by the line leader, the foreman, the official inspector, roving inspectors, spot inspections, and two final inspections after a guitar was finished. It was hard to imagine a guitar would get out the door if it wasn't up to Gibson standards.

But, was production low and scrap costs high because Hart and Abrams were ill? Did Hart's illness allow employee bitterness to escalate into an 'I don't give a damn attitude?' Probably, but there were other reasons for the losses.

Again, McCarty found that tools, dies, and fixtures were a mish-mash. Even in 1948, two years after the war had ended, and even after Maurice Berlin had ordered improvements to the plant in 1945, it remained unorganized. And Gibson suppliers were experiencing the same conditions. If just one supplier missed a schedule, a guitar would be just 98 percent complete – and that would not generate cost absorption.

Ted considered this a people problem. If he could get the "people issues" resolved, he could achieve the output to make a profit. And that's what he did; the millions of lost dollars Berlin described probably was not as bad as it sounded. Berlin probably knew that, and he knew if he could get the right man on the job, Gibson could be turned around in a short time. Ted knew that, too.

When Ted arrived in Kalamazoo, Guy Hart did not resist. Ted moved directly into Hart's office, and Hart stayed on as a lame duck. As promised, Berlin saw to it that Ted was elected General Manager and President of Gibson in 1950. Since '48, McCarty had been listed as the Vice President, General Manager, and Director of Gibson, Inc.

Gibson's officially announced that Hart retired, even if technically, he was elderly, in bad health, and had to be asked to leave. Berlin told Ted, "I want Mr. Hart's resignation on my desk Monday morning!" Ted asked, "Do you want me to set that up for you?" And Berlin replied to Ted, "No, you're going to do it." So Ted told Hart that although he was through as president, he would retain a seat on the Gibson board of directors.

Ted was thrilled with his appointment.

"The owner of *The Music Trades* came to the factory the day they made me President. He told me, 'Ted, you're the youngest president of a major company in this industry.'"

Ted McCarty and Julius Bellson in Ted's office in a 1953 photograph

The Gibson Years: Getting to Work, 1950

When Ted McCarty became CEO of Gibson in 1948, his boss, Maurice Berlin, did not insist on a rapid ramp-up of guitar production. Berlin told his salesmen to take an order if a store wanted to order a Gibson, but otherwise the salesmen were to promote other CMI products. But the policy didn't last, and once the Kalamazoo plant was fully functional, Ted began his own promotion.

Ted's first capital improvement was the 1950 expansion. *The Music Trades* covered McCarty's project, saying, "On July 14 (1950), Gibson, Inc. in its newly enlarged spacious modern factory, was host to almost 200 music merchants at a buffet luncheon. Following the luncheon, all those present made a tour of the entire factory in small groups of 10. Almost two hours were required by each group to inspect the varied manufacturing operations, which, in addition to fretted instruments, includes a complete string department and an amplifier manufacturing section.

"Under President Ted McCarty's direction, the program was intended to increase the dealer's knowledge of fretted instruments by showing the painstaking, precise methods employed in manufacturing," it continued. "Luncheon was served in the 14,000-square-foot modern wing completed in the spring and containing the fully air-conditioned general offices. The individual tours then began in the modern 15,000-square-foot wing completed in 1945 and devoted to cutting and shaping Gibson instruments. Housed on one floor, this section contains the most modern quality woodworking machinery obtainable. From there, the tour led to the original three-story plant containing 30,000 square feet of space. Here the visitors were able to observe at first-hand the painstaking hand-finishing and rigid inspection tests responsible for Gibson quality. Visitors learned that guitars contain from 146 pieces in the LG-2 model, 181 separate parts in the SJ-200 and in the normal course of manufacture, guitars and component parts are inspected more than 300 times.

"From the fretted instruments department the visiting merchants were then shown through the string manufacturing department and the amplifier manufacturing department. To meet the Gibson quality standard, amplifiers from the case and chassis on are manufactured in their own factory. Somewhat footsore from the long task, the Gibson company's guests enjoyed the facility of a well equipped bar until train departure.

"Visitors also learned that the Gibson Co. was founded in Kalamazoo 55 years ago."

"Gibson provided the following information:

Total production experience: 1,177 years (16% of the production employees have had over 15 years at Gibson; 39% of the production employees have had over 5 years at Gibson).

Total supervisory experience: 161 years (on an average of over 13 years per man; there were 12 supervisors)

Total inspection experience: 129 years (on an average of 18 years per man; inspector with the least experience 8 years; 7 inspectors).

Total office experience: 138 years (or an average of 9 years per person; 15 people worked in the office and in indirect support)

Total top management experience: 85 years (or an average of 14 years) (Note: six top managers – McCarty, Huis, Bellson, Comee, Werner, and Fuller)

Total employment: 200 people (Note: Management 6, Office Staff 15, Floor inspectors 7, Supervisors 12, and Production 160)"

After getting the plant and equipment up and running or modernized, Ted set about running the business. To do well, he needed two things; Kalamazoo was expected to promptly fill all incoming orders from CMI, and Ted was expected to continually generate new product that could be displayed at the two annual trade shows. Demand for guitars started to climb almost immediately.

Throughout Ted's 18 years at Gibson, he followed his "manage by walking around" style. "I went into the factory and talked to people. I was the boss, and they appreciated that. In fact, a couple of ladies said I was the best-dressed boss in the city. It was a very

The following pages show how complete the McCarty era Gibson product line was.

MODEL NUMBER	ITEM	LIST PRICE INCL. FED. EXCISE TAX
	GIBSON INSTRUMENT PRICES	
	FLAT TOP GUITARS	
LG-1	Guitar—Sunburst Finish	$ 87.50
LG-2	Guitar—Sunburst Finish	97.50
LG-3	Guitar—Natural Finish Top	107.50
117	Durabilt Case for above models	11.50
414	Faultless Case (Flannel) for above	35.00
LG-2¾	Guitar (¾ size)—Sunburst Finish	97.50
117¾	Durabilt Case for above model	11.50
	FLAT TOP GUITARS (Cutaway)	
CF-100	Guitar, Cutaway—Sunburst Finish	$142.50
CF-100E	Guitar, Cutaway Electric—Sunburst Finish	180.00
117	Durabilt Case for above	11.50
414	Faultless Case (Flannel) for above	35.00
	JUMBO FLAT TOP GUITARS	
J-45	Jumbo Guitar—Sunburst Finish	$125.00
J-50	Jumbo Guitar—Natural Finish Top	135.00
	J-45 and J-50 also available with Adjustable Bridge at no extra price.	
SJ	Southerner Jumbo—Sunburst Finish	155.00
SJN	Country-Western Jumbo—Natural Finish Top (SJN)	167.50
118	Durabilt Case for above model	12.50
514	Faultless Case (Flannel) for above	42.00
515	Faultless Case (Plush) for above	46.50
J-185	Jumbo Guitar—Sunburst Finish	225.00
J-185N	Jumbo Guitar—Natural Finish	240.00
514	Faultless Case (Flannel) for above	42.00
515	Faultless Case (Plush) for above	46.50
J-200	Super Jumbo Guitar—Sunburst Finish	370.00
J-200N	Super Jumbo Guitar—Natural Finish	385.00
609	Durabilt Case for above models	19.50
606	Faultless Case (Flannel) for above	42.50
600	Faultless Case (Plush) for above	52.50
	JUMBO FLAT TOP ELECTRIC GUITAR	
J-160E	Jumbo Electric Guitar—Sunburst Finish, with adjustable bridge	$189.50
119	Durabilt Case for above models	12.50
516	Faultless Case (Plush) for above	46.50

July 15, 1957 Price List page 1.

MODEL NUMBER	ITEM	LIST PRICE INCL. FED. EXCISE TAX
	GUT STRING (Classic) GUITARS	
C-1	Classic Guitar—Natural Spruce Top—Mahogany Back......	$ 99.50
C-2	Classic Guitar—Natural Spruce Top—Maple Back	175.00
C-5	Custom Classic Guitar—Natural Finish Top— Rosewood Rim and Back	275.00
117	Durabilt Case for above models	11.50
414	Faultless Case (Flannel) for above models	35.00
	CARVED TOP GUITARS	
L-48	Guitar—Sunburst Finish	$117.50
L-50	Guitar—Sunburst Finish	147.50
103	Durabilt Case for above models	12.50
514	Faultless Case (Flannel) for above....................	42.00
515	Faultless Case (Plush) for above	46.50
L-5	Guitar—Sunburst Finish	460.00
L-5N	Guitar—Natural Finish	475.00
609	Durabilt Case for above models	19.50
606	Faultless Case (Flannel) for above models..............	42.50
600	Faultless Case (Plush) for above models................	52.50
	CARVED TOP GUITARS (Cutaway)	
L-4C	Guitar, Cutaway—Sunburst Finish	$210.00
L-4CN	Guitar, Cutaway—Natural Finish	225.00
103	Durabilt Case for above models	12.50
514	Faultless Case (Flannel) for above....................	42.00
515	Faultless Case (Plush) for above	46.50
L-7C	Guitar, Cutaway—Sunburst Finish	265.00
L-7CN	Guitar, Cutaway—Natural Finish	280.00
L-5C	Guitar, Cutaway—Sunburst Finish	525.00
L-5CN	Guitar, Cutaway—Natural Finish	540.00
609	Durabilt Case for above models	19.50
606	Faultless Case (Flannel) for above....................	42.50
600	Faultless Case (Plush) for above	52.50
Super 300C	Guitar, Cutaway—Sunburst Finish	325.00
300	Case (Flannel) for above model.....................	45.00
400	Case (Plush) for above model......................	60.00
Super 400C	Guitar, Cutaway—Sunburst Finish	600.00
Super 400CN	Guitar, Cutaway—Natural Finish	625.00
400	Case (Plush) for above models	60.00
	ELECTRIC SPANISH GUITARS	
ES-125	Guitar—Sunburst Finish	$145.00
ES-135	Guitar—Sunburst Finish	175.00
103	Durabilt Case for above model......................	12.50
514	Faultless Case (Flannel) for above...................	42.00
515	Faultless Case (Plush) for above	46.50

July 15, 1957 Price List page 2.

MODEL NUMBER	ITEM	LIST PRICE INCL. FED. EXCISE TAX

THREE-QUARTER SIZE ELECTRIC GUITARS

Do not confuse these ¾ guitars with similar styles in regular models — these are ¾ in size and short scale.

Les Paul Jr. ¾	Guitar, Solid Body Cutaway	$120.00
115	Durabilt Case for above.	13.50
ES-125 ¾ T	Non-cutaway—Thin Body—Sunburst Finish.	145.00
ES-140 ¾ T	Cutaway—Thin—Sunburst Finish.	185.00
ES-140 ¾ TN	Cutaway—Thin—Natural Finish	200.00
116-¾	Durabilt Case for above models	11.50
533	Faultless Case (Plush) for above models	42.50

ELECTRIC SPANISH GUITARS (Cutaway) SOLID BODY

Les Paul Custom	Guitar, Solid Body Cutaway, Black Finish, with two built-in pickups and toggle switch	$375.00
537	Faultless Case (Gold Plush) for above.	47.50
Les Paul Model	Guitar, Solid Body, Cutaway, Gold Finish Top, with two built-in pickups and toggle switch.	247.50
535	Faultless Case (Plush) for above	42.00
Les Paul Special	Guitar, Solid Body Cutaway, with two built-in pickups and toggle switch	179.50
535	Faultless Case (Plush) for above	42.00
115	Durabilt Case for above.	13.50
Les Paul TV	Guitar, Solid Body Cutaway, Natural Finish, built-in pick-up	132.50
115	Durabilt Case for above.	13.50
Les Paul Jr.	Guitar, Solid Body Cutaway, with built-in pickup.	120.00
115	Durabilt Case for above.	13.50

ELECTRIC SPANISH GUITARS (Cutaway)

ES-175	Guitar, Cutaway—Sunburst Finish	$235.00
ES-175N	Guitar, Cutaway—Natural Finish	250.00
ES-175D	Special Guitar, Cutaway—Sunburst, two built-in pickups . . .	290.00
ES-175DN	Special Guitar, Cutaway—Natural, two built-in pickups	305.00
ES-295	Guitar, Cutaway—Gold Finish, two built-in pickups.	325.00
514	Faultless Case (Flannel) for above.	42.00
515	Faultless Case (Plush) for above	46.50
ES-5	Switchmaster Guitar, Cutaway—Sunburst Finish with three built-in pickups	450.00
ES-5N	Switchmaster Guitar, Cutaway—Natural Finish with three built-in pickups	475.00

(Continued on next page)

Bigsby True Vibrato Units available for conventional type Guitars, Solid Body Les Paul Models, or the new thin series. Specify type and model.

Regular Plating	**. . .$55.00**	**With Tune-O-Matic Bridge Saddle. . .$65.00**	
Gold Plating	**. 75.00**	**With Tune-O-Matic Bridge Saddle. . . 90.00**	

July 15, 1957 Price List page 3.

MODEL NUMBER	ITEM	LIST PRICE INCL. FED. EXCISE TAX
L-5CES	Guitar, Cutaway—Sunburst Finish, two built-in pickups	600.00
L-5CESN	Guitar, Cutaway—Natural Finish, two built-in pickups	615.00
609	Durabilt Case for above models	19.50
606	Faultless Case (Flannel) for above.	42.50
600	Faultless Case (Plush) for above	52.50
S-400CES	Guitar, Cutaway—Sunburst Finish, two built-in pickups	675.00
S-400CESN	Guitar, Cutaway—Natural Finish, two built-in pickups	700.00
400	Case (Plush) for above models	60.00

ELECTRIC SPANISH GUITARS — Thin Series

Byrdland	Guitar, Cutaway—Sunburst Finish, two built-in pickups	$575.00
Byrdland N	Guitar, Cutaway—Natural Finish, two built-in pickups	590.00
ES-350T	Guitar, Cutaway—Sunburst Finish, two built-in pickups	410.00
ES-350TN	Guitar, Cutaway—Natural Finish, two built-in pickups	425.00
603	Faultless Case (Plush) for above models.	52.50
ES-225TD	Guitar, Cutaway—Sunburst Finish, two built-in pickups	229.50
ES-225TDN	Guitar, Cutaway—Natural Finish, two built-in pickups	244.50
ES-225T	Guitar, Cutaway—Sunburst Finish, one built-in pickup	189.50
ES-225TN	Guitar, Cutaway—Natural Finish, one built-in pickup	204.50
ES-125T	Guitar, non-cutaway—Sunburst Finish, one built-in pickup. .	145.00
104	Durabilt Case for above models	12.50
519	Faultless Case (Plush) for above models.	46.50

TENOR GUITARS

TG-50	Tenor Guitar—Sunburst Finish.	$145.00
ETG-150	Electric Tenor Guitar—Sunburst Finish	190.00
103	Durabilt Case for above models	12.50
514	Faultless Case (Flannel) for above.	42.00
515	Faultless Case (Plush) for above	46.50

MANDOLINS

A-40	Mandolin—Available in Natural or Sunburst Finish Top. . . .	$105.00
A-50	Mandolin—Sunburst Finish	130.00
EM-150	Electric Mandolin—Sunburst Finish	185.00
101	Durabilt Case for above models	8.50
362	Faultless Case (Flannel) for above.	29.50
Florentine	Electric—Solid Body—Tune-O-Matic—Sunburst Finish.	205.00
A-5	Mandolin Acoustic, Florentine Shape—oval sound hole.	265.00
440	Faultless Case—Oblong (Plush) for above models.	43.50
F-12	Mandolin—Artist Model—Sunburst Finish	350.00
F-5	Mandolin—Artist Model—Sunburst Finish	485.00
371	Faultless Case (Plush) for above	32.50
440	Faultless Case—Oblong (Plush) for above	43.50

July 15, 1957 Price List page 4.

MODEL NUMBER	ITEM	LIST PRICE INCL. FED. EXCISE TAX
ELECTRIC STEEL GUITARS		
Skylark	(Student Steel) Guitar	$ 64.50
2	Hard Shell Case (for Skylark Guitar) plush lined	24.00
Skylark	Student Steel Outfit—(complete with 6-string guitar— GA-5 Amp and plush lined case)	144.50
BR-9	6-string Hawaiian Guitar	$ 75.00
9	Hard Shell Oblong Case for above	12.50
BR-9	Special Electric Steel Outfit—(complete with 6-string guitar—GA-9 Amp and case)	165.25
BR-6	6-string Hawaiian Guitar	99.50
6	Hard Shell Oblong Case for above	12.50
Century-6	6-string Hawaiian Guitar	139.50
Ultratone-6	6-string Hawaiian Guitar	189.50
1	Faultless Case (Plush) for above models	30.00
DOUBLE AND TRIPLE NECK GUITARS		
CG-520	Console Grande Double Neck—Natural Oak Finish	$287.50
19	Faultless Case (Plush) for above	57.50
C-530	Console Double Neck—Blond Finish	215.00
11	Faultless Case (Plush) for above	45.00
CG-523	Console Grande Triple Neck—Oak Finish	400.00
20	Faultless Case (Plush) for above	65.00
CL-4	Set of four regular legs for above models	12.50
CLA-4	Set of four adjustable, extension legs for above models	39.50
ELECTRAHARP		
EH-630	Electraharp—Four Pedals—8 strings	$520.00
EH-620	Electraharp—Six Pedals—8 strings	620.00
16	Faultless Case (Plush) for above models	75.00
EH-610	Electraharp—Six strings—Four Pedals—Oak Body—light weight	249.50
15	Case for above	50.00
MULTIHARP		
Multiharp	Three Necks—6 Pedals on Middle Neck—Ebony Finish	$795.00
17	Custom Construction Case (Plush) for above	100.00
ELECTRIC BASS		
	Electric Bass, solid body can be used with neck strap or in standing position with peg	$235.00
536	Faultless Case (Plush lined)	45.00
GA-200	Bass Amplifier (in. cover)	375.00
AMPLIFIERS		
GA-5	Skylark Amplifier	$ 59.50
5-C	Cover for above	2.25
Gibsonette	Amplifier	79.50

(Continued on next page)

July 15, 1957 Price List page 5.

MODEL NUMBER	ITEM	LIST PRICE INCL. FED. EXCISE TAX
GA-9	Amplifier	92.50
9-C	Cover to fit Gibsonette and GA-9 amplifiers.............	3.95
GA-6	Amplifier	122.50
GA-20	Amplifier	137.50
GA-20T	Amplifier with tremolo........................	169.50
20-C	Cover to fit GA-6, GA-20 and GA-20T amplifiers.........	5.75
GA-30	Amplifier—twin speakers	180.00
GA-40	Les Paul Amplifier with built-in tremolo	199.50
30-C	Cover to fit GA-30 and Les Paul amplifiers.............	7.50
GA-70	Country and Western Amplifier—15" speaker— features highs (inc. cover)	260.00
GA-77	Amplifier—15" speaker (inc. cover)	275.00
GA-55	Amplifier—twin 12" speakers (inc. cover)	250.00
GA-55V	Amplifier—twin 12" speakers with Vibrato (inc. cover)....	289.50
GA-90	Amplifier—six 8" speakers (inc. cover).................	340.00
GA-Super 400	Combo Amplifier Three Channels—two 12" Special Built Speakers (inc. cover)........................	435.00
GA-V1	Gibson Electronic Vibrato only....................	75.00
MAESTRO	Accordion Amplifier	235.00
40-C	Cover to fit...............................	7.50
Super Maestro	Accordion and Bass Amplifier with Vibrato..............	395.00
GA-200	Bass Amplifier	375.00
GA-85	Amplifier—Bass Reflex Cabinet—removable chassis........	289.50

TENOR BANJOS

TB-100	Tenor Banjo	$180.00
TB-150	Tenor Banjo	240.00
TB-250	Mastertone Tenor Banjo	290.00
120	Durabilt Case for above models	12.50
511	Faultless Case (Flannel) for above	40.50
509	Faultless Case (Plush) for above	42.50

5-STRING BANJOS

RB-100	5-string Banjo	$185.00
RB-150	5-string Banjo	245.00
RB-250	Mastertone 5-string Banjo	295.00
121	Durabilt Case for above models	12.75
521	Faultless Case (Flannel) for above...............	42.00
522	Faultless Case (Plush) for above	46.50

4-STRING PLECTRUM BANJOS

Models PB-100, PB-150 and PB-250 and cases are the same prices as corresponding 5-string models listed above.

July 15, 1957 Price List page 6.

MODEL NUMBER	I T E M	LIST PRICE INCL. FED. EXCISE TAX

UKULELE & TENOR UKULELE

Uke-1	Ukulele	$ 30.00
30	Chip Board Case for above model.	4.50
TU-1	Tenor Ukulele	45.00
111	Durabilt Case for above model.	6.00

FINGERREST PICKUPS

The following units will be attached to Guitar selected. See description of L7-CE (L7C with No. 102 pickup) in accessory circular.

100-SN	Single, Nickel (L-7, S-300)	$ 40.00
101-SG	Single, Gold (L-5, L-12, S-400).	42.50
102-SCN	Single, Cutaway, Nickel (L-7C)	40.00
103-SCG	Single, Cutaway, Gold (L-5C, L-12C, S-400C).	42.50
104-DN	Double, Nickel (L-7, S-300)	69.50
105-DG	Double, Gold (L-5, L-12, S-400).	72.50
106-DCN	Double, Cutaway, Nickel (L-7C).	75.00
107-DCG	Double, Cutaway, Gold (L-5C, L-12C, S-400C).	77.50

ZIPPER COVERS

ZC-5	Zipper Cover for 514 and 515 cases.	$ 23.00
ZC-6	Zipper Cover for 606 and 600 cases.	25.00
ZC-4	Zipper Cover for 300 and 400 cases.	30.00
ZC-3	Zipper Cover for 603 case.	22.50
ZC-LP	Zipper Cover for 535 Les Paul Guitar Case.	21.50
ZC-CLP	Zipper Cover for 537 Les Paul Custom Case.	21.50
ZC-22	Zipper Cover for 521 and 522 cases.	24.00
Gada-Kart	To transport amplifier or accordion, easily attached or removed.	19.95

Tenor Guitars and 4-String Plectrum Guitars available in some non-cutaway models on special order—$25.00 extra.

Write for prices and delivery dates on left-handed instruments.

ZONE 1

Effective July 15, 1957. All prices subject to change without notice. To improve the design, quality, and performance of our units and to make use of the best available materials at all times, we reserve the right to change specifications without notice.

July 15, 1957 Price List page 7.

July 15, 1957 Price List Cover.

pleasant period.

"Gibson started here in 1894 and had one little factory in 1918. That was the only building when I came to Kalamazoo, and we went from that small company to the fifth largest payroll in the city. There was a group of people in Kalamazoo that loved Gibson because it became known around the world."

Ted's other priority was to introduce new product. "We'd get busy in the late summer, developing something different we could show," Ted said. "Trade shows were a great time to consolidate sales strategy, and salespeople played a big part in determining new product. CMI had a large group of salesmen who created such a demand for our merchandise! And Gibson was one of the largest guitar factories in the United States, so I depended on these salesmen for ideas that we could develop for trade shows. During the late summer, my engineers did a fine job coming up with new models; later, we spent our efforts on manufacturing the new models."

The Gibson Years: Working With The Union

As CEO of Gibson, Ted's job was people and products. When it came to people, he was a master; he treated people as co-workers. But in the 1950s, one of every three private-sector workers belonged to a labor group. For these workers, control was in the hands of the union *and* management. The union was a major third party in any organized factory. Ted never avoided anybody – he prioritized direct interaction, was very mobile, and always favored action. This included his dealings with the union.

Kalamazoo, like most Michigan industrial towns in 1948, was a union town. Nationwide, union workers generally felt they didn't work for a company so much as they worked for their union. Most Gibson union workers were ambivalent toward union membership. Union issues in the 1940s and '50s were not particularly big for some Kalamazoo companies.

Ted's interaction with the United Steelworkers was perhaps his second-greatest accomplishment at Gibson. He never had a strike that lasted more than 24 hours (after he left Gibson in '66, the company was hit with a significant strike), and never had a serious issue with the union, even with all the changes and expansions.

Unionization in Michigan gained ground when the Congress of Industrial Organizations (CIO) targeted the automobile industry, and the United Auto Workers (UAW) was founded in Flint, Michigan, in 1936. But it wasn't until the war years that the CIO made gains as United Steelworkers' charters went into Kalamazoo companies like Atlas Press, Dutton, Clarage Fan, Kalamazoo Tank and Silo, Shakespeare, and Gibson.

In Gibson's case, factory output during the war changed from wood work to steel work due to government contracts. Unlike the unionization of the Chevrolet headquarters, the conversion to union labor was mostly transparent in Kalamazoo. The unions didn't have to push too hard, and employees didn't pay much attention. Union dues were perhaps the biggest complaint, but union workers were offered more fringe benefits, which was universally popular. Early on, unions in Michigan were more about working conditions and benefits than pay-scale issues.

Ted and the other company officials began to meet once a month in a hotel room, where they talked about who was getting taken by the union. Ted's eyes were opened by the union just five months after he arrived in Kalamazoo, when Shakespeare-Kalamazoo Reels, which made fishing tackle, was unionized.

The Shakespeare name was as great as Gibson's, and the company followed a path like Gibson. It was incorporated in 1905 after experiencing success as a smaller company named the Wm. Shakespeare, Jr. Company. Like Gibson, the incorporation was used to raise funds, in this case for $30,000 worth of automated machinery. Shakespeare was also a model for Gibson in that Shakespeare purchased land in north Kalamazoo and built a factory in 1913. Their location at 417 North Pitcher Street was one block east and four blocks south of the Gibson plant.

"The darkest chapter of the company's history unfolded on September 7, 1948, when the steelworkers union, of which only 30 to 40 percent of the employees belonged, declared a strike," said Shakespeare historian Eric Foster Jeska. "Management didn't recognize the union as representative of the majority, and the contract with the union was ended. All employees were invited back to work on September 11. Picketers clashed with 'scab' employees at the entrance, and several were injured. On December 1, a mob of 300 attacked the factory and wrecked the plant. Cars and trucks were overturned and set ablaze. Windows throughout the factory and office were smashed. Huge inventories of reel parts were destroyed. Michigan's governor was flown in and the National Guard was put on alert. On September 21, the courts ruled that the strike was illegal, and picketing ended on October 10."

Shakespeare was a true metal-working factory, while Gibson labor was organized during the war, when much of its work was war-related metal products. This created an opportunity for the Steelworkers to organize at Gibson. Six companies were organize by the Steelworkers during the War years in a concerted effort that saw most companies' employees receptive to unionization.

Ted faced just one serious challenge from his friendly Local.

"We had 150 employees in 1948 and we got to 1,200 by 1966, all union men and women. Well, the Dutchmen working at Gibson (Dutch heritage was common on the western side of Michigan) were anti-union. During one negotiation the Union said, 'The union does not want any more money for the employee. But the union *is* going to get is a closed shop. Gibson has 12 employees who don't belong to the union – everybody else belongs.' Ted said, 'That's anti-American. I won't do it.' The union replied, 'If Gibson won't give the union a closed shop, Gibson is going to have a strike, because we'll tell your employees all kinds of things about you and the rest of the people running this company, and they'll begin to hate you. And when we call for a strike count, we'll get it.' 'I want some time to find out who these 12 guys are,'" Ted told the union negotiator.

"So I called John Huis, who was a Dutchman, and told him to find out who these 12 guys were."

Ted discovered that when there was an increase in pay, there was an automatic increase in union dues. So the Dutchmen needled the union members, saying, "Ha! We get a raise, but we don't have to pay more dues!" This got back to union headquarters, which made the union determined to make Gibson a closed shop.

Ted spoke with the Dutchmen he knew in the plant, asking, "What have you guys got against the union? Why didn't you join?" They said, "It's against our religion." Ted said, "I know better."

Ted gave the Dutchmen a choice, telling them, "We're not going to have any control over a closed shop. If you join the union, you won't lose your job." They said, "We understand. We'll join."

So it was a done deal. Ted and the Local settled, and as Ted recalls, "That was the closest thing we ever had to a strike." Ted knew that when between a rock and hard place, a manager sometimes had to give in.

"But I got in on all the union negotiations," he noted. "We agreed to establish a pension fund for employees. But it was interesting that the women in the plant – which as about 40 percent of the workers – did not wish to have a union-paid pension. They wanted a little more in the paycheck. One time, it got to the point that there was going to be strike, so we got together to settle it – on a Sunday morning in my living room! I was proud of the fact that in 18 years, I never had a strike that lasted more than 24 hours.

"After I left, they had two strikes, and the end result was that Gibson moved out of town."

Ted left Gibson in 1966. Did he see the writing on the wall for Gibson and the United Steelworkers? He likely knew things were going to change, not only for Gibson, but other large Kalamazoo companies. In 1965 and '66, the automobile industry unintentionally created problems with unions in Kalamazoo when the newly built General Motors Fisher Body metal fabrication plant hired 3,000 new employees, severely tightening the labor market and giving the union an advantage in negotiations. There were several strikes in Kalamazoo in 1966, perhaps feeding off one another; the United Steelworks staged a strike at Gibson, Atlas Press, Brundage, and Clarage Fan. What would Ted have done to handle the situation? We'll never know, because by early '66 his days at Gibson were numbered. But Ted didn't leave because of the unions...

The Gibson Years: Lowrey Organ

Ted was always one of Maurice Berlin's favorite managers. He had the business side, the engineering side – he was essentially two men in one. But Berlin valued Ted's business side more, and he would be asked to wear many hats, including those of liaison and negotiator.

"Mr. Berlin and I worked together for 18½ years, and he'd come to Kalamazoo once a year on average," Ted recalled. "If we had a new building, he'd come see what it was."

In his tenure, Ted worked closely with Chicago Musical Instruments. During his time, CMI acquired a piano factory, and Ted played a role.

"In 1956, I heard there was a fellow interested in selling the Lowrey Piano and Organ Company. At Mr. Berlin's request, I got in touch with the Walter Andersen, Chief Engineer at Lowrey, and arranged to meet with the Lowrey people. Mr. Berlin, his attorney, John Huis, and I went to Chicago, and they indicated that they wanted $1 million. While we were discussing whether it was a fair price, Mr. Berlin said, 'I'll buy the company.' And we then discussed a reduced price – $250,000 – contingent on Lowrey supervising and building the first 1,000 units because they had the factory to do it. They quickly agreed, and I was appointed liaison.

"Mr. Berlin told me, 'We need these engineers in Kalamazoo, so it's up to you to hire them.' I had a meeting with the three men – the Chief Engineer (Walter Andersen), and his assistant (Chuck Welch), and the man that did the drafting (Harold Wheeler). I hired them and put them to work in a big laboratory close by the Gibson factory. They worked for CMI but were actually *my* employees, because I was paying their salaries through Gibson. I had them for about a year until we had another facility in Chicago. Lowry became the largest-selling organ in the U.S."

The Gibson Years: North Kalamazoo Race Riots

When Ted was CEO at Gibson, the buck stopped at his desk. Although he had a great guitar-building staff, he really had nobody with expertise outside of that realm. Ted handled all non-guitar related problems, and was a people person who believed face-to-face contact was the best way to get something done. But one issue that he could not have anticipated arose in 1963

The subject of African-Americans in Kalamazoo, and their effect on Gibson Guitars, has been overlooked by Gibson researchers. But over a period of decades, the north end of Kalamazoo became an increasingly rough neighborhood. This presented problems for Gibson and Ted McCarty.

Historian Catherine Larson says African-Americans were drawn to the north side of Kalamazoo.

"The North side has always had black residents, although at first the community was small, she said. "The first school on the north side, built sometime before 1866 on North Street just east of Walbridge, served the area's black children."

The north side really began to change after World War II, she adds. "The era after the war brought changes. An industrial boom encouraged the movement of millions of people from southern rural areas into northern cities in search of jobs. Many of these migrants were black. Those who came to Kalamazoo settled in the north side because older, cheaper homes were available there and were not covered by the restrictive covenants banning non-white residents, as was the case in newer neighborhoods. Segregation in housing was further encouraged by the Federal Housing Administration's refusal to insure mortgages for blacks in white neighborhoods, and vice versa. The north-side neighborhood began to shrink as white residents moved to the suburbs faster than blacks moved in. Between the 1950s and the 1990 censuses, population in the neighborhood dropped from 10,500 to 4,200.

"Many of those north-end residents left behind were those who were least able to help themselves. For many years, parts of the neighborhood were plagued by poverty and the problems often associated with it. Although problems persisted for many years, a turning point seemed to be reached in the 1963 picketing of the Van Avery Drugstore on North Burdick Street. Ostensibly because the Van Averys refused to hire a black clerk even though nearly half of their customers were black. Later opinions of the impact of the incident varied, but it did seem to mark the beginning of civil rights activities in Kalamazoo. It also helped to raise awareness of the problems in the neighborhood. Progress was slow at first, but an effort by many organizations and individuals eventually began to pay off."

Ted participated in the effort to improve the north end. In fact, he was ahead of his time when he began acting on minority issues in the 1950s, well before the 1963 Van Averys incident.

"There were no blacks working for Gibson in the 1950s, and we were having civil trouble on the north side of Kalamazoo," he said. "There was a small black-congregation church right across the street from the factory, and I got to know the minister. He used to come in and say, 'It's time for you to pay your due, Mr. McCarty!' I'd ask, 'What do you need?' and he'd say, 'More chairs for those kids in Sunday school.' So I made a phone call to Mr. Comee, in accounting, and asked him to make a check for $50. We did that with the church for years.

"Finally, I decided we were going to get a black into our factory. I called the minister and he said, 'I can get you some good men.' So he sent some men, and we hired one and put him in the shipping department. In those days, many people went through the shipping department – that's where they started.

"We got to where we had maybe four or five black men in the plant, but we didn't have any women. We thought we should have a black woman working in the string department, manufacturing strings, which was all women – they had private bathrooms and so forth. And we had some people around there who didn't like the blacks, who'd say, 'They're not going to have any in my department.' In the meantime, Gibson was tearing down buildings and homes on the next block, to build. There were 15 houses. I came up to one of the homes, the nicest investment in the place, I wanted to buy it and tear it down. So I went to talk to the lady who had it, an African-American woman named Josephine Sudduth. She said, 'Oh no, it's not for sale.' So I said, 'Where do you work?' She told me her husband had been a minister. I said, 'Why don't you come to work for Gibson?' She said, 'Could I do that?' I told her, 'Sure. Could you make strings?' She said, 'I think I can make anything you want me to make.' So we gave her good money for the house, and she came to work in the string department. We had a lady foreman in that department, and she told me, 'We haven't had any trouble. Josephine fits right in.'

"Josephine worked for us for years, and after she retired, she would visit me every year, and I'd get a big hug!

"So, my staff and I broke the color barrier at Gibson. It was my idea to do that because there was trouble in the area. One night there was a riot on the north end, near the factory, and they burned a few houses. So it was time to do something for that community. Oddly enough – and I checked this with Gibson – there had never been an application from an African-American to work for Gibson. Basically, as a group, African-Americans weren't woodworkers. They did other work. But we thought it was time to help the community. So we did."

The Gibson Years: Berlin Industrial Fair

Ted was the only person at Gibson who could handle non-guitar issues. His staff, great as they were, had grown up with Gibson making guitars the Gibson way. McCarty was a master's-level engineer who had worked in eight cities, doing everything imaginable, so it didn't take him long to meld into Kalamazoo's business community.

In Kalamazoo, the country club was one way to meet local business leaders. So Ted joined shortly after arriving in town. He also became a member of the board for the Kalamazoo Symphony Orchestra, which represented old Kalamazoo society and gave McCarty an opportunity to meet the city's VIPs.

When something like the Berlin Industrial Fair was presented to Kalamazoo, Ted was well-suited for involvement.

In 1958, Ted McCarty, Gibson, and Kalamazoo were honored by the Berlin Industrial Fair, held in Berlin. For the Fair, Kalamazoo was selected to represent the U.S. as an All-American City of Industry. The city's founders indeed had focused on making Kalamazoo a great place for industry. But it wasn't alone; Flint, Pontiac, Saginaw, and countless other Michigan cities competed with Kalamazoo to draw venture capital and new factories, looking to convert from farming and lumbering in order to grow and prosper. Beginning in the 1890s, smokestacks meant progress in Michigan. In '58, Kalamazoo won great recognition, something that could have gone to places like Flint, Lansing, or the others.

A month-long exhibit entitled 'Life and Work In Kalamazoo' was part of the Berlin Industrial Fair. The exhibit was one of the largest of more than 1,000 displays. In the late '50s, Gibson was on its way to being one of Kalamazoo's largest employers, and Ted McCarty was co-chair of American House at the Fair.

At the fair, his company displayed merchandise. "Gibson was very happy, and very proud, that we were able to do the fair. We displayed instruments while Rem Wall and Julius Bellson demonstrated them to crowds."

At the fair, the family of one Gibson's worker, Mary Lou Hoogenboom, was elected 'The Ideal Family' at the fair.

National and Local Leadership

Places like Kalamazoo, Flint, Pontiac, Battle Creek, and Saginaw had limited social calendars, and community leaders typically support their the public library, symphony, private dinner clubs, and perhaps a country club as places to network. Ted McCarty, being a very social man, pursued these organizations. His family joined the Kalamazoo Country Club by 1949, Ted joined the symphony early on, and he joined the local chapter of the Rotary Club. With these organizations, Ted's natural leadership abilities became an important asset; he was elected to the symphony board of directors in 1952, elected president in

'53, and served the board until '56. One of his accomplishments there was to bring Andrés Segovia to Kalamazoo.

"The concert was a success – it was a very big deal," said Ted. "And I always believed the guitar was a fine musical instrument – not something you just sit around and strum. I thought it could take its place with any other instrument in the business."

McCarty was also a leader on the national level. A prime example was American Music Conference (A.M.C.), a national non-profit association dedicated to promoting the importance of music, musicmaking, and music education. Based on his "unique and lasting imprint upon the world of music," McCarty was an honorary director of the A.M.C. He also served as President of the organization from 1961 to '63, remained a member through the '60s, and was Executive Director from 1970 to '76. According to Dan Del Fiorentino, historian for the National Association of Music Merchants, McCarty's leadership brought a new era in promoting musical instruments. McCarty believed that if a musical instrument was made part of the public's consciousness, many more people would want to play. McCarty's idea was to put the musical instrument in front of people, not just by way of a musical performer. His plan was to have cultural characters (like the Jolly Green Giant or Tony The Tiger) portrayed with musical instruments in ads for mainstream products (like green beans and breakfast cereal). Del Fiorentino recalls that McCarty and A.M.C. founder Henry Grossman (Grossman Musical Instruments) promoted the new idea in 1962. McCarty and Grossman devised an annual contest where advertising agencies created ads that included a musical instrument in ads for more mainstream products. The promotion was popular, and McCarty's concepts regarding accessibility remain alive and well today.

The Gibson Years: Leo Fender

From 1950 to '65, two men – Leo Fender and Ted McCarty – stood as the iconic heroes in the musical instruments industry. But with few exceptions, the two couldn't have been more opposite; neither could the play the guitar, both were accountants early in their careers, both liked radios, both were born in 1909 (Fender on August 10, McCarty on October 10), and both graduated high school in 1928. Fender was the reclusive inventor/entrepreneur, McCarty the professional corporate leader. Fender worked alone, McCarty never did. Fender was an outsider, McCarty an insider.

"I never knew anybody who got along with Leo," McCarty said. "He was a strange man. When he came along with his first guitars, Gibson, Martin, and Gretsch – owners of fine guitar brands – had a club, and we invited Leo to join. He said, 'Not interested.' He never got in with our group at any time, I think because he was afraid people would steal his ideas! The three guitar makers in Chicago – Harmony, National, and Kay – were members, and nobody would've thought about copying something from the other guys. We would have been ashamed, and we had our own ideas. We just didn't have any reason to cheat. All of those years, I never saw or heard of stealing an idea, except Leo, who got his start by

1952 Gibson GA-40 Les Paul amplifier front and back. Ted McCarty, Seth Lover, and Walt Fuller had a difficult time competing with Leo Fender's amplifiers. When interviewed, Ted McCarty and Les Paul remembered many details concerning the 1952 Les Paul Model guitar, but neither man could remember any specifics about the 1952 GA-40 Les Paul amplifier.

copying (Paul Bigsby's solidbody guitar). When Gretsch came out with the Sparkle Jet, Gibson didn't want to do that.

"CMI had a factory right next to Fender, on the north end of Los Angeles. Ours was the Olds brass-trumpet factory. When I was in L.A., I'd go to the Fender factory and see a fellow by the name of Forrest White, who would take me through the factory and show me what they were doing. We did that until CBS came in."

Still, McCarty admired Fender's accomplishments. As a CEO, he certainly was aware of corporate net worth, so when he found out that Fender sold his company to CBS for $13 million, he never forgot. He admired Fender for the success of his company's amplifiers, *and* because he became a multimillionaire.

"Don Randall put Fender guitars on the market – he was a salesman and a very good businessman. I'd see Don at trade shows, all over. You see, Leo always wanted to sue somebody, claiming they were infringing on some of his designs. So Don and I had to meet in various cities and we'd have attorneys with us. I'd be there, and Randall, Leo's attorney would be there. The last incident I remember, Leo was going to sue us because we made a guitar with an off-center C-bout. Leo had done that with one of his guitar designs, and he said we couldn't make a C-bout. We disagreed. So Fender got their attorneys and we had a meeting. They kept talking about their design being original, but we argued that Gibson mandolins had offset bouts. We had a mandolin at the meeting, and there were engineers and attorneys... So we presented a mandolin that was made 40 or 50 years before anything Fender was talking about. So our presentation ended the discussion about a lawsuit.

"After the meeting, Don Randall said, 'Ted, to tell you the truth, I would like to know how you make the (Les Paul model) solidbody guitar.' The Les Paul came out after the Fender solidbody became popular, but ours was not one solid piece of wood – ours was two pieces glued together. And they were different kinds of wood. The thickness of each was critical because that's where you got a lot of the tone. With the gold finish, Fender couldn't figure out the woods, and Randall was curious. He said, 'What is that body?' And I joked with him, 'It's gold!' I wouldn't tell him!

"Leo never really knew how to make a guitar – he was an amplifier man, and a darn good one – and most of the people who were working for him were not trained in making guitars. And Don Randall was a very good man – and I think was the reason for Fender's success.

"Leo drove me crazy, trying to out-build him on amplifiers. One thing Gibson has always had, even before I went there, was a good mellow instrument, and good mellow amplifier. Not this raucous tone. We didn't want a guitar like that, and we didn't want an amplifier like that. Leo came out with these amplifiers that just screamed. We made ours so they'd cut out before going wild. So, with their attitude, Fender was just building them, building them, building them. They were very popular.

"Leo had a little office in one corner of the factory. He'd get in there and change parts in an amplifier. He knew what he wanted, and he spent his time piddling around on amps, not the guitar."

The Gibson Years: C. Frederick Martin III and Others

McCarty prided himself on being a popular figure in the music industry. He counted as his friends nearly all the top men at the major manufacturers. It was a trademark quality he developed in high school where he participated in everything from sports to theater, all the while working at Kroger's Grocery.

In the music industry, McCarty was a bridge builder. He preferred nothing more than meeting face-to-face with peers at Epiphone, Gretsch, and the Chicago builders – Harmony, Kay, and National. He also had a great deal of respect for the industry's premier flat-top maker – Martin. While at Wurlitzer, he gained first-hand knowledge of the Martin Company.

"I got to know Fred Martin (C.F. Martin, III 1894-1986), who was a marvelous man. Fred and I were really good personal friends. He was very pleasant. He invited me to Nazareth (Pennsylvania) to tour their factory. At Wurlitzer, I learned that Gibson and Martin were both interested in quality products.

"When I first got to Gibson, I knew the leading acoustic guitar was a Martin, and the leading archtop builder was Epiphone. At the Rochester store, customers wanted Gibson. Wurlitzer handled Martins, Epiphone, Nationals, and some Harmony economy models. I wanted to get Gibson guitars into Wurlitzer stores, where Epiphone and Martin were our best sellers, but they were different types of guitars. Martin was strictly acoustic and they were very, very fine. But Epi was making the ones like the L-7 archtop in the Gibson line. I liked Gibson, and I thought Gibson would sell better than the Epi in our Wurlitzer stores. And Epi was beginning to get into trouble.

"After I was sent to Gibson in 1948, I finally got Mr. Berlin to put Gibson in all Wurlitzer stores. How'd I do it? Well, I knew the guy in charge of purchasing guitars at Wurlitzer, and Berlin knew him, of course. So I talked with Berlin about it and told him we should have a meeting with this fellow. At the meeting, in comes Berlin, and he sits next to the man, and finally Mr. Berlin tells him he is thinking about putting Gibson into Wurlitzer. And it was done."

The McCarty family (Ted, Elly, Sue and Ted) at their 2311 Glenwood Drive home in June 1953.

The Gibson Years: The 1950s, an interview with Susan McCarty Davis

Ted and Elinor McCarty's second child, Susan, was born in Cincinnati on March 13, 1940. She was 8 years old when the family moved to Kalamazoo. After attending college in Colorado, Susan and her husband, Elbert Davis, moved to Twin Falls, Idaho, where the couple raised two children and pursued careers.

If ever there was a Rockwellian story, Ted McCarty's life in the 1950s was it. Every day, the well-dressed dad left his beautiful colonial home, bound for work, and leaving two children and a lovely wife, driving his Cadillac to work. It was picture-perfect. On weekends, the family enjoyed its swimming pool, the country club, private dinner clubs, and the symphony.

What type of music did your dad listen to around the house in the 1950s? *He always preferred symphony music – he wasn't much for listening to western music, or rock music, or any of that kind of thing. He had some jazz records. He liked music, but we lived in Michigan and we didn't get much western music. And when I was little, rock wasn't even in yet. But my father didn't much care about rock music. He didn't listen to it much, even though he is responsible for most of the sound of rock music. It just wasn't his thing.*

What type of music did you listen to in the 1950s? *Oh, just the popular music.*

Bill Haley and the Comets? *Yes, that kind of thing.*

And Elvis? *Yes, my brother and I loved that sort of stuff.*

Would your dad say anything when you were listening to the radio? *No, he didn't. He kind of did his thing, and we listened to our music. I don't think one intruded on the other at all. It's kind of interesting that our father really didn't pay attention to rock and roll. Well, we all listened to popular music – Bill Haley and Elvis – but neither mother or father paid much attention.*

Did they get you interested in taking up an instrument? *My brother and I both took piano lessons starting in the first grade. He didn't take them very long, but I took until I was about 14. Of course, my mother was a very good piano player. She took piano lessons when she was a little girl, and she had perfect pitch – she was the musician of the group. She didn't play a lot, but she could play anything she heard. If there was a musical out like "The King and I," she could sit and play it.*

Did you have a grand piano, or an upright? *We had an upright.*

Do you recall the family going to the Kalamazoo Symphony? *Yes, in fact my father was president of the symphony board. He was very active in it. And there was a little theater company where we'd go to see plays. If we were in New York City and there was a good musical, we'd sometimes see that.*

Do you recall any famous people visiting your home? *Andrés Segovia came to the symphony one time, and came to our house. Of course, Les Paul and Mary Ford used to come to the house for dinner. And they may have stayed the night a time or two.*

What do you remember about Mary Ford? *She was the nicest, sweetest, prettiest lady, with the most beautiful speaking voice, as well as singing voice. She was just really a nice lady.*

How about Les Paul? *He was perfectly nice. Beyond that, I don't have much to say; he could play the music, which I liked.*

How about Maurice Berlin. Did you ever meet him? *Oh, yes.*

Les Paul and your dad very much agree that Mr. Berlin was the finest man ever! *He was a good man. I liked Mr. Berlin. Every Thursday, my father took the train to Chicago and met with Mr. Berlin. Sometimes he would drive, and mother and I would go shopping, then to Mr. Berlin's office. I was just a child, sitting there listening.*

What about the other fellows at Gibson – John Huis, Julius Bellson, Larry Allers, Seth Lover, Walter Fuller, and George Comee? *I knew their names, but the only ones I really knew were John Huis and Julius Bellson. John Huis and my father were good friends. They'd go hunting together and do things. We'd go to the Huis' once in a while for dinner, and they'd come to our house. And Margaret and Julius Bellson were really quite good friends for a lot of years. They came for Christmas one time, because they didn't have any children or family. And we'd go to their house, and my grandmother would go along with us too, at Christmas or something. We'd play games and have dinner. They were always very good to my brother and me.*

Christmas 1953, Ted, his son Ted, and Julius Bellson at the McCarty's.

John Huis and your dad went hunting then? *Yes, I believe they went duck hunting. My father loved fishing, too. If people invited him to go, he'd get himself together and go.*

Do you remember when your family joined the Kalamazoo Country Club? *I think they joined in the summer of 1948 or '49.*

Did your mom like to play, or was it just your dad? *No, my mother never liked to play golf. It was only my father. I played a little – father wanted me to – but I never could get the hang of it.*

Did your dad get home late at night, or was he pretty regular on hours? *He was always home in time to eat dinner. That always blew Paul Reed Smith's mind, that my father was home by 5:30 every night of the week. You could set your watch by dinner time at our house when I was a girl (laughs)!*

So, did he go in early? *Nope. Never. The only time I can ever remember him being at the factory any extra time was when there were labor negotiations with the labor union or there had been a fire at the plant. Dad used to take me and my friends to junior high and high school. There was a car pool, and he'd be the one who'd go to the school when it was our turn to drive. And we didn't go to school until about 8:15. He was not a "Go in early, stay late" or "Go in on the weekends" guy. He worked 9 to 5 and that was it.*

And he was a member of the Rotary Club... *He was President of the Rotary Club, and we were*

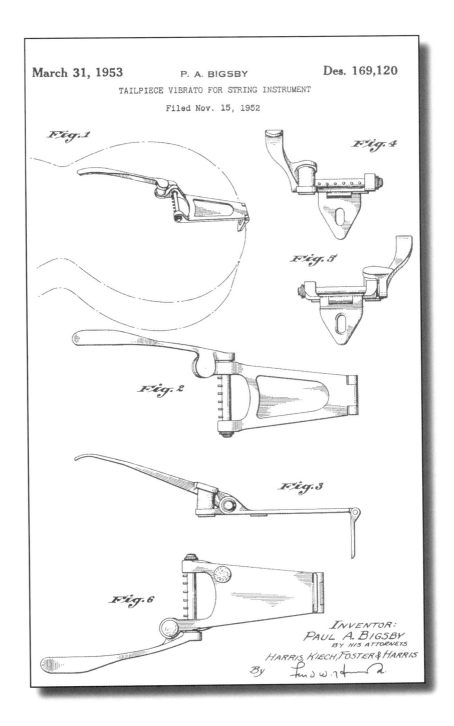

March 31, 1953   P. A. BIGSBY   Des. 169,120
TAILPIECE VIBRATO FOR STRING INSTRUMENT
Filed Nov. 15, 1952

Paul Bigsby's 1953 vibrato patent.

members of the Park Club and Beacon Club (dinner clubs). When I was a child, Kalamazoo county was dry, so there were quite a few dinner clubs, and they were the only really nice places to eat.

So, Sue Davis lived a normal, happy childhood typical of successful family in the 1950s. Her father had paid his dues early in his career – traveling, relocating, and working in eight cities. But the experience gave McCarty a strong sense of how he wanted things to be once he settled in Kalamazoo.

Bigsby Accessories: 1965

The 1950s were a prosperous time for Gibson and many other companies in Kalamazoo and other mid-sized cities like Flint, Battle Creek, and Pontiac. But the 1960s would not be like the '50s. Gibson grew so fast that by '66, quality control began to suffer. One reason was the departure of Ted McCarty.

There were several reasons why McCarty left Gibson that year.

"In 1965, I had an opportunity to buy Paul Bigsby Accessories, and at the time I did not particularly care for some of the things CMI was doing. There was new top management – Maurice Berlin was out, and Arnie Berlin was in. So I thought it was time to get out. I was looking for another opportunity, and it came from Paul Bigsby.

"Paul never made the Bigsby tailpiece in quantity, never made them to sell commercially. And I, as Gibson president, wanted to buy as many Bigsby vibratos as I could – I was the first one to put them on Gibson guitars. At first, Gibson said we couldn't use them because the handle was in the way. Paul had a cast aluminum tailpiece that was just a straight piece.

"So I called Paul and told him Gibson wanted to put vibratos on our guitars, but the handle was in the way. So Paul said, 'Can you design it so it will swing away? If you do it, I'll make it and put it only on Gibsons.' So I went to work, designed the thing, had one built by hand, and shipped it to him, and he figured out how to make it in profitable quantities. Well, the next problem was that nobody else could buy it. Fred Gretsch and a couple other guitar companies saw it, and they all wanted it. But it belonged to Gibson. So finally Fred Gretsch called and said, 'I want to put that vibrato on our guitars. I'd buy a lot of them, and Paul's business will grow. But you're going to have to give us permission – Paul won't do it without.'

'So I thought, "Maybe there's a way to do it. So I called Paul and I said, 'Can you think of anything we can work out, if you could sell (your vibratos) to anybody else, but somehow or another, we would be able to hang on to it?' He said, 'Well, I've been thinking... If you put in writing, you can buy yours for $20, and the rest will have to pay $22, you'll get a little money for designing it.'

"So I went to Mr. Berlin and asked, and he said, 'It sounds like a good deal. I'll talk to the attorney to see if it's legal.'

"So the companies poured in orders for 5,000 vibratos here, 4,000 vibratos there. And poor Paul, in his little plant, didn't want to get involved – he'd never been in the volume business. He tried for awhile, but he just got swamped, and that's when he called me (in November of '65) and said, 'I want to sell.' I said, 'But you're making a good business now.' He said, 'I've had a devil of a time in this factory, and I don't want to do it anymore. I want to sell.' Then I asked him, 'Are your talking to me as president of Gibson, or as Ted McCarty?' And he said, 'I thought maybe you'd like it. If you buy it from the ground up it would be better for the Bigsby Company than if Gibson bought it. I'm not going to offer it to anybody else.'

"I asked, 'How much do you want for it?' And he told me – a nice big figure. I told him, 'I'll tell you what, I'll be out there Saturday morning, and John Huis will be with me.'

"So John and I grabbed a plane and went out, and got there. It was about 6 o'clock Saturday morning, and we went to his factory, and we were there when they opened it at 7 o'clock. We talked with him, and I said, 'I want to see the books, and John is going out in the factory to look at the equipment and look at the way you make them.' Paul said, 'Alright.' So I said, 'Let me see the books.' And he said, 'I haven't got any.' I said, 'Paul, how can you run a business without books?' He said (in an irritated voice), 'Here's my books!' And he put down two piles, saying, 'Pay's on here and income's on there.' And I said, 'What do you do when the IRS comes around?' He said, 'Well, I give just what I gave you. There ain't no law that says I have to have books.' I said, 'That's good enough for me. But what do you do when the IRS wants a statement of your income and your profits?' Then he said, 'Oh, I have an accountant do that.'

"So John and I went to lunch, and decided to buy Bigsby. We were ready, because we knew changes were coming at CMI."

McCarty and Huis returned to Kalamazoo with a company – and a plan. Huis had enough years and experience to retire with a pension, so he would manage the plant. McCarty also had options; would he stay at Gibson, and lead Bigsby remotely, or would he leave?

Why McCarty Quit Gibson: 1966

The Kalamazoo Gazette, the major paper in the city, reported that Ted McCarty resigned from Gibson because CMI considered his ownership of Bigsby Accessories a possible conflict of interest. Although Gibson had been using several of its own vibrato designs, like the side-pull and Maestro, since the early 1960s, the company used Bigsbys on the ES-335, ES-345, ES-355, and other models as a factory option.

The Gazette covered McCarty's resignation by saying, *"Theodore M. (Ted) McCarty, president of Gibson, Inc., for the past 16 years, has announced his resignation from the top post in the Kalamazoo guitar manufacturing firm as of July 1.*

"McCarty will leave Gibson to devote full-time to Bigsby Accessories, Inc., 3221 E. Kilgore, a guitar equipment firm of which he has also been president since last January.

"McCarty and John Huis, another former Gibson executive, purchased the Bigsby firm last November. They moved its equipment from Downey, California, to Kalamazoo, and Huis left Gibson to direct Bigsby

as vice president.

"At that time McCarty tendered his resignation as president of Gibson Inc. to the Chicago Musical Instrument Company, of which Gibson is a subsidiary. The resignation... was not accepted until this week.

"Under McCarty's leadership Gibson Inc., experienced rapid expansion in the physical plant, employment and sales. Employment rose from 150 to 1,025 during his years as president. He had served as general manager of the firm for two years before being named president.

"McCarty, who resides at 2412 Bronson, states that he expects the Bigsby firm to expand into new phases of guitar industry production in the future. No successor to McCarty has been named by Chicago Musical Instruments Co."

Why did McCarty quit Gibson? Why did he purchase Bigsby? The fact is that he had already had plenty of opportunities to purchase companies such a Epiphone, which he could have done with little trouble and without stretching his wallet.

McCarty departed Gibson for the same reason he bolted from Wurlitzer – personal problems with management. In Gibson's case it was Maurice Berlin's son, Arnie, who replaced his father as president of CMI in the mid '60s. The appointment didn't sit well with McCarty, who became receptive to other opportunities. McCarty respected Maurice Berlin more than anyone, but he had no use for Arnie Berlin. There were 15 years between Maurice and Ted, and another 15 years between McCarty and Arnie, but in terms of management style and disposition, Ted was much more like Maurice. Arnie was an eastern-educated college boy who McCarty described as having "an MBA attitude."

"In 1966, I had good employees at Gibson," said McCarty. "We had more men who were assigned different responsibilities. Still,

PERFORMER REM WALL, A GIBSON EMPLOYE, GIVES GUITAR FINAL TEST
Gibson President T. M. McCarty, Vice President John Huis Look On —*Gazette photos*

Ted McCarty with Rem Wall and John Huis in a February 23, 1964, photo from the Kalamazoo Gazette.

I didn't find running Gibson was particularly difficult; my difficulty came with Arnie Berlin, who looked upon me as a 'country bumpkin' – and I had a five-year engineering degree. I even helped write his thesis for him because his father could get me to help him! And Arnie, as the new president, was doing things that were contrary to what I thought was proper. And it wasn't just Gibson – CMI had seven companies. I was at Gibson for 18½ years, it was unionized, and we never had a strike. There were six companies in Kalamazoo taken into the union during the war, and as far as I know, all five others had one or more bad strikes. People would say, 'Why hasn't Gibson had a strike?' And I'd say, 'Because we treat our employees like they're important. We don't make them feel like nobody gives a damn.'

"Arnie was a graduate of Princeton and Harvard, and in his opinion, everybody on the west side of the Hudson was an idiot. And he'd have nothing to do with his family.

"Well, Mr. Berlin called one day and said, 'So-and-so and his wife are coming through town on their way to California. They're going to stop in Kalamazoo to see the factory, and I want you to meet them, Ted – and turn on your usual charm. I think this guy would be a good man for our company.' So I picked him up in my Cadillac, took him to the factory, and spent the morning with him. Then I took him to the Beacon Club, and then back to the factory. So, we were sitting in my office, talking, and on my back wall was a portrait done by one of the finest photographers in the world – a picture was of Mr. Berlin.

"This man was looking around the office and he said, 'Who's the gentleman in the picture?' I said, 'That's Mr. Berlin, owner of most everything here.' The man said in a disconcerted tone, 'He looks like he's Jewish.' I said, 'Yes, his family is Jewish. They came from Russia.' The guy said, 'I know Arnie Berlin.' I told him, 'That's his son.' And he said, 'Arnie Berlin is this man's son?' I said, 'Yes. Why?' He said, 'I went to Princeton for four years, I went to Harvard for two years, and I never knew he was Jewish, and nobody else in the school knew he was Jewish.' I told him, 'His father is a prince of a man.'

"So, the next morning I get a phone call from Mr. Berlin. He told me that the guy and his wife didn't stop in Chicago on their way to California. I told Mr. Berlin that I wasn't surprised, and I told him what happened. Mr. Berlin told me, 'I understand.' I knew, because Mr. Berlin had told me that his son had serious personal biases against the Berlin family. But in spite of this, Mr. Berlin made his son president of CMI.

"I worked so closely with Mr. Berlin for years. We built Gibson up *together*. That's how we felt about it.

"I went to Chicago the day I got the letter saying Mr. Berlin was stepping down, but staying on as Chairman of the Board, and that Arnie was going to be president. So I went to Chicago, and I asked him, 'Can we talk?' like I usually did. I sat in his office and said, "I've always answered to you, but now Arnie is president of Chicago Musical Instruments? So, to whom do I report?' He said, 'Well, I'm here, am I not?' I said, 'Yes you are, sir.' He said, 'Well, that ought to be enough.'

"So I never for one minute answered to Arnie Berlin! I had no respect for him because Arnie was biased against his own family. His father came over as an immigrant and built himself up from nothing to become a multimillionaire with factories all over this country and sales around the world!

"Mr. Berlin sent me to Germany, because they were having a dispute over something. I said, 'Well now Mr. B., you can handle that, you know him the same as I do. But Mr. Berlin said, 'Yeah, but two Jews are never going to settle anything.' So I went to Germany, Switzerland, and France – whenever something like that was involved, he sent me.

"Another time, we were having a big argument with a distributor in England over merchandise going to Mexico. He was insisting that he should have Mexico, and we were making the same type of thing. But I got it, and CMI went into Mexico.

"I never had any use for Arnie Berlin. I put up with his appointment, but after about a year, I'd decided to get out. If you feel you cannot depend on the people you're working with, you don't belong. Then I got the call from Paul Bigsby saying he wanted to sell. So after John and I purchased Bigsby, I went to Chicago and resigned to Mr. Berlin. I was told Mr. Berlin was very upset and couldn't understand. But I told him, 'You and I got along great for all these years, and I did my best for you – you know it and I know it.' And he knew! Arnie moved Mr. Berlin out of his office into a little bitty place, and gave him a secretary. And that was it – the end – the reason for the downfall of CMI."

McCarty stayed on at Gibson until a replacement could be found. And according to Willie Moseley's 1999 interview with McCarty, Berlin offered to buy Bigsby from McCarty for $50,000 more than he paid. Negotiations also concerned McCarty staying on while keeping Bigsby (with Huis serving as manager). But the discussions ended with McCarty leaving under the "conflict of interest" umbrella.

Financial trouble was brewing when McCarty left Gibson. Product volume remained high, reaching its peak in 1965 before beginning to decrease due to lower demand and lost market share. Plus, new depreciation schedules were adding cost to product that were underabsorbed in pricing, creating a potential for a loss on the balance sheet. Conversely, added production increased cost absorption, which minimized lingering unabsorbed costs, and P&L losses were avoided. This all meant that more production was needed without an offsetting increase in variable cost. Gibson looked for ways to speed up its processes.

Arnie Berlin was slow to find a replacement for McCarty. He favored men in his age group; the two who replaced McCarty and Huis were not guitar men, and their textbooks were unable to cope with a guitar manufacturing business. The appointment of Arnie and his appointees marked the beginning of a 20-year slide at Gibson.

Sometime after McCarty left, losses began to reappear on CMI's books; The McCarty era was an island of profit between two oceans of financial loss. Gibson was losing money when McCarty joined in 1948, then after a couple months – and for the entire McCarty era – Gibson never showed a loss. After McCarty left, Gibson began reporting losses to CMI.

M.H. Berlin

John Majeski, Jr., former publisher of *The Music Trades*, and a walking encyclopedia on the music industry of the 1940s through the '70s, agrees that Maurice Berlin was the pivotal figure in the success of CMI, Gibson, and Ted McCarty.

Did you know Maurice Berlin very well? *Yes, yes, yes... I had many encounters with him. He was a brilliant man, so intuitively smart. He used to take me to lunch a lot and ask me questions. We used to go the Standard Club and the Union League. I lived in New York, but I used to go to Chicago [several times each] year.*

When did you first meet Berlin? *At the July trade show in 1946; I was just out of the Army, and my father (then publisher of The Music Trades) said 'You've got to meet M.H. Berlin,' because he was a very important man. Whenever I was in Chicago, I'd go see him. He was a very discerning man, and I was a young reporter – but I was also a grab-bag of information for him, which I did not appreciate at the time. He'd ask questions to get my reactions. He was always very, very nice to me.*

Do you remember talking with Berlin about the guitar business booming, especially once Leo Fender came in? *Oh, Leo was a fabulous guy – what I'd call an idiot savant. He did things with no formal training, no scientific background. But he was a lousy businessman, but a terrific inventor. And he was a very modest man. When Leo sold the Fender Company, he wanted just $1 million. Don Randall told him, "You're out of your mind!" and reminded him it's worth much more. So Randall sold it to CBS for $13 million.*

So Don Randall (Leo Fender's partner at Fender Sales) was a good businessman? *Don was a superb businessman – brilliant. And one of the most brilliant things he did was to learn how to fly an airplane because he wanted to fly from Fullerton to Las Vegas. He had a brilliant idea; at that time, Las Vegas was the music capital of the world. So he'd fly to Las Vegas with equipment and present it to everyone playing there. Everyone went to Vegas to play, and Don hit on the idea to service everyone who played there. He'd present them with guitars, and he really built Fender's relationships with artists. That was his real contribution to Fender.*

Do you think Leo Fender stole Paul Bigsby's solidbody electric guitar design? *I really don't think so. Leo was a very strange guy, with these wild, sensational notions about building things.*

You were about 29 years old when the first solidbody Fender came out in 1950. What do you remember about it? *Well, everybody else made fun of it – called it a canoe paddle. Ted called it a canoe paddle. But Berlin latched onto the solidbody really fast. He wanted a solidbody in his line.*

Was Berlin the one who pushed for a Gibson solidbody? *It's hard to be accurate on things where everyone has a different opinion. But Berlin was very cognizant about the importance of the solidbody electric, no question about that. I had a conversation with him about it, and he thought the solidbody was really great. It was Randall who thought the beauty of the solidbody was that every one had two sales; you sell a guitar, then the customer had to have an amplifier. It doubled your business. So Fender just grew like wildfire, and Gibson limped along behind.*

What did Berlin think about Gibson trailing Fender? *Berlin was incredibly generous. I never heard him complain about a competitor. He admired a competitor if they were doing something right and being smart. He was an unusual man.*

Berlin was born in Russia, and his parents were very poor. He started working at the age of 12 as a messenger boy for the Wurlitzer Company. He never had any education whatsoever. But a more brilliant gentleman you could not find. Every single person who ever worked for him thought he was great. He was absolutely a natural talent who signed up with the Martin band instrument company in Elkhart. Long story short, he changed the company name to the Chicago Musical Instrument Company.

Berlin's son, Arnold, was everything his dad was not. Arnie was better-looking, tall, a terrific tennis player, and had every social grace you could think of. But Arnold made a mess of CMI. He kicked his father out of the business and merged with ECL (later called Norlin). There was a proxy battle and M.H. Berlin graciously bowed out.

Did Maurice and Arnold Berlin get along? *No. A father and a son conflict in business is a very difficult situation.*

People say M.H. Berlin was a very trusting man. *I don't doubt that, but he was also awfully smart. I consider him the finest gentleman I ever met in my life, period!*

Anyone who knew M.H. Berlin had tremendous admiration for him. He had a way of buying companies – the way he took over Story & Clark Pianos (in 1961), Gibson (in 1944), and the big story was Lowrey Organ, which made CMI a viable institution on the stock exchange. That became more than 50% of CMI sales.

Lowrey organ was a brilliant merchandising idea. They brought out an organ for under $1,000 that was not a piece of junk, and just took the music industry by storm. Lowrey organ was the big story for M.H. Berlin and CMI. CMI purchased the Lowrey Organ business from Central Commercial Corporation. The minute the owner of Central Commercial died, his managers wanted to get rid of the organ business. That's when they called me up saying, "Who is in the business, who will buy this?" Those men went all around trying to sell the organ business and everyone laughed. Nobody would touch the business at all. And then Berlin heard about it. I remember him calling me, asking, "Who is this Central Commercial?" And as soon as he found out who they were he bought it.

The Bigsby Years: 1966-'99

Ted left Gibson because Arnie Berlin was handed the CMI presidency when his father, Maurice, moved into the shadows as a lame-duck chairman. At the time, Ted was 57 years old, Arnie was about 42, and Maurice Berlin was about 72. Maurice's retirement was understandable; he was getting old and the industry was changing rapidly. Ted McCarty and Les Paul, whose memories of just about everything seem to differ, agreed on one thing - Berlin was a great man. Workers at Gibson remember Berlin occasionally touring Parsons Street, and he, like McCarty, was unforgettably nice to the people of Gibson.

McCarty, as CEO of Gibson, had the greatest respect for what Leo Fender accomplished when Leo sold his company for $13 million. To Ted, that was a benchmark achievement. Like many CEO's, both then and today, Ted McCarty knew that fortunes were generally greater for those who owned a company. Fortunes were greater for entrepreneurs than they were for professional corporate mangers. Often times CEO corporate managers would watch as the owners of the company vendors and suppliers made much more money as a vendor than the CEO did as head of the corporation. McCarty, the quintessential

The Bigsby and Flex-Lite factory in November, 1998, when the business was still owned and operated by Ted McCarty.

bridge-builder, learned first hand at the Kalamazoo Country Club and the Kalamazoo Rotary, just how well local business owners were doing in Kalamazoo. McCarty spent a lot of time as a member of the Kalamazoo Golf Club on the golf course with his friends, local businessmen, and they'd talk about such things.

When Paul Bigsby, Ted's long time friend, called McCarty, Ted was mentally in a good place. It all seemed to fit. It seemed perfect. Ted, in his calm, cool style acted on the Bigsby offer quickly but not impetuously.

McCarty, "John and I went to lunch, and we decided to buy Bigsby. We bought it right there. We were ready, because we knew changes were coming at CMI. We had 1 ½ months to move Bigsby. This was just before Thanksgiving (1965). We had to find a place and get out of California by January 1st (1966). We had to have a factory. We got a hold of the realtor that they used at Gibson. This realtor had bought and torn down fifteen homes next to the Gibson factory, and he did it quietly.

"We bought the American Italian Society Club House building, and some extra land for expansion in the future. It was wide open and it had a kitchen. The price was right. John and I had 60% - 40% deal. We sent two moving trucks out to California. We bought everything, the machinery and the work-in-process."

"Paul's daughter came in for two weeks to show us how the vibrolas were put together. The first one was made on January 11th, and our first shipment to a guitar company was made. We worked seven days a week. I worked, my son worked, John Huis worked, and his son worked. We got a whole cadre of workers. They resigned from Gibson and went to work for us."

"We were selling vibratos to practically all the major companies. One day Fred Gretsch and I counted them at the trade show – we had 14 different models. Of all of our individual customers, Fred Gretsch was the biggest, but we were selling to other people, and the sales to the other people were greater than to Fred Gretsch. But the Japanese started to flood the country with cheap guitars and they practically put those four or five companies, including Harmony and Kay, out of business. The Japanese forced five companies into bankruptcy. The guitars that came in from Japan in the early 1960s were not good guitars. They were cheap. In the late 1960s, the Japanese were selling completed guitars for less than Harmony could pay for the wood! The Chicago companies couldn't compete, so they folded up, all of them. But Gibson was not getting any real pressure from Japan because Gibson was quality. I don't think Martin had any problem with them. Gretsch was in trouble too. Gretsch sold out to the big piano company, Baldwin. Then they went down the tubes."

"We had about 12 employees at Bigsby Accessories and initially things were going along very nicely. The Japanese nearly sank us. Their prices were so low. The Japanese prices were so low, that they put those Chicago guitar makers out of business. And those Chicago guitar makers used Bigsby vibratos. The Japanese guitar makers made their own vibratos, so they didn't use Bigsby vibratos."

McCarty faced a challenge when all the lower-quality American guitar makers went out of business. He managed to keep Bigsby afloat by taking on other jobs in consulting and administration, but he also invested in a company called Flex-Lite. During this time he was also associated with many organizations including GAMA (Guitar and Accessories Marketing Association) and the AMC (American Music Conference – see earlier report). Ted continued to be active in the Kalamazoo community, among other things, being president of the Kalamazoo Country Club in 1972.

Flex-Lite made small flashlights that were used in industry. Ted credits Flex-Lite with providing the cash flow to allow Bigsby Accessories to stay afloat during its business downturn. In the 1990s Bigsby vibratos became very popular again, and Bigsby's were really considered to be 'the one.' Bigsby Accessories business improved greatly and its income obtained a level that was near to the highly successful Flex-Lite venture's net income.

John Huis, who was about the same age as Ted McCarty, finally decided to retire again. Huis officially retired (he didn't quit or resign) from Gibson in 1966, but Huis started a new career with Ted at Bigsby Accessories. John originally owned 40% of the Bigsby Company. When John re-retired and moved to Florida, Ted bought John's share of Bigsby. Ted owned the Bigsby factory, which was leased back to the Bigsby Company.

As noted, in the late 1960s, McCarty knew he had a problem with Bigsby. He needed to diversify and buy another small company, a company that used the same type of machinery as was used at Bigsby. Just as a friend, Bill Gretsch surprised Ted pushing him towards Maurice Berlin in 1947, another friend came to Ted's rescue when he was in need. At a cocktail party, Ted and a friend were talking – Ted mentioned he needed to buy another small company – his friend said, 'I have one that I want to sell.' Once again Ted's broad base of friends and contacts paid off. Ted went over to investigate the Kalamazoo company, just like he had done with Bigsby. Without too much difficulty or concern Ted said, 'I'll buy it.'

Ted's purchase, Flex-Lite, was founded in Kalamazoo in 1947, specializing in flexible flashlights and inspection lighting tools. Ted, "Flex-Lite saved our lives. It was a specialty company that made many different models, for example Flex-Lite made a model for Cadillac, who ordered 1,800 units. We made a model that was a fishing light. Once we got Flex-Lite going, the number of models grew and grew. We added another little building doubling the size of our factory. Although we were not very large compared to Gibson, we doubled the size of our business. When I bought Flex-Lite they only made two models, we build that up to 30 different models."

While running Bigsby and Flex-Lite, Ted started consulting work with Paul Reed Smith Guitars in 1986. Ted was also busy attending to his wife Elinor's illness. Ted and Elinor moved out of their large home in Kalamazoo and into a condo located on Essex Circle in Kalamazoo, not far from the Kalamazoo Country Club. Elinor died October 23, 1989. Ted's eyesight was failing so his family asked Mable Sherrill to become Ted's live-in care taker. Mable, was the sister of Ted's daughter's husband.

In the 1990s, Ted split his time between Kalamazoo and his condo on Kihei Road, Kihei, Hawaii. "When I was in Kalamazoo, during the winter, I'd go into the office every day and try to develop things. In the summer, when I was in Hawaii for six months, I'd think about things that would improve my businesses. For Flex-Lite, I built the company up to the point that we were shipping product to about twenty foreign countries."

Ted, "By the early 1990s the vibrato business had been coming back strong. We were shipping vibratos to guitar makers in London, Sweden, Germany, Canada, and of course to the manufacturers in the United States. The Bigsby vibrato had once again been recognized as the only really good vibrato. When I originally purchased the company from Paul Bigsby in 1965, I managed to hold on to all the equipment – tools – dies – and forms - to manufacture vibratos exactly the way it had been done by Paul Bigsby when he owned the company."

"Walter Fuller, who designed Gibson's P-90 pickup, was a good friend of mine. When I went into business for myself, he used to work for us. I would hire him to come over and help us with the electronics."

At age 89, on May 10, 1999, Ted retired and sold the Bigsby business to the Gretsch Company. The sale to the Gretsch Company made perfect sense. Gretsch Guitars from the 1950s were very much associated with the Bigsby vibrato and as it was pointed out earlier, it was Ted McCarty that originally allowed Gretsch to use the swing-away Gretsch vibrato. When the sale of Bigsby to Gretsch was announced, Ted McCarty commented, "Fred Gretsch is the obvious person to take over Bigsby." It's ironic, too, that the new owner, Fred Gretsch III,was the son of Bill Gretsch, the very man that pushed McCarty to Maurice Berlin and Gibson Guitars.

The Paul Reed Smith Years: 1986-2001

In the mid 1980s, when Ted was in his late 70s, a guitar builder approached him with a deep, sincere interest in what McCarty had accomplished at Gibson. His name was Paul Smith.

"I had never met Paul," McCarty recalled. "Never heard of him, and didn't know anything about him. But he called and told me, 'I went to the Library of Congress, and made copies of all of the patents on guitars, and noticed that your name was popping up time and time again. So I decided to ask advice from the best person I could find, and I think that's you.'

"So, Paul asked if I would do some work for him. He wanted me to go to Annapolis, but my wife was not well at the time, and I didn't think I could travel alone. So he said, 'Well, if you can't come here, I'll go there.' I said, 'Well, I'll see to it that you get a full eight-hour day from me. So he came, with his superintendent, and we picked them up at the airport and went straight to the Bigsby factory. He told me what his problems were, and things that were bothering him.

"I asked him, 'Do you have problems with personnel? How often are you out in the factory?' He said, 'I go out there maybe once a month.' I said, 'Paul, you can't do it that way! That's a problem. You have to get out there every day to have those people know you're interested in them. Talk to them, find out what they're doing, see if they've got kids, whether they're married. Learn something about them as individuals.' He said, 'Okay, I'll do that.' I said, 'Look, for years I got in in the morning, took my overcoat off, hung it up in my cabinet, and I went out into the factory. I walked around and talked with people. I asked what they were doing, and whether we could help them do it better. People got to know me, and I knew them.' I told Paul, 'That's very important! You don't make the company, the people working for you and are interested in doing the job, they make the company.' So he tried it, and it worked!

"Paul made three trips here, and I've been to Baltimore a couple of times. Most of the stuff, like wood and engineering, he's very good at. But it was a question of handling people and machinery. We discussed finishes, plating, and a lot of things like that. For example, he was having bridges gold-plated, but they were aluminum. Not all the platers know how to do that, but I told him how to tell his plater. He called later and he said, 'It's cracking off.' I said, I told him, 'I'll call my plater here in Michigan. You send parts and ask him to apply 24-karat gold plate.' Well, I didn't hear from him, so I called and asked, 'Well, how is it working?' He said, 'They're beautiful. That's a great plater you have.' I said, 'Well, we taught him how to plate aluminum.'

"Sometime in the '90s, at a NAMM show in California, Paul walked in one day and said, 'I want your signature, Ted.' I said, 'What for?' He said, 'Well, I have a contract. I'd like to put your name on a couple of guitars, several of them which you designed.' I said, 'Nobody knows me. I'm not a player, I've never been onstage, and I've never been in any public thing playing a guitar or showing a guitar.' And he said, 'I know. But you don't know how much your name is worth on a contract.'

"My son-in-law and daughter were there, and I said, 'What do you think?' And they said, 'Go ahead, Dad. You can't lose.' So I signed, and Paul went out and got a copyright so nobody else can use my name on guitars."

PRS historian Dave Burrluck describes the PRS McCarty model, launched in 1994, as the best example of the classic PRS approach to the solidbody – the one that recalled the golden age of the electric guitar. While similar to the PRS Custom 22, it embodied changes Paul Smith had been working on in the early '90s.

Engineering of the McCarty model is credited to guitarist David Grissom, who was looking for an instrument that captured a sound reminiscent of Duane Allman. Grissom and Smith altered an existing PRS template with a thicker body, thinner headstock, lighter tuners, and different pickups. Other specs included a steeper headstock angle, wide/fat neck profile, longer heel profile, and 22 frets.

The result, according to PRS, was a guitar that sounded like vintage Les Paul models. The McCarty used red maple, which PRS called "Michigan maple" – the same used on 1950s Gibson Les Paul Standard models. It also used covered humbucking PRS Dragon Bass pickups, which had alnico magnets (also like vintage Gibson humbuckers) that varied from the exposed-coil pickups of the standard PRS solidbody. Another nod to McCarty's influence was the use of a three-way pickup selector, which replaced the standard PRS five-way rotary switch.

The McCarty's pickups were upgraded in 1995 with features that more closely resembled the PAF humbuckers of the McCarty era at Gibson. They were named the New McCarty Pickups.

"Ted taught us how to make PAFs," said Burrluck. "Paul said they were made like this, but Ted said no. All the ways people think they were made, Ted told us different."

In '94, PRS introduced the lower-priced all-mahogany McCarty Standard, and the McCarty Soapbar, with Gibson P-90-style pickups, debuted in '98. Smith wanted an authentic P-90 sound, and renowned pickup builder Seymour Duncan was a logical choice to help, given his close relationship with Gibson pickup designer Seth Lover.

In '98, PRS also introduced what Burrluck called the company's most innovative electric guitars at the time – the McCarty Archtop and McCarty Hollowbody. The design, credited to PRS' Joe Knaggs, was based on a Gibson L-5 while staying true to traditional PRS double-cutaway silhouette. This made for a smaller, more comfortable acoustic/electric archtop.

Smith celebrated his company's 20th Anniversary at the NAMM show in January, 2005. At the time, PRS had nearly 200 employees, not many more than the number McCarty led during his early years at Gibson. Smith described his company as a family, sounding very much like McCarty did at Gibson in the 1950s.

"At PRS, we've learned that we need each other, and we need each other's support," he said at the conference. "We all succeed by contributing hard work and good ideas to clear goals. For 20 years, this family has included talented craftsmen and women in the factory, loyal employees in marketing, advertising, sales, and administration, dedicated dealers and distributors, brilliant demonstrators and recording artists, hard working road reps, famous and gifted endorsers who could play *any* guitar but choose PRS guitars, supportive industry peers and press, and many other musicians, some of them famous, some obscure, but all part of the PRS family."

Paul Smith's American-made guitars are known for quality, just like the Gibson instruments that were built by Ted McCarty. At NAMM in '05, Smith was asked, "Why are PRS guitars so expensive?" Smith answered by noting, "If you take a group of very skilled people, and you ask them to dedicate their lives to the art of making guitars, they end up getting married they end up having children, they end up needing health insurance... And it's not like (making guitars) is a hugely profitable business. We earn a mild profit, just like anybody else, so the question for PRS is, 'Is this instrument worth the money we're asking?' The only way you're going to know that is to go and plug in and play it, and see if you can play music on it."

In conversation later, McCarty emphasized three important career accomplishments:

the Gibson Les Paul guitar, the building of the Gibson company to a record number of employees, and the PRS McCarty guitar.

Susan McCarty Davis recalled her father's affiliation with Paul Smith.

"I think Paul is a very smart businessman, very dedicated to what he's doing, and he genuinely admired and cared for my father. It was just good business for him to find dad and learn from him, then honor him.

"Paul came out to Twin Falls when my father was dying. He had dinner with us, then he went back to the hospital and played his guitar for dad. Paul genuinely cared about my father, no doubt."

The Heritage Guitar Company

Gibson left Kalamazoo in 1984, the most often noted reason being problems with the labor union. While its three-floor building was about 67 years old, most of the factory was only 24 years old. But north Kalamazoo had become a rough area, and some historical accounts suggest Gibson faced a tough decision when it came time to close either its Kalamazoo or Nashville plant. Nashville, the newer location, won out.

But very few Kalamazoo employees elected to transfer to Nashville. Many had extended families and were not interested in relocating. So when Gibson left town, many skilled craftsmen were left behind. Three of Ted McCarty's hires – Marvin Lamb, J.P. Moats, and Jim Deurloo – saw an opportunity for the Parsons Street factory, and founded the Heritage Guitar Company. While McCarty had no direct affiliation, he helped assure their financing through a local bank.

Lamb, a native of Huntsville, Alabama, was born June 25, 1939, and moved to Michigan in 1955. He was hired by Gibson in May of '56 as a sander and eventually held several jobs in the wood shop followed by a series of promotions, including in final inspection, foreman of the white-wood shop, then general foreman of finishing and final assembly. In '74, he became plant superintendent, a position he held until Gibson closed the plant in '84. Today, Lamb designs instruments, makes patterns and necks, and has produced various finishing ideas.

Moats was born in Moulton, Alabama, on February 10, 1936, and moved to Michigan in '52, where he began working in a paper mill. He joined Gibson in '57, where he worked in white-wood sanding, then final cleaning, followed by a series of promotions including final inspector, supervisor of buffing and finish-sanding, supervisor of inspectors, head of quality control, and head of wood inspection, simultaneous with head of repair and custom orders. Today, he is involved in design, wood selection, rim bending, and assembly.

Deurloo was born in Plainswell, Michigan, on April 17, 1939, and started with Gibson in August, 1958, sanding rims and necks. From there he went to machine operator and pattern maker in the mill room, followed by a series of promotions to general foreman of the pattern shop, and maintenance. Deurloo worked for Guild Guitars from 1969 to '74 before returning to Gibson as project engineer to help design the Nashville plant, including development of the production process, tooling, and purchasing of equipment. He became assistant plant manager at Gibson, then plant manager in 1978. Today, Deurloo serves as pattern maker, builder, and does machinery carving of tops and backs.

The Rock Walk Of Fame

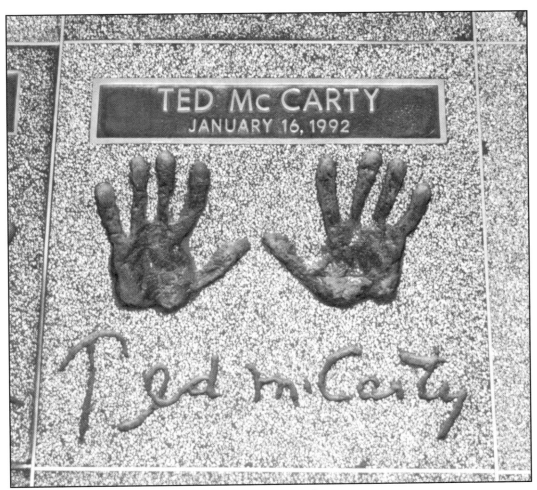

North Hollywood's Rock Walk dedication to Ted McCarty

The Rock Walk, located in the front of Guitar Center's North Hollywood store, was established November 13, 1985, to acknowledge the contributions of individuals who helped the music business. Inductees include Leo Fender, Les Paul, Chuck Berry, Larry Graham, Frank Zappa, Jimmy Page, and Jeff Beck. Ted McCarty was inducted January 16, 1992.

"Guitar designer Theodore M. McCarty, owner of Bigsby Accessories Inc., of Kalamazoo, and former president of Gibson Inc., was expected to be inducted today in Hollywood's Rock Walk of Fame," wrote the Kalamazoo paper. "McCarty, a Kalamazoo resident who was vacationing in Hawaii when notified of the award, will be honored as an innovator in the music industry.

"'The Rock Walk is a fitting tribute for a lifetime of music for Ted McCarty,' said David Crowley, a representative of the executive committee of Hollywood's Rock Walk of Fame.

"'It's an honor that should have come previous to this,' said Cindy Rooback, vice president and general manager of Bigsby Accessories Inc., which manufactures guitar accessories. 'He's being recognized for his involvement with Gibson and the fact he had patented well over a dozen different patents for different guitars and bridges.'

"The induction ceremony includes the placement of an inductee's handprints and signature onto the walkway of a sidewalk gallery on Sunset Boulevard.

"The most recent inductee was rhythm-and-blues singer Smokey Robinson on October 22. Other inductees have included Little Richard, B.B. King, Aerosmith, Leo Fender, Alice Cooper, Marvin Gaye and Elvis Presley.

"McCarty was inventor of designs for the Gibson Les Paul, Flying V, Firebird, ES-335, ES-345 guitars and the sole inventor of the now standard Tune-O-Matic bridge. He holds 12 patents in the music field.

"'Many of his guitars are considered collectors items," Roobach said. "The last Flying V that was sold went for $250,000.

"He was also past president of the National Association of Musical Manufacturers and head of the American Music Conference.

"At 82, McCarty is still very active with Bigsby Accessories, manufacturer of the famous Bigsby Tailpiece featured as a standard on Gretsch's Country Gentleman Guitar and has done extensive consulting for the fledgling PRS Guitars.

"McCarty headed Gibson, then headquartered in Kalamazoo, from 1950 to 1966 and led the company into it heyday when Gibson guitars helped put Kalamazoo on the map.

"When he started with the company, it had 150 employees and less than $1 million in annual sales. By the time he left, it had 1,200 employees and produced 100,000 instruments a year valued at $42 million in retail sales. Gibson guitars were used by the bands of Bing Crosby, Les Paul, Gene Autry, Roy Rogers and Merle Travis in the 1950s.

"Gibson, which was founded in Kalamazoo in 1894, moved its headquarters to Nashville, in 1981. The Kalamazoo operation was closed in 1984.

McCarty's contributions to the music business is listed in *Who's Who in America*, *Guitar Player* magazine, and *Encore* magazine."

Remembering Ted McCarty

McCarty passed away peacefully on April 1, 2001, in Twin Falls, Idaho. He was 91 years old. For several years prior to his death, he had suffered from a visual handicap and needed assistance. That help came in the form of Mable Sherrill, who in his final years spent more time than anyone with Ted.

Mable met McCarty in November, 1963, when Mable's brother, Elbert, married Mc-Carty's daughter, Sue. The wedding was held in a Presbyterian church in Kalamazoo, and the reception was at the McCarty home. The next time Mable saw Ted was 30 years later at Mable's nephew's wedding.

In the fall of '94, at the wedding of Elbert and Sue's son, Glenn Davis, the family offered Mable a job helping Ted. Things clicked with the two, and in January of '95, Ted hired Mable as his full-time caregiver, and she was soon introduced to Ted's other life – that of a guitar celebrity. Mable, Elbert, and Sue went to the NAMM show with Ted, and were there for the introduction of one of the PRS McCarty models. At the PRS display, Ted was the center of attention.

"People would come to the booth to see Ted, and they'd see the McCarty guitars and whatever else Paul had," said Mable. That summer, Mable drove Ted to the NAMM show in Nashville. And in '95, PRS opened a new factory so Mable drove Ted from the summer NAMM show in Nashville to the Annapolis factory. The two were dinner guests at Paul's home. That year, Mable drove McCarty 10,000 miles, including trips to visit Ted's brother and other relatives.

"To me, Ted was just Elbert's father-in-law. But at the NAMM show, I pushed him in the wheelchair and this man came up and said, 'You're Ted McCarty!? Ted said, 'Yes,' and the man said, 'I can't believe I'm talking to the real Ted McCarty!' So I pushed him around and we gave out autographs. Ted loved it; he'd visit with everybody.

"At NAMM we'd always look up the Heritage Guitar Company. Those guys were very, very nice, and were always happy to talk with Ted."

In '97, the Hard Rock Café in Baltimore built a 24-foot PRS McCarty model to place atop its building. They asked Paul Smith to play, and asked Ted to attend the grand opening. Mable drove Ted to Baltimore for the occasion

When Mable came aboard, Ted was still running Bigsby Accessories, and Flex-Lite.

"Ted wanted to spend six-months in Kalamazoo, running Bigsby, and six-months in Hawaii. He had a manager at Bigsby, and she ran it while he was in Hawaii. In Kalamazoo, I would take him to work every morning and pick him up every afternoon. He went to work every day. Ted loved recognition, and he used to tell everybody in Hawaii, 'Oh, I still work every day. Even though I'm 85 years old, I'm still working every day.' He needed to keep busy. He not only managed Bigsby, but he'd help put parts together. He was an amazing man.

"Around 1999, Ted knew time was pushing on, and knew he should get rid of Bigsby," Mable added. "So he put it up for sale. He had one guy ready to buy it, but the deal fell through. Then he worked and worked, and it took him about a year until finally Fred Gretsch bought it."

Mable attended to Ted during a very reflective period. Most of his major accomplishments were behind him, and in the mid/late 1990s, he would spend hours telling Mable about his career.

Ted McCarty in Obituaries

Thursday, April 5, 2001

TED McCARTY / GUITAR PIONEER
Former Gibson Guitar president lived in Hawaii
Associated Press

TWIN FALLS, Idaho Theodore M. "Ted" McCarty, a key figure in the development of the electric guitar and former president of Gibson Guitar Co., died Sunday in a retirement center. He was 91. McCarty, a part-time Hawaii resident, was the president of the Gibson Guitar Co. for 16 years, transforming a sleepy Kalamazoo, Mich., maker of acoustic musical instruments into the purveyor of guitars to the stars.

Nearly every virtuoso guitarist of the rock 'n' roll era at one time or another played a Gibson. McCarty's Les Paul series -- named for the blues guitarist who endorsed it -- is arguably the most famous guitar

ever made. It led to the Explorer series, widely used by both rock and country guitarists, and the radical Flying V. "It's fair to say that without him, our industry and the music would be different," said Paul Reed Smith, an acclaimed guitar designer who enlisted McCarty to help develop Smith's own brand. "I don't know how it would be different, but it would be." McCarty, in failing health, moved to Twin Falls last summer to be near his daughter, Sue Davis. He did not retire until age 89, when he sold his company that manufactured vibratos for guitars and custom flashlights. Private funeral services are planned in Hawaii, where McCarty lived part-time for 25 years.

Detroit News

The Detroit News

Friday, April 6, 2001

McCarty, key figure in development of the electric guitar, dies at 91

TWIN FALLS, Idaho -- Theodore M. "Ted" McCarty, a key figure in the development of the electric guitar and former president of Gibson Guitar Co., died Sunday. He was 91.

In his 16 years as president at Gibson, McCarty transformed the Kalamazoo, Mich.-based maker of acoustic musical instruments into the purveyor of guitars to the stars. The solid-body electric guitar was considered something of a gimmick when McCarty left the Wurlitzer Co. to join Gibson in 1948. He had a degree in commercial engineering and had been an engineering designer for the military during World War II. Despite not being musically inclined, McCarty saw possibilities in the electric guitar. At Gibson, he helped bring to life the Les Paul series, named for the blues guitarist who endorsed it, the Explorer series, widely used by both rock and country guitarists, and the radical Flying V. McCarty later bought the Bigsby Co., which manufactures vibratos for guitars. He sold the company and retired in 1999.

Tuesday April 10th, 2001

Farewell Ted McCarty

Former Gibson Guitar President Ted McCarty died last week at the age of 91. He led Gibson from 1948 to 1966.

Said current Gibson Chairman and CEO Henry E. Juszkiewicz, "Ted McCarty was the architect of a Golden period in Gibson's history. During his 18-year tenure, he helped to reestablish the company's historic leadership in the industry through a number of musical innovations that still resonate today.

Gibson mourns the loss of one of its great leaders, and will fondly remember Ted as a member of the Gibson family."

McCarty pioneered the development of several classic Gibson models including the three pickup ES-5, the classic ES-175. ES-175 "jazz box" and the semi-hollowbody design of the ES-335 which established a new genre of electric guitar design.

In 1952, McCarty collaborated with popular musical artist Les Paul to design what has become a standard of the industry and a legendary instrument--the Gibson Les Paul Goldtop. It was Gibson's first solidbody guitar and is still produced today.

McCarty's legacy remains in the hands of innumerable musicians worldwide and continues to inspire Gibson's master luthiers.

Gibson President Ted McCarty with (from left) Charles W. Bitters (Forbes Finishing Division/ PPG), Julius Bellson (Assistant Treasurer), Rollo Werner (Purchasing Agent), S.W. Lees (Forbes/PPG), and John Huis (Vice President) in a 1953 photo taken in McCarty's office.

Theodore Milson McCarty 1909 – 2001

SECTION II

McCarty Golden-Era Instruments

1957 Gibson Catalog cover

Introduction 26

Antonio Stradivari (1644-1737), the most famous instrument maker in history, wasn't an entertainer, performer, politician, or royalty. By age 70, he was treated like royalty because of his instruments.

A comparison can be made with Ted McCarty. Had he become President of Wurlitzer, today nobody would know his name. Had he become treasurer of Brach Candy, his name would have been buried with the rest of the accountants. But that didn't happen. Mc-Carty stayed in the music business, and his name is revered by guitarists all over the globe.

It wasn't McCarty, the man, who made the name. It was the instruments he built – the 1959 Les Paul Standard, the 1958 Explorer, the '58 Flying V, and '58 ES-335N. These are considered the Stradivari of electric guitars.

McCarty's incredible business skills made his appointment as Gibson's General Manager a brilliant move by CMI President Maurice Berlin. Was it Ted's guitar manufacturing brilliance that created his famous Gibson instruments? Yes, most of the credit has to go to McCarty – he put the plan together and guided Gibson until it became the largest company of its type. He had the experience, personality, and his timing and talent helped create a truly unique era. Much like the birth of rock and roll, the birth of rock and roll *instruments* could happen only once – and it happened on McCarty's watch at Gibson. All of his instruments were at the top – flat-tops, archtops, acoustic/electrics, solidbodies, basses, mandolins, steels, lap steels... For highly valued instruments, the McCarty era was the most prolific period in the history of the guitar industry.

The 25 most valuable fretted instruments in the vintage market are grouped below. These instruments were used to prepare Chart 1.

1950s Gibson Les Paul Standard electric guitar with humbucking pickups
1930s Martin Style-45 flat-top guitars (D, OM, 000)
1950s Gibson Explorer electric guitar with humbucking pickups
1920s Gibson Loar family instruments (F-5, H-5, L-5)
1930s Gibson Granada flat-head banjo (RB, TB, PB)
1950s Gibson Flying V electric guitar with humbucking pickups
1950s Gibson Les Paul Custom electric guitar with humbucking pickups
1950s Gretsch White Penguin electric guitar
1950s Gibson Les Paul (goldtop with Tune-O-Matic bridge) electric guitar
1940s/'50s D'Angelico New Yorker cutaway archtop guitar
1960s D'Aquisto New Yorker Deluxe cutaway archtop guitar
1930s Martin Style 28 flat-top guitar
1940s Stromberg Model 400 archtop guitar
1950s Gibson ES-335N electric guitar with humbucking pickups
1950s Fender Stratocaster electric guitar
1950s Fender Broadcaster and Telecaster electric guitar
1960s Fender Stratocaster and Telecaster Custom electric guitars in custom colors

These are the "holy grail" instruments of the market – the most expensive. The market is driven by supply and demand, and the demand for McCarty/"golden era" instruments exceeds all others. In this book, I have used market dollar values as the basis of market acceptance.

What does not tend to change in the vintage guitar market from year to year is the relationship between the values of vintage guitars. In the vintage market it is said, "A great guitar will always be a great guitar." Through the 1970s, '80s, '90s, and early 21st century, the same guitars have been highly valued –1954 Fender Stratocasters, '59 Gibson Les

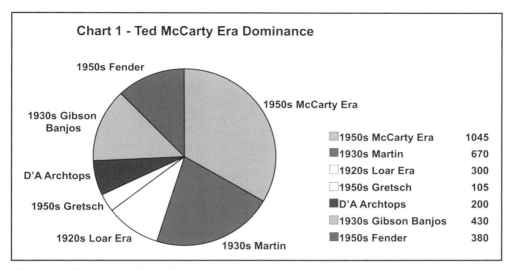

Chart 1 - Ted McCarty Era Dominance

1950s McCarty Era	1045
1930s Martin	670
1920s Loar Era	300
1950s Gretsch	105
D'A Archtops	200
1930s Gibson Banjos	430
1950s Fender	380

Chart 1 illustrates this dominance via the relative market values of various manufacturing periods. The "great eras" were the 1920s for mandolins, the '30s for flat-top guitars - archtop guitars - five-string banjos, and the 1950s for electric guitars. Within all of the great decades, the McCarty 1950s electric guitar era is the most dominant era among all the great eras. The market value for the McCarty era electric guitars exceeds any other era.

Pauls, '50 Fender Broadcasters, '59 Gibson ES-335Ns, and '40s Martin D-45. In 1995, the '59 Les Paul Standard was the most expensive, followed by the 1930s Martin Style 45s. The same relationship exists in today's market, and is expected to exist in the future.

If you consider all the listed models as a high-end collection, and assign the relative value to each, it is obvious how dominant McCarty era guitars are.

In a collection of the world's most valuable fretted instruments, McCarty era instruments would make up 33% of the collection's market value. The pie chart demonstrates that McCarty era instruments are more highly valued than any other group of instruments, including 1930s Martin flat-tops.

Comparing Stradivari and McCarty Instruments

The 1959 Gibson Les Paul Standard, nicknamed the 'Burst, is the model most often associated with the famous Stradivarius violins of the late 17th/early 18th Century.

Of the 1,000 Stradivarius violins (he made 1,200 total instruments including violas) thought to have been made, approximately 600 still exist. The violin was originally built as a folk instrument, not something of royalty. The first great violin maker was Andrea Amati (d. 1577). His sons and grandson, Nicholo (b. 1596), followed in the business, and over time, the violin became the great voice of composers, accepted by the royalty of Europe. Evidence suggests that Stradivari was an apprentice to Nicholo Amanti. Stradivari's violin

THE "GOLDEN" LOOK AND A REGAL PERFORMANCE

This golden beauty is truly a "royal" instrument . . . the entire body and neck are in gold finish, all metal parts are gold plated. Tone and action wise, the Gibson ES-295 measures up to its outstanding appearance; this instrument meets the demand for the slick action and sustaining power of a solid body electric in a regular-size acoustic guitar.

The combination bridge and tailpiece, by shortening the distance from the nut to the tailpiece, releases about 25% of the string pressure on the body, adding to the sustaining power and brilliancy of the instrument and giving faster and lower action. Every note in each chord has equal power and rings true without an abrupt ending of the tone.

- Two adjustable pickups have separate tone and volume controls.
- Three-way toggle switch activates either or both pickups, allows quick switching from rhythm to solo playing and accent of either bass or treble tones.
- Fingerrest and pickup covers of cream Royalite, with gold inlaid floral design on fingerrest.
- Florentine-style cutaway means ease in reaching all nineteen frets.
- Gibson Adjustable Truss Rod neck construction.
- Body size: 16¼" wide and 20¼" long.

ES-295 Electric Spanish Cutaway Guitar—Golden Finish—Cases to fit: 515 Faultless, 514 Faultless

1957 Catalog for Gibson ES-295

production started in 1666, but not all Strads were created equal. Strad violins varied as much as Gibson Les Pauls made from 1952 to '59. Stradivari was an experimenter, so different patterns were used, different sizes were produced.

During Stradivari's "golden period," designs became standardized. Stradivari made violins for 70 years. His instruments of the 'golden period' were known for their volume and projection, while the 'sweet tone' Amati violins were not powerful. The design of the Strad was deemed superior and most suitable for the composers, artists, and the enlarged concert halls of the era. For more than 300 years, the Strad's design and function was never outdone. The designed blossomed when used by virtuosos playing music from master composers. Instrument, virtuoso, and composer – the formula for the Strad's success.

A Strad-type evolution happened with the family of Les Paul Standards - those with the sunburst finish, made in the late 1950s. About 1,200 'Bursts are thought to have been made from '58 to '60. Of that, less than 1,000 are estimated to have survived in original condition. Initially, the Les Paul Standard was considered a very good design, but not vastly superior. It took a change in how the guitar was used to bring the '59 Les Paul Standard to

A NEW HIGH IN VERSATILITY
THE GIBSON ES-5 SWITCHMASTER

An increased range of performance, quality and playability, wonderful tone and beautiful appearance—all these features are destined to make the ES-5 Switchmaster a favorite among discriminating guitarists.

- Three separately controlled pickups with Alnico magnets for the greatest range of tone qualities.
- Six Controls—separate tone and volume control for each of the three pickups, permitting presetting of each.
- Four way toggle switch to activate each of the three pickups separately or all three simultaneously. At the "all on" position, by regulating volume controls, each pickup can be activated separately, any combination of two together, or all three.
- Gibson Tune-O-Matic Bridge for greater sustaining power.
- Body size: 17" wide and 21" long, 25¼" scale length.
- Individual gold plated enclosed Kluson machineheads with Keystone buttons.

Switchmaster ES-5 Electric Spanish Cutaway Guitar— Golden Sunburst Finish
Switchmaster ES-5N Electric Spanish Cutaway Guitar— Natural Finish

No. 600 Faultless. Plush-lined Case
No. 606 Faultless. Flannel-lined Case

ES-5 N

SENSATIONAL NEW BYRDLAND

The Gibson Byrdland is creating excitement in the guitar field with its thin body and narrow, streamlined short scale neck. Designed by famed guitarists, Billy Byrd and Hank Garland, this unusual Cutaway Electric Spanish Guitar incorporates all the features demanded by leading players as well as several important innovations.

- Two powerful Gibson pickups mounted close to the fingerboard and bridge for wide range of tone colorings.
- Three-position toggle switch on treble side activates either or both pickups.
- New modern design tailpiece.
- Gibson Tune-O-Matic Bridge and extra large individually adjustable Alnico No. 5 magnets, for greater sustaining power and accuracy of pitch on each string.
- Separate tone and volume controls for each pickup, can be preset to any desired quality and power.
- Gibson Adjustable Truss Rod neck construction.
- Body size: 17" wide, 21" long, 2¼" deep.
- Ebony fingerboard . . . 23½" scale length.

Byrdland Electric Spanish Cutaway Guitar—Sunburst Finish.
Byrdland N Electric Spanish Cutaway Guitar—Natural Finish.
No. 603 Faultless Plush-lined Case

Byrdland

1957 Catalog for Gibson ES-5 and Byrdland

ES-350T—"ARTIST APPROVED" FOR SOLO OR BACKGROUND WORK

The Gibson ES-350T Cutaway Electric Spanish Guitar has a reduced depth of body, a smaller, more streamlined neck and a shorter scale length—all requested features of the leading guitarists.

• Comfortable playing, easier, less tiring pick action with the body size: 17″ wide, 21″ long and 2¼″ deep.

• Faster and easier left hand fingering with the smaller, streamlined neck: 22 fret rosewood fingerboard, 23½″ scale length.

• Three position toggle switch on treble side activates either or both pickups.

• Powerful Gibson pickups with Alnico magnets and individually adjustable polepieces for better tone balance.

• Figured curly maple body and neck, finished with Gibson Golden Sunburst or selected Natural Finishes, accented by ivoroid binding on body, fingerboard and peghead.

ES-350T—Electric Spanish Cutaway Guitar—Golden Sunburst Finish
ES-350TN—Electric Spanish Cutaway Guitar—Natural Finish
No. 603—Faultless Plush-lined Case

ES-350 TN

1957 Catalog for Gibson ES-350T

the forefront; it happened when top artists began to use 'Bursts to play amplified music in loud settings in the mid/late '60s through the mid '70s. The scenario favored the punch of the thick maple-on-mahogany body Les Paul equipped with early (Patend Applied For, or P.A.F.) humbucking pickups. The instrument was almost universally accepted by virtuosos playing in large, loud venues. A better design has never surfaced, and the world's top performers continue to place the highest value on the Les Paul Standard made in the late '50s.

Great instruments are great because of their superior design. This applies not only to Gibsons, but to '50s Fender Stratocasters and Telecasters, and to '30s Martin dreadnoughts. Great instruments, played by virtuosos playing popular music was again the key to success. Great vintage instruments are valuable for the same reason that great violins were successful.

One of the key ingredients in the most valuable Gibson guitars is the humbucking pickups. The '59 Les Paul Standard, '58 Flying V, '58 Explorer, and '58 ES-335 are all equipped with P.A.F. humbucking pickups. The humbucking pickup is one of Gibson's most famous innovations and it affects vintage guitar values across the board.

The Gibson factory at 225 Parsons Street in Kalamazoo, Michigan, produced more high-quality instruments than any other facility. The Fender factory in California was great for solidbody guitars, but it didn't make quality flat-tops. The Martin facility in

Pennsylvania, the oldest American factory of its type, was great for flat-top acoustics, but it didn't make great archtops or solidbodies.

Every instrument built at the Parsons Street factory was made entirely by hand. It wasn't a small shop, but the number of apprentices and assistances was very small. In the 1950s, perhaps a dozen employees touched a single guitar. Work areas each had four or five skilled laborers, and any of the four could do hand work on a guitar as it passed through. And small groups of employees checked and evaluated peer performance. Within the Gibson system were three check points in each department. Those check points were the department 'leader' or sometimes called 'line leader', the department 'inspector', and the department 'foreman.' The hand-built process was rigorous. Demands for quality and a reasonable amount of output quantity were always equal parts of the process. While the guitars were made in a factory, the employees considered what they did during the McCarty era to be hand-building.

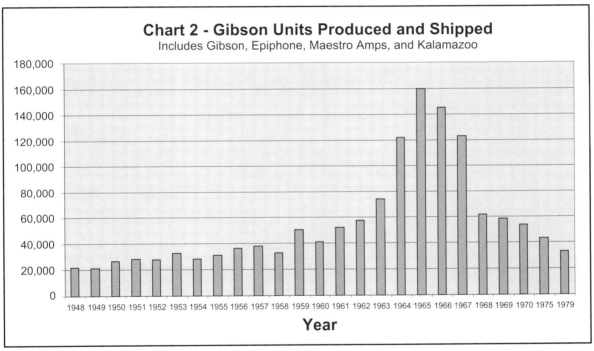

Chart 2 shows the units produced and shipped by the Kalamazoo factory from 1948 to 1970. For historical purposes, it also shows Gibson's unit volume (Kalamazoo and Nashville) in 1975 and '79. The chart shows production of Gibson guitars, basses, mandolins, banjos, steels, lap steels, and amplifiers peaked in '65 and includes all brands sold by Gibson, including Epiphone, Maestro amps, and Kalamazoo. Some of the '65 sales stayed on retail dealer shelves resulting in lower '66 production. The steep drop in volume in '68 reflects the discontinuation of amplifier production and scaling down of Epiphone, which was gone by late 1970. String-room production is not part of the chart, but that unit was also removed from Kalamazoo in '72. Lowered production meant the beginning of underutilized capacity. The chart also reflects the decline in volume in the late 1960s which was brought on by both lower overall demand and market share lost to the Asian importers. These two conditions – lower demand and lower market share – were catastrophic for American builders like Harmony and Kay. Gibson survived because, as McCarty liked to stress, Gibson meant quality.

In vintage-guitar circles, the shops of D'Angelico and D'Aquisto were the equivalent of the small, non-factory Stradivari shop. Those who operate in the collectible acoustic archtop market prefer such instruments; a '55 D'Angelico New Yorker cutaway has a value five to six times greater than a '55 Gibson Super 400 acoustic archtop. But the D'Angelico is an instrument of the past, not supported by popular music. That's not true of the Stradivarius violin, which is still considered the finest instrument.

McCarty and Stradivari instruments have a lot in common. They're both hand-built instruments made under rigorous supervision, used by top players playing the day's popular music.

Ted McCarty was president of Gibson during the "guitar booms" of 1958 and 1964. In '58, the Kingston Trio gained tremendous popularity playing a Martin flat-top, Martin tenor guitar, and Vega long-neck banjo. At the time, Martin guitars were nearly impossible to obtain, and Gibson benefited because it had a reputation as a quality builder of flat-tops. The second guitar boom hit as a result of the Beatles' "invasion" in 1964.

The Les Paul Model

Ted's most well -known accomplishment during the McCarty era is of course the design, development, and introduction of Gibson's first solidbody guitar – the 1952 Gibson Les Paul model. Maurice Berlin and his Chicago staff, as well as Ted McCarty, were well aware of what Leo Fender and Don Randall were doing in California. "They were eating our lunch!" Ted said. "We got involved in the Les Paul solidbody because Leo copied one of Paul Bigsby's guitars. And as soon as we heard he had a solidbody going on the market, I bought one for the company and we studied it. We had never made a solidbody – *and* he bolted the neck to the body, which was infamy as far as we were concerned. So we decided, about 1951, that we weren't going to let him have the whole market. So we decided to make a solidbody."

McCarty designed specifications for Gibsons solidbody; his name appears on patent number 2,714,326 with a file date of January 21, 1953. He wanted the instrument to have a carved top, something beyond what Leo Fender could do. He wanted it to have high-quality appointments that would make Fenders slab-body look plain. And he wanted the standard glued-in neck.

Before they could proceed, McCarty needed Berlin's approval. Legend has it Berlin suggested a violin-like carved top. Berlin was an entrepreneur, not a guitar man, so when McCarty asked for approval of ideas, Berlin quickly said, 'Sure, if that's what we need.'

The consensus concerning the design was that it was a group effort, including the important input from Les Paul himself. It's widely acknowledged that Les Paul selected the colors – a gold one and a black one – but according to Paul, Gibson got it backward because he asked for the Les Paul Standard to be black and the Les Paul Custom to be gold.

Gibson employees in the factory at the time suggest Larry Allers was a main contributor, too. Allers was Assistant Superintendent and Chief Engineer of woodworking, from the lumber yard and rough mill, to final white-wood cleaning. He reported to

"THE FRETLESS WONDER"
LES PAUL CUSTOM GUITAR

Here is the ultimate in a solid body Gibson Electric Spanish Guitar . . . players rave about its extremely low smooth frets and playing action, call it the "Fretless Wonder." Features clear, resonant and sparkling tone, with widest range of tone colorings.

Solid Honduras Mahogany body with carved top, size 17 ¼" long, 12 ¾" wide, 1 ¾" thick with graceful cutaway design; bound with alternating white and black strips on top and bottom of body. Mahogany neck, with exclusive Gibson Truss Rod neck construction; ebony fingerboard; deluxe pearl inlays.

Two powerful magnetic type pickups specially designed and engineered for this model; individually adjustable gold colored magnets, gold plated polepieces. Double combination Bridge and Tailpiece . . . adjustable both horizontally and vertically, Tune-O-Matic bridge, adjustable for each string length. This combination provides sustaining tone quality and precision adjustment.

Three way toggle switch selects either front or back pickup, or both simultaneously; each pickup has separate tone and volume controls; finest individual gold-plated Kluson machine heads; gold plated metal end pin and strap holder. Finished in solid Ebony color for rich contrast with gold plated fittings. Padded leather strap included.

Les Paul Custom Guitar

Case: 537 Faultless

BIGSBY TRUE VIBRATO

A new device for manually creating a true vibrato, this Bigsby model enables the player to sharp or flat the pitch one-half tone with an automatic return to normal pitch. The new swivel arm allows for convenient movement when desired. Two styles available to fit acoustical and solid body guitars. Will be installed at Gibson factory if desired; specify make, year and model of guitar when ordering.

Bigsby Vibrato for conventional type guitar

Bigsby Vibrato for Les Paul guitar models

1957 Catalog for Les Paul Custom & Bigsby vibrato

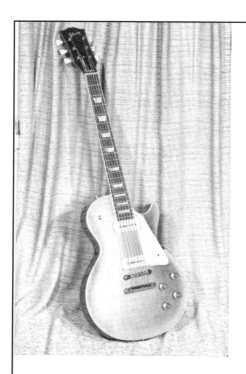

THE POPULAR "LES PAUL" SOLID BODY GUITAR

The famed "Les Paul tones" can now become a reality for all guitar players with this beautiful, solid body Les Paul guitar, incorporating many unusual Gibson features. Striking in appearance with its gold-finished, carved maple top, mahogany body and neck, the Les Paul name is in gold script on the peghead of this model.

Double combination Bridge and Tailpiece is another Gibson first . . . Tailpiece is adjustable for height, nickel Tune-O-Matic bridge adjustable up and down, and individual fine tuning adjustment for each string. This combination provides a new high in sustaining tone quality and precision pitch adjustment.

- Two pickups have separate tone and volume controls.
- Three position toggle switch activates either or both pickups.
- Tone can be pre-set to any desired quality and change from one pickup to another can be accomplished by a flip of the toggle switch.
- No dead notes—clear, sustaining tones in all positions with the 22 fret fingerboard.
- No buildup of synthetic tones or feed back.
- Body size—length, 17¼"; width 12¾"; scale length, 24¾".
- Gibson Adjustable Truss Rod neck construction.
- Padded leather strap included.

Les Paul Solid Body Electric Spanish Cutaway Guitar
Case: 535 Faultless

OUTSTANDING VALUE IN A SOLID BODY GUITAR

The new LES PAUL SPECIAL solid body Electric Spanish Cutaway Guitar incorporates the features that have made the Les Paul Model famous—tone, versatility, slender neck and low, fast action—with a moderate price. The appearance is rich and attractive . . . solid Honduras mahogany body and neck finished in limed mahogany shading . . . contrasting brown Royalite pickguard and unit covers . . . nickel plated parts . . . 22 fret, bound rosewood fingerboard with pearl dot inlays.

Other features of the Les Paul Special: Two powerful Gibson pickups with separate tone and volume controls for each; Alnico magnets and individually adjustable polepieces for each string; two position toggle switch activates either or both pickups; unique combination metal bridge and tailpiece, adjustable horizontally and vertically; individual Kluson machine heads; adjustable Gibson Truss Rod neck construction; padded, adjustable leather strap.

Les Paul Special Solid Body Electric Spanish Cutaway Guitar

Les Paul TV Model, Limed Oak— 1 pickup

Cases for Above Instruments: 535 Faultless, 115 Challenge

1957 Catalog for Les Paul Standard and Les Paul Special

NEW THIN MODEL ELECTRIC CUTAWAY

More brilliant tone, quicker response and greater sustaining qualities with the ES-225T—plus a new slim body design for easier and less tiring playing action. The rigidity and tone features of a solid body electric are combined with the light weight, easy-to-hold shape of the conventional electrics for an outstanding professional Cutaway Electric in the popular price field.

The ES-225T has a powerful single pickup with Alnico Magnets and individually adjustable polepieces to balance tone response from each string; original Les Paul style combination bridge-tailpiece for increased sustaining tone qualities and reduction of distortion and feedback; separate tone and volume controls; streamlined mahogany neck with Gibson adjustable Truss Rod; bound rosewood fingerboard with pearl dot inlays, side position markers and 20 nickel silver frets; laminated raised pickguard; nickel plated metal parts and fittings; body size 16¼″ wide, 20¼″ long, 1⅝″ deep with Gibson Sunburst finish top accented by cream colored top and back binding.

ES-225T Electric Spanish Cutaway Guitar—Golden Sunburst Finish

ES-225TN Electric Spanish Cutaway Guitar—Natural Finish

ES-225TD Electric Spanish Cutaway Guitar available with 2 pickups, 4 Controls and Toggle switch

No. 519 Faultless Case for Above Instruments

ES-225T

LES PAUL JUNIOR OUTFIT

LES PAUL JUNIOR GUITAR—Solid body Electric Spanish Guitar with fine tone, playing action and performance, at an unbelievable price for this instrument. The solid hardwood body is 17¼″ long, 12¾″ wide, and 1¾″ thick, with cutaway design. Slender Mahogany neck with exclusive Gibson Truss Rod construction, Brazilian rosewood fingerboard with 22 nickel silver frets, pearl position dots; powerful Gibson magnetic pickup with individual adjustable polepieces; new metal combination bridge and tailpiece, adjustable horizontally and vertically; separate tone and volume control; Kluson machine heads; Gibson Golden Sunburst Finish on top, dark brown Mahogany color on back, rim and neck. Complete with leather, padded strap.

Les Paul Junior Guitar; No. 115 Challenge Case

LES PAUL JUNIOR AMPLIFIER—Amazing quality and fine tone reproduction at a low price, true Gibson workmanship, performance and guarantee. Sturdy, compact ¾″ thick plywood construction, attractive beige covering, size 13½″ wide, 11¼″ high, 7″ deep. Slanted front panel, top mounted chassis with easily accessible control panel; three tubes, two instrument inputs; Rolla Oval Type speaker; jeweled pilot light, volume control and on-and-off switch.

Les Paul Junior Amplifier

5-C Cover

1957 Catalog for ES-225T and Les Paul Junior

A FAVORITE OF THE LEADING GUITARISTS

One of the finest electric Spanish guitars ever developed, the Super-400 CES has been given enthusiastic approval by the nation's outstanding musicians.

A definite factor in the quality of tone and responsiveness of the Super-400 CES is the carved spruce top, an unusual feature in an electric guitar. The finest spruce, curly maple and ebony add to the beauty of this instrument, available in Natural (as shown), or the Gibson Golden Sunburst finish.

- The two pickups are set close to the bridge and fingerboard for wider contrast in tone color.
- Modern cutaway design and small neck for fast, easy action.
- Gibson Tune-O-Matic bridge and extra large, individually adjustable Alnico No. 5 magnets give greater sustaining power and perfect accuracy from each string.
- Pickups have adjustable pole pieces and separate tone and volume controls which can be pre-set.
- Three-position toggle switch on treble side activates either or both pickups.
- Kluson Sealfast Pegs.
- Professional 20 fret fingerboard and Gibson Adjustable Truss Rod neck construction.
- Body size: 18″ wide and 21 ¾″ long.
- Decorative accents to the beauty of the Super-400 CES include gold plated metal parts, deluxe pearl inlays and alternate black-white-black ivoroid binding.

Super-400 CES Electric Spanish Cutaway Guitar—Golden Sunburst Finish.
Super-400 CESN Electric Spanish Cutaway Guitar—Natural Finish.
Case for Above Instruments—400 Faultless

Super-400 CESN

TONE AND BEAUTY FOR ARTIST PERFORMANCE

The depth and mellowness of the L-5 CES is winning acclaim for this fine guitar from the most discriminating artists. The tonal quality of the acoustic guitar and the advantages of an electric instrument are combined in this one superlative instrument.

Guitarists are singing the praises of the narrow, thin neck, the fast, easy action and the rich beauty of the carved spruce top, the curly maple back and rim, the pearl inlaid ebony fingerboard and beautiful ivoroid binding. Available in Natural Finish (as shown) or with Gibson Golden Sunburst Finish.

- Pickups are close to the bridge and fingerboard.
- Greater sustaining power and perfect accuracy of each string are achieved through the Gibson Tune-O-Matic Bridge and extra large, individually adjustable Alnico No. 5 magnets.
- Pickups have adjustable pole pieces and separate tone and volume controls which can be pre-set.
- Three-position toggle switch on treble side activates either or both pickups.
- Kluson Sealfast Pegs.
- Professional 20 fret fingerboard and Gibson Adjustable Truss Rod neck construction.
- Body size: 17″ wide and 21″ long.
- All metal parts are gold plated.

L-5 CES Electric Spanish Cutaway Guitar—Golden Sunburst Finish
L-5 CESN Electric Spanish Cutaway Guitar—Natural Finish
Cases for Above Instruments
606 Faultless   600 Faultless

L-5 CESN

1957 Catalog for Super 400CES and L-5CES

V.P. of Manufacturing John Huis, was known to be creative, and was the person who designated assignments to patternmakers. The patternmakers were generally responsible for prototypes, and they built the first guitar from any new design.

Wood was one important consideration for the solidbody. The team tested different kinds and Allers worked with patternmakers on different types of bodies using different woods. An all-maple body had great sustain, but was deemed too heavy. An all-mahogany body didn't have enough sustain. So they tested various combinations to see how long a string would vibrate on a test fixture. McCarty described the test as simply attaching a string to two mounts on the body, plucking it, and measuring how long it would vibrate. In some cases, the string would vibrate for too long a period, and others for too short a period. Eventually, they found a suitable combination.

McCarty and his staff also had to decide what sort of sound they wanted the guitar to make. How many pickups should it have? How deep should the pickup routings be? What type of controls should it have? What type of bridge?

McCarty was a strong advocate of mellow tone. He didn't want the solidbody to sound "harsh," like he thought came from a Fender solidbody. His instructions were clear – the tone needed to be mellow and full. Leo Fender, on the other hand, wanted a Spanish-style guitar that sounded like a Hawaiian steel guitar. McCarty wanted to keep the mellow tradition Gibson was known for.

McCarty always acknowledged that Leo Fender had a good ear. He also acknowledged that West Coast musicians liked the Fender sound, and that it was becoming popular. Still, its sound just wasn't for McCarty.

It took about a year to develop the Les Paul guitar, from parts design to tooling, then making dies, molds, etc. Near the end of the process, the question became, 'How should we market this?'

Gibson decided that Les Paul should market the guitar.

"The team decided to find an outstanding player who could play it in public and thereby get it known. The most talented guitar player in the U.S. at the time was a fella by the name of Les Paul. He and his wife, Mary Ford played in various places. So I took the guitar to New Jersey, to meet with Les and his wife. Les' financial manager, Phil Braunstein, drove up from New York.

"Les and Mary loved it, so we came up with a contract, which we were satisfied with, all sides, and the plan was to not introduce the guitar until the summer of '52. I showed the contract to our lawyers, and Les showed it to his."

Contrary to popular myth, from the start, the plan was for the Gibson name to be on the headstock of the Les Paul. And from the start it would have had Gibson's trademark sunburst finish (as the prototype built for Les Paul's examination did) were it not for Les Paul's request for a gold top on another guitar. "Les Paul had a friend in the hospital," said McCarty. "He came to me and said, 'Ted, could you make a gold guitar? I'd like to have one to take to my friend.' I said, 'No problem.'" McCarty painted an electric archtop in gold, and the idea would eventually become the ES-295.

But to McCarty, sunburst is Gibson and Gibson is sunburst. The earliest Fenders were natural-finish – that was Leo's color. The classic Martins were also natural. But classic Gibsons were sunburst, be it a '30s flat-top, '20s F-5 mandolin, or late-'50s Les Paul

Standard.

McCarty acknowledges that the Les Paul was his most significant professional achievement and that the '59 version represented the pinnacle of the model. He was pleased that the Les Paul Standard used what he called "Michigan fiddle-back maple." Later, PRS would use Michigan Red Maple on its McCarty model.

Whenever McCarty talked guitars in his later years, the Les Paul model seemed to come up. Here's an example from one of the interviews for this book.

When did you come upon the idea that you needed to make the solidbody? *1950. The solidbody guitar was practically unknown – Leo Fender borrowed a guitar that Paul Bigsby made for one of the players. And he saw the guy playing it on the stage and asked the fellow if he could borrow it. So he went back, copied it, and he made his first guitar. That was in 1949. I started at Gibson in early 1948, so all of this was happening at about the same time.*

Was it Maurice Berlin's idea, or your idea to get into solidbodies? *It was my idea. because we weren't making solidbodies. We didn't consider it, the people at Gibson felt a guitar had to have a body that would vibrate. So Leo started making a solidbody, and we thought it was junk. The neck was bolted to the body, which was nothing more than a plank. That was not what we considered a good guitar.*

How did you hear about it? Did you see it at one of the NAMM Shows? *Oh no, no, no. It used to be that the music industry was very close-knit. If something happened in California, we heard about,*

Les Paul, the man, in June 2002.

and they heard about it in New York. Everybody told everybody everything. Also, we had an organization so we kept up on things. But we also heard it through the grapevine. Leo's solidbody was known, and it was different and unusual.

Paul Bigsby had already been making solidbody guitars before 1949. He made them for individuals. When Leo started to sell these things, we were keeping an eye on it because it was new. We were wondering if it was going to catch. During the 18 years I was President of Gibson, Mr. Berlin never told me about any guitar. He didn't know anything about them. So I decided to make a solidbody, but different from Leo's. I called our engineers and said, 'We've got to get a good solidbody."

Was that your direct staff? *It was my engineers in the factory (note: Ted's "engineers" were generally the most skilled woodworkers and their supervisors). I said, 'We want to make a solidbody guitar, but we want to make it different than Fender's. The boys said, 'Okay, what do we want?' I said, 'We want a carved top and a neck set in the body.'"*

Did you give them the direction as to what type of wood? *Yes. I told them, 'It's not a solid block of wood. It's two kinds of wood glued together, making a sandwich.' The top is maple and the bottom is mahogany. We wanted to get plenty of vibration from this thing, but we didn't wish to have it go forever. If you make it out of solid maple, it's too harsh and it rings too long. So we made several bodies with different thicknesses of maple and mahogany, and finally got one like we wanted, with a carved top.*

By '51 we had a guitar that had everything in it that we liked and wanted, then brought in musicians to play the guitar in our boardroom, and we'd listen.

Did you ever contemplate not putting the Gibson logo on it? *No way! We were proud of it – it was a Gibson guitar... So then we had to find somebody to play the guitar in public I talked with Les and said, "I have something to show you."*

So I went this hunting lodge where Les was living and took out the guitar and I handed it to him. He played it for a little bit, and then he played it some more. He was happy with it. Then he said, "I want Mary to hear this."

I told Les, the idea was to have his name on it – a Les Paul model – and we'd pay him a royalty on every one that we make. Les yelled, "Mary, come down here." Les then handed Mary the guitar and said, "Ted wants to put our name on their guitar. What do you think of it?" She played it and said, "I like the way it feels. It's easy to handle, it's very comfortable, and it has beautiful tone. It's a great guitar." She went back upstairs and Les said, "Okay, let's go."

So I had to draw up a contract. We stayed up all night, and finally, around 6 o'clock in the morning we had a contract we thought covered everything. His finance man wanted a clause that said Les would not receive any money until the end of the contract. I asked why and he said, 'Because Les and Mary are getting $10,000 a night. They don't need money. Les says he'll always be able to do this, but like everybody else in this industry, there comes a time when it's time to get out. Maybe he'll need money then, but right now his tax to Uncle Sam is about 70% of what he makes. So we put that in the contract.

Then Les said, 'I have one of my Epiphones with a round-bar tailpiece, that the strings come down and wrap around that. I think it's better.' So I said, "Okay. We'll put it on the guitar and replace that one."

The contract, said Les was not allowed to be seen playing any guitar except a Les Paul. If he did play another brand, he lost all of his accumulated money. I knew he was popular, and I wanted him to do the work for us.

We went along for a couple of years, and I decided his trapeze tailpiece was stupid. We didn't get complaints from players, but it just didn't make sense. We had the stoptail, which was much more functional, solid, and better all-around. In 1954, we started bringing out more models.

After four years I got a call from Ted's finance man. He said, "We want to cancel the contract and re-write a new one for another five years."

Gibson discontinued the single-cutaway Les Paul Standard in 1960. It was replaced with a much lighter all-mahogany guitar of a very different design, but still bearing the Les Paul name. The contract expired in 1962, and the Les Paul SG Standard was renamed the SG Standard.

There was a lot of money involved by then, and the contract said Mary was to get 50%. And Les was accusing Mary of being unfaithful. I don't know if his accusations were accurate, but Mary told me, "I want to stay home with my kids. I'm willing to sing and play and do anything, if I can stay home."

So Les and Mary got a divorce, and Gibson divided the royalties. Mary was a wonderful woman who deserved to get her share. But we had to cancel the contract in order to split it and pay it off.

So we came out with the SG model – SG meant solid guitar. We put SG on everything that had been a Les Paul.

A less-often discussed detail regarding the solidbody guitar is how the Les Paul pushed Fender into building the Stratocaster. In *The Stratocaster Chronicles*, author and historian Tom Wheeler quotes Fender

Les Paul and Mary Ford in an August 1953 photo

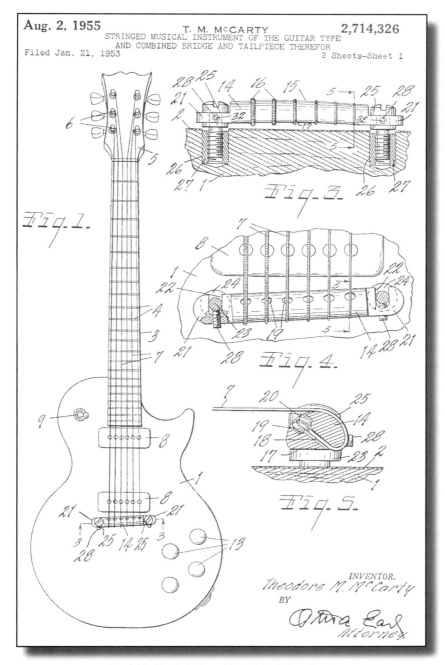

Aug. 2, 1955   T. M. M^cCARTY   2,714,326
                    STRINGED MUSICAL INSTRUMENT OF THE GUITAR TYPE
                    AND COMBINED BRIDGE AND TAILPIECE THEREFOR
Filed Jan. 21, 1953   2 Sheets—Sheet 1

Ted McCarty's Les Paul Model patent

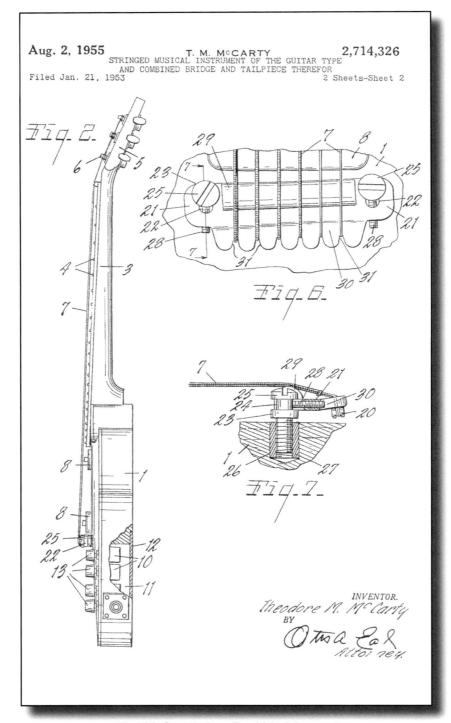

Ted McCarty's Les Paul Model patent

1957 Gibson Les Paul Special – Serial Number 7 7414

Sales chief Don Randall, "(It) was market driven. We had a very plain-Jane Telecaster. Gibson came out with the Les Paul. It was a nice-looking instrument. It was pretty, and we needed an upgrade in our own instrument. And we prevailed on Leo to say we've got to make the next step up. So we eventually developed the Stratocaster guitar."

Wheeler also quotes Randall as saying, "(Fender's first sunburst finish) was another market consideration. All of our competitors had (a sunburst finish); we were the only ones that didn't. I thought a sunburst finish would make the Stratocaster a little more business-like, if you will – fancier."

The Humbucking Pickup

The McCarty era's second great contribution to the guitar world was the humbucking pickup, though McCarty's opinion of the engineering breakthrough was decidedly "business as usual" – a matter of responding to customers, rationalizing a fix, and assigning responsibility.

Leo Fender took a monumental step with the introduction of the first commercially successful solidbody guitar in 1950. Gibson reacted with the Les Paul solidbody. As first-rate as the Les Paul model was, it was also a simple marketing response, devoid of true innovation. But innovation did indeed show up when Gibson introduced the first commercially successful humbucking pickup.

In 1954, Leo Fender was content with his single-coil pickup mostly because it had the tone he was striving for. Likewise, Gibson people were pleased with the sound of the single-coil P-90. But what displeased Gibson was the single-coil's penchant for amplifying electrical interference! The nasty noise bothered customers, and therefore bothered the CMI sales staff.

Additional motivation came from Gibson boss Maurice Berlin. During weekly meetings with Berlin in Chicago, McCarty and V.P. Marc Carlucci told Berlin about the dissatisfaction with the noisy P-90. Carlucci heard about it from sales, McCarty from celebrity clients who would drop by 225 Parsons. And both heard about it from professional players at the New York NAMM shows.

Part of the problem related to the increasing power of the guitar amplifiers, especially Fender amps. Not only were Fender amps becoming more powerful, they were voiced to augment the treble end of the tone spectrum. That meant more (and louder) hum. The problem was delegated to Gibson's electronic lab supervisor, Walter Fuller, and his assistant, Seth Lover.

All things electric went through Fuller, who had joined Gibson in May of 1933 in the machine shop, but was quickly promoted to cost estimator/time keeper. In '35, Fuller was named "electrical engineer," where he pioneered some of Gibson's earliest electric guitars, and for which he holds five patents. During World War II, he supervised Gibson's military subcontracts for electrical assembly; the work was done on the second floor of the Parsons Street factory.

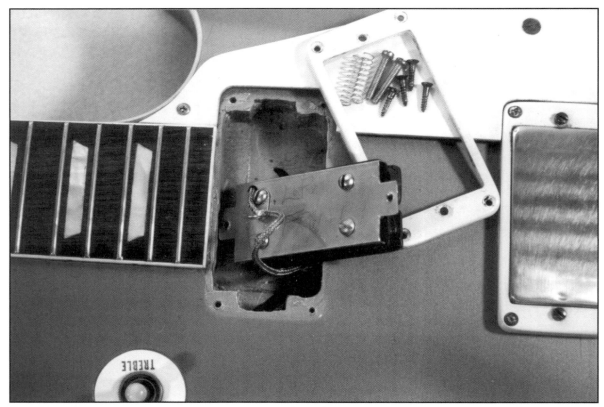

The 1955 Gibson Les Paul Humbucking Pickup Test Guitar pickup mounting assembly was designed in 1955 for this guitar. Originally the humbucking pickup was not going to have adjustable pole pieces so Gibson designed this assembly that allowed for the pickup height to be adjusted at each end of the pickup. This original 1955 Gibson design has become the universally accepted standard and this design has appeared on millions of guitars.

In 1941, Fuller asked Seth Lover to join Gibson as a troubleshooter for Gibson-branded amplifiers the company was getting from Chicago. Fuller's hiring of Lover was not unusual. In those days, and until about '55, a Gibson foreman was responsible for hiring his own department (on John Huis' approval).

Kalamazoo-born Seth Lover began playing with radio technology shortly after the commercial introduction of the radio in the early 1920s. By the mid '30s he was building amplifiers for local Kalamazoo musicians. He joined Gibson in 1941, left during World War II to become a radioman in the Navy, then after the war returned to Gibson for three years before re-joining the Navy. Lover said the moves were about pay; whoever paid the most was where he went.

In '52, Gibson needed Lover's skills. The electric era was beginning to boom and Gibson was masterminding its new GA (Gibson Amp) series. McCarty made an offer Lover couldn't refuse, and he became Gibson's amp guru.

When Lover returned, Gibson had a new electronics lab. There, Fuller and Lover did their work, and it was there that the first humbucking pickup was developed.

When Lover started work on his humbucker, the concept of eliminating the noise was not new. A vaguely similar design dated to three patent applications were submitted in 1935, '38, and '39. The term "humbucker" was not part of those applications, as Lover invented the term. Another element that worked against earlier hum-canceling pickup design was noisy amplifiers. When listening to a guitar and amp made in the 1930s, one might not be able to distinguish single-coil hum, field-coil speaker hum, or miscellaneous amplifier hum.

Lover's profound practical experience with radios gave him a fine background for the humbucker assignment. His early work with amps included the study of an amplifier humbucking choke-coil. Lover knew the P-90's problem was the electromagnetic pickup's sensitivity to external energy, exaggerated by the guitar amplifier. Part of the problem was generated by the amplifier's own power transformers – the pesky "60-cycle hum."

Lover's experiments led him to double-coil pickup construction such that the interference induced by the external sources could be cancelled while the signals generated from the vibrating strings were retained. Lover designed a pickup that had two coils combined into one unit. Each coil was reverse-wound so the hum from the first coil cancelled the hum from the second. Seth also opted for having the two single-coil bobbins wired in series, hence producing a more powerful signal to send to the amplifier. How fortuitous for '70s rockers, who pushed the humbucker to stratospheric volumes!

Lover pursued three humbucking designs, but chose the one that allowed for efficient assembly in the factory. It also was the most successful for maintaining the required high and low frequencies, plus providing consistent performance.

Lover's invention was not so much groundbreaking technology but rather a specifically engineered hum-canceling device, which became known as the Patent Applied For (P.A.F.) pickup. Lover and Gibson did not have exclusive rights to hum-canceling technology, but they did have sole rights to the specific P.A.F. design.

The prototype humbucker was designed to fit into a modified plastic P-90 pickup cover. Gibson liked the sound and size of the P-90, so using it as a model made sense. Hum-canceling designs of the 1930s and '40s had a tendency to produce a dull, vague tone.

Gibson wanted to retain the P-90 sound. Lover used as many P-90 attributes as possible, including slicing the P-90 bobbin in half to make two black bobbins.

"After Seth finished the job, he came into my office and put the pickup on my desk," McCarty said in a 1999 interview for this book. "He said, 'Here's the humbucker.' And I said, 'Put it on a guitar!'"

They selected a solidbody Les Paul to be the test guitar because a solidbody transfers pure string vibration to the pickups, as opposed to an acoustic/electric, which is affected by the vibrating top and sound-chamber.

Two more pickups, built like the first, were taken to the patternmaker's bench in the northwest corner of the Parsons Street basement. A complete guitar was pulled off the white-wood rack in the first floor mill – an early-'55 model. The guitar's pickup cavity was deepened because although the dual-coil design's length and width were equal to the P-90, it was deeper. After the handwork was accomplished, the guitar was taken to the spray booth, then down to the stockroom, where some of the hardware was installed.

Shielding paint and foil were added to the control and toggle-switch cavities. The engineers did not want hum generated from those areas. Lover also reversed the two individual pickups so that they were out-of-phase with each other, again going the extra mile to avoid hum.

Out of immediate necessity, the model makers designed a new mounting ring for the test guitar's humbuckers. The new humbucking

The 1955 Gibson Les Paul Humbucking Pickup Test Guitar and a rare 1955 Gibson GA-55V amplifier with two 12" speakers and true vibrato. Photo: Ward Meeker/Doug Yellow Bird.

pickup mounting assembly was simple, consisting of a plastic trim ring, two P-90 polepieces used as mounting/height adjustment screws, four trim-ring mounting screws, and two lightweight coiled springs. This engineering breakthrough, though often overlooked, first appeared on the humbucker test guitar. Since 1955, this design has been used on millions of guitars, and is still in use today.

As soon as the humbucker test guitar was ready, a meeting was scheduled in the conference room a few steps from McCarty's office. Kalamazoo legend/Columbia recording artist/Gibson employee Rem Wall was asked to play the guitar for McCarty, Lover, Fuller, Huis, and Julius Bellson. Bellson and Will Marker were also asked to test the guitar, as were two other specialists from engineering and final inspection.

"The guitar worked without any hum and was immediately approved. Moldings needed to be made, tooled and ordered, for the windings, and stampings for German nickel-silver."

The humbucking pickup, patent number 2,896,491, was dated June 22, 1955. Berlin empowered McCarty to assign patent holders and he generally gave credit to the lead designer. Lover was given credit for the important features of the Gibson humbucking pickup and his name is now legendary in the vintage guitar community.

Other than the mounting rings, the test guitar's pickups reconcile perfectly with the patent and with Lover's prototype, which is now owned by Seymour Duncan. The humbucker patent drawing depicts a flat magnet resting beneath two bobbins with the bobbin assembly polepieces directly touching the sides of the flat magnet. It also shows non-adjustable polepieces, which also matches the prototype and the test-guitar pickups. The patent was filed for Gibson by its attorney in Kalamazoo, who unfortunatley did not file for a trademark for the humbucking pickup logo.

Even though 1957 is commonly considered the date of the humbucker's introduction, the year was actually late 1955. Gibson's revised Consolette steel guitar was first shipped in late '55 and advertised in the catalog with "new powerful hum-bucking pickups eliminate all electronic disturbances."

Gibson's humbucker debuted on a production guitar in very early 1957. The guitar was an ES-175, possibly a nod to those original jazzers who created some of the buzz about the hum. Per historian Walter Carter, there is an entry in the Gibson ledger on February 18, 1957 – "ES-175N #A-25000" with annotation "H.B. Pickup starts here."

 Epiphone

The third great accomplishment of the McCarty era was saving the Epiphone brand name. Initially, CMI's idea was to offer another quality guitar line to retailers frustrated by Gibson territory agreements that protected Gibson dealerships.

Epiphone was established in 1923 by Epaminondas "Epi" Stathopoulo (1893-1943), a third-generation luthier. Located in Manhattan and Queens, Epiphone borrowed from the Gibson Master Model/Mastertone name when he introduced what would become the era's greatest competing model line in the Epiphone Masterbilt. In the '20s, Manhattan was a strong Gibson territory, so there was a lot of head-to-head competition between them.

Epi's brothers, Orpheus Stathopoulo (1899-1973) and Frixo Stathopoulo (1905-'57) were also active in the business. When Epi died, Orpheus became President, and Frixo was made Vice President.

"When I came to Gibson, the biggest competition we had was Epiphone," said Ted McCarty. "Epiphone made quality guitars, but it was one of those things; Epi died, and Orphie was put in charge. Then, the company got hit by a bad labor strike. Orphie had never been more than a shipping clerk, and he didn't know how to run the business. They put Frixo in charge, but he was a motorcycle man, and he went over the handlebars into a tree, head-first. He damaged his brains and from then on didn't know if he was on foot or horseback. So Epiphone went down, down, down.

"Purchasing Epiphone was another one of those things that just happened. I knew the Epiphone family, and I told Orphie once, 'If you ever want to sell the doghouse-bass business, I'll buy it. Yours is better than ours.'

Artwork from Epiphone's 1965 Catalog

"I was in California, looking at lumber, and I got a call from Orphie. He said, 'I want to sell out, but I'm just not able to. Frixo isn't capable of doing anything - Epi is gone - it's just not working.' I said, 'I'll be back next week and I'll talk with Mr. Berlin.'

"So I came back and told Berlin, 'This is a great thing if we can do it. Because, dealers are wanting Gibson guitars and we can't sell to all of them. Epiphone is a quality line.' Mr. Berlin said, 'What would you do?' I said, 'I'd move Epiphone to Kalamazoo, rent a building, and get a couple of our men to do the work, and we'd get all of Epiphone's tools, dies, and fixtures.' He said, 'Well, can you buy it for a reasonable price?' And I said, 'I can buy it cheap, believe it or not.' He said, 'Orphie is setting a price for us?' I said, 'I could give it to him out of my pocket!'

"So we brought Epiphone to Kalamazoo and put Ward Arbanas in charge of it. We put the Epiphone name on the factory and assigned a salesman from CMI.

"Then we put in another big building in 1960, and moved the Epiphone people there. Now we had another address, at the north end of the Gibson factory. The new street address was Bush Street. People all over the world don't know Parsons Street for Gibson from Bush Street for Epiphone. Sales really jumped because of Epiphone; when I left in 1966, we were doing $3 million a year in Epiphone."

The 1963 Epiphone catalog

The 1963 Epiphone catalog

CRESTWOOD CUSTOM

CRESTWOOD DELUXE

WILSHIRE

The 1963 Epiphone catalog

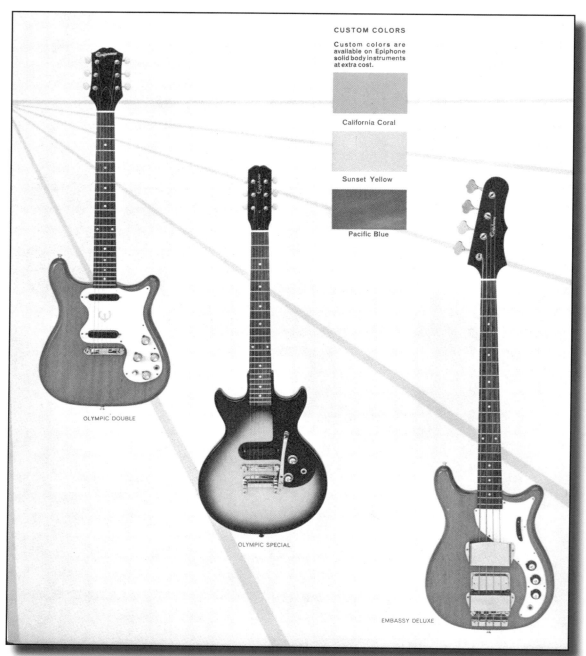

The 1963 Epiphone catalog

The 1963 Epiphone catalog

The 1965 Epiphone catalog

The 1965 Epiphone catalog

ELECTRIC BASS

NEWPORT

EMBASSY DELUXE

RIVOLI

The 1965 Epiphone catalog

The 1965 Epiphone catalog

12 STRING

RIVIERA 12

WILSHIRE 12

The 1965 Epiphone catalog

The 1965 Epiphone catalog

The 1965 Epiphone catalog

The 1965 Epiphone catalog

VENETIAN MANDOLIN

ZENITH

DELUXE

TRIUMPH

The 1965 Epiphone catalog

The ES-335

McCarty felt the ES-335 was right behind the Les Paul solidbody as his most important body design. The ES-335 was the McCarty era's fourth great product line accomplishment. Ted was proud that his double-cutaway thin hollowbody was heavily copied by other companies, including Fender, Guild, Gretsch, Harmony, and the Asian builders.

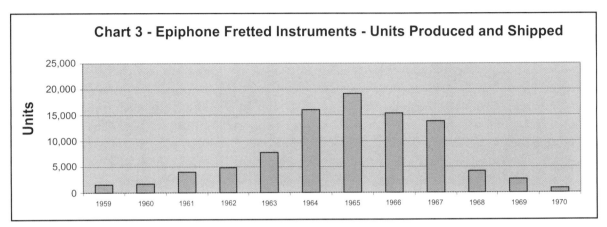

Chart 3 - Epiphone Fretted Instruments - Units Produced and Shipped

Chart 3 shows the number of Epiphone fretted instruments made between 1959 and 1970. The production ramp-up in the mid '60s was not unlike the Gibson brand volume increases. McCarty left in '66 and within two years Epiphone volume dropped to below 5,000 units. Epiphone was never considered a peer of the Gibson brand, and by 1970, CMI's new management decided to outsource the name plate to Japan.

Always challenged to come up with new instruments, McCarty came up with what some people consider his finest design.

"I thought we should have a new instrument that would have some of the sharp tone you get from a solidbody instrument, and some of the mellow tone from an acoustic hollowbody," he said. "I came up with the idea of putting a solid block of maple in an acoustic model and then make the pickups rest on the solid block. It would get some of the same tone as a regular solidbody, plus the instrument's hollow wings would vibrate and we'd get a combination of an electric solidbody and a hollowbody guitar."

According to PRS Guitars' Doug Chandler, the ES-335 was McCarty's proudest achievement.

"He always said that (his proudest achievement) was the ES-335, because it was almost entirely his idea and was an immediate success. Ted told me he thought that the solidbody guitars people were making back then sounded too sharp and, while he liked the idea of a larger hollowbody, he didn't like the feedback. Hence the 335."

The Flying V and Explorer

1964 Gibson ES-335TD SN 66582 with a 1964 Gibson GA-79RVT Multi-Stereo amplifier

Upon their introduction, Gibson's Flying V and Explorer models weren't widely accepted. But time has validated them. Jim Deurloo remembers a rack of white-wood Flying Vs sitting along the plant aisle near the main office from 1959 to '62. That must have been an awkward reminder to management...

McCarty's motivation with the Flying V was a 1958 trade show. When he sat at the drawing table, he wanted something very different, but within reason from an engineering sense. "But what to do?" he asked himself. He started by used simple geometric designs, then took them to the limit. At the drawing table, it was reasonable; his first design was a simply triangle – a triangle with a guitar neck. He knew it would be too heavy, so he "cut out" some of the wood by drawing more straight lines. The result was the Flying V. He expanded on the idea and started drawing more straight lines intersecting in unusual places. The result was the Explorer.

"Leo Fender was traveling around the country, and somebody would mention Gibson to him, and he'd say, 'Oh, that old fuddy-duddy outfit. They haven't had a new idea in centuries.' Friends were always telling me about that kind of stuff," said McCarty. "The only thing that Gibson could do was come up with something *way out*.

"So I got busy and we showed the design to some of the engineers and said, 'Can we make something like this? What do you think of it?' We had a number of people who were

106

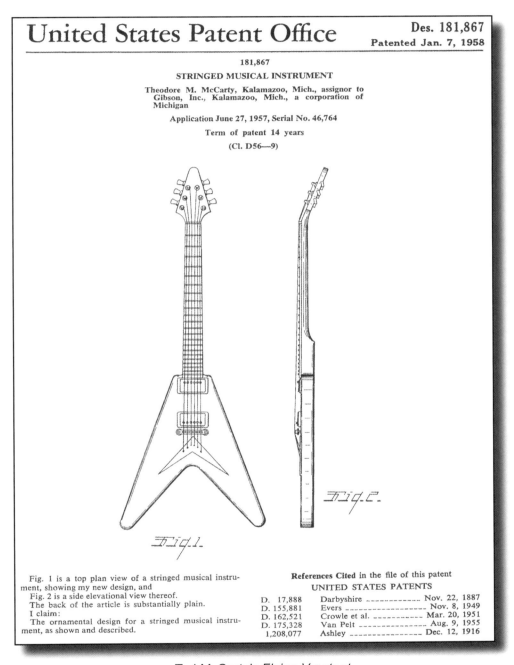

United States Patent Office

Des. 181,867
Patented Jan. 7, 1958

181,867

STRINGED MUSICAL INSTRUMENT

Theodore M. McCarty, Kalamazoo, Mich., assignor to Gibson, Inc., Kalamazoo, Mich., a corporation of Michigan

Application June 27, 1957, Serial No. 46,764

Term of patent 14 years

(Cl. D56—9)

Fig. 1 is a top plan view of a stringed musical instrument, showing my new design, and
 Fig. 2 is a side elevational view thereof.
 The back of the article is substantially plain.
 I claim:
 The ornamental design for a stringed musical instrument, as shown and described.

References Cited in the file of this patent
UNITED STATES PATENTS

D. 17,888   Darbyshire _____ Nov. 22, 1887
D. 155,881   Evers _____ Nov. 8, 1949
D. 162,521   Crowle et al. _____ Mar. 20, 1951
D. 175,328   Van Pelt _____ Aug. 9, 1955
1,208,077   Ashley _____ Dec. 12, 1916

Ted McCarty's Flying V patent

United States Patent Office

Des. 181,865
Patented Jan. 7, 1958

181,865

STRINGED MUSICAL INSTRUMENT

Theodore M. McCarty, Kalamazoo, Mich., assignor to Gibson, Inc., Kalamazoo, Mich., a corporation of Michigan

Application June 20, 1957, Serial No. 46,674

Term of patent 14 years

(Cl. D56—9)

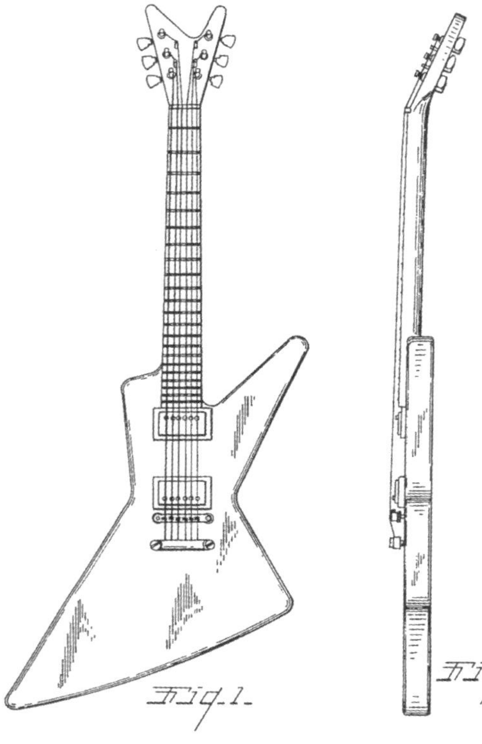

Fig. 1 is a top plan view of a stringed musical instrument showing my new design, and

Fig. 2 is a side elevational view thereof.

The back of the article is substantially plain.

I claim:

The ornamental design for a stringed musical instrument, as shown and described.

References Cited in the file of this patent
UNITED STATES PATENTS

D. 17,888	Darbyshire	Nov. 22, 1887
D. 155,881	Evers	Nov. 8, 1949
D. 162,521	Crowle et al.	Mar. 20, 1951
D. 175,328	Van Pelt	Aug. 9, 1955
1,208,077	Ashley	Dec. 12, 1916

Ted McCarty's Explorer patent

players, like Julius Bellson, and we showed it to them. We showed it to John Huis, who would know how to make it. When Seth Lover saw it, he said (laughs), 'It looks like a Flying V'. And the name stuck.

"We thought, 'What can we do with this Flying V design?' Gibson was a big name – a hundred years of building fine instruments – and here we come out with this thing. And then we made two more guitars with unusual shapes. So we had the Explorer, the Flying V, and another one we had to name. We thought, 'Well, it's a *modern* guitar.' So we just called it a Mod-Dern. And somebody came up with the name 'Explorer,' maybe somebody in CMI sales. We worked closely with sales – CMI had the finest group of salesmen in the country. In the late 1950s, those guys were making $40,000 a year on straight commission. They were good.

"We took the guitars to the trade show that January, and put them in a prominent place so people would see them. I wanted get people talking about them, saying, 'Those crazy guitars.' So I walked around to see what was going on, and I ran into some fellas saying, 'Did you see that crazy stuff down at Gibson's room?' And that went through the whole show. We actually sold maybe 40 of the Flying V. People didn't buy it because it was a *guitar*, they bought it to hang in their store window in New York or Chicago, to get attention and have people come into the store and say 'What is that thing?'

"It went into production and we made 81 of them the first year. We also did a second run of Flying Vs – we just made them, we didn't bother with orders. Our salesmen were out selling, and telling people whether the models were good, bad, or indifferent. It didn't matter if they sold the Flying V.

"The Flying V was clear limba wood; everybody used mahogany, so the Flying V had to be something nobody ever saw before. And we wanted a wood that we wouldn't have to finish to a color. Limba wasn't used in the guitars at the time, so I got some and found out it could work very well. And it wasn't difficult to find.

"The people who sold the limba called it Korina; limba is the African name, but the people who cut it and sold it gave it the name Korina. And I don't remember if it was more expensive. We bought it because it's a pretty wood and has the same basic appearance as mahogany, but almost white. In those days there was quite a demand for natural finishes, and limba was the best thing we could come up with. If it was a little more expensive, you didn't care because you needed a material that would do what you wanted to do. With the Flying V, what we wanted to do was to shake 'em up. And boy, we really shook them up at that show!"

The SG

The SG is another classic model from the McCarty era. Although it has undergone many name revisions, the basic double-cutaway SG is one of Gibson's longest running models. Initially, there were problems with its neck-to-body joint. Building the model produced more scrap wood, and warranty returns were higher than normal until Gibson responded with a firmed-up design. Designers also goofed with the infamous side-pull vibrato, developed from the idea that a vibrato should function in the same direction as a player strumming a guitar. The side-pull ranked as one of Gibson's greatest failures. It was physically heavy and caused problems with tuning stability.

The SG's various issues perhaps were signs that things were getting stressed circa 1960. The guitar market was booming, and more floor space and capacity were required. Gibson rented a plant on Eleanor Streetin Kalamazoo, and along with the Plant 1 expansion in 1960, the company effectively doubled its capacity. A rearrangement saw the finishing department moved off the third floor, a new Custom Shop was created on the third floor, and much of the mill was relocated.

The double-cutaway, lightweight SG did satisfy market demand, and sales of the Standard, Custom, and Special variants increased by about 33% when the SG version was introduced in '61.

"We made the SG because players were asking for a double-cutaway," said McCarty. "They wanted to use their thumbs on the sixth string, and couldn't on the single-cutaway."

When the SG Standard sold in '61, it was a little more expensive than the prior year's single-cutaway Les Paul Standard. Gibson's September 1, 1961 price list called for a $290 price for the SG Les Paul Standard. In Gibson's May 1960 catalog, the single-cut Les Paul Standard listed for $265.

The Firebird 34

The Firebird is another McCarty-era classic. While he didn't design it, he in effect was its creator. As President of Gibson, McCarty wanted to keep Gibson on top, not only for business reasons, but for personal reasons. He was proud of being top man at Gibson, proud of his team, proud of Kalamazoo, the place he called home.

The Firebird's name originally came from a proposed bright red finish that was to be applied to the model. But by the time it made it to price lists and catalogs, it was offered only in Gibson's sunburst, with custom-color options. The vintage market often calls this model's shade Cardinal Red instead of its original name, Firebird Red. According to McCarty, the model's Phoenix-inspired firebird-image pickguard was a secondary thought suggested by designer Ray Dietrich.

It has been said that the Firebird was designed to compete with the Fender Stratocaster. Other research suggests it was actually introduced to compete with the Jazzmaster.

"I paid Ray Dietrich to design it," said McCarty. "He was an very good engineer who designed bodies for automobiles. He and his wife lived in Kalamazoo, and I heard him lecture at one of the clubs in town. He talked about making these expensive cars, and I loved to hear him explain things. He believed in straight lines and doing this, that, and the other things.

"After his speech, I got the idea that I could get him to make me a guitar. We always needed a new model – something new, something different – for the next trade show in

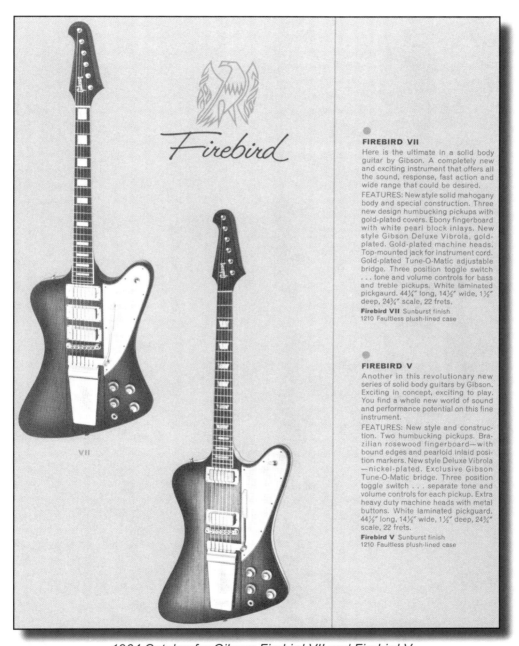

Firebird

FIREBIRD VII

Here is the ultimate in a solid body guitar by Gibson. A completely new and exciting instrument that offers all the sound, response, fast action and wide range that could be desired.

FEATURES: New style solid mahogany body and special construction. Three new design humbucking pickups with gold-plated covers. Ebony fingerboard with white pearl block inlays. New style Gibson Deluxe Vibrola, gold-plated. Gold-plated machine heads. Top-mounted jack for instrument cord. Gold-plated Tune-O-Matic adjustable bridge. Three position toggle switch . . . tone and volume controls for bass and treble pickups. White laminated pickgaurd. 44¼" long, 14½" wide, 1½" deep, 24¾" scale, 22 frets.

Firebird VII Sunburst finish.
1210 Faultless plush-lined case

FIREBIRD V

Another in this revolutionary new series of solid body guitars by Gibson. Exciting in concept, exciting to play. You find a whole new world of sound and performance potential on this fine instrument.

FEATURES: New style and construction. Two humbucking pickups. Brazilian rosewood fingerboard—with bound edges and pearloid inlaid position markers. New style Deluxe Vibrola —nickel-plated. Exclusive Gibson Tune-O-Matic bridge. Three position toggle switch . . . separate tone and volume controls for each pickup. Extra heavy duty machine heads with metal buttons. White laminated pickguard. 44½" long, 14½" wide, 1½" deep, 24¾" scale, 22 frets.

Firebird V Sunburst finish
1210 Faultless plush-lined case

1964 Catalog for Gibson Firebird VII and Firebird V

111

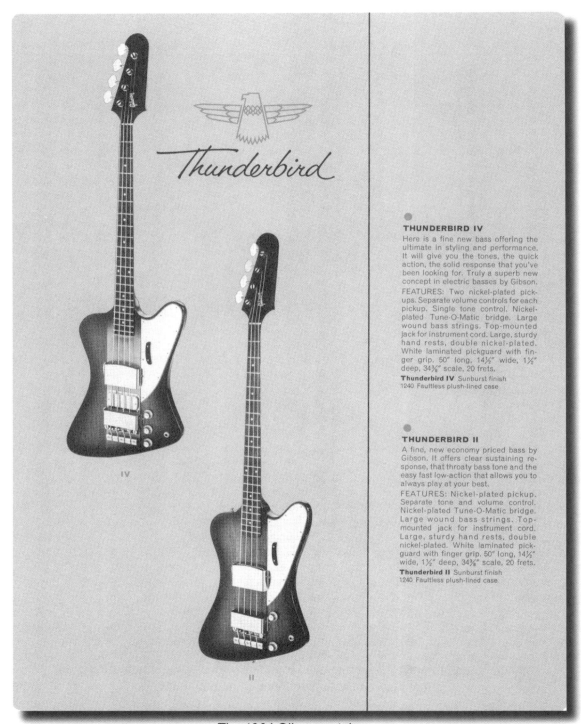

THUNDERBIRD IV

Here is a fine new bass offering the ultimate in styling and performance. It will give you the tones, the quick action, the solid response that you've been looking for. Truly a superb new concept in electric basses by Gibson.

FEATURES: Two nickel-plated pickups. Separate volume controls for each pickup. Single tone control. Nickel-plated Tune-O-Matic bridge. Large wound bass strings. Top-mounted jack for instrument cord. Large, sturdy hand rests, double nickel-plated. White laminated pickguard with finger grip. 50" long, 14½" wide, 1½" deep, 34⅜" scale, 20 frets.

Thunderbird IV Sunburst finish
1240 Faultless plush-lined case

THUNDERBIRD II

A fine, new economy priced bass by Gibson. It offers clear sustaining response, that throaty bass tone and the easy fast low-action that allows you to always play at your best.

FEATURES: Nickel-plated pickup. Separate tone and volume control. Nickel-plated Tune-O-Matic bridge. Large wound bass strings. Top-mounted jack for instrument cord. Large, sturdy hand rests, double nickel-plated. White laminated pickguard with finger grip. 50" long, 14½" wide, 1½" deep, 34⅜" scale, 20 frets.

Thunderbird II Sunburst finish
1240 Faultless plush-lined case

The 1964 Gibson catalog

112

January. I looked him up, introduced myself, and told him how much I enjoyed his speech. I said, 'Did you ever make any guitars?' And he said (laughs), 'No, Ted, I've never made guitars. But I'd like to.' And I said, 'Well, how would you like to make your guitar for me?' He said, 'I'd love to.' I said, 'Well, what's it going to cost me for your talent?' And he quoted me a figure, and I said, 'That's reasonable. We'd like you to make one.' And we gave him carte blanche.

"One of the things he did was make a neck that came all the way back to the tail. That was his idea. And it was a beautiful thing. Then he designed the pickguard for it. And it turned out the design was expensive and difficult to make, so we changed it in 1965. All of the rest of our models had glued-in necks, so in 1965 we changed the Firebird design to that type of neck. I think Ray retired shortly after that, they moved to Texas. Ray was a very fine man and a really capable guy. He had a very fine wife, I liked her very much, and she was a very nice lady. I kept in contact with them after they moved away."

It's interesting that McCarty decided to go for outside engineering for the Firebird. Since joining Gibson, one element he always kept in mind was the introduction of a new model each year to be a focal point at trade shows.

In the early '60s, McCarty and Gibson had a near-miss with the SG, and in McCarty's mind its problems may have created a bit of doubt about in-house design. Documentation and anecdotal evidence suggest the SG neck design was developed by Larry Allers. Unfortunately, the Dietrich design was similarly flawed; the headstock/neck joint was weak, and misplaced tuners caused many neck breaks. It proved to be a more fragile design than even the SG.

The Firebird was also an expensive design to make, likely a factor of outside engineering. Typically, designs were done in-house and were finalized by woodworkers who knew what would work and what wouldn't. The initial SG neck heel was a problem, and others occasionally surfaced, but generally speaking, the use of in-house engineers and model builders worked exceptionally well.

By late 1964 or early '65, the engineers had had enough of the difficult/expensive-to-build Firebird, so the design was changed. This change signaled the emergence of a new plant emphasis. Production speed and costs were becoming more important.

Another major change in product design happened with the ES-335 in 1965, also to address production speed and cost issues. In early '65, the famous stud tailpiece was removed from the 335, replaced by an easy-to-install trapeze tailpiece. The trapeze negated a key concept in the design of the 335 – the bridge bolted into solid wood. With the change, the semi-solid 335 became a thinline acoustic archtop.

The Johnny Smith model

Johnny Smith was McCarty's favorite guitar play. Smith's tone was smooth and easy, without excess brightness and fret noise. Johnny Smith tone was the Ted McCarty benchmark. While Leo Fender favored the honky-tonk tone of a steel guitar, McCarty

JOHNNY SMITH

TAL FARLOW

BARNEY KESSEL

...THE FRETS HEARD AND

PREFERRED AROUND THE WORLD

THREE OF A KIND!

...all guitar greats...all perennial poll winners...and all agreed about their guitar: it's a Gibson, and it's the finest.

Each of these famous guitarists served as the inspiration for a special Gibson model—designed by him, for his kind of music, for his guitar technique, for his special sound. And they're very special sounds...lively, brilliant, poetic...unique with each artist on his special Gibson.

Gibson makes the world's widest selection of models. Jazz guitars, solid bodies, classics, flat tops, folk models, country and

western, acoustic, amplified. All these instruments have their special properties—yet they're *all alike* in one important respect: their Gibson quality. Quality that has made Gibson the most sought-after guitar in the world for over half-a-century.

In every model, Gibson enhances the performance of the player. Its action is fast and easy, encouraging to the beginner. Its tone is pure and brilliant, challenging to the artist. Its response is perfect, a boon to anyone.

Today...there's a great and growing interest in guitar playing. You find it everywhere. The campus. The coffee house. The home. Every gathering place. And this makes Gibson doubly important, for Gibson is the world's most complete line of guitars, for every type of music.

Johnny Smith was Ted McCarty's favorite guitar player. He is shown here in a 1964 advertisement with Tal Farlow and Barney Kessel.

favored the mellow muted sound of chord-melody jazz. These biases became one of the most obvious differences between Fender and McCarty.

"Another company made a Johnny Smith guitar, and Johnny wouldn't play it. He said it was no good. That's when he came to me and said, 'Can you make me a good guitar, the way I want it?' I said, 'Sure. You tell us how you want it and we'll make it.' I had been in Hawaii, this was 1960, and on the way back, my wife and I stopped in Colorado, because my daughter, Susan, was going to Colorado State University. It was time for her to go to school and she had left her car in Denver.

She got off there, and we went down to Colorado Springs, where Johnny lived.

"Johnny had other guitars, but the ones he loved to play were a Gibson L-5 and his D'Angelico. So basically those were the instruments we used for his model. Johnny and I took the measurements of everything on his guitars. I had brought with me my instruments to measure his guitars. I wrote down what he wanted, why he wanted it, and all the rest of it. I went back to Kalamazoo and made one in the factory just like he asked for. He wanted 21 frets but we had enough room for 22 frets so we put 22 frets in it. Afterwards he said, "I don't want 22, I want 21." He had no tone control. He only had a volume control, because he felt he could get his own tone. He didn't need a button for tone. He didn't want a switch for it. He didn't want it that way."

"After the guitar was done, I sent it to him. The day after he got it, he telephoned me, and he said, 'Ted, I did something last night that I've never done in my entire career! I played that guitar on the stage the day I got it. I never took a new instrument without breaking it in first.' He said, 'This thing was so perfect. It was exactly what I wanted.' I said, 'Okay, I'll send you $1,000 to prove that we made it for you as an endorser.' So we sent him $1,000 and he took the check and went down and bought himself a studio. Johnny was the finest jazz guitarist in the country, as far as I'm concerned."

The Everly Brothers **36** and others flat-tops

McCarty always felt it was a great honor to be President of Gibson Guitars. He would casually say that it wasn't particularly difficult to run Gibson, and he didn't need to do too much with Gibson's flat-top designs. Flat-top guitars at Gibson reached their pinnacle in the 1930s. There wasn't much for McCarty to do in the flat-top field.

McCarty did order the production of a square-shoulder jumbo based upon Martin's D-style dreadnought. Wilbur Fuller, working in the Parson Street basement mandolin building and instrument repair department was asked by Larry Allers, chief engineer, to copy a Martin D-style. Fuller was given an actual Martin dreadnought and asked to pencil out an outline. Then he was to build a Gibson like it. The design debuted as the 1958 Epiphone Frontier, but it was quickly integrated as the 1960 Gibson Hummingbird.

The McCarty era also saw the introduction of the 'adjustable bridge' for Gibson flat-tops. Being able to adjust the height of the saddle seemed like a good idea. But the design deadened tone. The attempt was an example of trying to come up with an improvement and something new. The design of a 1930s Martin and Gibson flat-top was already about as good as it could get. McCarty's top engineer, Larry Allers, could not improve on something that was already proven to be 'near-perfect.'

Music celebrities liked to visit the Parson Street factory. Often they did it while on tour. When available, Gibson execs tried to treat the visitors like royalty and often some business was done. Some celebs would drop off their favorite instrument for repair. Others just wanted to snoop around and enjoy the place. Others wanted to do business.

McCarty recalls, "Two brothers, the Everly Brothers came to see us. We wound up making them a special guitar model. We said, 'Well, what do you want?' The Everly Brothers said, 'We want something with our name on it.' Gibson had mutual agreements with all of the Galaxy of Stars. It was good for them and good for us."

Another McCarty-era success was the J-160E, introduced in 1954. "Introducing the J-160E was an astute business move on Gibson's part, said Eldon Whitford, David Vinopal, and Dan Erlewine in their 1994 book, *Gibson's Fabulous Flat-Top Guitars: An Illustrated History and Guide*. "Acoustic rhythm guitars were the preference of rock, pop, and country performers in the '50s, thus guaranteeing the success of the J-160E."

A sleeper in the McCarty era line-up was the B-45-12 acoustic flat-top. When introduced in the early 1961, there was no other 12-string folk guitar on the market. Gibson's first was made as a custom order, but it opened the company's eyes to the possibility for marketing a long-forgotten guitar model, the flat-top 12-string.

McCarty learned first-hand that Gibson made great flat-tops, when he served as sales manager of the Wurlitzer store in Rochester. The store didn't carry Gibson (it had Martin and Epiphone), but McCarty wanted Gibson. McCarty had customers in Rochester that wanted Gibson. McCarty sold flat-top and archtop acoustic guitars in the late 1930s, when acoustic guitar engineering and production were in their prime. As President of Gibson, he tried to improve on everything that was on the market. But when it came to acoustic flat-tops and archtops, it just couldn't be done. The finest ever made had already been invented.

The ES-175 and other archtops

McCarty gets credit for being in charge when Gibson's longest-running post-war model, the ES-175, was introduced in early 1949. Given that the typical startup of any model is more than one year, he didn't have influence on the model. Upon his arrival, Gibson had already joined an industry that was shifting from full-bodied archtops to single-cutaway archtops.

Acoustic and electric archtops were not McCarty's holy grails. The pioneering was done much earlier by Orville Gibson and Lloyd Loar. The pinnacle of success in the archtop world would be left for the small independent builders D'Angelico, D'Aquisto, and Stromberg. McCarty and his staff made sure that Gibson's acoustic archtops did fully receive cutaways and electronics.

McCarty's fame was actually built by pulling away from the traditional archtop. Had Ted followed the advice of the Grestch family, perhaps everything would have turned out differently for Gibson. Before the Les Paul model came out, the Gretsch family and others advised him not to build a solidbody. Of course, the Grestch family didn't follow their own advice, entering the small-body electric guitar market shortly after Gibson.

The McCarty era's great contribution in the archtop field was thinline models. In 1955, several thin electric archtops were introduced, including the ES-225, the Byrdland, and the ES-350T, and they helped influence McCarty in 1958 to introduce the world's first successful double-cutaway, semi-solid thinline – the ES-335.

Gibson Mandolins and Banjos

Where are the great Martin and Fender mandolins and banjos? It's a tough question, but it demonstrates the power of the Gibson legacy. Just as with Gibson flat-tops and archtops, Gibson's best mandolins and banjos are from earlier eras. The 1920s Lloyd Loar-era F-5 mandolin and '30s Gibson Mastertone flat-head five-string banjos are holy grails in their field, very often copied and imitated, just lilke Gibson Les Pauls, ES-335s, Fender Stratocasters and Telecasters, and Martin D-45s and D-28s are copied.

What's impressive is that McCarty was able to maintain superiority over other builders of mandolins and banjos. In the banjo market, in particular, Gibson did a great job just staying alive. During the McCarty era, only two nationally known banjo makers existed – Gibson and Vega – and the success of Gibson mandolins and banjos at the time underlines the overall power of the Gibson process. Since 1917, Gibson mandolins – which were the basis for the company's name – were built in the same location on Parsons Street. It was a strong tradition, passed through generations of woodworkers.

Gibson was late getting into the banjo market, but McCarty wasn't going to give up on it. He appreciated that they needed to make banjos. Plus, they had hired Julius Bellson, a recognized 20-year-old banjo phenom. Once aboard, Bellson wasn't about to let his instrument flounder at Gibson.

McCarty kept banjos going while his other innovations were being put in place. Bellson was the key. As the number three man in Kalamazoo, behind John Huis, the banjo advocate wasn't about to let his beloved instrument vanish. Bellson had McCarty's ear when he wanted it. In fact, Bellson tried to do the same thing for another one of his favorite instruments, the ukulele.

The Gibson Bass Guitar

McCarty always thought the bass viol was the true musical bass. While he was quick to react to Leo Fender's slab solidbody, he all but ignored Leo Fender's electric bass. Asked about Gibson bass guitars, McCarty would launch into a discussion of Epiphone's dog-house bass viol. His concern at Gibson was to avoid competing with Epiphone. Of course, that concern prompted several offers by McCarty to buy the Epiphone bass viol technology and equipment, and the unintended consequence of his concern was ultimately very good for both nameplates.

McCarty's vision of a proper solidbody electric bass was reflected in the EB-1, from 1953. Shaped like a small violin, it had a telescopic extension foot that allowed it to be played like a bass viol. While Gibson introduced several spin-off Les Paul models designed for all price ranges, it did not offer a single-cutaway solidbody Les Paul bass. Why? Les Paul, the man, used a bass viol player in his trio, as did most other country, bluegrass, folk, and jazz musicians. While McCarty was concerned about Leo Fender "stealing the take" in the solidbody market, he seemed unconcerned about the solidbody bass. Conversely, some historians feel Fender's greatest contribution to music was the solidbody Precision Bass. Part of Leo and Don Randall's vision was an instrument that would replace the bulky upright bass viol, and in that regard, the Precision was revolutionary, even if it didn't register with Ted McCarty, because in the mid '50s, McCarty was still focused on getting the Epiphone upright bass viol. While McCarty was quick to accept the business opportunity for the solidbody guitar, he seemed unconcerned about the solidbody bass business. Gibson sold 546 electric basses prior to building the EB-0 and EB-2. When they were introduced in 1958 and '59, however, production tripled.

So Gibson didn't effectively enter the electric bass market until the EB-0. Rather, it

NEW RHYTHM IN THE BASS SECTION WITH THE GIBSON ELECTRIC BASS

Leading combos and orchestras are adding new resonance to their rhythm sections with the Gibson Electric Bass, the perfect complement to any musical group.

The carved top, violin-shaped body of the Electric Bass is of solid mahogany; the mahogany neck, with the famous Gibson adjustable Truss Rod construction, has 20 frets and is joined to the body at the 16th fret. The scale length is 30½" and offers a full range of deep resonant tones. An important factor in the outstanding performance of this instrument is the Gibson designed metal bridge, adjustable for height and string lengths.

Conveniently located tone and volume controls have easy-to-set, numbered, clear plastic knobs; individual Kluson nickel plated pegs have white plastic buttons; the powerful Alnico magnetic pickup has brown Royalite cover.

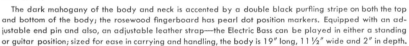

The dark mahogany of the body and neck is accented by a double black purfling stripe on both the top and bottom of the body; the rosewood fingerboard has pearl dot position markers. Equipped with an adjustable end pin and also, an adjustable leather strap—the Electric Bass can be played in either a standing or guitar position; sized for ease in carrying and handling, the body is 19" long, 11½" wide and 2" in depth.

Gibson Electric Bass

Case for Bass—536 Faultless

GIBSON FINGERREST PICK-UP UNITS

100-SN   *Single Nickel (L-7, S-300).*
101-SG   *Single Gold (L-5, L-12, S-400).*
102-SCN *Single Cutaway Nickel (L-7C).*
103-SCG *Single Cutaway Gold (L-5C, L-12C, S-400C).*
104-DN   *Double Nickel (L-7, S-300).*
105-DG   *Double Gold (L-5, L-12, S-400).*
106-DCN *Double Cutaway Nickel (L-7C).*
107-DCG *Double Cutaway Gold (L-5C, L-12C, S-400C).*

1957 Catalog of Gibson Electric Bass

118

treated the electric bass as a spin-off instrument that would be fashioned after its guitar bodies. That was true of the EB/SG series, the EB-2/ES-335 series, and the Thunderbird/Firebird series.

Because of the power of the Gibson name, EB and Thunderbird basses established a strong niche market. They were different, but not holy grails like the Fender Jazz and Precision basses made from the 1950s to 1965.

McCarty's administration over Gibson's solidbody basses indicated that he had a profound engineering influence within the organization. Looking at the organization during in the '50s, it was incredibly small at the top; McCarty provided most of the ideas, Huis oversaw manufacturing, Bellson oversaw personnel and administration, Walter Fuller presided over electronics, and Larry Allers did likewise in woodwork engineering. If McCarty was directly involved in instruments like the Les Paul and ES-335, the results were superior. If he wasn't heavily involved, as with amplifiers and bass guitars, the results were more average. Even with the introduction of the EB-2, it was Allers, not McCarty, who led the design and signed the patent.

The Tune-O-Matic Bridge

According to historian Tom Wheeler, the Tune-O-Matic bridge may well be the most recognizable McCarty-designed Gibson product. Wheeler points out that the term "tune-o-matic bridge" has become ubiquitous in the industry, much like the term "humbucker pickup" (coined by Seth Lover) is universally used for dual-coil hum-canceling pickup. Wheeler implies that had Gibson call the Tune-O-Matic the "McCarty bridge," his name would have been much more prevalent in the guitar lexicon.

In his interviews with McCarty, Wheeler discovered that Ted began to ponder a redesign of the bridge and tailpiece after he examined Les Paul's metal trapeze bridge. Les' design was used (albeit incorrectly) on the first production models of the 1952 Les Paul model. McCarty designed the stud bridge (also called the stop-tail or bar tailpiece) quickly in 1952 and it appeared on a patent filed January 21, 1953 for the Les Paul guitar, and naturally, Gibson and McCarty had every intention of replacing the metal trapeze tailpiece initially used on the Les Paul. Research a short while later by McCarty and his staff led to the development of the Tune-O-Matic design. As its name implies, the bridge allowed for improvement in guitar tuning capabilities. Even so, McCarty's stop-bar tailpiece is still used on instruments made by Gibson, Paul Reed Smith, and scores of other brands.

The Electric Uke

McCarty did a lot of delegating at Gibson. He was the final word on approval of designs, but often Larry Allers would do much of the engineering work. For larger creative assignments, McCarty was more involved. He'd sometimes say, "You can't go to the workers for that type of thing." The staff and model makers were great at tweaking, but breakthroughs were up to the boss.

One design that never appears on McCarty's list of major accomplishments is his electric ukulele. During his reign, it was not unusual for a recording star to ask the factory to make a special instrument.

"People would call or visit us at the factory and they'd say, 'I'd like you to make me a special guitar, how much would it cost?'" he said. "And we had a department that did nothing but make specials."

Ted McCarty's electric uke

One person who contacted McCarty was radio and television icon Arthur Godfrey. As a sailor, Godfrey learned to play the uke and brought the talent to his popular '50s radio and television shows. But his uke couldn't be heard with a band. Some members of the band were plugged in, and Godfrey wanted an electric uke that would match the volume of the electric guitar. So Godfrey went to McCarty.

"He wanted an electric ukulele, but he didn't want strings that were metal," McCarty noted. "But making an electric uke with nylon strings presented a real problem. I told my engineers what I wanted for the instrument, and they built it. But I took on the problem of designing the strings. You can't use regular nylon strings with an electromagnetic pickup, and Godfrey wouldn't have anything to do with metal strings. He didn't know any better, but that's what he wanted. So I talked with a couple of guys and they said, 'You can't do it, Ted!'

"So I tried and I tried... I had to get iron in the strings, somehow, and we couldn't get a string inside a string without having it get it too thick. So the only thing we could do was melt the nylon into a liquid, then run another string through a goo with iron powder. The way I did it was to get some plastic string material so I could melt it and get it into a liquid. I put in some iron-powdered metal and mixed it up really well. I ran the strings through that, and after they dried we milled them down to size. I made the strings, but didn't want to fool around with mass-producing them. It was time-consuming and expensive – and Godfrey was impatient. He wanted to know where his ukulele was, and I said, 'Well, we're working on it.'

"So I finally got it finished, and we sent it to the hotel where he stayed in New York. He called and said, 'Where is it?' I said, 'I sent it!'"

"Well, he got on the air and said, 'Ted McCarty, that used-to-be friend of mine, he promised me an electric ukulele, and I never got it!'

"I finally got so tired of him talking about me on the air that I called him and said, 'It must be in the hotel, because we sent it and we have the credit for having shipped it.' So he went and talked to them, and sure enough it was there, they just put it away.

"I heard he was overjoyed with it. He used to do the cigarette ads playing live music with his electric uke, and his studio musicians, and Mr. Berlin and I would sit in Berlin's office and listen to Godfrey's program. Godfrey sould say, 'My friend, Ted McCarty, from Gibson, and so forth and so forth,' every day. Mr. Berlin used to laugh and say, 'You and I made more air time for free than the cigarette company was getting.'"

In 1957, the only standard-sized uke in the Gibson price list was the Uke-1, listed at $30. It's interesting that Bellson, the jack-of-all trades personnel manager, was a huge fan of the uke and tenor banjo.

Accoring to McCarty, Bellson said, "Let's put ukuleles in the Kalamazoo schools. I'll teach 'em." So Gibson went to the school people just up the street from Gibson and they said we could.

"I don't think we used Gibson ukes for those kids, because they were expensive," McCarty said. "But we gave them a lot of ukuleles, and Julius actually taught those kids. It went on and on and on."

Gibson Amplifiers

McCarty cites the Les Paul guitar as his greatest achievement at Gibson. On the other end, something he would never claim was an ability to effectively compete with Leo Fender's amplifiers.

"To help us build amplifiers, I brought Seth Lover in from Chicago," he said. "And I always blamed him for not being able to beat Leo's amps. I told him (laughing), 'It's your fault.' I gave him a lab to work in and put him in-charge – he was top dog in amplifiers. We

A November 1955 Gibson amplifier advertisement that appeared in International Musician magazine

GIBSON'S FINEST PROFESSIONAL AMPLIFIERS

HIGH FIDELITY AMPLIFIER —SIX SPEAKERS

The GA-90 is the ideal amplifier for recording, broadcasting, or "on the job" playing—for clear, distortion free tones in a range from 20 cycles to 20,000 cycles. Perfect for any electric instrument, including electric bass or accordion with pickup. Sturdy, lightweight but powerful ¾" solid wood, lock-joint construction covered with dark brown buffalo grain fabric; large speaker baffle has rich grille with contrasting frame.

This High Fidelity amplifier has a normal output of 25 watts and a peak output in excess of 35 watts; six 8" matched Gibson Ultra-Sonic speakers. The pre-amplifier and controls are mounted in the top of the case, while main amplifier is at the bottom; two separate channels have two input jacks in each channel, with independent volume and voicing controls. Channel One is provided with a Gain Switch to allow use of either two microphones or two instruments; Channel Two with jacks for use with instruments; entirely different settings can be used for each channel. A standby switch maintains the 8 tubes ready for instant use while consuming a minimum of current in a standby position. Ground included with A.C. line cord; jeweled pilot light; three amp protective fuse. Size: 24½" wide, 20" high, 9½" deep; weight 38 lbs.

GA-90 Amplifier (Inc. Cover)

VERSATILE PROFESSIONAL TWO CHANNEL AMPLIFIER

A powerful, versatile professional amplifier, the GA-77 offers "High Gain" response in each of two channels: Channel One, with two inputs for electronic instruments or microphones, has separate volume and separate treble and bass controls for an unusually wide range of tone colorings and effects. Channel Two, with two inputs for electronic instruments, has a separate volume control and a combination tone control for "High Gain" response in the regular frequency range. Full 25 watts normal output, peak power in excess of 35 watts; top mounted chassis with easily accessible control panel; seven tubes; top quality 15" Jensen Speaker with Alnico No. 5 magnets; three position switch, on-off-standby.

An exceptional *Gibson First* feature of the GA-77 is the monitor jack for headphones for recording, "on the job" monitoring or practice. With the switch at the standby position, a tape recorder can be plugged into this jack, and recordings made free of room echoes and disturbing noises. The GA-77 is sturdy and compact of solid ¾" wood with lock-joint construction in rich two-tone covering of dark brown buffalo grain with contrasting mottled brown and grey; extra large speaker baffle of woven saran fabric; slanted front panel for clearer sound dispersement; jeweled pilot light, protective three amp fuse; special interwound primary and secondary low distortion output transformer; ground included with A.C. line cord. Size: 22" wide, 20" high, 10⅛" deep; weight 40 lbs.

GA-77 Amplifier (Inc. Cover)

1957 Catalog of a GA-90 and GA-77

"HIGH GAIN" TWIN TWELVE AMPLIFIER WITH BUILT-IN ELECTRONIC VIBRATO!

A "High Gain" amplifier with twin 12" speakers and a built-in true vibrato, the GA-55 V offers the discriminating artist top performance and appearance. The built-in vibrato features a neat, compact remote control box that plugs into the instrument jack and can be regulated for speed and intensity of vibrato and switched on or off at the player's fingertips.

Top mounted nine tube chassis with easily accessible top control panel; full 20 watts undistorted output, peak output 30 watts; wide angle sound dispersement with two top quality 12" Jensen speakers with Alnico No. 5 magnets. There are two instrument inputs, the first of which is hooked to the vibrato remote control; two microphone inputs which can be used for additional instruments; separate volume controls for instrument and microphone circuits; separate treble and bass tone controls for a wide range of effects and tone colorings. The amplifier case is of ¾" solid wood, lock-joint construction attractively covered in dark brown buffalo grain and contrasting mottled brown and grey; the extra large speaker baffle has a colorful grille of saran fabric; slanted front panel. Ground included with A.C. line cord, jeweled pilot light; three amp protective fuse; on-off-standby switch. Size: 26½" wide; 20" high; 10⅛" deep; weight 39 lbs.

GA-55 V Amplifier (Inc. Cover)

GA-55 Amplifier—The same as the GA-55 V described above, without the built-in vibrato. All of the other GA-55 features are retained, except for the 6 tube chassis and the weight which is only 37 lbs.

GA-55 Amplifier (Inc. Cover)

THE NEW "COUNTRY AND WESTERN"

A new Gibson design which produces unusually clear bell-like treble, with tremendous reserve volume and sustaining quality. The four inputs are in pairs with separate volume controls, and the combined voicing control has very wide range. "Standby" position on the main switch allows silent warm-up with instantaneous power available at a touch. Equipped with switching jacks for extension speakers. Top mounted chassis. SIX TUBES, of which two are double types, produce a nominal output of 25 watts with reserve up to 35 watts to cover peaks. The Jensen "15" Concert Series speaker has been specially engineered for top treble response. DIMENSIONS—22" x 20" x 10½". Weight 39 lbs. Finished in two-tone brown buffalo grained fabric with a striking "Country and Western" motif and gold lettering. Woven saran grille.

GA-70 "Country and Western" Amplifier—60 cycle

1957 Catalog of a GA-55V amd GA-70

A GIBSON AMPLIFIER FOR EVERY PURPOSE

THE POPULAR LES PAUL AMPLIFIER WITH BUILT-IN VARIABLE TREMOLO

Professional in performance, size and appearance, this Les Paul endorsed amplifier, complete with built-in variable tremolo, provides a top quality "High Gain" instrument with a clear, brilliant treble response. Powerful 7 tube chassis; 14 to 16 watt output; top mounted control panel; 12" Jensen speaker with Alnico No. 5 magnets.

A wide range of effects is possible with the built-in tremolo regulated by separate intensity and frequency controls and on-off switch mounted in foot pedal. Two channels; channel one with two inputs for microphone or additional instruments; channel two with two instrument inputs; separate volume controls; combination bass-treble voicing control. The amplifier case is of sturdy, compact solid ¾" wood lock-joint construction covered in dark brown buffalo grain and contrasting mottled brown and grey; slanted front panel; extra large speaker baffle, colorful dark grille of woven saran; jeweled pilot light; protective three amp fuse; off-on switch. Size: 22" wide, 20" high, 10⅛" deep; weight 34 lbs.

GA-40 Les Paul Model Amplifier. 40-C Cover for Above Amplifier.

DUAL SPEAKER AMPLIFIER FOR WIDE ANGLE SOUND DISPERSION

A dual speaker amplifier with all the features needed for top performance, the GA-30 offers a wide range of tonal qualities, "High Gain," and professional appearance. The case is a sturdy, compact unit of ¾" lock-joint construction covered with attractive two-tone brown and mottled brown and grey fabric with a large speaker baffle of woven saran fabric.

Twin Jensen 12" and 8" speakers with Alnico No. 5 magnets for faithful reproduction of high and low frequencies; full 14 watt output; powerful 6 tube chassis, easily accessible top mounted control panel; three input circuits for instruments, the fourth for microphone or an additional instrument. Separate volume controls for instrument and microphone circuits; combination treble and bass voicing control plus bass-treble tone expander for a wide range of tonal effects; jeweled pilot light; on-off switch; protective fuse. Size: 22" wide; 20" high, 10⅛" deep; weight 32 lbs.

GA-30 Amplifier

30-C Cover for Above Amplifier

1957 Catalog of a GA-40 Les Paul and GA-30

1955 Gibson GA-40 Les Paul Amplifier

built what we thought were damn good amps, and today you hear people say the old Gibsons are still very fine amplifiers. But ours was made such that it would not go into these real raucous tones.

"I worked on the amp *business*, not on amplifiers. When I got to Gibson, they were buying amps from some other company in town. So I got rid of that in a hurry. I thought we were a damn good woodworking factory, so we made our own amplifiers.

"During World War II, Gibson had contracts with the government to make electric things, including amplifiers," he added. "I don't know exactly what they were making, but when the war was over, they started ordering amplifiers from Barnes-Reincke. And I had our guys, Walter Fuller and Seth Lover, who could make amps just as well. I thought, 'Why pay someone when you have your own men here?' Fuller was in charge of the lab, and he and Lover did everything there. I worked with

1959 Fender Bandmaster Amp – Serial Number S03225. The Fender tweed amps of the 1950s established Fender as the premier amplifier company. Fender 'blackface' amps of the 1960s dominated the market and ultimately led to the discontinuation of Kalamazoo-made Gibson amplifiers.

1959 Fender Bandmaster Amp (back view)

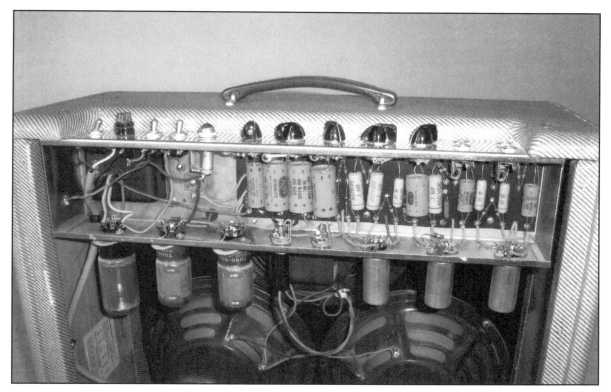

Inside the Fender amp is where Leo Fender did some of his best work. Ted McCarty considered Leo Fender to be 'an amplifier man' but not a guitar builder. Shown is an all original (including tubes, caps, everything) 1959 tweed Fender Bandmaster.

them on what kind of tone we wanted, and they worked on what kind of tubes to use, that kind of thing. And like I said, we didn't want to go for that loud, raucous sound. We wanted Gibson amps to have a real soft, genuine tone, not the real loud stuff.

"Gibson and Fender, had opposite ideas for what's right. They made theirs so harsh, sharp and whatnot, and we thought that they should not be able to go beyond where they would start to break down, to distort. Some of the musicians thought Gibson's should not just be good musical instruments, but that Gibson should try not to make them so they would break down. Gibson players wanted the mellow sound, while Fender players wanted the harsher sound. Gibson wanted the range of sound that would not be hard on your ears. But Fender didn't want it that way, and they were selling them, there's no question about it. Some of our salesmen said, 'We'd like to have some of that so-called harsh Fender kind of sound.'"

The loss of the amplifier business left a significant hole in the Kalamazoo plant, and of course a lot of fixed-cost absorption was lost. Loss of amplifier production was the first of three significant outsourcings that created an issue for Gibson's union committee. About 150 hourly jobs were lost when the amp business was discontinued. Another 55 hourly jobs were lost when the company closed the string room. And of course, the outsourcing of Epiphone to Japan created large job losses.

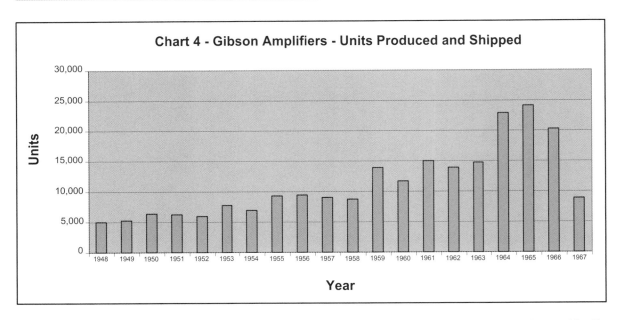

Chart 4 - Gibson Amplifiers - Units Produced and Shipped

Chart 4 – Gibson Amplifiers – Units Produced & Shipped shows units for amplifiers which specifically carried the Gibson logo. Gibson also made Epiphone, Kalamazoo, and Maestro (Bell) amplifiers, but those numbers are not in Chart 4. According to Paul Reed Smith McCarty finally decided that making amplifiers was a losing proposition. At the end of McCarty's tenure, Gibson ceased amplifier production and within a year, amplifiers were outsourced to CMI Chicago. Fuller transferred as part of the deal, and Lover went to work for Fender.

The Clavioline

The Clavioline is a little-known Gibson product, for good reason. Bellson described the instrument as, "The Clavioline, a unique keyboard electrical instrument, was manufactured for several years starting in 1952. This unusual musical innovation of French invention reproduced the sounds of a trumpet, trombone, cello, violin, and dozens of other instruments. It could be played as an individual unit but was at its best when attached to the treble range on a piano or organ keyboard, so that the left hand added bass accompaniment. The Clavioline was a remarkable single voice instrument. However, its initial popularity waned as electric organs were improved to include the ability to reproduce sounds of other instruments with complete harmony available at the artist's finger tips."

The Clavioline, as an instrument (and potentially profitable product), caught the attention of Maurice Berlin. As was often the case, Berlin called on McCarty to procure rights to the instrument. This had nothing to do with Gibson, per se. Berlin always considered McCarty as much an employee of CMI as he was of Gibson. He sent McCarty to France to get the Clavioline.

"The Clavioline was a keyboard instrument that would attach to the piano keyboard and make it sound like many different instruments all at one time. We produced that at Kalamazoo, and at one time we were up to about 35 a day."

The World's Greatest Guitar Factory

225 Parsons Street - Introduction

Ted McCarty called 225 Parsons Street the finest guitar factory in the world, in recognition of its longevity of high-quality production coming out of north Kalamazoo. Its competitors were limited to making flat-tops, solidbody electric guitars, or hand-built archtops, while Parsons Street produced great flat-tops, solidbodies, acoustic archtops, and in addition, as well as the finest mandolins and banjos. No factory could match the variety, quality, and quantity coming out of Parsons Street.

Three milestones cemented the reputation of the Gibson Guitar Company. First was the founding of the company by Orville Gibson in the 1890s. Gibson planned a commercial enterprise based on his new designs and skills. Second was the arrival of Sylvo Reams and Lewis Williams, who transformed Gibson from a shop to a factory while maintaining the highest quality. The third happened in 1917, when the Gibson Corporation built its state-of-the-art plant. The factory was situated in the Parsons Plat of north Kalamazoo, which was a mix of residences and factories. Several of the city's most important factories were within a few blocks of Parsons Street, including the fishing tackle maker Shakespeare-Kalamazoo Reels and Sutherland Paper Company, a waxed-paper/box giant. Parsons Street was just four blocks long, running east-west from Burdick on the west and Walbridge on the east, four blocks north of downtown, and only four blocks south of the northern city limits (Dunkley Street).

There was a church on the corner of Parsons and Edwards, but the name Parsons came from prominent businessman/educator and Civil War captain William F. Parsons. Shortly after the war, Parsons founded and operated a chain of business schools in Michigan towns such as Adrian, Jackson, Marshall, and Grand Rapids. In 1902, Orville Gibson's residence and workshop at the southeast corner of Michigan Avenue and Burdick Street were located one floor below a former site of Parsons Business College.

In the post-Civil War era, Michigan cities like Kalamazoo, Flint, Battle Creek, Saginaw, Pontiac, Port Huron, and others competed with each other for new industry; factories were synonymous with progress and prosperity, assuring jobs and growth. Kalamazoo historian Larry Massie cites a promotional pamphlet from 1912 that states, "Kalamazoo invites the world at large to come and see the city, to investigate its matchless opportunities for commerce and industry, its superior qualities as an abiding place."

Kalamazoo seemed destined to be a mid-sized industrial city. It was so successful in attracting industry that what started as a surplus of workers evolved into labor shortage. The city's paper companies were forced to recruit workers from southern states. And by the 1950s, a willing worker who was smart enough to adapt and learn could choose from several companies. It was certainly a "worker's market" labor environment that Ted McCarty, John Huis, and Julius Bellson dealt with at Gibson.

According to Kalamazoo historian Catherine Larson, the north side of Kalamazoo developed more slowly than other sections of the city. When Kalamazoo was settled, the north end was a floodplain forest and tamarack swamp. Local leaders and businessmen knew growth and prosperity were coming, and speculative land owners subdivided plots on the north side, holding the land as an investment.

Railroads, which were vitally important to Kalamazoo's development, cut through the north side of town, making the area ideal for business and industrial development.

"So much manufacturing required workers," Larson points out. "Housing to accommodate them rapidly filled in most of the rest of the (north end)."

Industry sites and residences grew up together on the north end of Kalamazoo.

In the first half of the 20th century, co-dependence of housing and factory work was typical throughout Michigan. Walking to work was considered beneficial, and many Gibson employees lived close to the Gibson factory. This proximity was beneficial because people could walk to the factory to get to the job, or even apply for a job. This contributed to factory loyalty; the factory was part of the neighborhood, part of their way of life.

The Daylight Plant

In 1915, plans were put in place at Gibson for corporate expansion after corporate capitalization was increased from $40,000 to $100,000. It bought land in the Parsons Plat, and according to Kalamazoo historians Massie and Schmitt, the plant built in 1917 was *the* industrial showplace of the city, and perhaps the most modern workplace in southwestern Michigan.

The plant was a three-floor facility designed to utilize daylight. Each of its three floors was lined with windows. The center of each floor served as a staging area where storage racks held in-process product. The east side housed workbenches, while the west side had an aisle that ran the length of the building and connected the freight elevator and the staging areas. Incoming and outgoing material was transferred to the center, where workers on the east side could access material in the center. The west aisle led to the bathrooms located on a west-wall alcove. The basement and third floor were the men's rooms, and the second floor was the women's room. The women's room was suited for the office workers at the front (south) end of the second floor. For years, the second floor was also the location of the

A 1953 photo of the second floor east-side windows of the "old building," where guitars were strung. The "daylight plant" was designed to maximize natural light.

string room, which was also populated by women.

Gibson built its factory so half of the first floor was below ground level – it was a semi-basement with windows that allowed the same amount of light as the other two floors. Because the bottom floor was below ground level, it was called the "basement" instead of the first floor. Being four feet below the ground also helped its foundation withstand hard-freezing winters.

The front of the building was at its south end. In the northwest corner of the basement were two ramps; one descended another half-floor down to an adjacent smaller-basement boiler room housing two large boilers that used a variety of fuels, including sawdust and scrap lumber. The other ramp led up to ground level and out the back of the building to the lumber storage facility. In Gibson's early years, wood was air-dried in wood storage areas.

Gibson's early board of directors were good planners, because the plant was designed for multi-floor expansion. And the plant was expanded several times, though never with additional floors.

In the plant's first year of operation, the company decided that a new lumber storage area would be the best way to improve operations. So it built an annex to the north end of the plant. It was a true first floor, not dug into the ground, and connected to the basement with the famous ramp.

In 1918, Gibson purchased two wood-frame houses just west of the plant. These were used for wood storage supplemental to the annex lumber-storage areas. Gibson expanded again in 1935, when they built a small annex for more wood storage space, and a kiln. The kiln was used until '59, when it was no longer able to keep up with the company's needs. In 1960, Gibson started buying pre-dried wood, which assured an adequate supply.

The plant's final expansion prior to McCarty joining Gibson was started in 1945, after Maurice Berlin purchased controlling interest in Gibson. This expansion and modernization of the mill and wood storage areas was added west of the powerhouse. Ordering these improvements late in the war may have been a great strategy, but in the post-war economy, when companies were converting from war work, Berlin and Gibson president Guy Hart encountered a difficult transition. Going from wartime to peacetime production created plant losses, which were compounded when Hart and his assistant, Neil Abrams, became ill. Also, skilled or experienced employees were scarce, as the men who returned from the war either found other jobs or retired from the workforce. And, the Gibson plant was unionized during the war, and although Gibson's union employees were not militant, they nonetheless forced a change in business for Berlin and Hart. McCarty remembers that the post-war period was marked by a transition when virtually all U.S. companies and workers didn't know what to expect from the nation's new social structure and its burgeoning post-war economy. Many factors contributed to Gibson's inefficient plant expansion of 1945, and things weren't really sorted out until McCarty's arrival.

The 1950 Expansion

Though he started with the company in 1948, the McCarty era began in earnest with the 1950 expansion. And, just as Gibson added administrative and manufacturing space, Leo Fender was bolting a guitar neck to a slab of wood, and calling it the Esquire.

Here again is Chart 2, which shows the number of units produced and shipped during the McCarty era at Gibson. The chart also shows the units produced and shipped by Gibson for 1966 to 1970, 1975, and 1979. The Chart includes units produced at all three factories in Kalamazoo.

When McCarty arrived, the Gibson factory building housed its administrative offices at the front of the second floor. A visitor would enter through the front door, walk up a half-floor stairwell, and greet a receptionist. The administrative offices were largely unchanged from 1917, so McCarty built new executive offices. Not only did they need a new administration building, the vacated space created new possibilities for plant layout.

McCarty hired local architects to design a new administration building. The end result was not ostentatious. Rather, it was reasonably done and befitting a '50s factory. The building was a single-floor structure that looked something like an elementary school.

The office's front door opened into a lobby filled with Gibson products, providing a great place for visitors to relax as they awaited their appointment. The office belonging to McCarty's secretary, Betty Meyle, was located to the right of the lobby. It fronted the lobby on the west side, with McCarty's office on the east side. A door connected the two offices.

McCarty's office was located in the southeast corner. It was large enough to suggest

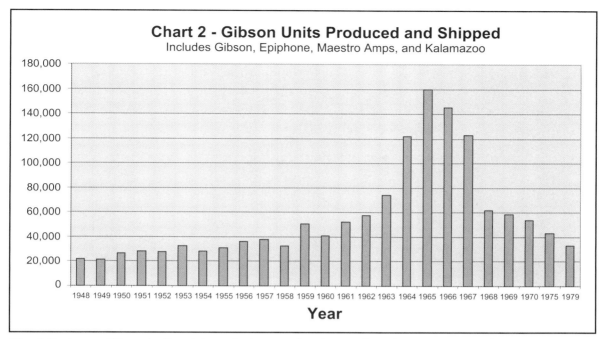

Chart 2 - Gibson Units Produced and Shipped
Includes Gibson, Epiphone, Maestro Amps, and Kalamazoo

Chart 2 shows Gibson's finest hour in terms of units produced and shipped. Generally, 1965 is considered Gibson's greatest year for manufacturing sales. Historians reference the 100,000-unit benchmark for fretted-instrument sales exceeded that year. Actual unit sales, including Epiphone, Kalamazoo, and Gibson, Maestro, and Kalamazoo amplifiers, was about 160,000. Chart 2 depicts all unit sales, for all Gibson-owned brands including Kalamazoo, Epiphone, and Maestro. It includes acoustic guitars, electric guitars, basses, steels, mandolins, banjos, and amplifiers. Nearly 1 million units were shipped during McCarty's tenure.
The chart demonstrates why Gibson needed to add capacity, which it did six times in the McCarty era – 1950, '59, '60, '62, '64 and '65. By '66, it had three plants and five warehouses.

good taste while being suitable for a chief executive. And it was beautifully appointed, with the finest wood paneling. But unlike the office of a CEO in Chicago or Detroit, it wasn't designed or decorated to impress visitors, as they would likely be more interested in the factory floor.

Just north of McCarty was the office of Julius Bellson. It was about half the size of McCarty's, and was also adorned with beautiful paneling. The shadow of Bellson's name still haunts the door, to this very day.

The office adjacent to Bellson belonged to John Huis. It was the same size and had the same paneling. Huis' office was next to the factory floor. As he walked into the plant, Huis passed the quality control office and Larry Aller's engineering office. Continuing north, he would have been among manufacturing employees doing amplifier final assembly (installing electronics and speakers into cabinets). To the west of that would be a large room where employees installed small parts, including neck inlay. The time office was also in this area.

Across from Huis was the office of Sylvia Howard, secretary to he and Bellson, and next to it was a space housing and displaying historical photos, as well as instruments and amplifiers. This was a convenient place to demonstrate product and was used as an office for visiting CMI employees. Down the west aisle was the office of purchasing agent Rollo Werner. Near him was a large conference room perfectly situated for business meetings, conveniently located near McCarty, Bellson, and Huis. George Comee, the office manager/ comptroller, had an office in the area. The windows at the front of the building were those of the conference room, purchasing office, the lobby, Meyle's office, and McCarty's office to the far right. The building also had a large area filled with desk after desk where accounting and administrative clerks processed their work.

A 1953 photo of the administration building and the "old building," from the Gibson employee manual

The main admin building also housed the office of payroll clerk Dorothy Kuras and telephone operator Katie Harris. A large walk-in vault was located on the north wall of this space. A walk-in safe/vault was typical of the era, and served as the space where accounting and records were maintained.

The expansion included more office and manufacturing space. Next to the admin office door connecting the administration office with the plant offices was the nurse's office, the quality-control office, plus engineering and expediting.

Everything else in the addition was manufacturing space which was mostly dedicated to small-parts manufacture, especially fingerboards, inlays, and pearl cutting. The foreman of that area was Gordon Wiley.

The north door of the small-parts department led to the mill woodshop, which included the 1945 addition. Mill machinery included shapers, band saws, routers, neck-fit equipment, rabbiting and binding equipment, belt and wheel sanders, and hand-sanding. Equipment in this area was soft-tooled, meaning it provided a flexible format for quick tooling changes. This allowed for variety. There was also an office for mill foremen Gerald Bergeon and Clarence Coleman. There was an office for the nurse station and restrooms.

A two-door dock was located between the first floor 1950 addition and the original building. The dock was part of the original building, but old photos indicate the dock was originally a three door dock. In the '50s this was the receiving and shipping dock. Received goods could easily be transported directly to the first floor mill, or to the elevator that took the packages to the second floor materials crib.

When the dock was used for shipping, finished goods could be easily rolled from the second-floor finished goods stockroom to the elevator. The elevator dropped the half-floor to the dock, where finished goods were delivered to parcel post. It has been reported that McCarty visited the shipping department nearly every day to verify shipments.

Workers entered the basement from the west door located near the truck dock. As a matter of security, employees were required to pass Dale Humphrey's guard shack, and would then walk to the west side doors and walk down a half-floor flight of stairs to the basement. As with all floors, the main aisle was on the west side, while material and racks were in the middle of the floor. The southwest corner of the basement housed experimental engineering where, among other things, development work for the high-speed glue machine was done. The machine, patented by Gibson, allowed wood to be glued and dried exceptionally fast. This was a great advantage in the production of the two-piece Les Paul body and other applications.

A 1953 photo of the boss and some of his skilled laborers in the small-parts department. The window in the background looks out to the shipping dock.

In the '50s, the repair department was located along the east windows of the basement. This is where service work was done, as well as mandolin manufacturing. A repairman would alternate between building mandolins and repairing returns. As standard procedure, most guitars returned in the '50s were given a new finish.

North of the repair department, about halfway along the east wall, was the patternmakers' shop. This was the heart and soul of the engineering department, where the work was done for prototypes. Gibson's best woodworkers – those who enjoyed a challenge – worked in this area, and it's where the 1951 Les Paul prototype was built, where the Flying V was made, and where the '55 Les Paul humbucker test guitar was prepared for the first humbucking pickups. If the factory has a "special" area, this is it.

The machine shop was located next to the patternmakers. Pattern making involved not only wood work, it involved working with metal and machine tools.

The cabinet-covering and grille department was west of the machine shop, just east of the ramp. In this area, leatherette and tweed covers were applied to the wooden cabinets. There was also an amplifier final assembly area in the 1950 annex, near the small-parts department. Here, chassis and speakers were installed into cabs.

Another ramp went to a low-ceiling aisle that led to the boiler room. Its two boilers were fueled by sawdust and wood scrap and located below Gibson's famous chimney.

The west wall near the ramp was lined with windows that overlooked a small courtyard between the old building and the powerhouse.

The elevator was next to the west-side stairwell, and was critical to the old-building layout. When racks of white-wood instruments were completed in the mill, they were taken down the ramp, rolled to the elevator, and taken to the finishing department on the third floor.

Beyond the old basement's north wall was the 1918 annex and beyond that another from 1935. The 1918 annex was used as the maintenance department, while the '35 annex housed the kiln. From 1948 to '59 wood was air dried and kiln dried. In 1960 Gibson began to purchase pre-dried wood from vendors.

When McCarty joined Gibson, the south end/front of the second floor housed the administrative offices, as it had since 1917, so the need to update was understandable. McCarty's new administration building was finished in 1950, and housed the offices. A new elec-

The east side of the "old building." Most of the workbenches were on the east side of the building. The middle of each floor was for racks and staging. The west side (not shown) was for the main isle way, restrooms, stairs, and freight elevator.

tronics area replaced the old offices. This was where some of Walt Fuller and Seth Lover's work was done. During the next rearrangement of the south second-floor area, a cafeteria replaced the electronics area. The electronics area, including amp-chassis construction, moved to the south end of the third floor.

The center of the second floor served as the materials crib that inventoried purchased parts like tuners, which were delivered to the loading dock and moved up via elevator. There was also a ramp that led from the dock to the second floor.

In the production process, the second floor received guitars that had been painted/finished and were ready for hardware, pickups, strings, etc. This was done near the stockroom crib, were there were also areas for final cleaning, string adjusting, fret filing, inspection, and

The 'annex' built in 1918 and added to in 1935 is the short building between the 'old building' and the 1960 expansion (at the right of the photograph)

final inspection. After a guitar was tested and approved by Rem Wall, it was tagged and sent to the finished-goods shelves. From there, it was boxed for shipment.

In the '50s, the third floor was the finishing department. In 1960, it was re-tooled and moved into the new annex. It was further updated in the '65 expansion. Some of the equipment from the '50s remained on the third floor and was used in the Customs Department, Gibson's first stand-alone custom shop.

The third floor followed the same pattern; the west side was the aisle, product and equipment could be moved across the floor, north to south, from the elevator, and racks and storage areas were in the middle of the floor. The finishing department was located along the east side. Racks of white-wood guitars would come up on the elevator from the first floor. The finishing process would begin with fill and staining, then move through to spray-painting in booths in the northeast corner. After final buffing, the guitars were ready for final cleaning and inspection.

While departments like the string room and electronics department were mostly women, the finishing department was mostly men. McCarty described the buffers as the toughest guys in the plant, and indeed, buffing did require a strong back.

McCarty was admired and respected by workers because among other things he was a true gentleman. Cursing and swearing were something McCarty would not tolerate. He recalled a particular occasion during a visit from Stan Rendell, at the time was CMI's newly appointed VP of Manufacturing.

"I had trouble with Rendell, because he was using the wrong kind of words and bad conversation," he said. "The F-word, every third word. We had all these women, 40% of our employees were women, and I had rules. Anybody I heard using obscene language or actions... they just retired. We were showing Rendell something and he was using this kind of conversation. So I said to him, 'You'll have to leave if you're going to do that, because we don't accept that around here. You'll never hear it in this factory.'

"So he shut up for the rest of that day. He couldn't say three sentences without using the wrong kind of conversation. For all of my 33 years, I never had it. The buffers (at Gibson) were the roughest guys we had, they were doing it, but not when I was around. I told one of them if I heard him, he was through. It's just an indication to me of poor vocabulary. Other words should be used."

In 1960, when the Customs Department moved to the third floor, the electronics department moved to the south end of the third floor. There were separate lines for each type of amp. In '62, the electronics department was moved to Plant II, and in '64, the electronics department was moved to Plant III, which served as the amp assembly's final home until the amplifier business unit was outsourced to Chicago in '68. In the late '60s, Gibson started to outsource products, the string room left, amplifier production left, and all Epiphone products were outsourced. This did not go unnoticed by the union. Shortly after McCarty left Gibson, the Kalamazoo factory had its first notable union strike.

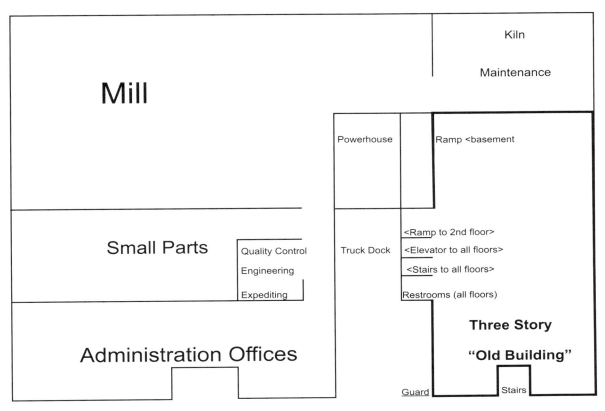

The Plant Layout in 1955 (general overview)

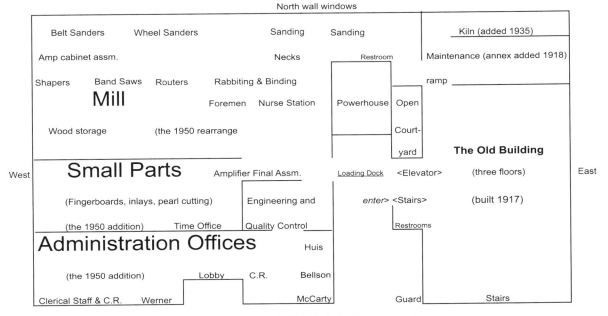

The Plant Layout in 1955 (detailed overview)

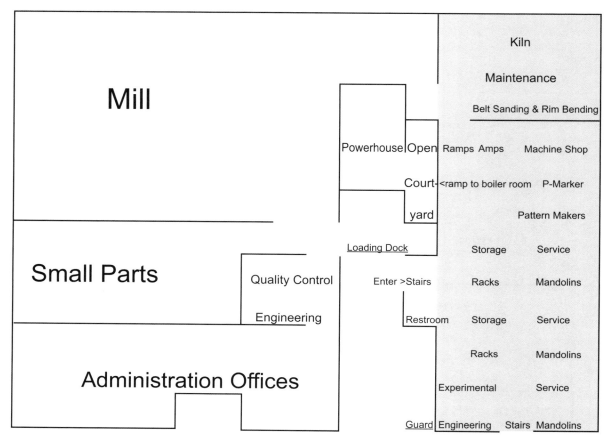

The Plant Layout in 1955 (basement)

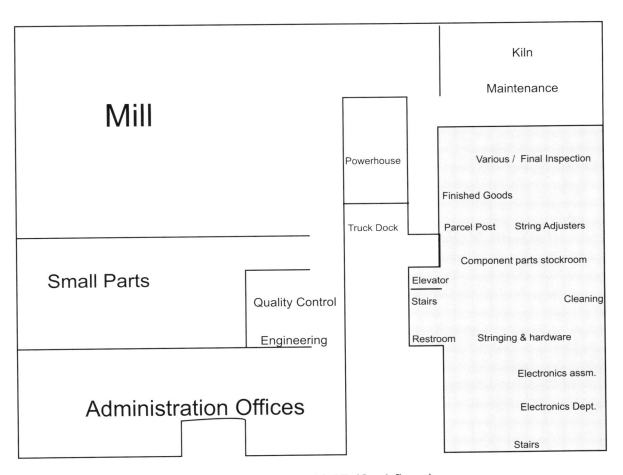

The Plant Layout in 1955 (2nd floor)

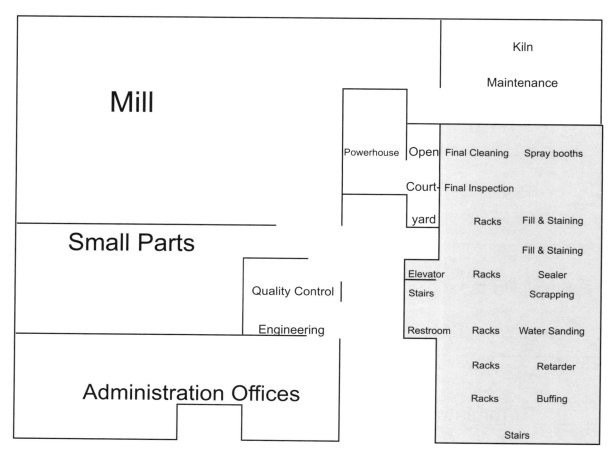

The Plant Layout in 1955 (3rd floor)

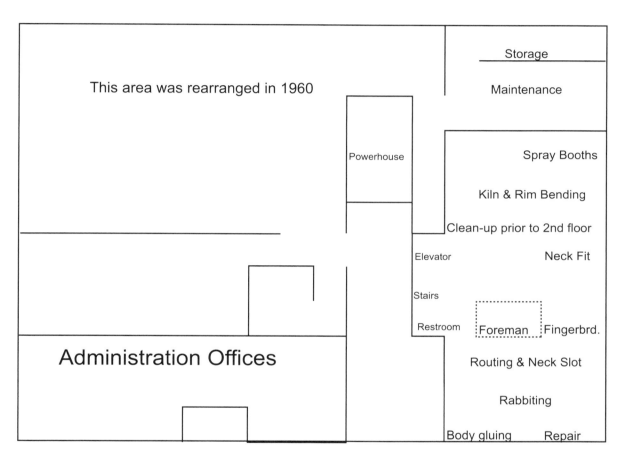

The Plant Layout in 1960 (new Customs Department 3rd floor)

Eleanor Street

The Eleanor Street Plant was a 1959 startup facility dedicated to Epiphone instruments. It was also a manufacturing facility for some Gibson solidbody models. Although the Eleanor Street plant has been described by historians as "the solidbody plant," employees suggest that some solidbodies were still made on Parsons Street. It has also been suggested that Eleanor Street built only lower-end solidbodies, and that finishing/painting of solidbodies continued on the third floor of the old building.

Eleanor Street was vacated with the completion of the 1960 annex. Epiphone production moved to Parsons Street and stayed until the line was outsourced to Japan in '69.

Epiphone's business address became Bush Street, a short street running parallel to Parsons, on the north side of the plant. The city of Kalamazoo closed Bush Street to all traffic except that generated by Gibson. McCarty intentionally used Bush Street to camouflage the fact that Gibson and Epiphone were the same plant. When customers contacted Epiphone, they thought they were dealing with a separate location. This fit into the business model; Epiphone was developed by Gibson in order to expand its dealer base. Historically, independent dealers were declined a Gibson dealership because of regional conflicts with established dealers. The Epiphone line gave these dealers a chance to work with CMI and have Gibson-like quality. Even so, some suggest Epiphone was designed by Gibson to be a half-step lower in quality. When demand dropped, Epiphone was outsourced.

Though seldom mentioned, and used for only about one year, Eleanor Street contributed an important legacy to one of Gibson's finest production years.

The 1960 Expansion

Gibson's largest expansion came in 1960, when the size of its factory doubled. This required a significant rearrangement, with nearly every department relocating in one fashion or another. The largest addition was directly north of the existing buildings. White-wood work, the material stores crib and the finishing department, all moved to the new space.

Moving the finishing department into the expansion created space on the third floor of the old building. This became the Custom Department, dedicated to special order, high-end instruments.

Custom instruments included the electric Spanish guitar Artist Series models such as the Johnny Smith, Barney Kessel, and Tal Farlow. It also included models such as the ES-400CES and CESN, L-5CES and CESN, the Byrdland sunburst or natural, the EDS-1275, EMS-1235, EBSF-1250, and Hawaiian EH-820, 810, 620, 630. Custom shop flat-tops included the J-200 and J-200N, and the classical models C-4, C-6, and C-8. Custom acoustic archtops included the 400C and CN, and the L-5C and CN. Custom-built mandolins included the F-5 and F-12.

The 1960 expansion. The high-bay areas were added in '65 and as part of the automatic paint conveyor installed that year. This view is from Bush Street which intersects the railroad tracks. Bush Street was the address used for Epiphone Guitars, although it was nothing more than the street parallel to Parsons Street on the north end of the plant.

Mac McConackie was the boss in the Customs Divison, Wilbur Fuller was assistant foreman in charge of finishing, and woodshop body building guru Clarence Coleman was the white-wood foreman. Some of the spray booths used so effectively in the '50s – those that painted all those great 'Bursts and 335s – remained on the north end, used for Custom Department finishing. The department also had a kiln, near the spray booths, as well as space for rim bending, buffing and water sanding, neck fit, fingerboards, a neck shaper, neckmaking, wood routing, rebutting, and body gluing, in addition to a clean-up station used before instruments were sent for final adjustment on the second floor. The foreman's office was located in the south center of the third floor, and a repairman (James Hanchett) was located in the southeast corner of the third floor (overlooking railroad tracks to the east and Parsons Street to the south). A high-frequency/high-speed glue machine, which was invented by Bill Gaut, sat in the southwest corner and was used to dry bodies in Gibson's microwave gluing machine – the first of its kind in the world.

As things progressed, Wilbur Fuller was named foreman, and soon named General Foreman, with three foremen reporting to him. With the retirement of John Huis in 1966, Mac McConackie was promoted to Plant Superintendent, a job that carried greater responsibility given that Gibson had doubled its productive floor space.

Plant II and Plant III

Plant II, also called the Electronics Plant, was opened in 1962. With the introduction of numeric factory identification, Parsons Street became known as Plant I. Plant II was relatively small 20,000-square-foot facility that built all pickups and housed an all-new amplifier production area. Walter Fuller was named manager of Plant II, and C. Richard Evans, was named Chief Electronics Engineer. In '64, Plant II transitioned to instrument production, when amplifier, electronics, and the string room were moved to another new facility – Plant III.

1966 Kalamazoo KG-2 and 1966 Kalamazoo Model 2 amplifier. Budget-level solidbody guitars were made in Plant II.

In August of 1962, employees were offered Gibson's first pension plan. Known as a "30 and out" plan, it required 30 years of service. It was improved year-to-year to the point that an employee could draw an early retirement pension at age 60 with as little as 15 years service. But full benefits started at age 55 with 30 years of service (known as the "85 points" system). About this time, employees also could carry over seniority. Previously, female workers lost seniority when they quit to raise a family. That changed circa 1962.

Plant III was located at Fulford and Alcott Streets, in Portage, Michigan, Kalamazoo's sister city. It was three times the size of Plant II, with 60,000 square feet of floor space. An older building, it was purchased, and opened in 1964 as the amplifier plant and the string room. Pickup production was also transferred to Plant III. Amplifier production remained at Plant III until '68.

The loss of the amplifier business was important. In the '50s, amplifier production was allocated to three different parts of Plant I – kind of squeezed into where it'd fit. With a stand-alone plant in '64, costs increased and the amplifier business became unprofitable. Two years after moving to Plant III, McCarty announced the end of amplifier production in Kalamazoo, and within two years, it was over. Loss of the amp business in Kalamazoo was ironic. McCarty considered Leo Fender the king of amplifiers, but thought "He didn't know how to build a proper guitar." But as Don Randall always said, the genius of the electric guitar was that you get two sales – a guitar and an amplifier. When Kalamazoo got out of the amp business, it gave up an important piece of the market. Historians say that Fender's Stratocaster and Telecaster sales were so-so in the mid/late '60s, but Fender's amplifier business was dominant at that time. Perhaps McCarty was right, because he thought Fender was an amplifier business that also made guitars. When Gibson gave up on amplifiers, the void was filled by a company that cloned the Fender Bassman in England – Marshall. Fender became the dominant company, competing with Gibson's guitars and Marshall's amps. Fender continued to be an amps-and-guitar company; Gibson became only instruments, while Marshall specialized in amps.

The new string room, under manager Walter Herman, remained at Plant III until the string business was closed in 1972. Employees considered the discontinuation of the amplifier business and the outsourcing of the string room as notable turning points in Gibson's history. The decisions to outsource may have been a result of two union strikes, a drop in demand for product, the inexperienced and lackluster leadership of McCarty's replacements, and of course the arrival of Arnie Berlin. Some employees and industry historians also gave Stan Rendell a bad score for the years he was president of Gibson from 1968 to '76. McCarty-era employees cite the dissolution of Gibson's quality control system during the Rendell era, specifically noting that he intentionally shipped substandard instruments in order to make quotas. Others who were there suggest that Rendell saved Gibson, but that story goes beyond the scope of this book.

The 1965 Plant Expansion

The 1965 expansion runs along the far west side of the site going north. To the right of the picture (but not shown) is the administration building.

The final (and ominously ill-timed) expansion to Plant I created more office space, a heat-controlled lumber storage area, mill room addition, overhead storage facility, and new loading docks. An overhead conveyor was built in the finishing department, changing the way mass-produced guitars were painted and dried.

In the vintage guitar industry, 1964 is generally considered the last great year for both Gibson and Fender. In January of '65, Fender Musical Instruments was sold to the Columbia Broadcasting System (CBS). McCarty purchased Bigsby Accessories in November of '65, and 1966 is considered the year quality began to decline at both companies. Coincidently, by the mid '80s, both were near financial collapse.

Along with the '65 expansion came new emphasis at Gibson for greater quantity and lower product cost. Two examples were the '65 Gibson ES-335 with trapeze tailpiece, and the '65 Firebird. Other negative changes included the automated spray conveyor in the northeast corner of the plant. The conversion also included new neck machines that reduced the famous Gibson 17-degree peghead pitch to 14 degrees. The new neck machines also produced Gibson's new (and what most deem inferior) neck profile, which was slimmer and shallower. At Fender, the CBS era brought the "large headstock" Stratocaster, which again many feel was a sign of digression.

The 1966 Downward Slide

The factory layout in 1966 – McCarty's final year at Gibson – included the fully expanded main facility (Plant I), Plant II for instruments, and Plant III for amps, electronics, and the new string room.

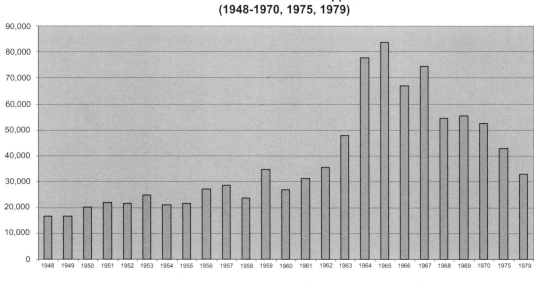

Chart 5 - Gibson Fretted Instruments
Units Produced & Shipped
(1948-1970, 1975, 1979)

Year

When McCarty left, things began to change. The industry saw demand for guitars begin to drop, tube amplifiers were considered passé as transistor technology tempted amplifier engineers, and industrial engineers and college-trained recruits introduced business models that were not based on the guitar industry's 50-year tradition of hand-building guitars. Some retail stores became overstocked, which led to smaller orders, and production of Gibson fretted instruments, as shown in Chart 5.

While demand for products dropped, demand for skilled and unskilled labor increased, and labor unions flourished. In Kalamazoo, the Fisher Body Division of General Motors built a huge new facility that quickly proved a boon for workers, offering auto industry pay and benefits. This put pressure on companies like Gibson. But McCarty wasn't going to be involved, at least not at Gibson. He resigned in June of '66, just as the business pendulum began to swing in an unfavorable direction for U.S. guitar makers. McCarty noticed the downturn in the music industry, and to keep Bigsby Accessories solvent, he had to purchase Flex-Lite.

The years 1966 to '68 saw the "Great Society recession," as the economy softened in reaction to domestic-spending programs launched while fighting a costly war in Vietnam. And of course, there was the impact of foreign imports absorbing market share.

In hindsight, it appears Gibson's final plant expansion was not necessary. But at the time, in a booming market, nobody in business would have taken the conservative road. But things changed in '65. Several unfavorable engineering changes were introduced, including the "non-reverse" Firebird, the trapeze-tail ES-335, the across-the-board shifts to a narrower nut width and reduced headstock angle, and high-speed finishing equipment.

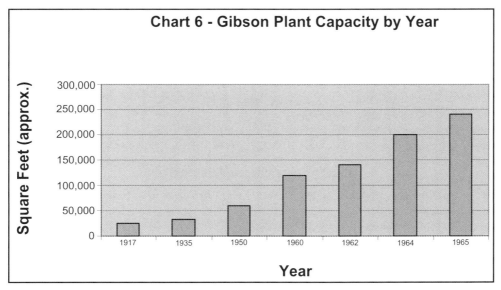

Chart 6 shows how Gibson's plant capacity increased in 1950 (for the McCarty administration building, mill upgrade, small-parts floorspace addition, amplifier floorspace addition), 1960 (for the large new plant addition, Epiphone floorspace absorption, the mill rearrange, the new Customs Division, the new spray room addition), 1962 (Plant II), '64 (Plant III), and '65 (for the new administration floorspace, new shipping and receiving room, general rearrange, and new finishing equipment).

149

Plant capacity doubled from 1935 to '50, then doubled again from 1950 to '60, and doubled once again from '60 to '65.

The Gibson Kalamazoo hourly workforce in 1965, McCarty's last year.

Plant 1 Parsons Street, first shift

Adjuster – Repair department	1
Body Completion	31
Custom Instruments & Basses	32
Custom Instruments Finishing	22
Custom Instruments Adjusting	10
Final Cleaning	35
Finishing	142
High Frequency & Body Assembly	16
Inspection	24
Lumber Yard	15
Machine Shop, Toolroom, Model Making	22
Maintenance, Sweepers, Millwrights	14
Mill Room	62
Neck Assembly	13
Shipping	13
Small Parts & Sub Assemblies	46
Truck Drivers and Warehousing	2
Receiving and stockroom	13
Red Ticket Repair	14
TOTAL	**527**

Plant 1 Parsons, second/night shift

Maintenance, Sweepers, Millwrights	6
Mill Room	39
TOTAL	**45**

Plant 2

Finishing	48
Inspection	4
K-2 Indirect	7
Maintenance, Sweepers, Millwrights	3
Woodwork Assembly	24
TOTAL	**86**

Plant 3 Electronics and String Room

Electric Services	1
Electronics 2200A	47
Electronics 2200 A-2	15
Electronics 2200 A-3	14
Electronics 2200 A-4	6
Electronics 2200 B	44
Inspection	11
Maintenance, Sweepers, Millwrights	4
Receiving and stockroom	4
Shipping	6
String Room	55
TOTAL	**207**

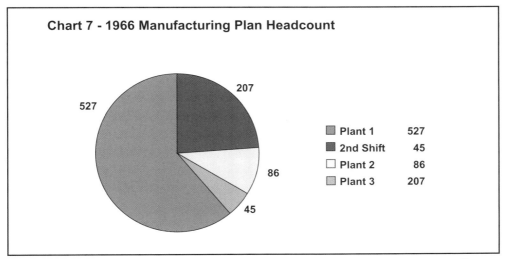

Chart 7 - 1966 Manufacturing Plan Headcount

■	Plant 1	527
■	2nd Shift	45
□	Plant 2	86
■	Plant 3	207

Chart 7 takes the above headcount information and summarizes it according to manufacturing plant. Plant III was the amplifier and string room facility. Plant II produced mostly economy solidbody instruments. Plant I (Parsons Street) handled most of the instrument building including the newly installed high-speed finishing equipment.

Ted McCarty left Gibson with 865 hourly employees. The chart shows that 527 of them were in Plant I, while Plant II had a relatively small workforce that built lower-end instruments. Plant III was the Electronics Plant that built Gibson's amplifiers, in addition to being Gibson's string room. By 1972, both of Plant III's products would be outsourced, along with the Epiphone line that was removed from Plant I. The second/night shift in 1966 was small, with the only productive department being the mill. At the time, Gibson's salary headcount was about 15% of the hourly headcount, making employment at Gibson when McCarty left about 1,025 people.

1966 was the beginning of a downward slide of the great guitar companies. As repeated many times in this book, a company like Gibson was built on decades of using the Gibson system, which was reinvigorated and restored by McCarty, whose company would not fall apart easily after he left. It took years to tear Gibson down. The fall of Gibson was primarily the result of mismanagement by Arnie Berlin and Norlin management, as well as a hostile environment for many American industries. In the '70s and '80s, cheap, inferior product allegations were echoed by customers against many American industries, including automobile manufacturing.

Gibson's ability to continue after McCarty's departure is a testament to the workers McCarty hired and trained. Most pre-McCarty employees were gone by 1973. The others – those hired since 1948 – would continue building guitars under deteriorating circumstances. In the post-McCarty period, most people say Gibson just got too big. Plus, the people who replaced McCarty were so ineffective in 1966-'67 that few remember who they were. These were Arnie Berlin's men, and McCarty predicted that he would cause the downfall of CMI and Gibson. His prediction, for what ever reason, became reality.

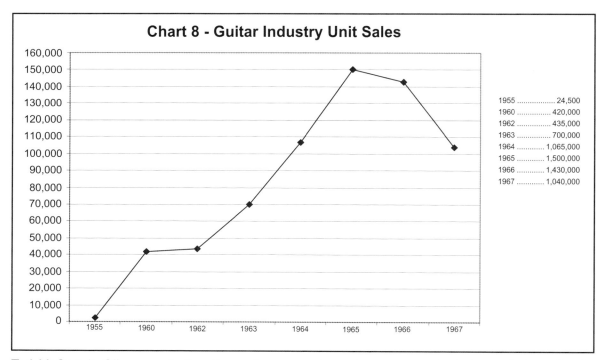

Chart 8 - Guitar Industry Unit Sales

Year	Units
1955	24,500
1960	420,000
1962	435,000
1963	700,000
1964	1,065,000
1965	1,500,000
1966	1,430,000
1967	1,040,000

Ted McCarty's Gibson and all guitar makers experienced an unprecedented growth in unit sales from 1955 to 1965. Unit sales in the industry began to drop in 1966. Gibson and Fender survived the industry recession while companies such as Kay and Harmony went bankrupt.

1966 aerial view of Gibson's Plant 1. This was Ted McCarty's photograph that he kept at Bigsby Accessories and at home in his study.

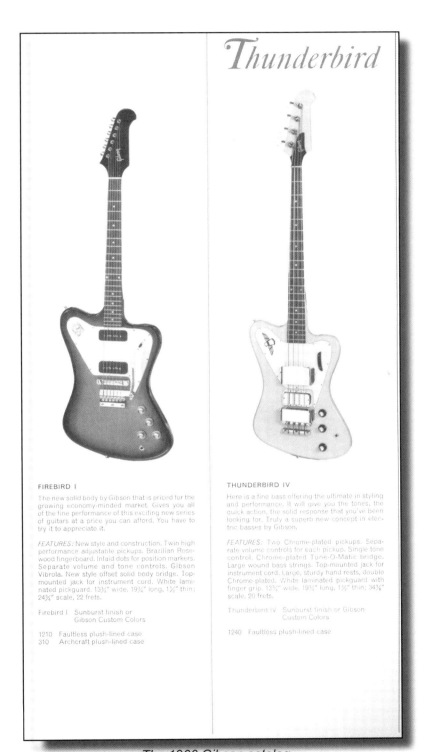

Thunderbird

FIREBIRD I

The new solid body by Gibson that is priced for the growing economy-minded market. Gives you all of the fine performance of this exciting new series of guitars at a price you can afford. You have to try it to appreciate it.

FEATURES: New style and construction. Twin high performance adjustable pickups. Brazilian Rosewood fingerboard. Inlaid dots for position markers. Separate volume and tone controls. Gibson Vibrola. New style offset solid body bridge. Top-mounted jack for instrument cord. White laminated pickguard. 13¼″ wide, 19¼″ long, 1⅜″ thin; 24¾″ scale, 22 frets.

Firebird I   Sunburst finish or
             Gibson Custom Colors

1210 Faultless plush-lined case
310   Archcraft plush-lined case

THUNDERBIRD IV

Here is a fine bass offering the ultimate in styling and performance. It will give you the tones, the quick action, the solid response that you've been looking for. Truly a superb new concept in electric basses by Gibson.

FEATURES: Two Chrome-plated pickups. Separate volume controls for each pickup. Single tone control. Chrome-plated Tune-O-Matic bridge. Large wound bass strings. Top-mounted jack for instrument cord. Large, sturdy hand rests, double Chrome-plated. White laminated pickguard with finger grip. 13¼″ wide, 19¼″ long, 1⅜″ thin; 34½″ scale, 20 frets.

Thunderbird IV   Sunburst finish or Gibson
                 Custom Colors

1240 Faultless plush-lined case

The 1966 Gibson catalog

153

The People of Gibson
/People Make the Company

"Ted McCarty was born to be a businessman with a great personality. When his help carried out his instructions, he let them know that he appreciated it. Through his perseverance, he enlarged the company many times over. During his tenure in office, 1948 to 1966, 1,398 employees were hired. The building expanded to include a full block, a large parking lot was added, and two more buildings. What an achievement for the President of Gibson Guitars. Ted gave a lot to the music industry and he continued to do so after he left Gibson."

Wilbur Fuller
May 10, 2001

Introduction

Guitar historians, archivists, and researchers have written about entrepreneurs and leaders in the music business. Books have shown hundreds of beautiful photos of Gibson vintage guitars. Skilled laborers have been mostly overlooked.

There's a legend that Gibson was great because of great woodworkers. Woodworkers were important in Michigan, that's true, as lumbering was the second great industry in Michigan. The first was fur trapping, followed by farming. The lumber industry required heavy-duty wagons. When presented with the opportunity, some Michigan wagon makers invested in the newfangled horseless carriage. The wagon makers became automobile makers, and the automobile industry was born in Michigan

The skill of Gibson's woodworkers came from the training established by Orville Gibson, Sylvo Reams, and Lewis Williams. It was a rigorous tradition. Great woodworkers were not born, they were created at the factory. The fact Gibson was in Kalamazoo was extremely important! It was a mid-sized city full of industrious, hard-working people with a proud history of working with their hands, whether in lumber, celery farming, copper mining, paper milling, or other industries.

Gibson built a system of self-audit, where each employee was an inspector. It had traditional inspectors, as well, but it was the individual workers who were responsible for quality

BOARD OF DIRECTORS

M. H. Berlin ....*Chicago, Ill.*

T. M. McCarty ....*Kalamazoo, Mich.*

E. P. Morse ....*Chicago, Ill.*

Guy Hart ....*Kalamazoo, Mich.*

C. E. Havenga ....*Chicago, Ill.*

OFFICERS

T. M. McCarty ....*President*

E. P. Morse ....*Vice President, Legal Counsel*

J. Huis ....*Vice President, in charge of Production*

C. E. Havenga ....*Vice President, Sales Manager*

M. H. Berlin ....*Secretary-Treasurer*

J. Bellson ....*Assistant Treasurer*

T. Naylor ....*Assistant Secretary*

EXECUTIVE OFFICES

GIBSON, INC. ....225 Parsons St., Kalamazoo, Mich.

SOLE DISTRIBUTORS

Chicago Musical Instrument Company
7373 North Cicero Avenue, Chicago, Ill.

Turner Musical Instrument Ltd.
9 Church Street, Toronto, Ontario, Canada

The Board of Directors and Officers as shown in Gibson's 1953 employee manual.

workmanship. If an employee underachieved, he or she would hear about it, not only from supervision, but from co-workers. Employee self-worth was based recognizable quality work. Sure, there was plenty of good-hearted kidding on the factory floor, but behind it was an understated sentiment that you were lesser if you can't do the job right.

In the McCarty/"Golden" Era, there was a lot of pride on the factory floor. Opportunity abounded. Workers who wanted more responsibility were often given it, and they could advance to supervisory roles if they wanted. Supervision did not necessarily mean a larger paycheck, but it signified a level of accomplishment and skill. To some, that was important, while others preferred their daily routine in which they could stay effective.

A great system and great people made great woodworkers, and they were provided the best tools, the best raw materials, and a great work environment. An oft-heard sentiment in the '50s was that Gibson was a friendly place to work, where everybody knew everybody else. Gibson employees would pull together. Even in a so-called union shop, people crossed classifications if needed. If a certain activity or line was caught up, it wasn't unusual for workers to go to the next department to offer help. "I'd even sweep the floor if that was what needed to be done," said one former employee.

Under McCarty, Gibson had a true work ethic. People helped each other, they cared about the next guy, they cared about the product, and they cared about the company. That's what McCarty wanted. His favorite quote was always, "People make the company."

Gibson's People

McCarty was responsible for introducing me to dozens of his former employees. He said, "You have to talk to the people that were there." My interviews were recorded for posterity. When looking for interviews I found that some of the older McCarty era employees were deceased. As Ted himself explained, all of his direct staff at Gibson were deceased by the late 1990s.

Quality was built in through the Gibson system. My interviews show how Gibson did it during McCarty's time. The interviews show how everyday, hardworking Michiganders were transformed into great woodworkers, stringmakers, electronic assemblers, etc.

After McCarty, the first employee that I talked with was Wilbur Fuller. Of all the people I talked with, Fuller seemed the most dedicated to preserving the history of Gibson Kalamazoo. In his time there, he worked his way up to Quality Manager. Wilbur likened Gibson to a friendly high-school environment where everybody knew everybody.

Rather than post interviews according to the date they occurred, I've listed them according to seniority date. My plan was to get most of the living employees hired prior to 1955. Then I obtained interviews from many people hired between 1955 and '60.

The center of the McCarty Era's Golden Years was 1952 to '59. 1960 to '64 is also part of the Golden Era, but in '60, the plant capacity doubled and Gibson did change somewhat. What's really astounding is that quality did not significantly slip from 1960 to '64, which is phenomenal for a company that experienced such exponential growth.

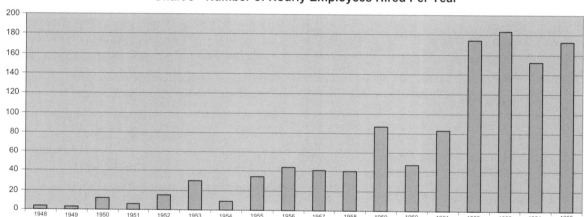

Chart 9 - Number of Hourly Employees Hired Per Year

Chart 9 displays the number of skilled hourly employees hired each year during the McCarty era. Employment ads in 1948 and '49 were small. In 1949-'50, a plant expansion added manufacturing floorspace and a new administrative office building. McCarty was proud of the 1950 expansion and he invited hundred of music dealers, and *The Music Trades* to Kalamazoo for a tour of the new facilities. You'll notice a jump in employment in 1950, and 1952/'53 employment increases reflect the addition of the Les Paul Model. 1954 ads reflect replacement of retiring workers. 1955-'58 saw steady additions to the workforce, some covering attrition and others representing new work. Employees were consistently added in small numbers during the 1950s. Gibson's system of training allowed new employees to be fully trained by leaders, inspectors, and foremen. 1959 increases reflect the addition of the Epiphone line at the temporary Eleanor Street plant. Most of the Epiphone line employees were new hires, except when a Parson Street employee might have volunteered to relocate to Eleanor Street. 1960 additions to headcount reflect the doubling of floorspace with the 1960 expansion. The entire plant was "leveled" allowing for seniority rights, but most employees did not choose to 'post' for new jobs. That was beneficial and it allowed high quality to remain during the plant rearrange. 1961 ads reflect increased volume. 1962 ads reflects the addition of Plant II at 416 Ransom Street. 1963 and 1964 reflects the rearrange of Plant II and the purchase of Plant III (at Fulford and Alcott). There were also other off-site warehouse additions. 1965 reflects the final expansion to southwest side of 225 Parsons Street.

During the '50s, employee additions were done systematically. The Gibson system of cross-training easily handled new incoming employees. The Gibson system operated without much stress all during the 1950s. In 1960 floorspace was doubled and significant department rearranges were required. In addition, the flagship of the solidbody line was changed from the heavy single cutaway Les Paul Standard to the new thin, lightweight SG Standard. The SG Standard had engineering problems with the neck-joint. (Note: To this day, it is difficult to find an early 1960s SG that has the original unrepaired, unmodified neck joint). Even with the plant rearrange and SG engineering and manufacturing issues, Gibson continued with a good record of quantity with quality.

Even with the rapid ramp-up of employees and floorspace from 1960 to 1965, quality remained admirable during the late McCarty days. That was a testament to the Gibson system that required deep inspection and cross-training of employees. No matter how many new influences were introduced the skilled employees maintained their quality rigor. As one employee explained it, "The employees during the early to mid 1960s did not know how to make a low quality product. They were trained to build quality and that is what they did." Quality was built in. This of course was a testament to McCarty's oversight. If a poor quality product was found during McCarty's reign, the product would be rejected. According to employees, quality and union happiness deteriorated very quickly shortly after Ted McCarty left Gibson in 1966. [Note: Product rejections would increasingly not be made after McCarty left in 1966. Employees who outlasted McCarty at Gibson clearly suggest that it was the new president of Gibson that intentionally allowed poor quality to be shipped in the post-McCarty days.]

SINCE 1894

HEARD AND PREFERRED

AROUND THE WORLD

While the guitar had its origin in antiquity the *modern guitar* really began in 1894 with Orville Gibson. It was he who first applied the principles and techniques of violin making to fretted instruments, tremendously enhancing the tone and enlarging the musical possibilities of these instruments. The improvements he initiated and the tradition of quality established and maintained through the years has brought the Gibson company an enviable world-wide reputation as a maker of the finest guitars and fretted instruments.

Gibson has been first from the first, continuously pioneering improvements for ever finer purity of tone, deeper resonance, greater flexibility and playing ease. Among many Gibson firsts: the electric guitar, truss rod neck construction, adjustable bridge, three-quarter size instrument, carved top and back, cutaway design and "humbucking" pickup.

First with the electric guitar, Gibson has continued to lead in musical electronics . . . developing amplifiers unequaled in projecting and amplifying musical sound without distortion and without "hum" . . . creating such exciting electronic instruments as the multiharp console . . . and most revolutionary of all, developing the first true stereophonic sound for the guitar. Continuous research and experimentation in the Gibson laboratories continues to bring the newest and finest electronic developments to the guitarist.

Guitar-making is a fine art at Gibson, where craftsmen of many years' experience create musical instruments of the highest order. Skill, patience, and integrity go into every Gibson instrument—from the selection of fine components to the final inspection. Today Gibsons are played by leading performers, recording artists, and enthusiastic amateurs who take pride in owning the very best.

1960 Gibson Catalog Introduction

158

Employee 54 Interviews

Employees and their dates of employment

Helen Charkowski (1941-'68)
Clara Van Noorloos (1943-'80)
Harriet Johnston (1944-'79)
James Hanchett (1945-'76)
Neal Walton (1947-'84)
Joyce Shelven (1952-'69)
Mary Lou Hoogenboom (1953-'84)
Wilbur Fuller (1954-'80)
Maxine Vette (1955-'70)
Vi Bradford (1956-'82)
Marv Lamb (1956-'84)
Ron Allers (1956-'80)
Huber Hill (1957-'84)
JP Moats (1957-'84)
Jim Deurloo (1958-'69, 1974-'84)
Hubie Friar (1959-'84)
Bob Knowlton (1959-'84)
Jacqueline F. Friar (1961-'84)

Interview 1
Helen Charkowski (1941-'68)

Of all of the people introduced me by McCarty, Helen Charkowski had the earliest seniority date, hiring into Gibson on April 1, 1941. As was the case for many women at Gibson in those days, she quit several times to raise a family, thus losing her seniority. That issue was solved when the union demanded that seniority be cumulative. Under the seniority rules, Helen's official seniority date was October 3, 1949. I have included the whole interview.

When did you hire into Gibson? *I started April 1, 1941. They kidded me about hiring in on April Fool's Day. I quit a few times to raise a family. I graduated in 1940 from Kalamazoo Central High School. In factories like Gibson, in the early 1940s, they would not hire you until you were eighteen. You had to be eighteen in order to work with machinery. I was seventeen when I graduated from high school so I worked for Grant's Department Store until I became of age. I made $0.25 an hour at Grant's.*

Why did you apply to Gibson? *Gibson was not too far from where I lived. I walked to work. Then I rode my bicycle to work. A girl friend and I both applied at Gibson. We were both friends at school and we were both out looking for jobs. We both filled out applications. My parents didn't have a phone, so I left my*

159

neighbor's phone number, and I specified that it was my neighbor's phone. My friend did not get a job there, but I did. It was April first and Gibson asked me if I could come in at 1 p.m. I said (emphatic tone), 'Yes!' I made $0.30 per hour. I thought it was wonderful. We were paid every other week.

Why didn't your friend get a job at Gibson? *They did not call her, and in the meantime she got a job at Sutherland Paper Company (Note: Sutherland was located close to Gibson. It was founded in 1917, the same year Gibson's Parsons Street Day Light Plant was opened. Sutherland began by manufacturing wax butter cartons. Kalamazoo's Sutherland, and other paper Kalamazoo companies of the era, produced more paper and paper products than any other city in the world.)*

What was your first job a Gibson? *My first job was in the string room. I worked on a machine making strings. In the early 1940s, the string room was on the second floor of the old three floor building. I could see the railroad track and the railroad workers could see me through the windows (Note - The railroad ran north-south and was located on the east side of the Gibson complex. The railroad was not used for Gibson shipping or receiving. Shipping and receiving was done by parcel post, or other truck delivery methods, delivered to Gibson's truck dock). My husband worked for the railroad. One day the railroad workers stopped the railroad engine, picked me up, and took me to the railroad round house (laughing). My first boss was Leonard and then Gerry Woodworth became boss. They were both nice bosses.*

What was the string room like? *When I first started I would say there were sixteen people in the string room and four were on coiling. There was one person per machine, and I think 12 machines, and four people coiling and boxing. The string room did not get much bigger until Gibson moved the string room to a new building. During the war, Gibson had to get into war work. I was the only one they had in the string room. Sometimes they sent me upstairs to sort little parts that were war work. Sometimes we had to work on Saturdays and got paid for that. Walt Fuller was the boss upstairs when I was doing war work. Walt Fuller was wonderful and a really nice gentleman. He was very nice to work for. During the war, some older men were still working at Gibson, for example, in the shipping department there were older men.*

A 1940s photograph of Helen Charkowski in the 2nd floor string room at Gibson. Helen was hired by Gibson in 1941. No one that was interviewed had an earlier hire-in date.

How did you do on the job? *My first couple of days I was terribly scared; I was so young. I used to pray that I could do it. Gibson had quotas and each string operator had to make so many strings. Each day you had to report what amount you did that day. At first I thought it was impossible. Every night I would go home and cry to my mother, but she encouraged me. I was very nervous about the whole thing, making my numbers. In the beginning I took my work home so that I could finish up my work. Gibson didn't dock your pay if you didn't make quota. After a couple of weeks, actually very quickly, I got used to it and I did fine and I always made my numbers. I liked working in the string room because I could make extra money if I exceeded my quota and I was doing very well. I didn't want to leave the string room or be reassigned because I was making so much extra money.*

Did you know Mr. Hart in the 1940s? *Mr. Hart was*

the 'big shot' when I hired in. He was a rather stern gentleman. He was not as sociable as Huis, Bellson, or McCarty. He was an elderly man at the time. We didn't see much of Mr. Hart. We knew who he was. I don't remember him coming into the string room. Mr. Hart was reserved. He had a business-like manner.

You said that you quit Gibson several times? *One day a couple of gals and I decided that we would take the afternoon off. Mr. Bellson wanted us to apologize for doing that. Rather than apologize, I decided to go to work for Shakespeare (known for fishing reels). Shakespeare paid about the same amount as Gibson. They were doing 'war work' at Shakespeare making pilot and co-pilot instrumentation.*

Then what happened? *After I had a baby boy, I called Julius Bellson to see if I could come back to work at Gibson. And Julius said, "We could use you." But it was too much to handle, so I quit again. Later Julius called me and asked if I could come in for a few months. By now my son was three years old.*

What kind of man was Julius Bellson? *Julius Bellson was in personnel. When my husband was on referral from the Army, he'd come down to the shop to see if I could get some time off. I did not know if I could, so I asked Julius Bellson and Julius said, 'Of course, yes!' Another time during the war, around 1943 or 1944, they were freezing jobs, and I asked Julius if I could get a leave of absence to go visit my husband. Julius gave me a leave without pay. I went down to Alexandria, LA because my husband was stationed there in the Army. Julius was responsible for allowing that leave. Julius used to say, 'Helen is one of my best favorite workers.' We were on incentive pay and I was making good money in those days. In those days, there was a receptionist in the front of the second floor of the old building. Julius had an office in the front of the old building. When my son was in elementary school, Mr. Bellson gave me the summers off – June, July, and August. I remember that Mr. Bellson was a bridge player; he played a lot of bridge tournaments. Unlike Mr. Huis and Mr. McCarty, Mr. Bellson did not come out in the plant a lot.*

Did Gibson want you to move to another department? *The war was not over, but Gibson was beginning to get more string work. Julius Bellson asked me if I'd like to be a supervisor. There were seven or eight girls in the department. But one of the girls was negative. I was young, and the girl's negative attitude towards a female supervisor made me feel uncomfortable. I was a supervisor for a short while but I felt that I shouldn't be a supervisor, so I told Julius Bellson that they should get a man as supervisor. So I helped the supervisor set things up. Then I went into coiling and boxing in the string room. One of the girls that was a coiler had to quit, and that's how I got on the coiler. That was still during the war. I would coil the strings and put them into an envelop, and then into a box, and then label them.*

What was John Huis like? *John Huis came around a lot to the string room. He wasn't stuck up. John hired in after I did (Note: Actually John originally hired into Gibson in 1926, but he returned from the war after Helen was already working). He was just a regular employee. Then he moved up to VP. He was a really nice man. John Huis always stopped and talked with me. I told John about a few friends of mine that were interested in a job, and he hired them, for example Stella Delach (seniority date September 16, 1955). I told Stella to come down to Gibson. John came over to see me and he told me about Stella - that she was hiring in.*

What was Ted McCarty like? *Ted McCarty was a friendly person. Ted would bring out celebrities to the plant. The celebrities were people that had bought instruments. Bill Monroe was one; I used to enjoy watching him on TV. When I was in coiling, Ted talked with me several times. Ted was very outgoing. Ted would query us about how we liked the job. He wanted us to be satisfied. (Pause) And I do remember Les Paul coming through the string room.*

Any other managers come to mind? *Wilbur Marker. He played the steel guitar. He was on the road for a while. He was a very nice guy. Everybody at Gibson was nice, except for Mr. Herman, who belittled my boss (refer to explanation later). Gibson was a nice place to work. I also remember Larry Allers who was a foreman and then became an engineer. His son (Ron) worked there too. I knew Rem Wall. His band, The Green Valley Boys, played on TV. They played for the Kalamazoo County Fair.*

The United Steelworks Union organized Gibson and several other Kalamazoo companies during the war. You were working at Gibson (in 1941) before the union came in. What do you remember about the start-up of Local #3596? *I don't remember anything specifically about the union start-up. I remember discussions about getting a union in. We had meeting to discuss the benefits. I had never had any problems at Gibson, but the union reps made me feel that I wanted a union, so I went along with the rest of them. At the time it seemed like a lot of people were trying to get unions. Hermin Meints was the Financial Secretary of the 3596 Local.*

What else do you remember about the union? *Having a union did not bother me. The union dues did not bother me. The seniority system did not seem to be important to me. I was only working in the string room, coiling and packaging. Those were the only jobs available in the string room. I never wanted to get out of the string room. I never thought about going into any of the other departments.*

Did the union ever help you? Did you ever notice a change in attitude by employees regarding the union? *During my years, I don't remember any change in attitude about the union or working conditions. I did not run into any problems that needed the support of the union. But I did have one problem. Gibson had a machine that made a special string. The foreman asked me to do that. We worked on an incentive. I told the foreman that I worked at Gibson because I needed the money. But there was no incentive pay on the special string machine. I liked the quota system because I could make more money. The other girls could have worked on the special string machine. I told the foreman that I had seniority and I should not have to work on the special string machine. The foreman resented that.* [Note: Incentive pay was not a basic motivational tool generally used at Gibson, but it was available in the sting room.]

Did you participate in the mid to late 1960s strikes? *I remember the first strike (ca. 1966 after Ted McCarty left). I was called to walk on the picket line. I don't remember why we were on strike. The strike was not too long. As a result of the strike, I don't recall a change in attitude in the string room.*

During the Gibson expansions the string room was moved. What was the new location like? *Gibson purchased the Ihling Brothers Building and moved the string room from Parsons Street to the Ihling Brothers Building (Gibson's Plant III). They also moved the electronics department over there, but I was only concerned with strings. Paul Lukins was the old string room boss at the old building. Gibson hired a new boss named Walter Herman (Manager of the String Division) from New York. He would say, 'Hurry, hurry' and he would belittle our old boss. By then I just wanted to quit. I did not like Mr. Herman at all. I decided, 'I don't think I want to work here anymore', so I quit. I retired September 28, 1968.*

Initially you walked to work. After you married your husband Earl and your son was born, how close to the plant were you? *We moved to a bungalow on Sunnyside Drive, about 3 ½ miles northeast of the Gibson.*

Interview 2
Clara Van Noorloos (1943–'80)

Clara Van Noorloos was one of the oldest employees I interviewed. She was born in 1924, making her 15 years younger than McCarty. Clara is another example of a woman who was hired, got married and quit, had a family, and returned.

How did you get to Gibson? *I originally was living in Comstock, Michigan working in a box factory. In 1943, I heard about Gibson so I went over there to find out about a job. They hired me right away. I was assigned to the string room, which was on the second floor over by the east side windows. I was put on the machine that made the plain string (unwound string). That wasn't for me so I ran the string machine (wound strings).*

How long did you stay at Gibson? *I quit work in 1947 when I got married. I didn't go back until 1955. They put me in the sanding department but I didn't like sanding, so they put me back in the string room. I liked the string room and I stayed in the string department most of my career. I quit in 1980 because I was old enough to retire.*

A 1953 photograph of Betty Meyle in the second floor finished goods stock room at Gibson. Betty was Ted McCarty's secretary in the 1950s. Information that accompanied this photograph indicated that the 1953 boom in guitar sales was a result of population increases, emphasis of music in schools, and increasing leisure time available to the public.

Interview 3
Harriet Johnston (1944-'79)

Harriet Johnston touched most of the Ted McCarty guitars that were built. Harriet worked in Gibson's general stores stockroom, thereby handling the outgoing hardware that was requisitioned by the guitar builders. Harriet also handled the outgoing guitar paperwork as the Parcel Post scheduler. Think of Harriet, the next time you strum your vintage Gibson. She's part of your Gibson's history; she is part of history!

How did you get to Gibson? Harriet Johnston: *When I graduated from Kalamazoo High School I went to work for Sutherland Paper. Then I had a family and quit. I intended to go back to work and when that happened I just went over to Gibson to get a job. I interviewed with Julius Bellson and he hired me right away. I worked full time, but I was a temporary hire (indicative of the war years).*

What was your first job a Gibson? *I hired into Gibson in late 1944. My husband was in the service. I was having a baby and living with my parents. Gibson started me on war work, radar work, on the second floor of the old building. Then I was laid off, but they called me back in 1946 for the string room. I was do-ing strings and coiling. My foreman was Gerry Woodworth. I had a family so I quit several times, and went back several times. I was laid off or quit in the summers to raise the family. I remember going back to work in 1949 and noticing that Gibson was getting bigger. By 1949 Gibson was definitely getting to be a bigger company.*

What was your second position at Gibson? *I re-hired into Gibson in early 1954. There was an opening for the stock room and I took it. The prior stock room clerk, Glenda, wanted to get out of the stock room and go into the electronics department. I became the single store keeper in the stockroom located in the middle of the second floor of the old building. My supervisor was Carleton Pease. I would issue pickups, tail pieces, bridges, machine heads for the guitars. I also did the parcel post, ½ a day I would issue stock, and ½ a day I would do parcel post.*

What was the stock room activity like? *I would receive all of the incoming component parts. In the 1950s there was no incoming inspection. I'd just received it and checked it in. I'd get the pickups from the electronics department and store them in the stock room. A person from each department would come over once a day to get the parts that they needed for that day.*

What happened to you during the 1960 expansion? *The stock room moved out to the new stock room in the new building. Since 1954 I've always worked in the stock room. I really liked working in the stock room. To stay on a job for 25 years you need to like it. Gibson was a wonderful place to work. It was like family there. Everyone knew everyone. But it wasn't the same after Ted McCarty left in 1966.. After Ted McCarty left it wasn't like family anymore.*

What do you remember about Julius Bellson? *At one time I wanted to get a guitar. I wondered what I should get. So I asked Julius Bellson, 'What kind of Gibson guitar should I get? I don't want a cheap one.' Julius said (laughing), 'Harriet, Gibson doesn't make a cheap guitar.'*

Interview 4
James Hanchett (1945–'76)

McCarty introduced me to James (Jim) Hanchett on August 21, 1999. He was one of the oldest employees I interviewed because even though he worked at Gibson for many years, he didn't join at a young age. Jim was one of a few Gibson employees who actually played guitar, a skill that drove him to Gibson and Gibson took advantage of that.

Jim was born in Minnesota but spent his school years in Michigan. After high school, he went to California, where he played steel and electric guitar professionally for 10 years. Jim returned to Michigan to work in a paper mill and a steel processing company. He joined Gibson in 1945.

How did you get to Gibson? *Jim Hanchett: I was a farm boy. I went to Idaho to play music in 1929, then to San Diego to play semi-professionally, then to Los Angeles to play semi-professionally on steel guitar. In the 1940s I came to Michigan to do war-work at another plant in Kalamazoo. I loved guitar and I wanted to keep with it, so I came to Gibson.*

You were there when Mr. McCarty joined Gibson in 1948. Do you remember that? *Not too much. Mr. McCarty was pretty busy there. What I remember most is my own work that I did at Gibson.*

What did you do at Gibson? *I was a guitar adjuster in the Service Department.*

Did you continue to play guitar when you worked at Gibson? *Yes, I played with several bands around the area, but I gave it up in the 1950s when rock & roll became popular. Guitar playing was useful to me when I worked in the Service Department. I love guitars and I love playing them. It was very enjoyable working at Gibson and being around all of those guitars, mandolins, and banjos.*

Interview 5
Neal Walton (1947-'84)

Neal Walton was one of the most experienced employees that I talked with. He hired into Gibson under Guy Hart and he was there when Ted McCarty joined Gibson. Neal was one of those employees that kept at what he was doing, particularly in the McCarty days.

Neal, his wife, my wife, and I met at one of the Gibson employee reunions. The following day we toured all of 225 Parsons Street. Neal pointed out where he worked and what was done in the different areas of the plant. I also did plant tours with Marv Lamb, Wilbur Fuller, JP Moats, and Helen Charkowski. And there were other instances where I toured the plant with building owner John Thingstad.

Did you start at Gibson right after high school? *Neal Walton: No. I left school after the eighth grade. I did not graduate but I got my GED. I worked in a plant making canopy frames in the heat-treating department. I stayed there for one year, then I joined the service. The war had already started. I joined the coast Guard in 1942. I stayed in 2½ years and got out in 1945. I started working in Sturgis, Michigan down by the state line.*

After the war, how did you get to Gibson? *I wanted a job and I was going to be a piano tuner. I had a good ear for piano. I took an aptitude test for piano tuning. Somebody took me over to Gibson. I was going to work for Gibson until I got my own piano tuning business going, but that never happened. Someone introduced me to Mr. Bellson, or I may have gone over to Gibson on my own. That was the first place that I went to. I don't remember if I interviewed or just got an application. I had not had any woodworking experience. I think my starting pay was $0.90 per hour. I worked at Gibson until they closed the Kalamazoo plant in 1984. My pay when the Gibson plant closed was about $8.00 to $10.00 per hour. Things went well at Gibson, so I dropped the piano tuning idea. I was always happy with the pay; the pay was pretty fair. I never thought about leaving Gibson. It was a pretty good place to work.*

Did you live close to the Gibson plant? *The Gibson plant area was mostly residential. The Sutherland Paper Mill was two blocks north of Gibson. The Shakespeare Kalamazoo Reel plant was about three blocks south (at Kalamazoo & Edwards). Clarage Fan was four blocks south. I hired in September 29,*

1947. I lived on East Ransom Street. That was about two blocks away from the plant. I walked to work. I had a single room. Then I got married and we moved to Vine Street, two miles away, and then to N. Park Street, which was pretty close. I walked to work. Then we got a permanent home on East G Avenue that was about three miles away. My wife would drop me off to work and I'd walk home, summer and winter. My wife worked at Allen Electric which was north of Sutherlands. Later she worked at the old American National Bank / Old Kent Bank.

Did you ever think the Parsons Street neighborhood was getting too rough? *I didn't think the neighborhood was getting too rough. I didn't pay too much attention.*

What was your first job at Gibson? *My first job was filling and staining. The guitar was built in the raw wood and we took some filler, especially for mahogany, and filled all of the pores. The guitar was already put together. It was all in one piece. In the 1940s and 1950s, the filling and sanding department was on the top floor in the old building on the side by the railroad (third floor east side windows). The guitars came up from the down stairs, on the elevator, in a rack of about 35 instruments. I would wipe them off with a paint brush; wipe them off to fill the pores. The filler liquid came in a 5 gallon can. We took the filler liquid out and we put some thinner on and then we brushed it on the instrument. For maple we used stain, maple is a non-porous wood. The rack was either all mahogany or all maple. I did both.*

Did you work on the Les Paul models? *The Les Paul had the maple top and mahogany back and neck. One person would fill and stain a Les Paul. I worked on a medium sized bench and I worked on one guitar at a time. I could look out the window and see the railroad tracks. It was a full-time railroad track; freight trains would go through. The railroad was not part of Gibson, everything at Gibson was by truck.*

How many guys were in the department? *There were three or four guys that were doing filling and staining. I had two bosses, but the one that I can remember was Case Triezenberg (legendary Gibson finishing department supervisor). After the pore filling, the guitars went and had a sealer coat sprayed on. One of*

two guys did that. Sometimes there was a natural finish guitar, and they would not do anything to that. For sunburst they'd spray on the yellow first, then they'd shade it for the sunburst. All of this happened on the top floor (the third floor). You could smell a lot of lacquer, and that lacquer really got to me. I was on that job for quite a while. In the 1950s, the old building (225 Parsons) would get hot in the summer, but it wasn't too bad in the winter.

Neal Walton (far left) and other skilled craftsmen put the finishing touches on Gibson guitars in a 1953 photograph. The west side windows in the rear of the photo show the courtyard to the brick powerhouse.

Did you ever consider another assignment at Gibson? *I had seniority but I did not care to move. When a job came up there was a posting board. Any job in the plant was posted in every department, and if you wanted it, you could bid on it. People at Gibson were generally pleased with their department and they would not change departments too often.*

Did you have a Skilled Trades union group that serviced the finishing department? *We had the guys from maintenance. They were all the same. They had their own place, but it didn't seem like they were a skilled trades group. [Note: In the 1950s, the maintenance department was located in the 1918 built annex which was just north of the old building's north basement wall.]*

You were there in 1948 when Ted McCarty came, and when the first McCarty plant expansion occurred in 1950. *In 1947, when I hired-in, there were two houses on Parsons Street to the left of the old building. Those buildings were the lumber yard (lumber storage). They tore those houses down in 1950 and put in the new single floor administration building. I remember Mr. McCarty coming through the*

Neal Walton (far left) and Howard Quibell (far right) in a 1953 photograph in the second-floor final cleaning department.

plant, but he never stopped to talk with me. He was really friendly. John Huis would walk through about the same, but he never stopped to talk with me.

In the 1950s, did you have other jobs in the third floor finishing department? *I became a buffer. That was on the same floor (third floor) in a group together. I posted for that (applied via a union job posting). After the finish was applied, the guitar went down the floor a ways and they scraped the bindings. The color on the bindings needed to be cleaned and scraped. Then they had the lacquer put on, in a different booth. There were a lot of smells up there. Then the guitars were water sanded to take off the 'orange peel.' All of this was on the top (third) floor. Then they put retarder to soften the finish, then we would buff it. The buffing was on a machine, a buffing wheel. They had maybe six or eight buffers. I was a buffer when they moved the buffing department out to the new building around 1960.*

What was your next assignment? *Then I became a cleaner. All the hardware was on, everything was on, and then we cleaned it up prior to shipping it out, so that the guitar would be in top condition. The cleaners were on the middle floor (the second floor of the old building) over by the railroad tracks (east side windows). There were maybe four cleaners, each working on their own bench. The boss supervised both departments, the finishing department and the cleaners, so the boss had to go upstairs – downstairs. After we cleaned the instrument, a gentleman would check the frets for buzzes. He would file it down. That was done right there on the second floor near the stock room.*

Where was the stockroom? *The stockroom was on the middle (second) floor. The stock room did not take too much room. I thought it was kind of small. They kept the guitars in the stockroom that were ready for shipping. They kept the component parts like machine heads and bridges in the stock room. There was one person (stock keeper Harriett Johnston) that took care of everything.*

What do you recall about the 1960 expansion? *Gibson moved the filling / staining / finishing / buffing department from the third floor of the old building to the new building. Everyone on the third floor went out to the new building. They put in the Custom Instruments department on the top floor (third) when the finishing department was moved (Note: The new Customs Department was designed and set up by Wilbur Fuller). I was a buffer when we went out to the new building.*

The union was there when you hired into Gibson in 1947. What do you remember about the atmosphere at Gibson during your career? *I don't remember any difference in the atmosphere in the '50s, '60s, '70s, or the '80s. I remember there was a weekend strike. The union called me to walk the line. I think I walked the line just once. The line was in front of where the trucks come in. We struck for more pay. We got it. The second strike was the same, I think it was for more pay. I don't remember the name of the union boss. I went to a few of the union meetings but I did not go to many.*

The string room had an incentive pay system that involved quotas. Did you have that in the finishing department? *I was never on a piece rate but I'd heard of a piece rate at Gibson. We had a bonus plan. We'd have to get out so many a day and so many a week. Some weeks were bad and we didn't get anything, and some weeks were good. I liked the bonus plan. It was fair. We would help each other out.*

What one individual do you remember working with? *I worked for Rem Wall for a while. That was when I was cleaning. He was an inspector. I knew he was a good guitar player, but I never heard him.*

You were among the last Kalamazoo employees to work at Gibson Kalamazoo. You worked from 1947 to 1984. That's 37 years of seniority. Why did Gibson leave Kalamazoo? *I don't know what happened to make Gibson move. I was kind of surprised when Gibson said they were closing. I had a good pension coming based upon my seniority. The timing was perfect for me, but I felt sorry for the other people.*

Interview 6
Joyce Shelven (1952–'69)

How did you get to Gibson? *I graduated from Kalamazoo Central High School in 1945 and got married in 1946. I first worked at Grace Corset Company and Kalamazoo Stationary. I worked outside picking grapes and I helped my husband build our house. He was a bricklayer and he built our house himself. My sister, Barbara Ledbetter (seniority date 8-24-50) worked at Gibson. I'm not sure why she went to work for Gibson; she needed a job I guess. [Note: The Grace Corset Company was an old Kalamazoo firm dating to the early 1900s. It eventually grew to be the largest corset factory in the world. Kalamazoo was full of niche industrial powers. Grace for corsets, Shakespeare for fishing tackle, Gibson for fretted instruments, to mention a few.]*

Did Barbara recommend Gibson to you? *Barbara talked favorably about Gibson. It's been so long ago, I think I just went over to Gibson and talked with somebody. I can't remember who hired me. Gibson was a very nice place to work. Gibson was one of nicest, most decent factories to work at. I never considered leaving Gibson. I think most people stayed at Gibson.*

What was your first job? *My first job, I was a hand sander. Hand sanding was near the mill, back against the north wall windows of the first floor addition (Note: From 1950–'60 the plant layout was as follows. The 'old building' had three floors that were called the basement, the second floor, and the third floor. There was no official first floor in the old building. The new 1950 addition that was added by Ted McCarty was called the first floor. From 1950–'60 there were windows on the north wall of the first floor. Those windows became the south wall of the 1960 expansion.)*

Did you sand all of the various models? *I sanded all of them. They were in the white wood. I was on that job for quite a while. Then I went to belt sanding. The men used to do the belt sanding and I guess I decided the girls could do it too. When I went to belt sanding it was a man's job, so I got a man's pay. I always felt my wages were satisfactory at Gibson. (Note: In union shops, various jobs had classifications. Often jobs that required less physical strength were called 'light classifications.' They paid less. Often women worked in the 'light classifications.' The belt sander classification was a 'regular classification' that paid more than a 'light classification.') The belt sanders were in a little room by itself in the same vicinity. When there wasn't any belt sanding to do, I went to another department and glued the amplifier boxes together. There were quite a few other things that I did, but I can't remember them. I tried rim sanding once. A guy said, 'Why don't you try it?' That was something!! I didn't like it.*

Some departments were on a piece rate? *When we got so much production out, we got a piece rate. The whole department got the piece rate if we got over the quota. When you would run out of work, you'd do something else; even sweep floors.*

A 1953 photograph of the mill hand sanding department located at the north end of the mill. Shown in the photograph is a rack that holds up to 40 guitars. These racks were referenced often by the employees that were interviewed. Many of the employees interviewed started in hand sanding.

Who did you work for? *Larry Allers was my first boss. He took me out and showed me how to belt sand. Then Clarence Coleman was my next boss; he was a good boss. He replaced Larry Allers.*

Is that how you learned your job at Gibson? *Yes, the boss showed me how it was done. The skilled workers would show you how to do it, so the skill was passed from worker to worker.*

What was your next job? *I transferred up to Customs (Gibson Custom Instrument Department, established in 1960 by Wilber Fuller). There was an opening, so I transferred up there. (Note: The Custom department was located on the third floor of the old building. It was established there when the former finishing department was relocated to the new finishing room in the new 1960 plant expansion. A few of the old finishing booths were retained in the third floor Custom department and used to finish the instruments made there). Wilber Fuller was my boss. I went to the Custom department to belt sand. I tried to water-sand (the process after the finish was applied). I did dry sanding and I did belt sanding. This was on the third floor of the old building. I think I liked it up there better than in the mill. There weren't so many people up there. I was up in the Custom department until I retired in 1968. I worked long enough to get my pension.*

What do you remember about the union? *For the union, you had to wait so many days or weeks and then you had to join the union. The union hall was down on Westnedge & Main, across the street from St. Augustine Food. The union would hold meetings there and people would go to those. I was in a strike. I can't remember why we struck. I went down and took my turn at picketing. I brought rolls and coffee. I was a guard at the union meetings. I had people sign in. I helped make sure nobody was there that shouldn't be there. One lady used to say, 'You better stick with the union or we will go broke.'*

A 1953 photograph of the automatic buffing and leveling operation in the mill.

KENNY BURRELL

TAL FARLOW

MUNDELL LOWE

HERB ELLIS

JIM HALL

in the **Gibson** *Galaxy of Stars*

Fine guitarists demand fine instruments . . . that's
why there are so many stars in the Gibson galaxy,
why so many fine musicians everywhere choose Gibson.
They appreciate Gibson tonal perfection, superb response,
and ease of playing—so fast and low and light.
They appreciate, too, the beauty of their instruments.
Top performers in the guitar world are shown throughout
this book—they're Gibson artists all!

3

The 1960 Gibson catalog

BARRY GALBRAITH

JIMMY RAINEY

in the **Gibson**
Galaxy of Stars

TINY TIMBRELL

ANDY NELSON

AL VIOLA

HOWARD ROBERTS (WITH BOBBY TROUP)

4

The 1960 Gibson catalog

Electric Spanish Guitars — THIN BODY MODELS

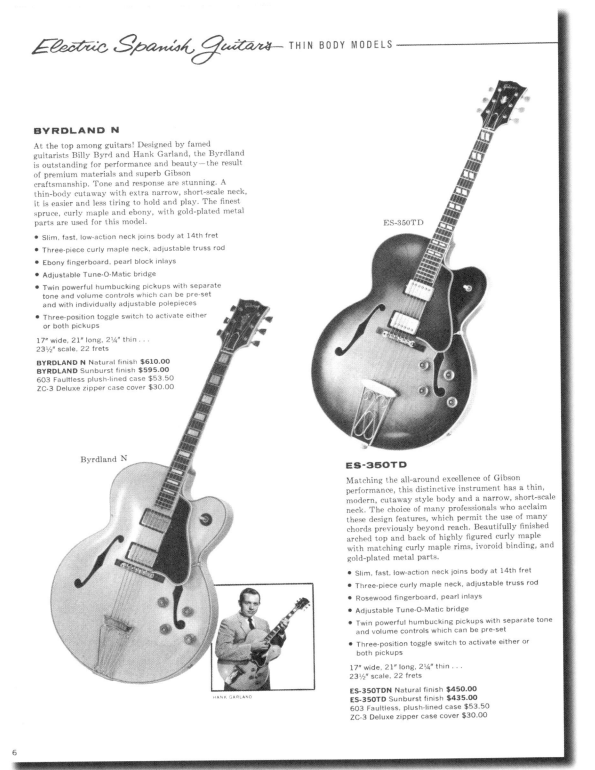

BYRDLAND N

At the top among guitars! Designed by famed guitarists Billy Byrd and Hank Garland, the Byrdland is outstanding for performance and beauty—the result of premium materials and superb Gibson craftsmanship. Tone and response are stunning. A thin-body cutaway with extra narrow, short-scale neck, it is easier and less tiring to hold and play. The finest spruce, curly maple and ebony, with gold-plated metal parts are used for this model.

- Slim, fast, low-action neck joins body at 14th fret
- Three-piece curly maple neck, adjustable truss rod
- Ebony fingerboard, pearl block inlays
- Adjustable Tune-O-Matic bridge
- Twin powerful humbucking pickups with separate tone and volume controls which can be pre-set and with individually adjustable polepieces
- Three-position toggle switch to activate either or both pickups

17" wide, 21" long, 2¼" thin . . .
23½" scale, 22 frets

BYRDLAND N Natural finish **$610.00**
BYRDLAND Sunburst finish **$595.00**
603 Faultless plush-lined case $53.50
ZC-3 Deluxe zipper case cover $30.00

Byrdland N

HANK GARLAND

ES-350TD

ES-350TD

Matching the all-around excellence of Gibson performance, this distinctive instrument has a thin, modern, cutaway style body and a narrow, short-scale neck. The choice of many professionals who acclaim these design features, which permit the use of many chords previously beyond reach. Beautifully finished arched top and back of highly figured curly maple with matching curly maple rims, ivoroid binding, and gold-plated metal parts.

- Slim, fast, low-action neck joins body at 14th fret
- Three-piece curly maple neck, adjustable truss rod
- Rosewood fingerboard, pearl inlays
- Adjustable Tune-O-Matic bridge
- Twin powerful humbucking pickups with separate tone and volume controls which can be pre-set
- Three-position toggle switch to activate either or both pickups

17" wide, 21" long, 2¼" thin . . .
23½" scale, 22 frets

ES-350TDN Natural finish **$450.00**
ES-350TD Sunburst finish **$435.00**
603 Faultless, plush-lined case $53.50
ZC-3 Deluxe zipper case cover $30.00

6

The 1960 Gibson catalog

Did you live close to Gibson? *It took about twenty minutes to get to work. I was in a car pool. You could park in the street or in the parking lot across the street.*

Did you know Ted McCarty? *I remember Mr. McCarty walking through. I don't think he stopped to talk with me. He wasn't the boss of me. He was always friendly and he'd say hi to you. He was always at the get-togethers when they had them, when he could make it.*

Did you know John Huis? *John Huis was friendly. I remember when I was working in the belt sanding room near the mill. By that time there were three girls in belt sanding. One time the girl that I worked with could not get in, and I was sick also. So John called at home and said who ever isn't the sickest should come in. One other time my daughter was sick and I wanted to take her to the doctor and John said, 'My wife will take her', but he was not serious. John was more serious than Ted McCarty, but I didn't talk with McCarty that much.*

Did you ever hear of Mr. Berlin? *I'd heard of Mr. Berlin.*

Gibson had a discipline policy called 'blue slips. *I got a lot of blue slips, maybe ½ dozen, usually for not calling in, or leaving work before the bell rang. (Note: It was common in Michigan corporations, even for salary workers, to start and end their day at the ring of a bell. Workers, including salary, were expected to be at their work station when the starting bell sounded, and when the ending bell tolled. For some companies, this policy continued into the 1970s). Gibson was not unfair with the 'blue slip' policy. You only got one if you needed it. [Note: If an employee received so many 'blue slips' they were disciplined and they could be fired.]*

Did you play guitar? *No one in my family played guitar.*

What happened when the plant expanded in 1960? Was the union involved? *My husband helped build the new factory. He did some of the brick work for it. Everything in the new factory was based on seniority.* (Note: When a large reorganization takes place at a union shop, such as the 1960 factory addition, the plant is 'leveled' which means nearly every job is available to anyone who is qualified, and high seniority people have first choice as to where they want to work. For the 1960 expansion few people posted for new jobs.)

The union stuck behind you on that...

Interview 7
Mary Lou Hoogenboom (1953–'84)

How did you get to Gibson? *Mary Lou Hoogenboom: I was a waitress and I wanted to try to get into Gibson. I got an application at the Gibson guard shack by the truck entrance. I started at $1.05 an hour. I started in wood working, rim binding, in the mill working for Larry Allers.*

Where else did you work? *First I worked at rim lining for one week. Then I transferred to High Frequency (in the experimental department in south east part of 'the basement.') I chiseled my thumb, so I went to dry sanding, where I met Joyce Shelven. Then John Huis transferred me to Electronics in the 'old building.' I worked there until Plant 2 opened (in 1962).*

GIBSON STEREO

ES-355TD-SV

ES-345TD

Exciting to play, thrilling to hear! This new Gibson can produce *any* sound you've *ever* heard from *any* guitar. The Vari-tone selector switch produces 18 separate sounds and creates hundreds of voices when coupled with tone controls. Though marvelously versatile, it is uncomplicated . . . may be used with stereophonic, monaural, or two-channel amplifier. A thin, double cutaway with finest sustain and tone color, and Gibson's low, fast, professional string action. Semi-solid body construction. Curly maple arched top and back, ivoroid binding, gold-plated metal parts. Deluxe padded leather strap included.

- Slim, fast, low-action neck joins body at 20th fret
- One-piece mahogany neck, adjustable truss rod
- Rosewood fingerboard, pearl inlays
- Adjustable Tune-O-Matic bridge and adjustable tailpiece for perfect intonation
- Twin humbucking pickups with separate tone and volume controls which can be pre-set
- Three-position toggle switch . . . stereo wiring and Y cable
- Vari-tone built-in tone selector . . . six pre-set tonalities at each position

16″ wide, 19″ long, 1¾″ thin . . .
24¾″ scale, 22 frets

ES-345TDN Natural finish **$400.00**
ES-345TDC Cherry finish **$380.00**
ES-345TD Sunburst finish **$365.00**
519 Faultless plush-lined case **$47.00**
ZC-19 Deluxe zipper case cover **$30.00**

ES-355TD-SV

This magnificent jazz guitar reflects all the beauty and skill of the guitar maker's art. Made with semi-solid body construction to the Gibson wonder-thin silhouette, it's easy and comfortable to hold; its feel is just right. The slim low-action neck makes strings seem feather-light and the double cutaway provides easy access down to the very last fret. With tone ranging from a clear treble to a throaty bass, with thrilling vibrato and instant response, it offers the jazz artist everything. The new Gibson cherry-red finish on curly maple with gold-plated metal parts makes it a beauty. Deluxe, padded leather strap included.

- Slim, fast, low-action neck joins body at 20th fret
- One-piece mahogany neck, adjustable truss rod
- Ebony fingerboard, pearl block inlays
- Adjustable Tune-O-Matic bridge
- Twin humbucking pickups with separate tone and volume controls which can be pre-set
- Three-position toggle switch to activate either or both pickups
- Vibrato tailpiece for added effects

16″ wide, 19″ long, 1¾″ thin . . .
24¾″ scale, 22 frets

ES-355TD Cherry finish **$550.00**
ES-355TD-SV with Stereo and Vari-Tone (shown above), cherry finish **$600.00**
519 Faultless plush-lined case $47.00
ZC-19 Deluxe zipper case cover $30.00

ES-345TD

GIBSON STEREO

1960 Catalog for ES-345TD and ES-355TD-SV

Did you know John Huis? *Yes. One time, when I was working in electronics, John Huis and Les Paul came around. John showed Les Paul what I was doing and he said, looking over my shoulder, 'Now this is making Mary Lou a little nervous.'*

You stayed at Gibson until the end? *When Gibson began to close down the plant, I was one of the last people to go. We (the employees) were going to have 'give backs' in 1983 & 1984 but it didn't work.*

You were also involved in the Berlin Fair which promoted Kalamazoo and Gibson? *Our family was called the 'ideal family' for the German Fair.*

Interview 8
Wilbur Fuller (1954–'80)

Wilbur Fuller is perhaps most easily identified as the cousin of Gibson's former electronic and pickup guru Walter Fuller. But cousin Wilbur Fuller has more than just a famous Gibson name. Wilbur Fuller worked at Gibson from December 14, 1954 to December 31, 1980. Among other things, he crafted several important Gibson products including the late 1950s Gibson square shoulder flat top, the late 1950s Florentine sharp cutaway, and later on, the highly regarded Gibson Kalamazoo Award archtop. Wilbur Fuller, a truly dedicated Gibson employee, who loved and admired his fellow employees, is an unsung Gibson hero. Wilbur's interview, like the rest of the interviews, goes no farther than 1966, the year Ted McCarty left Gibson. Like some others interviewed, Wilbur advanced to senior management during the post-McCarty years.

What was your background prior to joining Gibson? *Wilbur Fuller: I graduated from Marcellus High School, over in Cass County (about twenty miles southwest of Kalamazoo) in 1936. After I graduated from high school I went to work at the Bill Parker Saw mill, and this was hard work. I ran a crate saw with a big steam engine. It was over by Marcellus, MI. Then I went to work making radio cabinets in a furniture factory for Spartan Radio Cabinets. It was a Chicago firm. That was in Cassopolis, Michigan. I moved up (got promoted) there and got to be a foreman over shipping. But in the late 1930s they moved out and went back to Chicago. After they went back to Chicago I went to work for a building contractor in Marcellus, building houses and so forth. Then I decided to go out on my own. I built two nice houses but I had trouble with my back.*

What did you do after you could no longer build houses? *There was a farm up by Schoolcraft, Michigan (ten miles due south of Kalamazoo). It was 300 acres of nice level ground. I decided to go up there and lease from this lady. I started farming in 1951 and left there in 1953. From 1953 to 1954 I worked around as a carpenter doing wood work. We were still at the house in Schoolcraft, MI, when we moved north to Lawrence, MI to my wife's uncle's place in 1954. Lawrence, MI was my wife's home town. That's where I met her. We could have moved back to Marcellus, MI, but my wife's folks lived in Lawrence, and that was a benefit.*

How did you find Gibson? *Most people did not know about Gibson. If somebody was not interested in instruments and music, Gibson did not mean much. I had a cousin that worked up there at Gibson. And his father had been there at Gibson for a number of years as the janitor. I imagine that's why my cousin, Walter*

Fuller, decided to go to Gibson. I think Walter went to work at Gibson really early, probably right out of high school. Walter was always interested in electronics. There were four or five year's difference in age between Walter and myself. His father and my father were brothers.

So Walter Fuller introduced you to Gibson? *I became interested in Gibson after hearing Walter talk about Gibson. That got me to want to go up there. I'd always been interested in wood. I'd been interested in wood ever since the old saw mill. So I went out and applied for a job. I think they hired me really quickly. I think Julius Bellson hired me. I just filled in an application, and I don't remember doing any interviewing. I put down on the application that I was a woodworker.*

Gibson was hiring a lot of people in 1954? *They hired nine people in 1954. It wasn't too pushy right then. In 1955 and 1956 Gibson's hiring commenced to pick up. I went to work for Gibson in 1954. This was before Gibson started to grow and expand. I saw Gibson grow from one factory, to three factories, with a seniority list of around 1,000 people. Because of the hand labor, every job was a skill of its own.*

What was your first job? *Removing the finish from instruments in the repair department was my first job. The repair department was in the basement of the old building along the east wall windows. On my first job, I started at the bottom, zipping and sanding. I removed the finish on every guitar that came in that needed a new finish. Then I moved up to Repairman 'A'. In the repair department there was a steady flow of instruments coming in for repair. For example, a guitar's top had been broken or something. I was on that job for probably two or three years. I was happy with that job. It was very interesting. I was happy with the pay.*

You liked it a Gibson right away? *Gibson was a great place to work. It was like going to high school everyday. Everybody was so friendly to one another you know. Everyone seemed to enjoy their work. My boss in the repair department was Ray Peldon. He was responsible for the repair department, the whole works. Once in awhile Ted McCarty would come walking through. The repair department was in the basement of the old building. To get there, you'd normally enter by going up and around the shipping bank, and then go down the stairs. The basement was one floor down. Along with the repair job, I would work on making mandolins in the back of the repair department, or whatever was needed. For mandolins, you'd do the whole thing. I build a lot of F-5, F-12, and A-5 mandolins. So I got some building experience. (Pause) Some of the people working along with me in the basement were, R.L. Kingsly (pattern maker), Frank Abnet (rims, seniority date August 8, 1926), Ralph Diehl (repair), Gene Berg (repair and mandolin maker), Steve Stozicki (repair), Ivan Reed (repair) and Hartford Snider (repair). North of the repair department, along the windows was the pattern makers and machine shop. Some of the people working there were George Menne (pattern maker), Basil Raynes (pattern maker), Gar Bos (machinist), Jake Doorenbos (machinist), Jake Tuke (machinist, seniority date June 15, 1943), Rose Mary Welch (machine operator), and Bill West-man (pattern maker). Some of these employees were involved in designing and building of the first Les Paul Model. [Note: Because no written records have been uncovered concerning the Les Paul prototype, it is certainly possible that anyone of Wilbur's co-workers mentioned above could have participated in the Les Paul prototype build, as well as in the 1955 Gibson Les Paul Humbucking Pickup Test Guitar.]*

In the basement of the old building, in the 1950s, there was the repair department, the machine shop, the pattern maker's benches, and a lab. Did they build the amplifier cabinets in the basement? *Yes. When I came there in 1954 Gibson was building amps. They were built in the basement on the north end (close to the ramp). They built amps there until the new factory was used. The amp lab in the 1950s was located in a small room built into the basement, over in the south corner. [Note: My*

Electric Spanish Guitars — THIN BODY MODELS

ES-335TD

ES-330T

A wonderful instrument with truly magical tone available in single and double pickup models. The double cutaway body and thin silhouette make it wonderfully easy to hold and play. The new slim neck provides fast, low-action and perfect response. A beautiful guitar in the finest curly maple and rosewood and nickel-plated metal parts.

* Slim, fast, low-action neck joins body at 16th fret
* One-piece mahogany neck, adjustable truss rod
* Rosewood fingerboard, pearl dot inlays
* Adjustable Tune-O-Matic bridge
* Powerful pickup with individually adjustable polepieces
* Separate tone and volume controls
* Available in single or double pickup models
* Three-position toggle switch to activate either or both pickups on double pickup models

16″ wide, 19″ long, 1¾″ thin . . .
24¾″ scale, 22 frets

Single Pickup Model
ES-330TN Natural finish **$225.00**
ES-330T Sunburst finish **$210.00**

Double Pickup Model
ES-330TDN Natural finish **$265.00**
ES-330TD Sunburst finish **$250.00**
519 Faultless plush-lined case $47.00
ZC-19 Deluxe zipper case cover $30.00
104 Durabilt case $13.25

ES-335TD

THIN, DOUBLE CUTAWAY—a newsmaker from its first appearance, this model offers outstanding performance for ensembles, recording, radio and TV at an amazingly modest price. It offers all the advantages of Gibson's thin-body design with its ease of handling, easy fingering, and fast action . . . its sparkling sustaining tone and instant response. Semi-solid body construction. Beautiful curly maple arched top and back, pearl dot inlays, and nickel-plated metal parts.

ES-330T

* Slim, fast, low-action neck joins body at 20th fret
* One-piece mahogany neck, adjustable truss rod
* Rosewood fingerboard, pearl dot inlays
* Adjustable Tune-O-Matic bridge
* Twin humbucking pickups with separate tone and volume controls which can be pre-set
* Three-position toggle switch to activate either or both pickups

16″ wide, 19″ long, 1¾″ thin . . .
24¾″ scale, 22 frets

ES-335TDN Natural finish **$295.00**
ES-335TD Sunburst finish **$279.50**
519 Faultless plush-lined case $47.00
ZC-19 Deluxe zipper case cover $30.00

1960 Catalog for ES-330T and ES-335TD

178

ES-125TC

An outstanding guitar in the popular price field, this thin-bodied cutaway model is ideal for home or professional playing. It is light in weight and easy to hold, made in the Florentine cutaway style. Has fine arched maple top and back with matching maple rims and nickel-plated metal parts.

• Slim, fast, low-action neck joins body at the 14th fret
• One-piece mahogany neck with adjustable truss rod
• Rosewood fingerboard, pearl dot inlays
• Powerful pickup with individually adjustable polepieces
• Separate tone and volume controls

16¼" wide, 20¼" long, 1¾" thin . . . 24¾" scale, 20 frets

Single Pickup Model
ES-125TC Sunburst finish **$189.50**
Double Pickup Model
ES-125TCD Sunburst finish **$225.00**
519 Faultless plush-lined case $47.00
ZC-19 Deluxe zipper case cover $30.00
104 Durabilt case $13.25

ES-125TC

ES-125T

ES-140T¾

ES-125T
ES-125T 3/4

Thin, very light weight, easy to hold, and ideal for the professional or student who requires fine quality and top performance in a popular priced instrument. Available in single or double pickup models. Beautiful maple arched top and nickel-plated metal parts.

• Slim, fast, low-action neck joins body at the 14th fret
• One-piece mahogany neck, adjustable truss rod
• Rosewood fingerboard, pearl dot inlays
• Adjustable rosewood bridge
• Powerful pickup with individually adjustable polepieces
• Separate tone and volume controls which can be pre-set
• Toggle switch to activate either or both pickups on double pickup models

16¼" wide, 20¼" long, 1¾" thin . . . 24¾" scale, 20 frets

Single Pickup Model
ES-125T Sunburst finish **$159.50**

Double Pickup Model
ES-125TD Sunburst finish **$195.00**
519 Faultless plush-lined case $47.00
ZC-19 Deluxe zipper case cover $30.00
104 Durabilt case $13.25

Also available in ¾ size with 22¾" scale and 19 frets

ES-125T ¾ Sunburst finish **$159.50**
533 Faultless plush-lined case $42.50
116 ¾ Durabilt case $12.25

ES-140T 3/4

Gibson's exciting innovation, the ES-140T ¾ with its eye-catching Florentine cutaway design provides big performance for youngsters or adult guitarists with small hands and fingers. Many professionals find this unique three-quarter size instrument ideal for their work. It offers unusual ease and speed in fingering due to its short-scale, narrow, short slim neck and extra low string action. The finest all maple body with arched top and back, and nickel-plated metal parts.

• Slim, fast, low-action neck joins body at 14th fret
• One-piece mahogany neck, adjustable truss rod
• Rosewood fingerboard, pearl dot inlays
• Adjustable rosewood bridge
• Powerful pickup with individually adjustable polepieces
• Separate tone and volume controls

12¾" wide, 17¼" long, 1¾" thin . . . 22¾" scale, 19 frets

ES-140T ¾ Sunburst finish **$195.00**
533 Faultless plush-lined case $42.50
116 ¾ Durabilt case $12.25

1960 Catalog

Spanish Guitars

SOLID BODY MODELS

LES PAUL CUSTOM

Here is the ultimate in a solid body Gibson Electric Spanish Guitar—players rave about its extremely low, smooth frets and easy playing action, call it the "Fretless Wonder." Now with three humbucking, adjustable pickups and the adjustable tailpiece, this new and improved "Custom" guitar has increased power, greater sustain, and a clear, resonant, sparkling tone with the widest range of tonal colorings. Three-way toggle switch provides a new method of tone mixing: top position selects top pickup for rhythm; center position activates the center and lower pickups simultaneously for extreme highs and special effects; lower position operates lower pickup for playing lead. Finished in solid ebony color for rich contrast with the gold-plated metal parts. Deluxe, padded leather strap included.

* Slim, fast, low-action neck—with exclusive extra low frets, joins body at 16th fret
* One-piece mahogany neck, adjustable truss rod
* Ebony fingerboard, deluxe pearl inlays
* Solid Honduras Mahogany body with graceful cutaway design and carved top
* Adjustable Tune-O-Matic bridge
* Three powerful, humbucking pickups with unique wiring arrangement
* Separate tone and volume controls
* Three-way toggle switch specially wired

12¾" wide, 17¼" long, 1¾" thin ...24¾" scale, 22 frets

Les Paul Custom Ebony finish
$395.00
Les Paul Custom with gold plated Bigsby **$470.00**
537 Faultless gold plush-lined case
$47.50
ZC-CLP Deluxe zipper case cover
$30.00

LES PAUL STANDARD

This beautiful solid body guitar incorporates many unusual Gibson features. Cherry sunburst carved maple top, mahogany body and neck. Combination bridge and tailpiece is a Gibson first. Tailpiece can be moved up or down to adjust tension. Tune-O-Matic bridge permits adjusting string action and individual string lengths. Finish in the striking cherry sunburst. Nickle-plated metal parts and individual machine heads with deluxe buttons. Deluxe padded leather strap included.

* Slim, fast, low-action neck—with exclusive extra low frets, joins body at 16th fret
* One-piece mahogany neck, adjustable truss rod
* Rosewood fingerboard, pearl inlays
* Graceful cutaway design
* Adjustable Tune-O-Matic bridge
* Twin powerful humbucking pickups with separate tone and volume controls which can be pre-set
* Three-position toggle switch to activate either or both pickups

12¾" wide, 17¼" long, 1¾" thin ...24¾" scale, 22 frets

Les Paul Standard Cherry sunburst finish
$265.00
535 Faultless, plush-lined case
$42.50
ZC-LP Deluxe zipper case cover
$30.00

10

1960 Catalog for Les Paul Custom and Les Paul Standard

interviews indicate that the basement was used to apply the leatherette and tweed coverings to the amplifier cabinets. The white wood cabinets themselves were built in the mill, then moved via 'the ramp' to the basement, and then moved again via 'the ramp' to the annex where the amp chassis and speakers were installed. In general, most Gibson employees knew a lot more about the guitars than the amps. Ted McCarty, himself, knew considerably more about the guitars than the amps. My conclusion is that the Gibson Guitar Company was a guitar company that happened to build amplifiers. Ted McCarty always claimed the Fender Musical Instruments Company was an amplifier company that happened to build guitars. As you'll find out later in the book, these considerations become important as both companies evolved.]

You seemed to enjoy the repair department and the variety of work there. *Yes. Larry Allers, the chief engineer, would sometimes bring me something to do. For example, in the late 1950s he had me change over the small shallow rounded horn archtop cutaway to a deep sharp horn for a new model. He said, 'Come up with something with a sharp horn.' After I was done, the pattern makers came and picked up the specs and the sharp corner block. I thought this to be quite a privilege, being that I only had about four years seniority. [Note: Pattern maker assignments were doled out as they were received. It is very likely that all the pattern makers were overbooked when Larry Allers needed the work done on a sharp horn cutaway. The repair department workforce was also very skilled. It is likely that supervision had noticed that Wilbur had skill and he was ready for a new challenge. Skilled workers, if they aspired for variety and responsibility, could move up in the organization rather rapidly.]*

Any other assignments come from Chief Engineer Larry Allers? *In the late 1950s Larry Allers brought over a Gibson flat top with the round shoulders and he also brought a Martin flat top with square shoulders. Martin dreadnoughts had more or less of a square shoulder at that time. Larry came to me and wanted me to use the benders and bend the rims and change Gibson's style over to the square shoulder. Larry was the engineer. He told me what to do, to copy Martin, so I had to copy Martin. He gave me a Martin guitar and he told me to copy it.*

How did it go? *I just took the measurements. I did a silhouette of it. I copied if off first and then put it in the bender. I changed the bender by hand. There was not a lot of trial and error as long as I followed the pattern and bent it to form. After it was bent – the guitar could be made. Then I cut the top and the back to size. The first one was successful. Once the guitar was to size, it went on through to the wood shop. Once it was to size, that's all I had to do. I made it to size, I cut it and I made the body. Then it was sent to the wood shop. It was a body that was in the 'white wood.' The wood shop finished it on up. In wood shop it had to be 'rabbitted' – cut it out for the binding. They did the routing for the neck slot. They made the neck and put that on it. Then I imagine they tested it for Mr. McCarty.*

Then the square shoulder went into production? *Then three pattern makers came out and asked me about it. This was normally their job to have done the bender and pattern. But Larry Allers asked me (laughing). So the pattern makers came to me to find out how I did it. The pattern makers were on the north part of the basement of the old building. The pattern makers were experimenting along with engineering. What ever the engineers wanted, they asked the pattern makers to do it. And the pattern makers made the first ones and then it went on to production. I was glad that Larry had the confidence in me.*

In the 1940s and 1950s there were just foremen running the plant. *Yes, it was just foremen. When Gibson started getting bigger (ca. 1960) they started assigning general foremen (Note: A general foreman would supervise a number of departmental foremen).*

SPECIAL
SPECIAL 3/4

Two ways new! A lovely new finish in a new shade of limed mahogany or Gibson's new cherry red . . . an ultra-modern new shape—the solid body double cutaway design that provides easy access to *all* 22 frets. Outstanding for its tone, versatility, and low fast action at a modest price. Very graceful and sturdy with beautifully finished, nickel-plated metal parts. Enclosed individual machine heads. Leather strap included.

Available also with three-quarter size neck and fingerboard that joins the double cutaway body at 15th fret.

- Slim, fast, low-action neck—with exclusive extra low frets, joins body at 22nd fret
- Rosewood fingerboard, pearl dot inlays
- One-piece mahogany neck, adjustable truss rod
- Combination metal bridge and tailpiece, adjustable horizontally and vertically
- Twin powerful pickups with separate tone and volume controls which can be pre-set
- Three-position toggle switch to activate either or both pickups

12¾" wide, 17¼" long, 1¾" thin . . . 24¾" scale. 22 frets

SG-R Special Cherry-red finish **$195.50**
SGC Special Cream finish **$195.00**
SG Special ¾ Cherry-red finish **$195.00**
535 Faultless, plush-lined case **$42.50**
ZC-LP Deluxe zipper case cover **$30.00**
115 Durabilt case **$14.25**

TV

The graceful double cutaway design emphasizes the latest in modern appearance with beautiful limed-mahogany finish and incorporating unusual quality, features and performance at a popular price. Its easy, low playing action, slender neck, and clear sustaining tone make it a favorite with students and advanced players. Bright nickel-plated metal parts and quality machine heads. Leather strap included.

- Slim, fast, low-action neck—with exclusive extra low frets joins body at the 22nd fret
- One-piece mahogany neck, adjustable truss rod
- Rosewood fingerboard, pearl dot inlays
- Combination bridge and tailpiece, adjustable horizontally and vertically
- Powerful pickup with individually adjustable polepieces
- Separate tone and volume controls which can be pre-set

12¾" wide, 17¼" long, 1¾" thin . . . 24¾" scale, 22 frets

SG TV Limed-Mahogany finish
$132.50
535 Faultless plush-lined case
$42.50
ZC-LP Deluxe zipper case cover
$30.00
115 Durabilt Case **$14.25**

LES PAUL AND MARY FORD

11

1960 Catalog for SG Special and TV

What was your next assignment? *The factory enlarged in the early 1960s and Gibson now took in the whole block. The repair department moved out there next to the mill room. R.L. Kingsley was now our boss, because the other fellow retired. Gibson created an all new Custom Instruments Department upstairs on the third floor of the old building, where the finishing department had been. This was the first time that Gibson had a Custom Instruments Department. Before, custom work was just combined with everything. Previously custom work would be done in each separate department. The Custom Department included custom carved and advanced instruments, and consisted of neck building, body building, and on through to final assembly. [Note: In the early 1950s Wilbur Marker was head of the custom build activity. There wasn't a department per se. The custom instrument was built along side all of the other instruments, but a custom instrument was not in a rack of dozens because it was a one off.]*

You became a part of the new Custom Instruments Department? *Gibson moved me to the Custom Instruments Department and gave me the job of helping to line everything up. I helped lay out the department. I set up a continual line for movement of guitars along with the component parts to build them. I was made assistant foreman at that time. My boss was Mac McConachie. Clarence Coleman, an older employee, had the woodwork part of the upstairs Custom Department. The woodwork part would build the custom guitar. I helped Clarence on his end, getting it lined up. I had the finishing end. I was assistant foreman. Then I was made foreman of finishing and final assembly.*

What was your next assignment? *The next year (1961) I was made general foreman of all of the Custom Shop and I had three foremen under me. Mac McConachie, the former general foreman became the superintendent of the factory. [Note: John Huis had been a superintendent. Huis was VP of Manufacturing, to whom the superintendent reported.] There was just one superintendent for the whole factory at that time. The middle floor of the old building had the stockroom, and also the string and adjustment part of the Custom Department. So as boss I was upstairs – downstairs.*

Did Ted McCarty visit the new Custom Instruments Department? *I remember when we got the upstairs custom instruments department set up. I remember Ted McCarty coming up and making the trip around. He came back and I was by the stairs. Ted McCarty said, 'Okay. You have done a wonderful job of setting this up. I love this department' (Wilbur laughs with pride).*

Because it was a custom department, did any special customers come through? *Yes. One day Bill Monroe (Bluegrass legend) came into the Custom Department. But people were not allowed to travel around our department because customer's custom instruments were there and management did not want anybody looking at them and picking them up. Bill Monroe had his mandolin up there, and he had special rules that his mandolin had to be done a certain way, and that nothing else be touched on his mandolin. So Bill Monroe came through the Custom Department and somebody told me, 'Bill's down there, Bill Monroe!' And I said, 'I have to go down there and talk to him.' So I went down and talked to him, and I said, 'Nobody is allowed in here – to walk through – if you would please move on.' He paid no attention to me, he just walked around and looked at this and that. And I said, 'Bill you have to leave.' But he paid no attention until he got out of there (Wilbur laughing).*

Any other celebrities that you can recall? *Ernest Tubbs came through with his bus parked out in front. He came into the office. He didn't go around the plant. We'd get celebrities up in the Custom Department once in a while.*

Ted McCarty told me that the north end of Kalamazoo was kind of a rough neighborhood

Electric Spanish Guitars—

SOLID BODY MODELS

LES PAUL JUNIOR
LES PAUL JR. 3/4

A best seller that's now even better—with
its handsome new cherry-red finish and
its highly desirable new double cutaway
design, and its very low popular price. You
get Gibson quality and top performance.
A small, thin, sturdy, solid body guitar, its
beautiful cherry-red finish on the finest
mahogany. Nickel-plated metal parts
and quality machine heads. Leather
strap included.
Available also with three-quarter size
neck and fingerboard that joins the double
cutaway body at the 15th fret.

* Slim, fast, low-action neck—with exclusive
  extra low frets, joins body at the 22nd fret
* One-piece mahogany neck, adjustable
  truss rod
* Rosewood fingerboard, pearl dot inlays
* Combination bridge and tailpiece,
  adjustable horizontally and vertically
* Powerful pickup with individually
  adjustable polepieces
* Separate tone and volume controls
  which can be pre-set

12⅜" wide, 17¼" long, 1¾" thin
. . . 24¾" scale, 22 frets

Les Paul Jr. Cherry-red finish
$132.50
Les Paul Jr. ¾ Cherry-red finish
$132.50
115 Durabilt case $14.25

MELODY MAKER
MELODY MAKER 3/4

Greatest value ever in a Solid Body
electric with full-size neck and scale
length. Acclaimed by players, teachers
and students for its fine sound, big tone,
sensitive pickup, feather-light touch,
and beautiful sunburst finish. Expert
workmanship and finest materials are
used throughout to produce this top
quality low-priced instrument. Nickel-
plated metal parts. Cutaway style.
Leather strap included.
Available also with three-quarter size
neck and fingerboard that joins the
body at the 12th fret.

* Slim, fast, low-action neck—with
  exclusive extra low frets, joins body
  at the 16th fret
* One-piece mahogany neck, adjustable
  truss rod
* Graceful, cutaway design
* Rosewood fingerboard, pearl dot inlays
* Combination bridge and tailpiece,
  adjustable horizontally and vertically
* Powerful pickup near bridge with
  individually adjustable polepieces
* Separate tone and volume controls

12¾" wide, 17¼" long, 1⅜" thin
. . . 24¾" scale, 22 frets

Melody Maker Sunburst finish
$99.50
114 Durabilt case $10.75
Melody Maker D with two pickups
$135.00
Melody Maker ¾ Sunburst finish
$99.50
114¾ Durabilt case $10.75

12

1960 Catalog for the Les Paul Junior and Melody Maker

184

Electric Spanish Guitars — ACOUSTIC MODELS

SUPER 400 CES

A crowning achievement! Developed through years of research, the luxurious Super 400 CES has been acclaimed by outstanding musicians everywhere as the finest electric Spanish guitar. Superior materials and superb Gibson craftsmanship produce its clear, clean-cut powerful tone and dependable performance. A modern cutaway design . . . hand-graduated carved top of finest spruce, carved back of highly figured curly maple with matching rims, black and white ivoroid binding, exclusive pearl-inlaid peghead, hand-bound custom pickguard, gold-plated metal parts, and deluxe individual machine heads.

- Slim, fast, low-action neck joins body at 14th fret
- Three-piece curly maple neck, adjustable truss rod
- Ebony fingerboard, pearl block inlays
- Adjustable Tune-O-Matic bridge
- Exclusive Super 400 adjustable tailpiece
- Twin, powerful humbucking pickups with separate tone and volume controls which can be pre-set
- Three-position toggle switch to activate either or both pickups

18″ wide, 21¾″ long, 3⅜″ deep...
25½″ scale, 20 frets

Super 400 CESN Natural finish **$775.00**
Super 400 CES Sunburst finish **$750.00**
400 Faultless plush-lined case $60.00
ZC-4 Deluxe zipper case cover $35.00

L-5 CES

Super 400 CES

L-5 CES

The inherent quality, versatility, and rich, impressive appearance of the L-5 CES have won acclaim from the most discriminating artists. Guitarists everywhere praise the slim, comfortable neck, the fast, easy-playing action and quick response. A beautiful modern cutaway guitar with hand-graduated, carved top of select close-grained spruce, arched back of highly figured curly maple with matching rims . . . white-and-black ivoroid binding, stunning pearl-inlaid peghead, gold-plated metal parts, and deluxe individual machine heads.

- Slim, fast, low-action neck joins body at 14th fret
- Three-piece curly maple neck, adjustable truss rod
- Ebony fingerboard, pearl block inlays
- Adjustable Tune-O-Matic bridge
- Exclusive L-5 adjustable tailpiece
- Twin, powerful humbucking pickups with separate tone and volume controls which can be pre-set . . .
- Three-position toggle switch to activate either or both pickups

17″ wide, 21″ long, 3⅜″ deep...
25½″ scale, 20 frets

L-5 CESN Natural finish **$665.00**
L-5 CES Sunburst finish **$650.00**
600 Faultless plush-lined case $53.50
606 Faultless flannel-lined case $42.50
ZC-6 Deluxe zipper case cover $30.00

14

185

by the 1950s. I spent 30 years around Flint, Michigan and Flint's north end was very rough. Was the area around the Gibson factory a rough neighborhood? *Yeah. The stores in the area went out of business because they were losing too much money. People were stealing. Those people never broke into our cars, because Gibson had plant security. I remember one of the ladies was walking to work and two young fellows from school, they ran into her, knocked her down, and took her pocketbook. That was the only thing I ever recall.*

You talked about the engineer coming out in the 1950s and giving you the Florentine cutaway assignment and the square shoulder dreadnought assignment. I understand the engineers were really just highly-skilled wood workers who were promoted to be engineers. They weren't college degreed engineers. They learned their skills on the job. Was there one main engineer in the 1950s? *In the 1950s they had at least two, sometimes three engineers. The engineers were responsible to make new designs. They made prototypes. If someone in the plant had any problem with a design, they'd go to the engineer.*

Did the engineers work in the administration building with Ted McCarty? *No, they had their own section. The office was over there (Wilbur points to chart). Larry Allers, when he was involved as Chief Engineer had an office over here (points to Engineer's office) but the rest of the engineers worked out in the plant. Larry Allers was an engineer in 1954 when I came in. He was one of the engineers for the Les Paul.* [Note: Allers probably was promoted to chief engineer of woodworking in about 1953. Employees recall that Larry was a supervisor over body building and sanding in 1952.]

Like everyone else who was 'on hourly', you were a member of the union. *At Gibson, 'the salary people' (salary workforce) were still paid by the hour. I was 'an hourly' even as a foreman (and general foreman). All I got was $8 an hour, whether it was supervisor or whether I was on the bench. The pay always stayed the same.*

Who were the true salary employees? *I don't know. [Note: Wilbur indicated that even supervisors were hourly employees. Apparently, salary non-exempt status didn't really begin until an employee was on the manager's staff. In the 1950s, in other union plants, such as General Motors, even though a person was considered 'salary', the person was pretty much paid by the hour. If extra hours were required the person was paid overtime. If a 'salary employee' came into work on a Saturday, then even though they were not technically 'hourly' they were paid on an hourly basis for their Saturday work.]*

Why did the union strike Gibson? *There were two strikes during the time I was at Gibson. Money, they struck for more money. I was still in the union, even as a general foreman, the strikes were before 1970, because 1970 was when I became a staff member as head of quality control. James Ferrell was the union boss. The union mainly wanted the union dues. There weren't a lot of union meetings. [Note: The first strike was shortly after McCarty left in 1966. McCarty was replaced by two outsiders. They were not Gibson people. They were not guitar people. They were 'management specialists' each with their own niche. It was reported by employees that the two years after McCarty left were considered to be a 'dark period.']*

In modern guitar making facilities, some of the companies let their employees make one free guitar a year. Did Gibson have that? *I never heard of that. One time I had a mandolin that was made for me. I had one of my repairmen fix it up. Then I went to Julius Bellson with it and then he let me have it for less than what they were asking for them. Otherwise, I never heard of an employee building their own guitar. [Note: The author observed that a small % of the 1940s & 1950s employees actually knew*

ES-5 SWITCHMASTER

This beautiful guitar introduces many new and exclusive features, bringing the guitarist an increased range of performance, the latest electronic advances, and exciting "playability." Modern cutaway design with arched top and back of highly figured curly maple, matching maple rims and black-and-white ivoroid binding . . . attractive laminated pickguard, exclusive tailpiece design, gold-plated metal parts, and individual machine heads with deluxe buttons.

- Slim, fast, low-action neck joins body at 14th fret
- Three-piece curly maple neck, adjustable truss rod
- Rosewood fingerboard, pearl block inlays
- Adjustable Tune-O-Matic bridge
- Three powerful, humbucking pickups with separate tone and volume controls which can be pre-set
- Four-way toggle switch to activate each of the three pickups separately, a combination of any two, or all three simultaneously

17" wide, 21" long, 3⅜" deep . . .
25½" scale, 20 frets

ES-5N Natural finish **$525.00**
ES-5 Sunburst finish **$495.00**
600 Faultless plush-lined case $53.50
606 Faultless flannel-lined case $42.50
ZC-6 Deluxe zipper case cover $30.00

ES-175D

The Florentine cutaway design provides easy access to the entire fret range. Easy to play and comfortable to hold, it produces a brilliant distortion-free tone. Beautiful arched top and back of select maple with matching rims, black-and-white ivoroid binding, exclusive tailpiece, nickel-plated metal parts, and individual machine heads with deluxe buttons.

- Slim, fast, low-action neck joins body at 14th fret
- One-piece mahogany neck, adjustable truss rod
- Rosewood fingerboard, pearl inlays
- Adjustable rosewood bridge
- Twin, powerful humbucking pickups with separate tone and volume controls which can be pre-set (double pickup models)
- Toggle switch activates either or both pickups on double pickup models

16¼" wide, 20¼" long, 3⅜" deep . . .
24¾" scale, 20 frets

Double Pickup Model
ES-175DN Natural finish **$325.00**
ES-175D Sunburst finish **$310.00**

Single Pickup Model
ES-175 Sunburst finish **$249.50**
515 Faultless plush-lined case $47.00
514 Faultless flannel-lined case $42.00
103 Durabilt case $13.25
ZC-5 Deluxe zipper case cover $30.00

ES-125

The unusual all-around performance, appearance, and value of the Gibson ES-125 has made it one of Gibson's most popular models. Only the best in parts and workmanship are used in this outstanding instrument. Made with arched top and back of select maple, mahogany rims with ivoroid binding, and nickel-plated metal parts.

- Slim, fast, low-action neck joins body at 14th fret
- One-piece mahogany neck, adjustable truss rod
- Rosewood fingerboard, pearl dot inlays
- Adjustable rosewood bridge
- Powerful pickup with individually adjustable polepieces
- Separate tone and volume controls
- Full body size

16½" wide, 20¼" long, 3⅜" deep . . .
24¼" scale, 20 frets

ES-125 Sunburst finish **$159.50**
515 Faultless plush-lined case $47.00
514 Faultless flannel-lined case $42.00
103 Durabilt case $13.25

ES-5

ES-175 D

ES-125

15

1960 Catalog for ES-5 Switchmaster, ES-175D and ES-125

EB-2

Bass-ically your hard work is done! This new thin-model double cutaway Gibson doesn't use bulk for a fine bass sound. It's one-tenth the size (and a fraction of the cost) of a fine string bass, with volume to fit the need. New body construction—with solid fitting neck, pickup, and tailpiece bridge—provides the solidity to produce a clear, resonant response. The EB-2 offers great facility and handling ease for all string bass effects . . . tremendous sustain and tremolo, fast plucking and slap bass. It even adds a baritone voice with its new Vari-tone switch, which operates easily and quickly to provide two entirely different tonal characteristics. Arched top and back are curly maple with matching rims and pearloid binding.

- Slim, fast, low-action neck joins body at 18th fret
- One-piece mahogany neck, adjustable truss rod
- Rosewood fingerboard, pearl dot inlays
- Combination bridge and tailpiece, adjustable horizontally and vertically
- Powerful humbucking magnetic pickup
- Vari-tone pushbutton switch for variable frequency resonating response

16″ wide, 19″ long, 1¾″ thin . . .
30½″ scale, 20 frets

EB-2N Natural finish **$300.00**
EB-2 Sunburst finish **$285.00**
538 Faultless plush-lined case $57.50

EB-2

EB-0

A new, economy priced bass by Gibson—it offers clear sustaining bass response, easy and fast playing action, and modern cherry-red finish. Double cutaway body brings the entire length of the fingerboard within easy reach. Expensive bass style machine heads further enhance the value of this instrument. Once you hear its throaty bass tone and feel the quick easy response, you'll agree—the EB-0 gives the professional artist the quality he wants.

- Slim, fast, low-action neck joins body beyond 17th fret
- One-piece mahogany neck, adjustable truss rod
- Rosewood fingerboard, pearl dot inlays
- Combination bridge and tailpiece, adjustable horizontally and vertically
- Powerful humbucking pickup with separate tone and volume controls

13″ wide, 16½″ long, 1¾″ thin . . .
30½″ scale, 20 frets

EB-0 Cherry finish **$195.00**
127 Durabilt case $20.25

EB-0

EB-6
Electric Six-String Bass

Like the EB-2, but with six strings, giving a full octave lower guitar tuning on a regular bass scale length. Neck joins body at the 18th fret, providing easy access to all frets on all six strings.

EB-6 Sunburst finish **$325.00**
538 Faultless plush-lined case $57.50

16

1960 Catalog for EB-2 Bass and EB-0 Bass

Custom-built Doubles

DOUBLE 12

A completely new and exciting instrument . . . the Double 12 combines the conventional six-string guitar neck with a twelve-string neck—six strings double strung which can be tuned either in thirds or an octave apart for reinforced resonance and unusual tonal effects. The Florentine double cutaway design provides easy access to the entire fret range of both necks. Has arched top of fine-grained spruce, back and rims of select maple, attractive laminated pickguard, and nickel-plated metal parts.

- Two slim, fast, low-action necks
- One-piece mahogany necks, adjustable truss rod
- Rosewood fingerboards, pearl inlays
- Adjustable Tune-O-Matic bridges
- Twin, humbucking pickups on each neck with separate tone and volume controls for each neck
- Three-position toggle switch to activate either or both pickups
- Neck selector switch to activate either neck

Custom-built to order only
17¼" wide, 20" long, 1⅜" thin . . .
24¾" scale, 20 frets

Double 12 Sunburst, solid white,
 or solid black **$550.00**
1275 Faultless plush-lined
 oblong case $90.00

Double Mandolin

Double 12

DOUBLE MANDOLIN

Tailored to meet specific unique requirements, the Gibson Double Mandolin lends conspicuous quality to any performance . . . character that commands attention. Combining a six-string guitar neck and a mandolin neck with six strings tuned an octave higher than the regular guitar tuning. this instrument offers solid tonal brilliance with many unusual and interesting effects. The Florentine double cutaway design permits easy access to entire range of both necks. Made with arched top of fine-grained spruce, back and rims of select maple, attractive laminated pickguards, and nickel-plated metal parts.

- Two slim, fast, low-action necks
- One-piece mahogany necks, adjustable truss rod
- Rosewood fingerboards, pearl inlays
- Adjustable Tune-O-Matic bridge on guitar neck
- Special combination, adjustable bridge on mandolin neck with rosewood base and nickel-plated saddle
- Twin humbucking pickups on guitar side and one on mandolin side with separate tone and volume controls for each neck
- Toggle switch to activate either or both pickups
- Neck selector switch to activate either neck

Custom-built to order only
17¼" wide, 20" long, 1⅜" thin . . .
Guitar neck, 24¾" scale, 20 frets
Mandolin neck, 15½" scale, 24 frets

Double Mandolin Sunburst, solid white,
 or solid black **$495.00**
1235 Faultless plush-lined oblong case $90.00

17

The 1960 Gibson catalog

SKYLARK OUTFIT

The sensational performance and attractive appearance of this latest Gibson creation gives the beginning student or advanced player the finest in quality, tone, and value—at an extremely low price.

SKYLARK STEEL GUITAR—Solid body construction, high quality natural Korina finish. New powerful pickup unit; specially designed peghead, nut, and bridge produce a clear, powerful, resonant tone with unusual sustaining qualities and extra reserve volume. Special design and numbering of 29 fret fingerboard is most helpful in locating any position. Separate tone and volume controls for simplified "fingertip action." Attractive, nickel-plated metal parts $75.00

No. 2 SKYLARK CARRYING CASE—Hard shell construction with Spanish gold covering material, leather trimmed with attractive beading and stitching, crushed red plush lining $24.00

SKYLARK AMPLIFIER—See page 25 for full description $64.50
5-C Amplifier Cover $2.75

Skylark Outfit—(6-string guitar, plush-lined case, GA-5 amplifier) **$163.50**

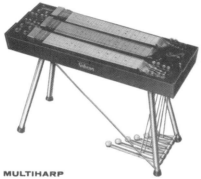

MULTIHARP

One of Gibson's most exciting firsts, providing eye-catching audience appeal, plus versatility, tonal brilliance, and harmonic reproduction beyond comparison. Combining the eight-string six-pedal Electraharp and two additional eight-string necks, the Multiharp offers the equivalent of more than nine separate necks.

Features: First neck permits tuning for extreme treble and special effects. Middle neck is the eight-string, six-pedal Electraharp with feather-touch pedal action and adjustable stops (to lower or raise any string 1½ tones; eight individual string rollers at both nut and bridge.) Third neck is for bass tunings, essential to individual performance, and in small or large combos. Powerful humbucking pickups with separate tone and volume controls for each neck, and four-way toggle switch. Reversible controls for instant tone change from bass to treble or treble to bass. Audio cut-off switch for added tonal effects.

14⅜" wide, 36⅜" long, 4⅜" thick . . .
22½" scale, 36 frets

Multiharp Ebony finish **$895.00**
17 Custom construction, plush-lined case $120.00

ELECTRAHARP EH-620

Gibson Electraharps are the ultimate in steel guitar development offering an infinite range of voicings and organ-life effects with exciting tonal brilliance and clarity. Available in two models. Six-pedal model has seven related chord patterns; four-pedal has five separate chord settings. Both made with lightweight aluminum frame and beautiful curly maple case.

Features: Eight-string neck . . . fast, fingertip action. Feather-touch pedal action. Adjustable stops to lower or raise any string 1½ tones, Eight individual string rollers at both nut and bridge. Powerful humbucking pickup with separate tone and volume controls. Reversible controls for instant tone change from bass to treble or treble to bass. Audio cut-off switch for added tonal effects. Four detachable legs fit into carrying case.

9⅞" wide, 36⅜" long, 4" thick . . .
22½" scale, 36 frets

EH-620 Electraharp Six-pedal, sunburst finish **$695.00**
EH-630 Electraharp Four-pedal, sunburst finish **$595.00**
16 Faultless, plush-lined case $75.00

18

The 1960 Gibson catalog

CENTURY-6

The graceful design of the Gibson Century six-string steel guitar makes it easy to hold and play. Powerful new pickup with Alnico magnets and individually adjustable polepieces. Separate volume, bass and treble controls provide a wide range of dynamics. The Century has contrasting colors of bittersweet and beach white. Removable plexiglas combination hand rest and bridge cover design to permit picking both in front and in back of polepieces for added variety of tone colorings; individual, enclosed machine heads with white buttons.

Century-6 Six-string steel guitar—exclusive finish **$149.50**
No. 1 Faultless plush-lined case $30.00

ELECTRAHARP EH-610

A versatile instrument for the student of the six-string steel guitar, offering all the fine sounds of a pedal guitar without switching to eight-string tunings . . . in range and sound selection the equivalent of five six-string guitars built into one. A beautiful instrument with modern laminated limed-oak body, brown Royalite unit cover, and nickel-plated metal parts.

Features: Six-string neck . . . fast, fingertip action. Easy, positive pedal action. Powerful humbucking pickup provides tonal clarity, eliminates electrical interference. Conveniently located tone and volume controls. Collapsible for easy carrying. Weight 35 lbs.

9" wide, 37⅞" long, 2" thin . . .
22½" scale, 36 frets

EH-610 Electraharp Four-pedal, limed-oak finish **$269.50**
15 Faultless plush-lined case $52.50

CONSOLE GRANDE CG-520

A top flight, amazingly versatile multiple-neck steel guitar with immense power and the widest range of dynamics and tone colorings. Made with sturdy, richly finished oak body, handsome black-and-white bindings, and nickle-plated metal parts.

Features: Two eight string necks . . . fast fingertip action. Two-step construction for easy accessibility to each fingerboard. Steel tuning framework for accurate tuning at all times. Gibson ''4-8-4'' highly specialized, magnetic, high impedance, powerful pickups. Separate tone and volume controls for each neck. Four-way tone-selector toggle switch on each neck. Reversible controls for instant tone change from bass to treble or treble to bass. Audio cut-off switch for added tonal effects.

11¾" wide, 34⅞" long, 3½" deep . . .
24¾" scale, 36 frets

CG-520 Double-neck, oak finish **$325.00**
19 Faultless, plush lined case $67.50
CL-4 Set of four regular legs $14.50
CLA-4 Set of four adjustable legs $42.50

CONSOLE C-530

This compact version of Gibson's double neck console steel guitar uses a revolutionary method of laminated hard maple construction to achieve the heights of tonal purity . . . adds many features for wide range tonal effects. Finished in lustrous blond with matched glare-resistant fingerboards. Lightweight, easy to carry.

Features: Two eight-string necks . . . fast fingertip action. Two-step construction for easy accessibility to each fingerboard. Powerful humbucking pickups with separate tone and volume controls for each neck. Conveniently located toggle switch activates either or both pickups. Reversible controls for instant tone change from bass to treble or treble to bass. Audio cut-off switch for added tonal effects.

10¾" wide, 29¾" long, 2" deep . . .
22½" scale, 36 frets

C-530 Double neck, blond finish **$239.50**
11 Faultless, plush-lined case $45.00
CL-4 Set of four regular legs $14.50
CLA-4 Set of four adjustable legs $42.50

19

The 1960 Gibson catalog

GA-SUPER 400
Three channel high fidelity sound

Clear, powerful, undistorted performance. Premium quality in every component assures great reserve power, tone projection, and trouble-free service. Highly recommended for the electric bass as well as all other electric instruments.

Features: High fidelity sound reproduction from 40 to 20,000 cycles. Two fine quality 12″ twin cone speakers. Three channels . . . separate volume and wide-range tone controls for each, two inputs for each . . . remote speaker outlet. Two-unit chassis . . . 12 tubes . . . 60 watts output . . . extremely low hum level. Built-in compression circuit prevents overloading. Three position switch: on—off—standby. Polarity switch and ground clip eliminate interference. Solid redwood lock-joint case . . . finest twill vinyl covering.

28″ wide, 20″ high, 10½″ deep

GA-400 Amplifier **$429.50**   400-C Cover $15.00   Gadakart $25.00

GA-200 RHYTHM KING
Two channel high fidelity sound

If two channels serve your playing or your group, this is your amplifier. Fully equal in quality to the GA-400 with premium components and great reserve power. Great for use with the electric bass.

Features: High fidelity sound reproduction from 40 to 20,000 cycles. Two 12″ twin cone speakers. Two channels . . . separate volume and wide-range tone controls for each, two inputs for each . . . remote speaker outlet. Two-unit chassis . . . 11 tubes . . . 60 watts output . . . extremely low hum level. Built-in compression circuit prevents overloading. Three position switch: on—off—standby. Polarity switch and ground clip eliminate interference. Solid redwood lock-joint case . . . finest twill vinyl covering.

28″ wide, 20″ high, 10½″ deep

GA-200 Amplifier **$365.00**   200-C Cover $15.00   Gadakart $25.00

GA-86 ENSEMBLE
Unique removable control panel

Unsurpassed for design and performance in its price range. Mellow tone, especially for jazz players who want a flat response. Permits placing control panel near player with speaker located for the best tone response.

Features: Striking case with smart, durable fabric cover and contrasting grille. Detachable top-mounted chassis with convenient 15-foot extension cable. 12″ best-quality speaker . . . 7 tubes. Two channels . . . separate volume controls . . . four voicing controls, separate bass and treble controls in each channel. 25 watts output with 35 watts for peaks. Polarity switch and ground clip eliminate interference. Monitor headphone jacks. Three position switch: on—off—standby. Equipped with jack for adding extra speaker.

17¾″ wide, 26″ high, 10″ deep

GA-86 Amplifier **$289.75**   86-C Cover $8.75

21

The 1960 Gibson catalog

GA-80 "VARI-TONE"
Six exciting pre-set tone colors

In a class by itself — with widest possible selection of tone colors. Vari-tone pushbuttons give six distinctly separate amplified musical sounds at a touch.

Features: New styling with slant grille. A 6-in-1 amplifier with improved tremolo. New built-in Vari-tone selector switch. 15" heavy duty Jensen auditorium speakers. 7 tubes—3 dual purpose. 2-channel, high gain 25-watt output chassis . . . 4 input jacks. Separate controls for volume, depth, and frequency of tremolo. Polarity switch and ground clip eliminate interference.

22" wide, 20" high, 10⅛" deep

GA-80 Amplifier **$315.00**
80-C Cover $8.75

GA-77 VANGUARD
High gain channel

Bell clear reproduction with brilliant highs and a profusion of tonal effects for the professional guitarist. Two can play through this amp and each can achieve as much bass or treble as he wants.

Features: All new Gibson styling—slant grille, twill vinyl covering, lock-corner case. 15" best-quality speaker . . . 6 tubes. Two channels . . . separate volume and tone controls for each . . . two inputs for each. High frequency filter for brilliant highs in channel #2. Standby polarity switch and ground clip eliminate interference. 25 watts normal output, over 35 at peak.

22" wide, 21⅛" high, 10½" deep

GA-77 Amplifier **$287.50**
80-C Cover $8.75

GA-40T LES PAUL MODEL
With built-in variable tremolo

Endorsed by leading artists for its thrilling tremolo and brilliant treble. Outstanding in its price range for power and distortion-free sound reproduction, for flexibility and ease of handling.

Features: Handsome case with top-mounted control panel . . . . woven Saran grille cover . . . jeweled pilot light. Tremolo with separate intensity and frequency controls . . . on-off switch in foot pedal. 12-inch Jensen speaker . . . 7 tubes. Two channels . . . separate volume controls for each . . . bass-treble voicing control . . . two inputs for each. Polarity switch eliminates interference. 16 watts output.

22" wide, 20" high, 10½" deep

GA-40T Amplifier **$215.00**
80-C Cover $8.75

22

The 1960 Gibson catalog

GA-30 INVADER
Dual speakers for bigger voice

A wide range of tonal qualities with ample power and a big voice from its two speakers make this the choice of many professionals. Handles three instruments and microphone with ease.

Features: Modern styling with woven Saran grille cover . . . jeweled pilot light. 12″ and 8″ best-quality speakers. 6 tubes . . . 16 watts output. Combination treble and bass voicing control plus tone expanders. 4 input circuits: two for instruments or microphones, two for instruments only . . . separate volume controls for each. Combination polarity switch with off-standby-on positions.

22″ wide, 20″ high, 10⅛″ deep.

GA-30 Amplifier **$195.00**
80-C Cover $8.75

GA-20T RANGER With built-in tremolo
GA-20 CREST

Clear, clean tones and solid undistorted response plus a wonderful built-in tremolo—that's GA-20T, a favorite of professionals and students. Can easily handle three instruments and microphone. GA-20 CREST—same amplifier without tremolo (6 tubes)

Features: Sleek new slant grille, twill-vinyl covering. Maximum high-gain distortion-free tone. Built-in tremolo gives greater variety. 12″ heavy duty speaker . . . 7 tubes. Two channels with separate volume controls and combination bass-treble voicing control . . . two inputs on each channel. Full 16 watt output power.

20″ wide, 16″ high, 9″ deep

GA-20T Amplifier **$189.50**
GA-20 Amplifier **$147.50**
18-C Cover $7.00

GA-18T EXPLORER
With built-in tremolo and tremendous voice

Small in size, but powerful of voice . . . with a tremolo that regulates from extremely fast to a slow wobble. It adds fine tone quality and wide sound range to make it second to none for its size and low price.

Features: Smart new slant grille, lock-corner case. Wide swing tremolo and powerful sound. 10″ heavy duty concert speaker. 5 tubes—2 dual purpose. 3 input jacks . . . 14 watts output. Quick-change controls for volume, tone, depth and frequency of tremolo. Foot control switch for tremolo.

20″ wide, 16½″ high, 9″ deep

GA-18T Amplifier **$149.50**
18-C Cover $7.00

23

The 1960 Gibson catalog

GA-6 LANCER
Light and serviceable

Plenty of power for professional performance and plenty of quality to meet the exacting requirements of discriminating players. Clear, clean, undistorted tone and flexibility.

Features: New styling with slant grille and twill-vinyl covering, lock-joint case. Top quality 12" speaker. 14 watts output . . . 5 tubes. 4 input circuits: two for instruments or microphones, two for instruments only . . . separate volume controls for each. Combination bass and treble control. Two channels.

20" wide, 16" high, 9" deep

GA-6 Amplifier **$135.00**
18-C Cover $7.00

GA-14 TITAN
Compact two-channel model

Powerful response, tonal qualities that are clear and clean, professional performance, top quality materials, and a moderate price make this an outstanding value for the exacting player.

Features: Attractive styling with slant grille and twill-vinyl covering, lock-joint case. 10" heavy duty concert speaker. 14 watts output . . . 5 tubes, 2 dual purpose. Two channels. 4 input circuits: two for instruments or microphones, two for instruments only . . . separate volume controls for each. Combination bass and treble control.

20" wide, 16" high, 9" deep

GA-14 Amplifier **$119.50**
18-C Cover $7.00

GA-88S STEREO-TWIN
Two separating speakers for true stereo sound dispersal

Widest range of tonal effects and greatest versatility! One nested unit separates into bass and treble speakers and control panel . . . enabling the guitarist to create a symphony of warm, full stereophonic sound.

Features: A single compact unit with handsome luggage-style lock-corner case. Two 12" special heavy duty speakers. Removable two-circuit amplifier . . . separate bass, treble, and volume controls for each channel . . . 35 watts output. 8 tubes—3 dual purpose. Polarity switch and ground clip eliminate interference. Stereo, monaural, or two-channel operation.

Closed: 22" high, 23¾" wide, 8¾" deep

GA-88S Amplifier **$450.00**
88-C Cover $10.00
Gadakart $25.00

24

The 1960 Gibson catalog

GA-5 SKYLARK
GA-5T SKYLARK With built-in tremolo

The ideal student amplifier—yet powerful enough for professional use. Light weight, easy to handle, with easily accessible top-mounted control panel. Amazing quality and fine tone reproduction.

Features: Attractive gold covering, new slant grille. ¾" solid wood lock-joint construction. Top-mounted, nickel-plated chassis. Quality 8" speaker. 4½ watts output . . . three tubes. Two instrument inputs.

13½" wide, 13½" high, 7¼" deep

GA-5T Amplifier with tremolo **$79.50**
GA-5 Amplifier **$64.50**
5-C Cover $2.75

GA-8 GIBSONETTE
GA-8T GIBSONETTE With built-in tremolo

Fine tonalities, a powerful voice and a thrifty price make the Gibsonette one of the fastest selling amplifiers on the market—to both amateur and professional guitarists. Sturdy case—lock-joint construction.

Features: Smart new styling with slant grille and gold patterned fabric cover. Lightweight, easy to handle and carry. Top-mounted, nickel-plated chassis. Faithful 10" best-quality speaker. 9 watts output . . . 4 tubes. Separate volume and tone controls. Two instrument inputs.

20" wide, 16" high, 9" deep

GA-8T Amplifier with tremolo **$119.50**
GA-8 Amplifier **$87.50**
18-C Cover $7.00

GA-83S STEREO-VIB
Stereo sound and true vibrato

The most advanced single-cased stereo amplifier with marvelous flexibility for the discriminating player. Five speakers, placed to give full 360° stereo sound, may be used in any combination . . . built-in electronic true vibrato.

Features: Smart luggage-style, lock-corner case. Five heavy duty speakers—four 8" and one 12". 360° stereophonic sound. Two-circuit amplifier . . . separate bass and treble controls for each circuit . . . 35 watts output. 13 tubes—8 dual-purpose. Polarity switch and ground clip eliminate interference. Stereo or monaural operation.

21½" high, 26¼" wide, 10½" deep

GA-83S Amplifier **$425.00**
83-C Cover $10.00
Gadakart $25.00

The 1960 Gibson catalog

for accordions

Made by Gibson . . . these four top quality amplifiers
are designed especially to reproduce and enhance the
"living sound" of the accordion as well as the guitar.
Ideal for the professional accordionist . . . for
the man who plays both instruments . . . and for
the combo or orchestra that includes the accordion.

STEREO MAESTRO
True stereo sound dispersal

One nested unit separates into three component parts to create a symphony of warm, full stereophonic sound. Speakers may be set for as much bass or treble as the player wants. Two 12" special heavy-duty speakers (bass and treble) . . . 8 tubes—3 dual purpose—equaling 11-tube performance . . . three-way operation—stereo, two channel, monaural . . . input jacks . . . 35 watt output. A single, compact, easy-to-carry unit with handsome, luggage-style case . . . 23¾" wide, 22" high, 8¾" deep.

GA-87 Stereo Maestro Amplifier **$450.00**
88-C Cover $10.00
Gadakart $25.00

SUPER MAESTRO

A high gain amplifier with built-in tremolo and powerful, distortion-free sound reproduction for all lower and middle frequency ranges. Finest heavy-duty components assure great reserve power and trouble-free operation. Two 12" twin cone speakers . . . 10 tube chassis . . . 4 input jacks . . . 60 watt output . . . foot pedal "on-off" switch . . . two channels with bass and treble tone controls . . . 3 position "on-off-standby" switch. Remote control outlet. Attractive case equipped with jeweled pilot light . . . 28" wide, 20" high, 10½" deep.

GA-46T Super Maestro Amplifier **$395.00**
400-C Cover $15.00
Gadakart $25.00

MAESTRO STANDARD

A high gain four-speaker amplifier with built-in tremolo . . . engineered to reproduce the full powerful tones of the lower and middle frequency ranges. Free of distortion, plenty of reserve power. Four 8" best-quality speakers . . . 7-tube chassis . . . 16 watt output . . . two channels with two inputs in each channel and separate volume, treble, and bass controls. Foot pedal "on-off" switch. Deluxe modern case . . . 22" wide, 20" high, 10½" deep.

GA-45T Maestro Amplifier **$249.50**
80-C Cover $8.75

MAESTRO VISCOUNT

A full-sized amplifier with powerful voice . . . quick-change controls for volume, tone, depth and frequency of tremolo . . . 10" heavy-duty concert speaker . . . 5 tubes—2 dual purpose—giving 7 tube performance . . . 3 input jacks . . . 14 watt output. Designed for perfect tone reproduction, its full sound range, wide-swing tremolo make this newest Maestro Amplifier the most desirable unit of its size to be found anywhere. Smart new slant grille —20" wide, 16½" high, 9" deep. And the low price makes it truly exceptional.

GA-16T Maestro Viscount Amplifier **$165.00**
18-C Cover $7.00

26

The 1960 Gibson catalog

Flat Top Guitars • JUMBO MODELS

J-200 N

Called "King of the Flat Top Guitars" for its dramatic beauty, booming resonance, and penetrating carrying power . . . built with an extra large tone chamber and many exclusive design features. Very showy in appearance, flawless in workmanship, outstanding in performance.

Features: Finest close-grained spruce top with highly figured curly maple back and rims. Decorative black-and-white ivoroid binding, multiple inlaid purfling rings. Slim, fast, low-action neck—three-piece curly maple with adjustable truss rod. Bound rosewood fingerboard with large pearl inlays. Pearl-inlaid rosewood bridge. Gold-plated enclosed individual machine heads with metal tuning buttons.

17" wide, 21" long, 4⅞" deep
25½" scale, 20 frets

J-200N Natural finish **$410.00**
J-200 Sunburst finish **$395.00**
600 Faultless plush-lined case $53.50
606 Faultless flannel-lined case $42.50
ZC-6 Deluxe zipper case cover $30.00

SJN COUNTRY WESTERN

Country-Western artists have no greater favorite! They praise the SJN's traditional jumbo size and shape, its deep resonance, powerful tone and deluxe appearance, and its Gibson quality.

Features: Top of natural finish selected spruce; back, neck, and matching rims of rich red Honduras mahogany. Handsome multiple white-black-white binding and purfling rings. Slim, fast, low-action neck—one-piece mahogany with adjustable truss rod. Bound rosewood fingerboard with large parallel pearl inlays. Gibson special rosewood bridge. Large tortoise shell finish finger rest and nickel-plated enclosed individual machine heads.

16¼" wide, 20¼" long, 4⅞" deep
24¾" scale, 20 frets

SJN Natural finish top **$179.50**
515 Faultless plush-lined case $47.00
514 Faultless flannel-lined case $42.00
118 Durabilt case **$13.25**
ZC-5 Deluxe zipper case cover $30.00

SJ SOUTHERNER JUMBO

A special favorite with southern balladiers, but preferred by many Country-Western artists, too, especially for its dramatic appearance. The SJ has all the outstanding features, the tonal response, and quality workmanship of the SJN.

Features: Top in a glowing golden sunburst finish with rims, neck, and back in rich red Honduras mahogany. Multiple white-black-white binding and purfling rings. Slim, fast, low-action neck—one-piece mahogany with adjustable truss rod. Bound rosewood fingerboard with large parallel pearl inlays. Gibson special rosewood bridge. Large tortoise shell finish finger rest and nickel-plated enclosed individual machine heads.

16¼" wide, 20¼" long, 4⅞" deep
24¾" scale, 20 frets

SJ Sunburst finish **$165.00**
515 Faultless plush-lined case $47.00
514 Faultless flannel-lined case $42.00
118 Durabilt case $13.25
ZC-5 Deluxe zipper case cover $30.00

32

The 1960 Gibson catalog

ELECTRIC JUMBO MODEL

J-50 Adj.

A popular-priced jumbo guitar with exceptional resonance and response. Made of finest materials, with Gibson proved engineered bracing and construction.

Features: Selected spruce top, Honduras mahogany back and rim, with attractive ivoroid binding and purfling. Slim, fast, low-action neck—one-piece mahogany with adjustable truss rod. Rosewood fingerboard with pearl dot inlays. Gibson special rosewood bridge or adjustable bridge. Tortoise shell finish finger rest. Nickel-plated enclosed machine heads.

Gibson's much-acclaimed adjustable bridge is available with this model at no extra cost. Please specify model J-50 Adj.

16¼" wide, 20¼" long, 4⅞" deep
24¾" scale, 20 frets

J-50 Natural finish top **$145.00**
J-50 Adj. Natural finish top **$145.00**
515 Faultless plush-lined case $47.00
514 Faultless flannel-lined case $42.00
118 Durabilt case $13.25

J-45

Golden sunburst version of the popular jumbo J-50 with the same fine resonance and response, the same superb Gibson quality, the traditional size and shape.

Features: Selected spruce top, Honduras mahogany back and rim, with attractive ivoroid binding and purfling. Slim, fast, low-action neck—one-piece mahogany with adjustable truss rod. Rosewood fingerboard with pearl dot inlays. Gibson special rosewood bridge or adjustable bridge. Tortoise shell finish finger rest. Nickel-plated enclosed machine heads.

Gibson's much-acclaimed adjustable bridge is available with this model at no extra cost. Please specify model J-45 Adj.

16¼" wide, 20¼" long, 4⅞" deep
24¾" scale, 20 frets

J-45 Sunburst finish **$135.00**
J-45 Adj. Sunburst finish **$135.00**
515 Faultless plush-lined case $47.00
514 Faultless flannel-lined case $42.00
118 Durabilt case $13.25

J-160E

Here it is—the popular jumbo flat top that's electric—and the only guitar of its type with the adjustable bridge that gives perfect action plus much more power and sustaining quality to the tone. An exceptional amplified instrument, popular with Country and Western artists.

Features: Finest spruce top, Honduras mahogany back and rim, attractive ivoroid binding and purfling. Slim, fast, low-action neck joins body at the 15th fret for easier playing in the upper register. Bound rosewood fingerboard with large pearl inlays. Adjustable bridge. Compact magnetic pickup with adjustable polepieces. Conveniently located tone and volume controls.

16¼" wide, 20¼" long, 4⅞" deep
24¾" scale, 20 frets

J-160E Sunburst finish **$199.50**
516 Faultless plush-lined case $47.00
119 Durabilt case $13.25

33

The 1960 Gibson catalog

Flat Top Guitars

LG-3   LG-2   LG-1   LG-0

LG-3

A grand concert flat top guitar with rich, mellow tone, extra power and deep resonance . . . more compact and easier to hold than jumbo models. Has a slim, fast, low action one-piece mahogany neck with adjustable truss rod . . . rosewood fingerboard and bridge. Made with specially selected spruce top in natural finish, Honduras mahogany back and rims . . . ivoroid binding and purfling ring, pearl dot inlays, tortoise shell finish finger rest, and nickel-plated enclosed machine heads.

14¼″ wide, 19″ long, 4½″ deep   24¾″ scale, 20 frets

LG-3 Natural finish Top **$115.00**

LG-2
LG-2 3/4

Popular for its rich, deep mahogany finish and golden sunburst top . . . for its mellow, resonant tone . . . for its fine Gibson quality at a modest price. Has slim, fast, low-action one-piece Honduras mahogany neck with adjustable truss rod . . . selected spruce top, rosewood fingerboard and bridge . . . pearl dot inlays, large tortoise shell finish finger rest, and nickel-plated enclosed machine heads.

14¼″ wide, 19″ long, 4½″ deep   24¾″ scale, 20 frets

LG-2 Sunburst finish **$105.00**
LG-2¾ (¾ size) Sunburst finish **$105.00**

LG-1

Top value and low price make this Gibson flat top a popular seller. Quality materials and expert craftsmanship combine to produce its fine responsive tone and rich sunburst finish. Features Gibson's slim, fast, low-action one-piece mahogany neck with adjustable truss rod . . . rosewood fingerboard and bridge. Top is selected spruce, back and rims Honduras mahogany. Attractive trim . . . ivoroid binding and purfling ring, pearl dot inlays, tortoise shell finish finger rest, and nickel-plated enclosed machine heads.

14¼″ wide, 19″ long, 4½″ deep   24¾″ scale, 20 frets

LG-1 Sunburst finish **$95.00**

LG-0

A top seller, favored by students, teachers, strolling players and anyone who wants to have fun with the guitar. Brings you Gibson quality at Gibson's lowest price. Has slim, fast, low action one-piece mahogany neck with adjustable truss rod . . . rosewood fingerboard and bridge . . . full size satin finish mahogany body. The small, narrow neck is easy to finger, the action is easy, the tone full and round with deep base quality.

14¼″ wide, 19″ long, 4½″ deep   24¾″ scale, 20 frets

LG-0 Mahogany finish **$75.00**

Cases for guitars on this page:
415 Faultless plush-lined case $42.00 • 414 Faultless flannel-lined case $37.50 • 117 Durabilt case $12.25 • 117¾ Durabilt case $12.25

34

The 1960 Gibson catalog

Classic GUITARS

C-6 CUSTOM
Richard Pick Model

The finest in classic guitars, developed in co-operation with and named for Richard Pick, the famous American classic guitarist. Choice pretested woods, a scientifically designed tone chamber, a hand sculptured neck, and separate hand-crafted parts help make the custom C-6 the masterpiece it is.

Features: Traditional classic size and shape. Two-piece spruce top with shell trim and rosewood purfling, two-piece rosewood back and rims. Three-piece mahogany neck joining body at the 12th fret. Rosewood facing on peghead. Ebony fingerboard of classic width with smooth nickel-silver frets (extra low and wide), rosewood bridge and special combination open fret and string spacer nut. Gold finish machine heads, finest quality nylon strings, lightweight construction.

14¼" wide, 19" long, 4½" deep   25½" scale, 19 frets

C-6 Natural finish top **$325.00**
415 Faultless plush-lined case $42.00
414 Faultless flannel-lined case $37.50
117 Durabilt case $12.25

C-2

Gibson's answer to the demand for a fine classic guitar in the middle price range is this superb instrument with all the classic features, easy playing action, richness of tone, and beauty expected only in a custom model.

Features: Selected two-piece spruce top in natural finish with inlaid purfling rings, two-piece maple back and rims. One-piece mahogany neck of full classic width joining the body at the 12th fret. Rosewood fingerboard, slotted peghead with engraved nickel-plated machine head and large string posts. Rosewood bridge with bone saddle, and special combination open fret and string spacer nut. Nylon strings and lightweight construction.

14¼" wide, 19" long, 4" deep   25½" scale, 19 frets

C-2 Natural spruce top **$195.00**
415 Faultless plush-lined case $42.00
414 Faultless flannel-lined case $37.50
117 Durabilt case $12.25

C-1

Here are the traditional classic features, lightweight construction, easy playing action, and clear resonant tone of top finger-style guitars at an unusually low price. Ideal for playing classics or folk music . . . for country-westerns, ballads, Spanish rondos, or calypso strumming!

Features: Two-piece natural-finish spruce top, two-piece Honduras mahogany back and rims. One-piece mahogany neck of full classic width joining body at the 12th fret. Rosewood fingerboard, slotted peghead with engraved nickel-plated machine heads and large string posts. Rosewood bridge with bone saddle and special combination open fret and string spacer nut. Fine quality nylon strings.

14¼" wide, 19" long, 4½" deep   25½" scale, 19 frets

C-1 Natural spruce top **$110.00**
415 Faultless plush-lined case $42.00
414 Faultless flannel-lined case $37.50
117 Durabilt case $12.25

35

The 1960 Gibson catalog

Acoustic Guitars.

Super 400 C

SUPER 400 C

A superlative instrument, flawless in appearance and performance. Designed with carved top and back in modern cutaway style, its rare beauty, response, and magical tone are the fruits of Gibson's expert craftsmanship.

Features: Carved top of finest close-grained spruce, and carved back of highly figured curly maple with matching rims and white-black-white ivoroid binding. Slim, fast, low-action, three-piece curly maple neck with adjustable truss rod. Ebony fingerboard and peghead with large pearl inlays. Rosewood adjustable bridge. Exclusive Super 400 adjustable tailpiece. Gold-plated metal parts and Sealfast individual machine heads with metal buttons.

18" wide, 21¾" long, 3⅜" deep . . .
25½" scale, 20 frets

Super 400CN Natural finish **$675.00**
Super 400C Sunburst finish **$650.00**
400 Faultless plush-lined case $60.00
ZC-4 Deluxe zipper case cover $35.00

L-5CN

The L-5 has held its enviable position as an exceedingly popular orchestra guitar for many years . . . a wonderfully rich tone, easy playing action, and beautiful cutaway styling are among the reasons.

Features: Carved top of finest close-grained spruce, carved back of highly figured curly maple with matching rims, and white-black-white ivoroid binding. Slim, fast, low-action, three-piece curly maple neck with adjustable truss rod. Ebony fingerboard with black pearl inlays. Rosewood adjustable bridge. Hand bound pickguard. Exclusive adjustable tailpiece. Gold-plated metal parts and Sealfast individual machine heads with metal buttons.

17" wide, 21" long, 3⅜" deep . . .
25½" scale, 20 frets

L-5CN Natural finish **$580.00**
L-5C Sunburst finish **$565.00**
600 Faultless plush-lined case $53.50
606 Faultless, flannel-lined case $42.50
ZC-6 Deluxe zipper case cover $30.00

L-5CN

L-5 CT Thin Body Cutaway

Developed expressly for George Gobel with the same fine features as L-5CN . . . plus thinner body in gleaming cherry-red finish.

17" wide, 21" long, 2⅜" thin . . .
24¾" scale, 20 frets

L-5CT Cherry finish **$565.00**
603 Faultless plush-lined case $53.50
ZC-6 Deluxe zipper case cover $30.00

37

The 1960 Gibson catalog

Acoustic Guitars — CARVED TOP MODELS

L-7C

Extremely popular for orchestra use for its modern cutaway design, handsome appearance, exclusive features, and rich vibrant tone . . . an outstanding example of Gibson superior quality.

Features: Hand-graduated carved top of selected spruce, arched curly maple back and matching rims, attractive white-black-white ivoroid bindings. Slim, fast, low-action neck—three-piece curly maple with adjustable truss rod. Rosewood fingerboard, pearl inlays. Rosewood adjustable bridge. Special Gibson tailpiece. Nickel-plated metal parts, and enclosed individual machine heads with deluxe buttons.

17″ wide, 21″ long, 3⅜″ deep . . . 25½″ scale, 20 frets

L-7C Sunburst finish **$285.00**
600 Faultless, plush-lined case $53.50
606 Faultless, flannel-lined case $42.50
609 Durabilt case $20.25

L-4CN

Designed for easy playing . . . the compact size, medium scale length, and Florentine cutaway styling permit faster action throughout the entire range. Top quality materials, expert workmanship, and rich resonant tone.

Features: Hand-graduated carved top of selected spruce, arched maple back with matching rims, attractive white-black-white ivoroid binding. Slim, fast, low-action neck—one-piece mahogany with adjustable truss rod. Rosewood fingerboard with inlay design. Rosewood adjustable bridge. Nickel-plated metal parts, and enclosed individual machine heads with deluxe buttons.

16¼″ wide, 20¼″ long, 3⅜″ deep . . . 24¾″ scale, 20 frets

L-4CN Natural finish **$240.00**
L-4C Sunburst finish **$225.00**
515 Faultless, plush-lined case $47.00
514 Faultless, flannel-lined case $42.00
103 Durabilt case $13.25

L-50

A notable guitar! Proud owners boast of the L-50's brilliant response, fast easy-playing action, beautiful appearance and value . . . all the result of selected quality materials, expert workmanship, and the many famous Gibson features offered in this instrument.

Features: Hand-graduated carved top of selected spruce, arched maple back with matching rims, attractive ivoroid binding. Slim, fast, low-action neck—one-piece mahogany with adjustable truss rod. Rosewood fingerboard with large pearl inlays. Rosewood adjustable bridge. Nickel-plated metal parts, and enclosed individual machine heads with white buttons.

16¼″ wide, 20¼″ long, 3⅜″ deep . . . 24¾″ scale, 20 frets

L-50 Sunburst finish **$157.50**
515 Faultless, plush-lined case $47.00
514 Faultless, flannel-lined case $42.00
103 Durabilt case $13.25

38

The 1960 Gibson catalog

203

L-48

One of Gibson's best-selling acoustic guitars—for its rich tone, easy playing action, attractive appearance, sturdy construction and outstanding value. The popular-priced L-48 is ideal for the student guitarist.

Features: Arched laminated mahogany top for strength, matching mahogany rims, arched laminated maple back, and attractive ivoroid binding. Slim, fast, comfortable low-action neck—one-piece mahogany with adjustable truss rod. Rosewood fingerboard with pearl dot inlays. Rosewood adjustable bridge. Tortoise shell finish pick-guard. Nickel-plated metal parts and enclosed machine heads.

16¼" wide, 20¼" long, 3⅜" deep . . . 24¾" scale, 20 frets

L-48 Sunburst finish **$127.50**
515 Faultless, plush-lined case $47.00
514 Faultless, flannel-lined case $42.00
103 Durabilt case $13.25

ETG-150
TG-50

The top choice of guitarists who prefer a four-string tenor style on an amplified instrument. The Gibson ETG-150 is outstanding in performance and appearance, offering a clean, clear lovely tenor tone. TG-50 is acoustic model with same features.

Features: Arched maple top and back with mahogany rims, ivoroid binding. Slim, fast, low-action neck—one-piece mahogany with adjustable truss rod. Rosewood fingerboard with pearl dot inlays. Adjustable rosewood bridge. Powerful humbucking pickup with individual adjustable polepieces and separate tone and volume controls. Nickel-plated tailpiece and metal parts.

16¼" wide, 20¼" long, 3⅜" deep . . . 22¾" scale, 19 frets

ETG-150 Sunburst finish **$210.00**
TG-50 Sunburst finish **$160.00**
515 Faultless, plush-lined case $47.00
514 Faultless, flannel-lined case $42.00
103 Durabilt case $13.25

TG-O

This four-string flat top tenor guitar is the same in size and features as the LG-O but with a four-string tenor neck. It's the perfect answer to the player who wants to step up from the ukulele—tenor or baritone—to the four-string guitar. The TG-O may be played as a tenor guitar or with ukulele tuning—for soloing or voice accompaniment. It has Gibson's famous slim neck, easy fingering, and fast action plus a fine, full round tone. TG-OB has baritone tuning.

Features: Full size satin finish mahogany body. Slim, fast, low-action one-piece mahogany neck with adjustable truss rod. Rosewood fingerboard and bridge. Beveled pickguard. Gibson Mona steel strings.

16½" wide, 20¼" long, 3⅜" deep . . . 22¾" scale, 19 frets

TG-O Mahogany finish **$75.00**
TG-OB Mahogany finish **$75.00**
117 Durabilt case $12.25

39

The 1960 Gibson catalog

F-5 ARTIST

There is no finer design than is represented in the Gibson F-5 Artist Model Mandolin. Gibson craftsmen produced this superb instrument with its clear tone and its unsurpassed rich cremona brown finish with beautiful golden sunburst shading on top, back, rims and neck.

Features: Artist style body and peghead design. Hand graduated carved top of finest selected air-seasoned spruce. Highly figured curly maple back with matching curly maple rims. Alternate white-black-white ivoroid binding. Curly maple neck with adjustable truss rod. Bound ebony fingerboard with block pearl inlays. Gold plated metal parts, engraved tailpiece, enclosed machine heads with pearloid buttons, adjustable rosewood bridge, and raised finger-rest.

10" wide, 13¾" long, 1¾" deep . . . 13⅞" scale, 29 frets

F-5 Sunburst finish **$550.00**
371 Faultless plush-lined case $37.50
440 Faultless plush-lined oblong case $48.00

F-12 ARTIST

The Gibson F-12 Artist Mandolin is recognized as one of the world's finest. Its design and quality materials have made it a masterpiece among string instruments.

Features: Artist style body and peghead design. Hand graduated carved top of selected spruce. Highly figured curly maple carved back with matching curly maple rims. Ivoroid binding. Curly maple neck with adjustable truss rod. Bound rosewood fingerboard with pearl dot inlays. Gold plated metal parts and fittings, engraved tailpiece, enclosed machine heads with pearloid buttons, adjustable rosewood bridge, and raised laminated finger-rest with attractive border.

10" wide, 13¾" long, 1¾" deep . . . 13⅞" scale, 24 frets

F-12 Sunburst finish **$395.00**
371 Faultless plush-lined case $37.50
440 Faultless plush-lined oblong case $48.00

A-5 FLORENTINE

A new Gibson Florentine Mandolin with the traditional oval sound hole. Acoustically engineered to produce brilliant, full-bodied tone.

Features: Rich red mahogany finish on rims, back, and neck with golden sunburst top. Ivoroid binding, including the sound hole, with multiple ivoroid purfling. Hand graduated carved top of select spruce, with carved curly maple back and matching rims. Mahogany neck with adjustable truss rod. Bound rosewood fingerboard with pearl dot inlays. Nickelplated metal parts, engraved tailpiece, enclosed machine heads with pearloid buttons, adjustable rosewood bridge and raised, laminated finger-rest with attractive border.

9⅞" wide, 12¾" long, 1¾" deep . . . 13⅞" scale, 24 frets

A-5 Golden sunburst finish **$275.00**
440 Faultless plush-lined oblong case $48.00

40

The 1960 Gibson catalog

EM-200 FLORENTINE ELECTRIC

A solid body electric mandolin with full 24 fret range. Grace-fully styled of solid Honduras mahogany with carved top and contrasting white ivoroid trim.

Features: Slim mahogany neck with adjustable truss rod. Bound, rosewood fingerboard with pearl dot inlays. Artistic scrolled peg-head with distinctive pearl inlays. Special combination, adjustable bridge with rosewood base and gold-plated saddle. Gold-plated metal parts, enclosed machine heads with pearloid buttons and engraved tailpiece. Laminated pickguard with white-black-white border. Powerful, magnetic pickup with adjustable polepiece spe-cially engineered and located to reproduce mandolin tonal quality. Separate volume and tone controls. Attractive sunburst finish.

9⅜" wide, 12½" long, 1¾" deep . . . 13⅜" scale, 24 frets

EM200 Sunburst finish **$225.00**
440 Faultless plush-lined oblong case $48.00

EM-150 ELECTRIC

An amplified mandolin, the EM-150 combines quality parts, Gibson workmanship, the latest features of electronic ampli-fication, easy playing action, and strikingly beautiful appear-ance with its Golden sunburst finish.

Features: Carved spruce top, arched maple back and matching maple rims. Contrasting ivoroid binding. Slim mahogany neck with Gibson adjustable truss rod. Bound rosewood fingerboard with pearl dot inlays. Powerful pickup with Alnico magnets and adjust-able polepieces. Separate tone and volume control. Enclosed ma-chine heads and nickel-plated metal parts. Laminated pickguard with white-black-white border.

10¼" wide, 13½" long, 1¾" deep . . . 13⅞" scale, 20 frets

EM-150 Sunburst finish **$195.00**
362 Faultless flannel-lined case $33.00
101 Durabilt case $9.50

EM-200   EM-150

A-50

The A-50 mandolin features superior quality and expert crafts-manship at a moderate price. This beautiful sunburst instrument is acoustically engineered to produce strong bell-like tones.

Features: Carved spruce top with curly maple arched back and curly maple rims. Attractive ivoroid binding. Mahogany neck with adjustable truss rod. Rosewood fingerboard with pearl dot inlays. Nickel plated tailpiece and enclosed machine heads, adjustable rosewood bridge, and laminated finger-rest with attractive border.

10¼" wide, 13½" long, 1¾" deep . . . 13⅞" scale, 20 frets

A-50 Sunburst finish **$145.00**
362 Faultless flannel-lined case $33.00
101 Durabilt case $9.50

A-40

The A-40 mandolin combines the usual famous Gibson features of quality materials and workmanship. Has a clear, powerful tone and beautiful finish.

Features: Carved spruce top, arched mahogany back with ma-hogany rims. Ivoroid top binding. Mahogany neck with adjustable truss rod construction. Rosewood fingerboard with pearl dot inlays. Nickel plated tailpiece and enclosed machine heads, adjustable rosewood bridge, and shell finger-rest.

10¼" wide, 13½" long, 1¾" deep . . . 13⅞" scale, 20 frets

A-40 Sunburst finish **$112.50**
A-40N Natural finish **$112.50**
362 Faultless flannel-lined case $33.00
101 Durabilt case $9.50

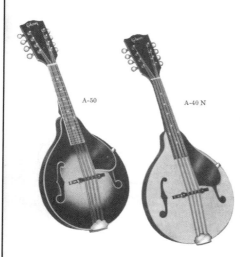

A-50   A-40 N

41

The 1960 Gibson catalog

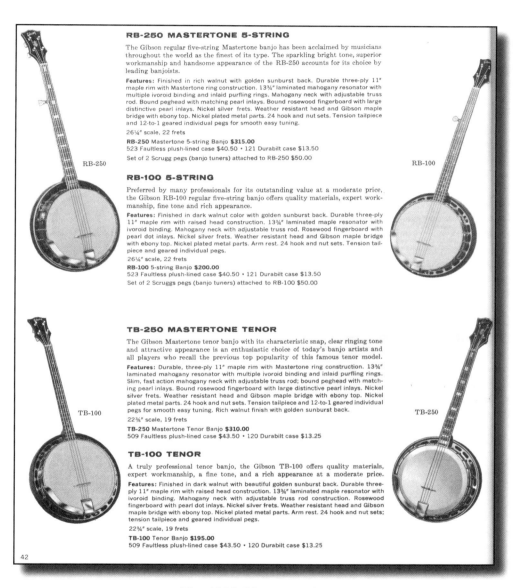

RB-250 MASTERTONE 5-STRING

The Gibson regular five-string Mastertone banjo has been acclaimed by musicians throughout the world as the finest of its type. The sparkling bright tone, superior workmanship and handsome appearance of the RB-250 accounts for its choice by leading banjoists.

Features: Finished in rich walnut with golden sunburst back. Durable three-ply 11" maple rim with Mastertone ring construction. 13¾" laminated mahogany resonator with multiple ivoroid binding and inlaid purfling rings. Mahogany neck with adjustable truss rod. Bound peghead with matching pearl inlays. Bound rosewood fingerboard with large distinctive pearl inlays. Nickel silver frets. Weather resistant head and Gibson maple bridge with ebony top. Nickel plated metal parts. 24 hook and nut sets. Tension tailpiece and 12-to-1 geared individual pegs for smooth easy tuning.

26¼" scale, 22 frets

RB-250 Mastertone 5-string Banjo **$315.00**
523 Faultless plush-lined case $40.50 • 121 Durabilt case $13.50
Set of 2 Scrugg pegs (banjo tuners) attached to RB-250 $50.00

RB-100 5-STRING

Preferred by many professionals for its outstanding value at a moderate price, the Gibson RB-100 regular five-string banjo offers quality materials, expert workmanship, fine tone and rich appearance.

Features: Finished in dark walnut color with golden sunburst back. Durable three-ply 11" maple rim with raised head construction. 13¾" laminated maple resonator with ivoroid binding. Mahogany neck with adjustable truss rod. Rosewood fingerboard with pearl dot inlays. Nickel silver frets. Weather resistant head and Gibson maple bridge with ebony top. Nickel plated metal parts. Arm rest. 24 hook and nut sets. Tension tailpiece and geared individual pegs.

26¼" scale, 22 frets

RB-100 5-string Banjo **$200.00**
523 Faultless plush-lined case $40.50 • 121 Durabilt case $13.50
Set of 2 Scruggs pegs (banjo tuners) attached to RB-100 $50.00

TB-250 MASTERTONE TENOR

The Gibson Mastertone tenor banjo with its characteristic snap, clear ringing tone and attractive appearance is an enthusiastic choice of today's banjo artists and all players who recall the previous top popularity of this famous tenor model.

Features: Durable, three-ply 11" maple rim with Mastertone ring construction. 13¾" laminated mahogany resonator with multiple ivoroid binding and inlaid purfling rings. Slim, fast action mahogany neck with adjustable truss rod; bound peghead with matching pearl inlays. Bound rosewood fingerboard with large distinctive pearl inlays. Nickel silver frets. Weather resistant head and Gibson maple bridge with ebony top. Nickel plated metal parts. 24 hook and nut sets. Tension tailpiece and 12-to-1 geared individual pegs for smooth easy tuning. Rich walnut finish with golden sunburst back.

22¾" scale, 19 frets

TB-250 Mastertone Tenor Banjo **$310.00**
509 Faultless plush-lined case $43.50 • 120 Durabilt case $13.25

TB-100 TENOR

A truly professional tenor banjo, the Gibson TB-100 offers quality materials, expert workmanship, a fine tone, and a rich appearance at a moderate price.

Features: Finished in dark walnut with beautiful golden sunburst back. Durable three-ply 11" maple rim with raised head construction. 13¾" laminated maple resonator with ivoroid binding. Mahogany neck with adjustable truss rod construction. Rosewood fingerboard with pearl dot inlays. Nickel silver frets. Weather resistant head and Gibson maple bridge with ebony top. Nickel plated metal parts. Arm rest. 24 hook and nut sets; tension tailpiece and geared individual pegs.

22¾" scale, 19 frets

TB-100 Tenor Banjo **$195.00**
509 Faultless plush-lined case $43.50 • 120 Durabilt case $13.25

RB-250

RB-100

TB-100

TB-250

42

The 1960 Gibson catalog

how to play the guitar. There would therefore be no particular reason to allow a person to build their own 'employee guitar.']

Even though Gibson is known for its woodworkers, it doesn't appear that Gibson ever tried to recruit woodworkers? *I don't know if they ever combed the area for somebody that worked in wood. They probably just interviewed them.*

You received many promotions during your tenure with Gibson moving all the way up to staff head of quality control. Why do you think they promoted you? What qualities did you have? *One was that I was always digging in, working hard. The quality of work that I put out was a factor, and when I was building mandolins in the 1950s they measured you by how many you could put out in a certain amount of time and still have great quality. I liked to talk with the old timers and find out how they did things. Then I would try the same thing out to see how it worked. I was able to rediscover things that had been lost and we put those things back into production.*

It seems like Gibson had a very little turnover. *People seemed to stay at Gibson. Once in awhile, a person would leave Gibson, and they would come back. Most of the people stayed.*

John Huis was a key person at Gibson. Many people have confirmed this. What do you remember about John Huis? *He was Ted McCarty's No. 1 man. John was very straight in what he did. He was serious. To me it seemed like he was more serious (than other people). I had to call John Huis one time. I was upstairs (customs department supervisor) and one of the fellows had an air hose and he was shooting paper wads with this air hose. And the paper wads would sting. And he was at the top of the stairs and he stung this guy when he came up the stairs. So they were having quite an argument and I said come on in the office. We got in the office and one fellow told the other, he said, 'Now we're both going outside and only one of us is coming back.' And the other fellow, he's a minister now, said the same thing. So I said, 'Lower your voices in my office, and don't talk loud.' So we talked a little more and I reached over and picked up the phone. I called John, the Superintendent, and asked him to come up. And John came up and they said the same thing. I told John what the one fellow said and that the other fellow said the same thing. So John said, 'Now neither one of you are going out the door, and you are both going back to work, and you're not going to ever speak to one another anymore. And you're going to do your job.' 'Now', John said, 'Get back to work.' And that was the last trouble they had. John was very straight forward.*

How about Ted McCarty compared to John Huis? *Now Ted was softer. Ted would do what he said, but he wouldn't be like John. Ted was a better communicator. That was one of his skills.*

Some employees have talked about 'piece rate' and quotas. *In November of each year, we had what was called 'John Huis Day.' John was Vice President. The work force was put on a piece rate. The highest piece rate bonus ever paid at Gibson was in our Custom Department. All 73 employees received a $100 bonus for this one week's work.*

Interview 9
Maxine Vette (1955–'70)

Where did you work at Gibson? *When I was first there, I changed jobs. I worked for Larry Allers in wood work. Then I worked in the machine shop, but it was too dirty down there. Then I worked up in electronics. It was cleaner up there. I soldered the harnesses, upstairs in the old building.*

Where did you live? *Lawton, Michigan (20 miles southwest of Kalamazoo).*

Did you know Mr. McCarty? *Yes, I'd see him when he came around the plant.*

Interview 10
Vi Bradford (1952 - 1982)

Viola (Vi) Bradford's background is a bit different in that she didn't come from Kalamazoo. Many people that hired into Gibson in the 1940s and 1950s were from Kalamazoo. Many lived on the north end of Kalamazoo near 225 Parsons Street.

Other well-known names, like J.P. Moats and Marv Lamb did migrate from the south. Like Vi, they found a good paying job in prosperous Kalamazoo.

How did you get to Gibson? *Vi Bradford: I graduated from England High School, in 1950, down south in England, Arkansas. I worked for two years for the Timex watches/U.S. Times Company in Little Rock. I worked in the Timex factory making watch parts. I just applied out of high school and I had a cousin that worked there who helped me.*

How did you get to Michigan? *I came to Pontiac, Michigan on a two weeks vacation. Through a friend I met my husband, and I never went back to Arkansas. Six months later we were married (at the time of the interview they marked their 48th wedding Anniversary). He worked at International Paper in Kalamazoo. That's the International Paper Company on Sprinkle and Miller Road on the southwest side of Kalamazoo. He worked at Gibson briefly. He left that job and went to work for Eaton, on Mosel Avenue, and he retired from that job.*

How did you get to Gibson? *I worked at Jolly Kid Togs children's wear. I worked there for about two years. I didn't even know about Gibson. A friend of my husband's at Eaton told my husband that Gibson was hiring.*

How were you hired? *A guy by the name of Clarence Coleman hired me. I went to the factory and went in the front door. They sent me to the guard shack. Dale Humphrey was the guard on duty and Clarence Coleman came out to the guard shack. I filled out an application, and he took me out to the plant and showed me around. He hired me right then. It was a courtesy thing, to take me out to the plant. He wanted me to start working the next day, but I finished the week out at Jolly Kid. At that time, the foreman could hire people. That stopped shortly after that. After 1955, the hiring process had to go through the front office.*

How was the starting pay? *$1.65 an hour was my starting pay. At the time, my husband was making $1.85 an hour at Eaton. I was making $0.85 an hour at Jolly Kid. $1.65 was indicative of industrial pay in the city. It was a benefit to go from office work into the factory because I could double my pay.*

Many employees that I've talked to lived close to the plant. *We were living out at Osthemo, Michigan, a little place outside of Kalamazoo. My husband dropped me off to work. The hours were 7 a.m to 3:20 p.m, with lunch from 12:00 to 12:30. Gibson was just running one shift. (Note: The Gibson first shift hours were very typical for Michigan business. Some companies started their first shifts at 6 a.m or 6:30 a.m. Michigan second shifts would start about 3 p.m. allowing for some cross-coordination between shifts. Most Michigan employees very much enjoyed having first shift start and end early, allowing them to have some daylight to do things after work.)*

What was your first job? *They started me hand sanding. That was in the back of first floor. You'd pass by the guard shack at the truck entrance, go through the side door, and walk straight back to the row of windows at the back. They did away with the north end windows when they expanded in 1960. I was at a work bench. There were about six dry sanders. They were all women. It used to make me mad, the men doing the same job as you, were paid more. Not much more, $.05 an hour, but $.05 was a lot back then.*

How did you get your training? *The boss showed me how to dry sand. He just showed me. He stopped by quite a bit to see how I was doing. I sanded all different types of instruments, mandolins, guitars, solid-body guitars, flat tops. All sanding went through our department including banjo rims and banjo necks. When you are dry sanding the technique is pretty much the same.*

Did you join the union right away? *I worked 30 days. You had to work out your trial period. Then everyone had to join the union. The union dues were not much, maybe $3 a month in the mid 1950s.*

What was your next assignment? *I went to belt sanding which was a man's job and I got a man's pay. It was posted and I applied for it. My boss, Clarence Coleman, put pressure on me to apply for the posting. He said that men's hands were too heavy and they sanded through the tops of the instruments. I wasn't in dry sanding too long, about three months. I was in belt sanding for 8 years. I didn't like hand sanding. I hated it. Some of the girls were on hand sanding for many, many years, but not me, I hated it. In 1957, I had a baby, my son Mike was born. I went back to work after six months, but I lost seniority because you couldn't retain your seniority back then.*

You belt sanded all types of instruments? *All guitars got belt sanded. The mandolins did not. Archtops were belt sanded but they were a challenge. There were three belt sanders, then only two when Gibson started cutting down. We sanded the guitars before they put the neck in. A different department did the necks. We did rough sanding, then the top of the instrument, then they would dry sand, and then we would do fine sanding. Hand sanding was done when the neck was on and the instrument was all put together.*

What happened in the 1960s? *I stopped belt sanding in June of 1962, when my son Mike was 5 years old. I was pregnant again. I took a leave of absence. When I returned, November, 1962, I went back to the belt sander. My supervisor was still Clarence Coleman. In 1960, we left the location at the rear of the first floor and we went out into to the new plant. The department was kind of in the middle of the plant. Clarence Coleman was the full time supervisor because he had a huge department. He had belt sanders, hand sanders, binders, and rim benders. We were all together in the plant. [Note: Coleman was also associated with the body building in the Custom Department on the third floor.]*

A lot of Gibson women left work to have a baby and raise a family. You did that too. *When I came back to work after my first son was born there was no opening on the belt sander. They weren't required to take me back, but my foreman, Clarence Coleman gave me a good recommendation. Gibson had to take me back (new union rule in place by 1963) after my second son was born. They had to take me back but they didn't have an opening on the belt sander.*

What was your next job? *Shortly after I came back in 1962 I went over to the machine shop, where they made the bridges, truss rods, and truss rod covers. I ran the screw-machine and a punch press. Wait was the foreman. I didn't mind the work. The screw machine was the dirtiest job (machine oil) in the department. They would rotate us on that. The screw machine made just truss rods; we cut them and put the threads on them. The machine shop was in the basement of the old building along the railroad tracks (northeast side). There were windows that were near the ground. I didn't mind it over there. It was cleaner than belt sanding, other than the screw machine. I was there for about a year and then I went to electronics in 1965.*

Why electronics? *There was an opening and it was so much cleaner in electronics. Henry Penning was the supervisor. In the early 1960s the electronics room was on the third floor of the old building, but the electronics room moved over to a separate building (in 1962 Plant II and then again in 1964 Plant III). Amps and all the electrical parts were there.*

Did you know Ted McCarty and John Huis? *Ted McCarty and John Huis came through the plant quite often. I talked with Ted McCarty a lot of times. He was a nice guy. Usually it was, 'How are things going?' I never made a complaint. Ted was a little nicer than John. John was more serious. John came through by himself a lot. Ted always seemed to be in a good mood. I don't remember seeing him in a really bad mood.*

Who else from management came into the plant? *Bellson would come into the plant too. He would stop and talk with the people. He was the personnel man. Wilbur Marker, I didn't see him too much. Larry Allers, I'd talked to him. When I first went to the machine shop, he was over the machine shop. I think he went to engineering. Then Jim Deurloo took over; he's a nice guy.*

What did you do for lunch at Gibson? *In the 1950s, I'd go down to (Bill's) little café down at the corner of Parsons Street. It was across from the church. I'd have lunch down there. The Gibson cafeteria, when they had it, was on the second floor. They served mostly sandwiches.*

Did you ever get a disciplinary 'blue slip'? *I never got a 'blue slip.' If a person got too many 'blue slips' they would be fired.*

When the new factory was built, what did you do? *When the new factory was built (the last expansion of 1965) I was in electronics. I made pick-ups, controls, and terminal boards. It was a cleaner place to work; it was clean and quiet. I posted for that job and got it.*

Several employees have said to me that they participated in the two strikes. Did you? *The second strike I walked the picket line. Gibson didn't want to give us a pay raise, or health insurance. We had health insurance but we wanted better. The strike wasn't long, one or two weeks.*

You worked at Gibson during the glory days of the 1950s on through to the 1980s. What happened to Gibson? *At first, in the 1950s, Gibson was kind of small, and everybody knew everybody else, and it was kind of like family. But then it got so big – you just went and did your job. But I never thought about leaving Gibson. But even in the 1950s Gibson wasn't for everybody. A girl I worked with at Jolly Kids – I recommended Gibson to her, but she didn't last very long. I think she had always worked in the office. At Gibson she missed getting dressed up and going into the office. I didn't mind the factory work. I like factory work better than I did the office work, and oh yes, the factory always paid better.*

You and others have told me about the jobs for women and the jobs for men. *In the early years, men and only men did the routing, bending, necks, and binding. The wood shop was all men; they made the necks. It was a hard, dangerous job. You could lose a finger easily. My husband was a fiddler (refer Green Valley Boys) and he worked in the Gibson woodshop for a while. And he looked around and saw the missing fingers and he quit. That was before we were married. He worked there about two weeks.*

I've heard from others that the north side of Kalamazoo where Gibson and the other factories were located started to become a 'rough neighborhood.' What do you remember about that? *Even when in the mid 1950s, it was kind of a rough neighborhood. My husband took me to work my whole career. I never had any trouble but I knew to be careful. Sometimes the windows would be broken in the factory from people throwing stones.*

Interview 11
Marv Lamb (1956 - 1984)

Marv Lamb is a co-founder and co-owner of Heritage Guitars, Kalamazoo, Michigan. Heritage guitars are built at 225 Parsons Street, utilizing the basement and third floor of 'the old building.'   Heritage still uses some fixtures and machines that were used by Gibson. Heritage uses the same third floor spray booths as used by Gibson and the Gibson Customs Department. The two other founders of Heritage, J.P. Moats and Jim Deurloo, were also interviewed. Lamb, Moats, and Deurloo all hired-in Gibson within two years of each other. They all started in white wood sanding. They all progressed to positions of senior management in the 1970s.

Take me from your high school days to going to Gibson. *My father worked at Gibson. I was working at a bakery in Kalamazoo in 1956. He started at Gibson in January, and I got him to get me a job. I'd come right from the South. I came from Huntsville, Alabama, that was my home. My family had a big cotton farm down south. My folks farmed the final crop and then they sold out. I was the youngest child in the family. I was the last one to leave, and when I left, well they said, 'Well, we're going north too.'*

How did your dad decide on Kalamazoo? *I had a brother and a sister living here. They had been working in Detroit at a bakery. The company had a bakery in Detroit and Kalamazoo and my brother-in-law got transferred to Kalamazoo. My brother came up from the south and went to work for the bakery, and when I got out of school I came up to work for the bakery. So that's how we got here. I had two other sisters that lived in Detroit. We grew up on a farm, and you know how 'you want to get away from the farm', you know how that is (laughing). And then my dad came up and went to work for Gibson. Gibson was the first place that he got into. And I told him to get me a job at Gibson. And that's how I started.*

Why did he choose Gibson, instead of Kalamazoo Reel, or one of the paper plants, or some of the other places? *He knew a gentleman that worked there. That was a guy by the name of Bob Parsons. Bob Parsons worked there and he told my dad that Gibson was hiring; Gibson was going to hire some people. So my dad kept going to Gibson every morning and asked if there was anything open. Finally Gibson realized that he wanted a job, so they took him in.*

Did he talk with anybody, or did he just talk with the guard shack? *He talked with the guard shack. Dale Humphrey was the gentleman's name, the guard at the guard shack. Julius Bellson was the personnel manager. Dad probably went to see Julius or John Huis.*

What was the first job your dad started on? *Dad started working in the lumber yard (seniority date February 14, 1956). That is where they cut the lumber in the 'rough mill.'*

Was that because that was the position that was available? *That was the position that was available, yes sir.*

Then what positions did he work? *He ended up being an assistant millwright; he got into the maintenance department. He got hurt, he had a heart attack, he came out of it fine, but he was about 60 years old and he retired on a disability. He worked there about 16 or 17 years so that was about 1970.*

Your dad suggested that you come over to Gibson? *Yeah. I was working nightshift at the bakery. And at a bakery you'd never know what hours you'd work. I selected the bakery because my brother-in-law was working there. He'd been transferred there out of Detroit. And my brother was working at the bakery too. They got me a job. That was just when I got out of school and I came north.*

Your dad said, 'Hey, Gibson is pretty good'? *Yeah, and I wanted a day job. I wanted to know when I'm going to work and when I'm getting off. So that was pretty well the reason I came to Gibson.*

Then did you go to the guard shack too (to apply for a job)? *No. My dad talked to one of the foreman, a guy by the name of Clarence Coleman. He got me down there and interviewed me. He called me down and talked to me because my dad had told him that he had a son that wanted a job. I probably went out to talk with him and then made the application out.*

Did he Clarence Coleman let you tour the work area? *I think we toured it and then they hired me.*

Then did you come in to work at Gibson the next day? *I'll tell you what I did. The bakery works on holidays, so I think I worked 16 hours at the bakery on Memorial Day and I started to work at Gibson the next day, May 31, 1956.*

Where did they start you out? *Clarence had the guitar bodies, the work after the mill but prior to finishing, and yeah, that's where I started out in hand sanding.*

Was there a 'leader' in that department? *Yes, a guy by the name of Tom Fries (seniority date August 2, 1950) or George Merica one of those two guys. They were both leaders while I worked on the hand line. Gibson was starting to boom about that time. I believe George Merica was the line leader, and when he left, Tom Frieves took over. Then George went over into the tool crib making sanding belts and things like that. Clarence Coleman was the foreman.*

Was there a general foreman, or did Clarence Coleman report directly to John Huis? *There was an assistant superintendent. That was Larry Allers. And Larry reported directly to John Huis.*

It may depend on what year we're talking about, but I have heard about Larry Allers being called the (chief) engineer. *Yes, he was also put in charge of engineering. When I went there in 1956 he was the assistant plant superintendent. John Huis was a very nice guy. We had more dealing with those two guys, Larry Allers and John Huis, than we did with Ted McCarty.*

When you first hired in where did you live relative to the plant? *I lived on the south side of Kalamazoo over in the Washington Square area. I drove to work, and if you timed all the red lights, I could probably be to work in five or six minutes. It wasn't very far. At the time I wasn't married, in the early years when I started there. My mother and father and I had an apartment on Portage Street. I and my dad drove in together a lot. After I got married I moved on a little side street right off Portage Street, and my wife and I raised our two kids there.*

Did your wife work? *She did not at first. She went to work in 1966 for Kalamazoo Gas & Light, or Humphrey Products. That was factory work. It was located on the south side of Kalamazoo. She could be to work in ten minutes. It took me five or six minutes going north and she would go south for ten minutes. [Note: All large city dwellers might appreciate the fact that it took about 15 minutes to drive from Kalamazoo's northern city limit to Kalamazoo's southern city limit. This was not unusual for mid-sized Michigan cities like Flint, Kalamazoo, Port Huron, and Pontiac. To most employees that was a benefit.]*

Why did she go there and not to Gibson? *Well, it was just our choice not to work together.*

Where did you park during the 1950s and 1960s? *My dad and I rode together a lot from 1956 to 1959. We just used to park on the street. They allowed parking anywhere on the street. The parking lot was usually assigned out. They started adding more parking lots in later years. I had my own parking spot when I was Plant Superintendent (after 1974).*

Going back to the 1950s, where did you go to work after sanding? *After about a year, or a year and a half, I went to work in the neck department. Making necks, belt sanding necks.*

Who was the supervisor there? Who was the group 'leader? *Clarence Coleman. He had that area. I worked for Clarence for a lot of years. For the 'leader' in that group, I won't swear, but I believe there was not a 'leader' in that group.*

So Clarence provided the 'leader' role showing each new employee what to do? *Well each guy working there did. Your co-workers did. A lot of the guys had been there quite a while, and I wanted to learn everything that I could possibly learn. Which I did. I tried to learn to do anything that I could.*

Did Gibson ask you to move to the neck department, or did you apply for the neck department? *I believe there was a job posting and I applied for it. I just wanted to learn everything that I could.*

I know the sanding department was along the north wall where the windows used to be before the 1960 expansion replaced the windows with a wall. Relative to the sanding department, looking out of those north windows, where was the neck department? *The sanding department was right on that north wall and the neck department was just directly south. It was just a short ways. In those days, the lumber yard was outside (along the west edge of the Gibson property), then there was the mill room (east of the lumber yard, but west of the neck department), then the body and neck assembly were all right there together.*

Was there a saw or something to carve the neck? *It was done by hand. The necks came from the mill room in a rough shape. We would take them and glue the fingerboards on them, glue head veneers on them. Then I would take and shape that neck with a slack-belt sander. And we had a guy that would carve the heels; the heels were kind of square. He'd use a spindle-carver; it was like an eight blade knife sticking out on a spindle. He would carve the heel and the flair. Then I would take and roll the neck on that slack-belt sander, and round the neck. Then sand it up. Then I'd go over to a spindle sander, which was basically like a spindle carver. Then I'd have a tube sander, and I'd sand it up some more.*

Now you had quite a bit of control over the shape of the neck then? *Absolutely. I hand shaped a lot of necks. The C-6 model for example. The C-6 was a classical guitar, we had to hand shape it. We had to use various gauges that it fit to. I used to scrape them and sand them, and that C-6 had to be shaped after those templates.*

Let's talk about shaping a neck, in that year, which is about 1958. If a neck that came through for a Les Paul versus a neck that came through that was going to be a flat top J-50. Did you know that was the case? Did you do anything differently? *Yeah, they were completely different necks.*

So there was a little note saying that this was a Les Paul? *They only ran them in batches of 30 or 35. And there would be a tag with it saying J-50, which was a flat top. And there would be 35 J-50s because there would be 35 J-50 bodies. And they would come through in batches and certain guys would put fingerboards on them, put veneers on them, and I would do my job, and the next guy would do his job. And the Les Paul would be very well the same way. A batch would come through the same way. We had gauges to measure the thickness and we had radius gauges for the curvature of the neck – the roundness. There were certain gauges for certain necks, and certain fixtures for certain necks. And as much hand work as we did on them, I promise you, they varied. But we got them as close as you could, once you learned how to do the thing, you'd get them pretty consistent.*

When was the truss rod put in? *It was put in before the fingerboard was put on. That was done in the mill room department where they made the rough blank of the neck.*

Was the mill separate? Or could you see the machines and hear all the noise? *There were just different lines. There was the mill room, and there was the body & neck assembly, and hand sanding. At that time (late 1950s) there were no walls between them.*

So it was just one huge room? *It was just one huge room. They had shapers, routers and things in the mill room. They'd do the rough work. They would take a blank, my dad and they would saw it up into a plank (lumber yard, rough mill). The mill room would take the plank and make it into whatever. Then it would come to us and we would build the body. They'd make a top, they'd make a back for the flat top, and then there'd be a rim built. Then there was an area where they glued the top and back on it and it became a body. Then they rabbitted it for binding, they'd bind it, and hand sand it. Then there'd be a neck made and it would be glued together.*

At your work station, could you look around and see all of what you described? *I could see a lot of it (laughing).*

So you could see most of the operation? *You could see a lot of it. Some areas you couldn't see, over against the far wall or something.*

Clarence Coleman wasn't foreman of the mill room too? *No. Gerald Bergeon was the foreman of the mill room. And another guy was named Ed Rosenberger, my dad's boss was the foreman of the rough mill. In the 1950s there were three foremen: the foreman of the rough mill, the foreman of the mill room, and the foreman of the body building, neck building and hand sanding. When they were finished hand sanding, they would go downstairs, down the ramp into the basement (of the old building). They'd go in a rack that held 35 to 40 guitars. Then they'd go in an elevator in the basement up to the third floor and that's where they'd finish them.*

All of those three foremen reported to Larry Allers, the Assistant Superintendent, in the late 1950s? *Yes, I'm almost positive. Larry Allers was a great guy. He was in that area a lot. And John Huis was too.*

I ask everybody about Ted McCarty coming through the plant. You saw him some? *I saw Ted quite often, sure. He'd come through, but he always went out to the shipping department. I think he kept a pretty close check on shipping. You know that's where the dollars were coming out of (laughing). Actually, I got to know Ted better in later years. In the 1950s when he came through he was pretty well all business. He'd go out and take care of what he wanted and then he'd go back to his front office. Most of the time, he would walk out by himself. Ted and John didn't walk out together. Later on, after he got Bigsby, we became better friends. I'd see Ted at Gibson employee reunions, I'd see Ted at music trade shows, things like that. He'd act like we'd known each other all those early years, but yet I never had a lot to do with him during the earlier years at Gibson (1956–'66).*

Did he ever stop and talk with you about the neck department operation or anything? *Not Ted, I mean John Huis did it. M.H. Berlin (CEO Chicago Musical Instruments, Ted McCarty's boss from Chicago), would take a tour of the plant, he'd stop and talk to you. I talked with M.H. Berlin; he was a super, super guy.*

Was that in the 1950s? *Yeah, I'm sure it was. It was either in the late 1950s or the early 1960s? [Note: It was probably 1960 when the factory doubled in size. Ted McCarty stated that Mr. Berlin would normally come over from Chicago when a new building was added.]*

He came out with Ted? *No. They would come over from CMI, and they would come through in groups with different people. A lot of times, maybe Ted and M.H. would be together, because Ted was President and M.H. the head man at CMI. But if Ted or somebody got sidetracked – I remember they got sidetracked and M.H. was right near me, and he just walked over and started talking to me.*

He talked about the job? *Yeah, he talked about the job, and a lot of things. He just seemed like a down to earth kind of guy.*

Okay, you were working in the neck department, and where did you go from there and when was that? *I became the 'leader' of the sanding line. I was the lead person.*

Why did you do that? *Well, more money. The 'lead person' was basically in-charge of ten or twelve people. You couldn't hire or fire, but you kept (your employees) in work.*

Did Gibson ask you to do that, or did you post for that? *They got me to sign for that job, because I guess I was pretty good at that type work at that time - at hand sanding. And I remember Clarence Coleman definitely wanted me to have that 'leader' job. And Clarence kind of coached me into signing. And like I said, it was more money for me.*

What year was that? *It's been a long time (laughing). You see I would do anything that Gibson wanted me to do. If they needed somebody to fill in a job, then I'd go do it. Like I said, my goal was to learn to do anything that I could learn to do in the white wood, in Clarence's area. I didn't go into the rough mill at that time. I did rim sanding, I did belt sanding, bodies and thing like that. If somebody was absent, Clarence knew he could depend on me. I thought the world of him. All he had to do was to ask me and I would do anything that he'd ask me to do.*

Was the rabitting in that area too? *Yes, a guy by the name of Fern Russel (seniority date October 26,*

1948). He was a little guy, and they built a box for him to be up high, so he'd be high enough to look at the cutter. He did that job for so long that he could actually look at everything that was going on, and be talking to people, and also be rabbitting that thing. We called him 'Pinky.' He did that a lot of years. To the best of my recollection, he retired out of that job.

Then different guys did the bindings? *Yes, that's right. There were totally different guys that did that. A guy by the name of Dick Mitchell (seniority date September 4, 1956) was binding, a guy by the name of Kenny Wait (seniority date August 31,1955), and Wesley Beatty (seniority date August 21, 1958) did some binding. All those guys worked on hand sanding. I broke them in when I was the 'leader' and then they signed (signed up for the position, based on an opening posted on the bulletin board) for the binding jobs because it paid a little bit more money. Those are three guys that just come off the top of my head.*

It sounds like the white wood guys, the people, kind of stayed in white wood, unless there was a good reason to leave. *Yeah. Unless there was a job that opened up that may have been in a cleaner area. I remember J.P. (Moats) he didn't like the hand sanding, he did it, but he wasn't crazy about it. For J.P. a job opened up in the 'final cleaning.' That's where you buff and polish the guitar. He went there. J.P. didn't like the sanding job. Guys would make job changes like that.*

What was you next job after 'leader'? *They made me assistant foreman. I was a 'line leader' but I did repair too. I did the repair in the department. I'd put a new piece of binding on a guitar, take the fingerboard off and replace the fingerboard. Things like that, in the immediate area.*

Who was the inspector of the sanding area in the late 1950s? *I remember the first two inspectors, a guy by the name of Jim Ferrell (seniority date August 22, 1950), and Jim Drower. They would come down and inspect the white wood sanding. Then they'd take them down to the ramp to the basement, to the elevator. One inspector would come down for two weeks. Then he'd go upstairs and inspect his own work. Both of them would do that. Jim Drower would come down and inspect for two weeks, then he would go back upstairs to the third floor finishing area and inspect those same guitars that were going through the system. So later on, he'd be looking at a lot of stuff that he had inspected. Then Jim Ferrell would come down when Jim Drower went back upstairs. So, the two would rotate. After that, Jim Drower became an assistant foreman to Clarence Coleman in body building after the 1960 expansion. [Note: Marv has described another McCarty-era quality clue. A final inspector would follow his own work through the factory. If a problem was found by Rem Wall, at the end of the process, then one final inspector could be identified as having inspected the guitar from the mill through finishing.]*

What happened with the 1960 expansion? *I was doing all that white wood work and neck work during that period 1956–'59 (on the first floor of the original 1950 building). When I went out to the new area (the 1960 expansion area), I was still a 'line leader.' At that time, we hired a lot more people. I had several women and several guys working under my line.*

The 1960 expansion? *Yes. I was the 'line leader' in hand sanding. At that time, they had trouble with the neck department (Note: Refers to the Les Paul Special double cutaway and new SG double cutaway models). Drower became assistant to Clarence Coleman when they made that first expansion in 1960. Then they made Drower the foreman of that area and Clarence Coleman was moved up to the new Custom Shop. Clarence Coleman took the white wood body building area of the Custom Shop and Wilbur Fuller had the finishing area of the Custom Shop. At that time I became foreman of the neck department. They moved the body building and all of that into the new expansion (the 1960 expansion), the belt sanding, etc. But they put the neck line right along that north wall where the hand sanding used to be. So I became the first foreman of that. [Note: Les Paul Standard 'Burst owners are well aware that the 1960 Les Paul Standard's neck has a pronounced flat profile versus the rounder U-shaped neck of the 1959 'Burst. Other guitars like the ES-335 also have the same change in profile in 1960 versus 1959. The neck machines were relocated in late 1959/early 1960 at the same time the neck profiles changed. Neck profile changed back to the U-shaped rounder profile in 1963. The greatest change in neck profile occurred in 1965 when the final 1965 rearrange was made and new neck machines were installed in 1965.]*

Then what? *I did that for six months and I said, 'I don't want this foreman's job.' So I went back into the bargaining unit (Note: Supervisors/foremen were not part of the union, when a person was promoted to fore-man, they dropped out of the union. An employee always had transfer rights to return to hourly status. The employee would re-joint the union, aka bargaining unit.).*

This October 1, 2001, photo shows Marv Lamb (right), Wilbur Fuller, and J.P. Moats (left) with a vintage Gibson rim-bending machine. The men are standing in the northwest corner of the basement where the ramp goes up to the 1st floor mill. Lamb and Moats, along with Jim Deurloo are co-founders of Heritage Guitars located at Parson Street.

Why didn't you like it? *I don't know. Young. Crazy. Anyway, I went back to hourly and I went into inspection. There was a grace period there, where you could leave the union, but you had a grace period to go back to the union and not lose seniority. I was pretty well liked by both sides, the union and management.*

While we are talking about the union, it seemed like it was a good relationship, the union and Gibson, while Ted was there? *Yes it was. When I was still in the union ,before becoming a fore-man, I was one of the union stewards. I was still back in the bargaining unit (the union) and they (Gibson) kept after me to come back to supervision. And finally I just threw up my hands and I said, 'I will, but if I go back, I won't go back into the bargaining unit, I'll go out the door!' I went back and I stayed in manage-ment* (Note: Marv became Plant Superintendent in 1974, under then Gibson President Stan Rendell).

When Ted left in 1966 it sounds like you were still the 'leader' in the new addition? *I believe I was, it was a long time ago. Either that or an inspector.*

How did you like inspection? *I liked it, yeah. I got along well with the people, the 'leaders', I knew all the people. I worked with them, I knew how to do the job, and if they did anything wrong I'd take it back and show them, and help them. Gibson kept on growing, and growing, and growing, more and more people. That was hard. It made it more difficult.*

Who followed Ted McCarty when he left, before Stan Rendell? There is not much written about who directly followed Ted. *There was Al Stanley and another guy by the name of, oh, I can't think of his name. But Al Stanley was an accountant who had worked over in Chicago. He was a young Ivy-League-type guy. I don't know... things just didn't happen. He didn't last long. Then there was an older guy that came in behind Al Stanley (but before Stan Rendell).*

One of the things I have been asking people about was the neighborhood around the plant in the 1950s. Was the neighborhood getting a little bit rough? *Yeah, it started getting that way. I remember, we used to do 'fire watches.' I'm sure you heard that. There was a lot of Molotov cocktails into some of the houses. You know, the racial thing. That was in the 1960s.* [Note – It is assumed this was post-McCarty, circa April 4, 1968, during the national race riots.] *In the 1950s, it was not bad. People lived in the area and it wasn't too bad. I recall in the 1950s, walking around the area. When the racial thing got stronger, that's when it got really bad. We had to watch. Back in the 1960s, the foreman had to go in all night, we'd take shifts.*

Going back to 1959, some authors say that the solidbodies were made in another plant. *Only a part of them. They made Melody Makers and some of the lower lines, but still some of the solid-bodies were made over at the Parsons Street.*

Do you believe the Les Paul with the two piece top (maple over mahogany) was still made at Parsons Street? *I believe it was. I don't remember too many Les Pauls being built at the temporary plant.*

Epiphone? *Epiphone was over on Eleanor Street. I worked some over there, when they first moved in there. I went over and worked on the big basses, the stand-up basses. I worked on a few of them. That was a whole different world. I did some hand sanding on them. They needed some help over there, so they ask me to go over there. I didn't stay a long time. I had a brother that worked over there. Another guy was Howard Davis, he was a maintenance supervisor, and I believe they made him kind of in charge of the manufactur-ing. Howard Davis was mostly the maintenance supervisor at Gibson, because my dad worked for Howard Davis. Ward Arbanas was over there too; he kind of ran that plant.*

Tell me about your brother. When did he hire in? *His name is Robert Jr. My father was Robert Senior. He hired in a year or two after I hired in. John Huis and Case Triezenberg hired him. Case Triezen-*

berg was a finishing man. My brother hired in as a buffer. He also was in final clean up in the finishing department. That was the opening that Gibson had. He liked it up in cleaning, but he liked to party too. He stayed a couple of years.

Anyone else work there? *My sister-in-law worked there. Robert's wife. She hired in right about the time that I did. She started off on that hand sanding line. Most everybody started there. She did hand sanding on guitars. She was there a couple of different times. She left and then she came back. She also worked at Bigsby.*

Did you know Rollo Werner back in the 1950s and 1960s? *Yes I did. Rollo was the Purchasing Agent. He was a super guy. He used to like to party. We used to party together. He was a good buyer.*

He did a lot of the wood buying? *Yes, he had a lot of connections. He knew a lot of people. He had a girl that worked for him, she was excellent too, Kathy Fleetwood.*

Did you know George Comee? *He was the office manager. I didn't have a lot to do with him. I knew George. Later on, we'd go to dinners. Gibson was a fantastic place to work. Gibson was good to me over the years.*

How about Julius Bellson? Did you do much with him while Ted was at Gibson? Did he come out in the plant? *I knew Julius well; he was more of the personnel director. Any problem that came up, he was a super, super, super man.*

That's what I keep hearing. *Oh yeah. Great guy. He was friendly, he'd come out to the shop. He'd walk out there and he'd stop and talk to you. He always acted like a shy person. He'd talk to you, but he'd turn his head kindly and look off. He was never a direct eye contact type of person, but still just a super, super guy. I don't think you'd hear one person, that worked at Gibson say anything bad about him. There were close to 1,100 people there, in the office and on hourly and you'd never hear any one person ever say anything bad about him.*

When they came out with the SG, the thin-style double-cutaway SG, they switched from the old style single cutaway Les Paul. Do you remember any problems with that conversion? *I remember a neck-joint problem. I remember that there were a lot of necks broken. They 'jointed' it right at the end of the fingerboard. It just didn't have enough meat and wood in there to hold it. It just wasn't the strongest neck joint.*

They discovered that pretty early when they were building them? *It didn't take long (to discover the problem), but they still built a lot of them.*

You mean, the neck joints actually broke in the assembly process? *Yeah. That was called a Les Paul (SG Les Paul Standard).*

Do you know who had the idea to come up with that engineering? *No.*

Because there is a lot of history of quality engineering and quality building and all of a sudden here comes the SG. *It's just my opinion (hesitant voice), it's just my opinion, that Larry Allers (the head Engineer of guitar products) was involved in that. That's just an opinion. Larry was pretty innovative in those type things (during the 1950s and 1960s). Just like Seth Lover and Walt Fuller were the big guys on the humbucker pickups.*

Did you know Seth Lover? *I knew him. I didn't get up to the electronics department in those days. I didn't travel around (the plant) in those days; I was young and I was learning my job.*

I was wondering, when did the second shift go in? *When I hired in there was no second shift. But when I became a foreman, I became a foreman on the night shift. I can't tell you exactly when, but it was probably close to the early 1960s, because we were running a lot of solidbodies on the night shift.*

The volume just exploded in 1962, 1963, and I know there was a second shift in 1965. I was just wondering when that second shift started? *You're probably close to right, because there was three of us guys, Gordon Wiley was the night foreman of the mill room, I went into the white wood body building line as the night foreman, and then a guy by the name of Jim Hitchcook was the night foreman of the finishing department.*

And it was a regular 8 hour second shift? *Yeah.*

And you got 5% premium (more pay than the first shift)? *I think so. You got a little bit of premium for that.*

Did you mind the second shift, and how were the employees on the second shift? *They were good. You know, we had to work with them. We had a few people that signed on the second shift (volunteered and posted for the job), but most of them were new hires. It was tough breaking those people in, but we managed.*

You (and Gibson) must have really done a great job, because nobody really talks about the falling down of quality at Gibson between 1960 and 1964. That's when all these new people were coming in, and all of this tremendous volume was happening. But the guitars seemed to be pretty good. *At that time, you could sell anybody a Gibson. If you just named it a Gibson guitar, there was somebody there willing to buy it.*

Why do you think that could happen? That you could have such an increase in volume, new plants, new people, and still things seemed to be of pretty good quality? *Well, I think there were a lot of good experienced people there to work with those new people, to train those new people.*

It was a good training process, wasn't it? Using leaders and the foremen, that system seemed to be able to handle all the new people? *Like I said, it was kind of a close knit group of people. People seemed to help each other, you know, which was kind of nice.*

Even with all the new people coming in? *In 1963 and 1964, a whole bunch of new people came in. There was a lot of them. I always thought that there were too many people, but, you know, that wasn't my decision. They (Gibson) decided to put them on (laughing). But yeah, the quality seemed to stay pretty good. It was the later years that the quality started getting worse. In the later years, there were a lot of things going on.*

Anything else about the McCarty years? *Well, they were good years. That's all I can say. Like I said, Ted became a friend in the later years (the Bigsby years). In the earlier years (1956–'66) I didn't know Ted too well. He was kind of a private individual, but I'm sure you've found people that did know him. He seemed to take care of business, and that's what he was supposed to do.*

Interview 12
Ron Allers (1956–'80)

Ted McCarty's Gibson allowed for extended families to work at Gibson. This was not unusual for Michigan industry in the 1950s and early 1960s. During the 1950s there was a rather sever labor shortage in Michigan. In Flint, Michigan, the home of General Motors, recruiters would actually cruise Saginaw Street, downtown Flint, calling out from their car, "Do you want to go to work at Buick?" Buick, AC Spark Plug, Fisher Body, and Chevrolet would talk people into working in the factories and have them start on as-soon-as-possible basis. This type of thing was happening in the other mid-size Michigan cities. In Kalamazoo it was the paper mills that were most active in daily recruiting. Mid-Michigan cities enthusiastically welcomed family members into the factories. Extended families seemed to be very loyal to their employers. Ron Allers and his dad Larry Allers, and Marv Lamb and his dad Robert Lamb were examples of this at Gibson.

Larry Allers, Gibson's plant superintendent and chief engineer, was responsible for designing the Les Paul Model, flat top adjustable bridge, D-style Gibson flat top, Florentine cutaway archtop, EB-2 bass, just to mention a few. He was one of the most important people in Ted McCarty's organization. For more on Larry, please check the "Other Employee Histories" Section that follows later on.

Ron Allers was Larry's son. Ron gave me the background on his father Larry which is shown later in the book. Here is Ron's history.

When did you start at Gibson? *I started at Gibson in 1956. I swept floors because I wasn't old enough to run a machine, because I was still in high school. When I graduated from school, I went to work full time at Gibson, and that was 1958.*

Did you go to Kalamazoo Central High School? *No, I went to Portage.*

What job did you start on? *When I started full time I build amplifier cabinets. That was on the first floor in the middle of the building, right in the woodshop.*

Was that near the sanders? *Yes it was.*

Near the neck carvers? *Yes, it was all in the woodshop right there. Amplifier cabinet making was south of the neck carvers. Then south of the cabinet building was the rough material wood, where they buy in the lumber and they cut the lumber to size. That was the first part of the mill. That was in 1958 and 1959 and my dad, Larry Allers, was the Chief Engineer and I used to go and visit him in his office all the time.*

Well your dad must have been pretty talented to move up in the organization from wood worker to the position of foreman, superintendent, and the chief engineer? Did he love wood working? *Yeah, he did. I had a lot of people tell me when I was working there, that Gibson would have never have been where it was if it wasn't for him.*

Yeah, your dad was there really early, he came to Gibson in 1937, and Ted McCarty came in 1948, so your dad was there eleven years before Ted McCarty. Did your dad ever talk about Guy Hart (the Gibson President who preceded Ted McCarty)? *Yes, I remember him mentioning his name, but I don't remember anything that was said about him.*

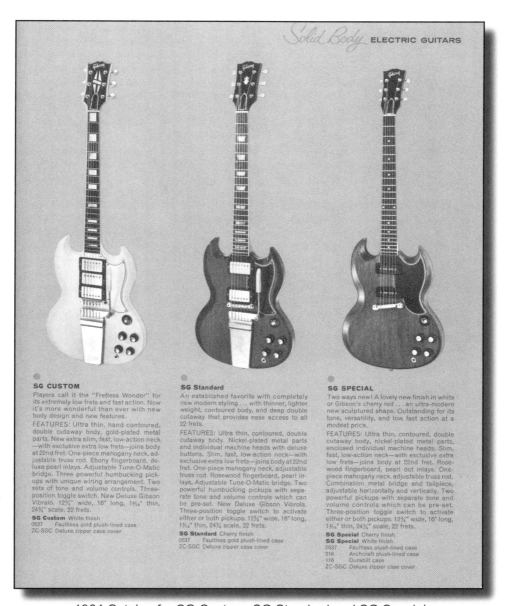

1964 Catalog for SG Custom, SG Standard and SG Special

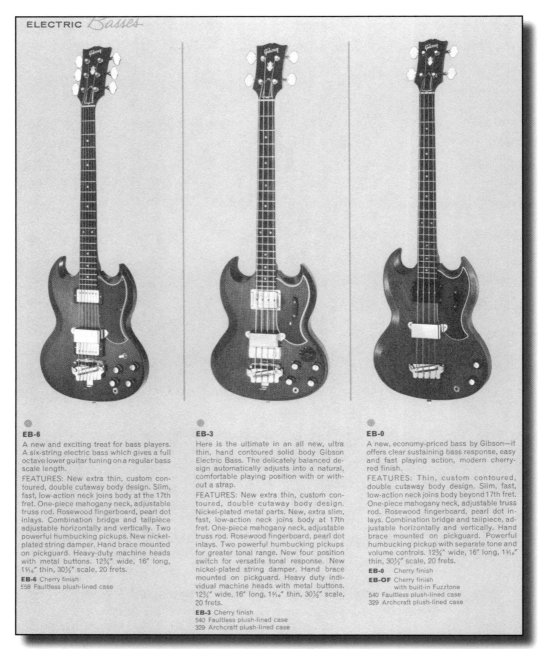

ELECTRIC *Basses*

EB-6
A new and exciting treat for bass players. A six-string electric bass which gives a full octave lower guitar tuning on a regular bass scale length.

FEATURES: New extra thin, custom contoured, double cutaway body design. Slim, fast, low-action neck joins body at the 17th fret. One-piece mahogany neck, adjustable truss rod. Rosewood fingerboard, pearl dot inlays. Combination bridge and tailpiece adjustable horizontally and vertically. Two powerful humbucking pickups. New nickel-plated string damper. Hand brace mounted on pickguard. Heavy-duty machine heads with metal buttons. 12¾" wide, 16" long, 1⁵⁄₁₆" thin, 30½" scale, 20 frets.

EB-6 Cherry finish
558 Faultless plush-lined case

EB-3
Here is the ultimate in an all new, ultra thin, hand contoured solid body Gibson Electric Bass. The delicately balanced design automatically adjusts into a natural, comfortable playing position with or without a strap.

FEATURES: New extra thin, custom contoured, double cutaway body design. Nickel-plated metal parts. New, extra slim, fast, low-action neck joins body at 17th fret. One-piece mahogany neck, adjustable truss rod. Rosewood fingerboard, pearl dot inlays. Two powerful humbucking pickups for greater tonal range. New four position switch for versatile tonal response. New nickel-plated string damper. Hand brace mounted on pickguard. Heavy duty individual machine heads with metal buttons. 12¾" wide, 16" long, 1⁵⁄₁₆" thin, 30½" scale, 20 frets.

EB-3 Cherry finish
540 Faultless plush-lined case
329 Archcraft plush-lined case

EB-0
A new, economy-priced bass by Gibson—it offers clear sustaining bass response, easy and fast playing action, modern cherry-red finish.

FEATURES: Thin, custom contoured, double cutaway body design. Slim, fast, low-action neck joins body beyond 17th fret. One-piece mahogany neck, adjustable truss rod. Rosewood fingerboard, pearl dot inlays. Combination bridge and tailpiece, adjustable horizontally and vertically. Hand brace mounted on pickguard. Powerful humbucking pickup with separate tone and volume controls. 12¾" wide, 16" long, 1⁵⁄₁₆" thin, 30½" scale, 20 frets.

EB-0 Cherry finish
EB-0F Cherry finish with built-in Fuzztone.
540 Faultless plush-lined case
329 Archcraft plush-lined case

1964 Catalog for EB-6, EB-3 and EB-0

Do you remember any of the names that your dad was working with back in the 1930s? *I remember the name Harlan Clair (seniority 1928–'73; see his history later in the book).*

Well, let's get back to your career. You were building wood cabinets. How did you happen to end up on that job? *I just signed up for it. When a job became open, you just signed up for it, and you got it according to seniority.*

Did you have a line leader in that department? *No, my foreman was Gerald Bergeon. Clarence Coleman was also a foreman in the woodshop.*

Who else worked side by side with you there? *I was kind of all by myself.*

Would you take four piece of wood, and dovetail them, and glue them together? *No, they were already all dovetailed in the mill. I glued them and I put them together.*

Did you put the tweed covering on them? Did you put the speaker baffle in? *No, I didn't do that. Both of those were done after they left me. I just put the four sides on, the back, and the wood part that held the grille cloth part.*

Did they have a certain expectation of you that you needed to get so many amp cabinets made in a certain time? *Yes, but I don't remember the amount or number of them.*

Were you the only one putting the cabinets together? *Yes.*

So you did all of them. If there was an amp cabinet made in that year, you did it? *Yes.*

How long did you stay on that? *I stayed on that a year. Then I went to scrape binding. That's where, after they had the rough finishing on the instrument, then you had to scrape the binding to get the paint off the binding, and then they sent it in for lacquer.*

Okay, so you went up to the third floor. Where on the third floor was your work station? *It was on the far north side. The spray booths were there too. At that time Case Triezenberg (seniority 1926–'73) was the foreman of the scrapers. There were about six of us, six scrapers.*

What were you scraping off? *They put a rough stain on it. It was like a filler. Then we had to scrape that off, then it went for lacquer, to spray over it again. I was doing that around 1959.*

So you were doing Les Pauls and 335s? *Yeah, I was doing everything, everything that came through there.*

You were over by the east windows? *Yes, the window was right in front of me. Everybody had a bench.*

How many spray booths were there then? *Let's see, I think about seven or eight.*

Each spray booth had one guy working in it?   *Yeah.*

Do you remember any of the names of any of the guys that were doing the spraying? *Well, one of the guys I've mentioned, Harlan Clair (seniority 1928–'73). He was actually doing the spraying.*

Did you ever want to spray them? *No, I didn't. It never interested me that much.*

Did the guys that were in the spray booths, did they seem to like it? *They seemed to like it, yeah.*

When you went up to the scraping job, why did you leave amplifiers and go up there? *Well, it paid more money.*

That was posted and you signed up for it? *Yeah.*

Was there a line leader up there? *Yes, Paul Vallier (seniority date January 9, 1948) was the line leader.*

How long did you stay on that? *Probably about a year, and then a job became open for a roving inspector. That's where you'd go around and inspect any department were they needed an inspector. So I went from scraping to roving inspector. There was a posting and I signed for that.*

When you were a roving inspector, did they actually call you, to tell you they needed an inspector, or did you just walk around and decide what to do? *No, they'd call me and let me know. Like if they needed me in the wood shop, they'd tell me to go down there. Wherever they needed me, they'd let me know first thing in the morning.*

I know that there were inspectors that inspected the white wood, and then they followed the racks right up to the finishing department, and then they inspected those instruments after they were finished. But you were a different type of inspector? *Yes, I'd be capable of inspecting whatever they did to the instruments. I had to be able to inspect them after they got done with them.*

Why did you take that job? *It also paid more money.*

And who was your supervisor there? *Back then, it was J.P. Moats. He was over all the inspectors at that time. I worked there for about a year, roving inspector, and then a job became open for final inspector, and that really interested me, because I play guitar. So I was final inspector until I quit there. As a final inspector, you had to play every fret, every string, and play the guitar to make sure it played good.*

So you were up there with Hubie Friar and with Rem Wall? You were all there together? *I took Rem Wall's job when they made him a foreman. He was a final inspector, so when they made him foreman, I took his job. When I got into final inspection, all the musicians were kind of close. Hubie Friar, he played bass for Rem Wall, we were close friends. I'd say our department was probably the closest department down there at Gibson. It was just like family there.*

Did they reject a lot of guitars? *No, not too many.*

Because they were well built by the people? *Yeah they were, yeah.*

I got a sense while Ted was there the quality control was quite good because there was a lot of inspection. Everybody would inspect the instrument, then the line leader would inspect it, then the supervisor would, then the inspectors, and there were all of these triple check procedures. *Yeah, there were.*

When did you start to play guitar? *When I was seven, my dad taught me how to play.*

Did your dad (Larry Allers) play? *Yeah.*

That's fantastic. That must have really helped him out, because he designed all these guitars (from the 1952 Les Paul Model to the 1958 EB-2 Bass). *Oh yeah!*

Did he play in bands around town? *He had a band when he was younger, not around Kalamazoo, but around South Haven, Michigan when he was living there. He just played on the weekends.*

Do you think that could have been a reason he came to work for Gibson? *It could have been, because he was interested in guitars, yes. He liked guitars and playing guitars.*

What kind of guitar was he playing? *A Gibson LG-1 (Note: The Gibson LG-1 was introduced in 1943). That's what I learned on. He bought me my first guitar.*

You started really early if you started at seven years old? *Oh, yeah. I had a band for 42 years, Ron Allers and the Rhythm Masters (Note: 1960 to 2002). We played in a bunch of bars around Kalamazoo, for example, The Home Bar, that's the one we played the most. We played country. We played at all the clubs around Kalamazoo, The Eagles, and The Moose Club. I was on Rem Wall's Show a lot in the 1960s. I sang with the Green Valley Boys. (Ron pausing) In 2003 I got inducted into the Rockabilly Hall of Fame. That was quite a surprise for me. That's in Tennessee. Your can pick it up online. They have 16 pages on me.*

Did you record then? *I recorded a song in 1962, which is the one that made it on the Rockabilly Hall of Fame. It was called "Heartless Woman."*

Were you able to tour with that, or were you tied down with Gibson? *No, I was tied down pretty much at Gibson. I sold a lot of records around Michigan and Indiana. But I never did make it big with it, or anything like that.*

What kind of guitar were you using then? *I was using a Gibson Trini Lopez (Note: Introduced in 1964).*

Who was the lead guitar player in your band? *Greg Allen. He worked at Gibson for a short while, about two years, in the 1960s. But he wanted to go into playing music full time.*

It is interesting that you are a guitar player, because most people that worked at Gibson didn't play guitar. *I know it (laughing).*

But it seemed that most of the people that did play guitar ended up in final inspection. *Yep, in the final end of it.*

Because they could test them out. Did you enjoy playing all of those guitars? *Oh yeah! I loved my job, it was a good job.*

During that time, there were guitars that had a little "2" on them. They were called 'seconds.' Can you tell me something about that? What was a 'second? *A 'second' was based on the quality of the finish.*

In the 1950s and early 1960s, a "2" on the guitar would have been a finishing problem? *Yes.*

Who made that decision? *The inspectors. The "2" was impressed into the wood.*

When was the serial number put on the back of the headstock? What part of the operation? *Towards the end of the line in the finishing department. It was just before they put the lacquer on.*

When did you leave Gibson? *I left there in 1980, I started a guitar repair shop. I just really wanted to do that. I was really into repairing guitars.*

You still had seniority. You could have stayed if you wanted? *Oh yeah.*

That was when lower-seniority people started losing their jobs. But you could have stayed right until 1984 (when Kalamazoo closed and production relocated to Nashville)? *Yeah, I could have.*

Going back to the 1950s, what did your dad have to say about John Huis? *He was good friends with John.*

Did they do anything on the outside, like go hunting or fishing, or was it just in the workplace? *I think they played cards, once in a while, together.*

Was there anyone else that your dad was particularly friendly with at work? *Gerald Bergeon was one. And the co-owner of the Heritage Guitar Company, Jim Deurloo was another one. Jim was just under my dad, when my dad was chief engineer.*

Yes, and Jim Deurloo speaks very highly of your dad. Did your dad ever mention anything to you about the development of the Les Paul guitar, or designing the Les Paul Model? *No, but then people started talking about it, and that's how I learned.*

Your dad has a patent for the EB-2 bass. *Yes, and I know he's got a patent for the adjustable bridge.*

Now I believe your dad was the head engineer on the SG model too? *Oh yes.*

Your dad's office, when he was chief woodworking engineer, was near to the door that would go into John Huis' office? *Yes, he was about two doors from there? The quality control office was also there at one time. And the nurse's office was right there too.*

Did Ted McCarty come out and talk with you when he did his plant tours? *Oh yes! Ted was a really friendly guy. He was well liked.*

Do you remember any specifics? Like when you were in the amps, or when you were scraping, or when you were inspecting? *No. He'd just come by and see how you were doing, and to see how everything was going, and to see if you had any complaints.*

Was John Huis normally with him, or were they by themselves? *They would be by themselves when they'd come through. Once in a while they'd come together, but not very often.*

How about Julius Bellson? Did he come out; what can you tell me about Julius? *He just pretty much stayed in his office. He didn't get out in the plant too much.*

When you hired in did you have to go see Mr. Bellson? *No my dad hired me in. He was over the maintenance too. He had a lot of responsibility. He really enjoyed his job.*

Did you know Rollo Werner, the purchasing guy? *No I didn't. I know my dad and him took a couple of trips together for Gibson to look at wood and things like that. My dad would go out on buying trips for the wood with Rollo.*

Did your dad ever talk about the Fender Company? *No, I just remember him saying they were one of our top competitors. [Note: This reply concerning Fender was very typical of the Gibson hourly workers that I talked with. I asked many of them this same question and about all they would say was that Fender was 'the' competition. They all seemed to know they had to do a good job in order to compete with the Fender Company.]*

Any other thoughts about Ted McCarty? *I know at Christmas time they used to take everybody out to the Gull Harbor Inn for dinner. After Ted left, that all stopped. That was on Gull Lake in Richland,, Michigan, which was about 10 miles from Kalamazoo.*

Everyone in the plant? *Yes, everyone in the plant. Oh yeah it was a big affair. It was really something. It was a sit down dinner. The wives didn't come. I don't think they were invited. It was just the employees*

Would Ted get up and speak? *Yeah, him and John (Huis) both. Ted just wanted to do something for the people once a year.*

Well I'm happy to get the information on you, and particularly the information on your dad Larry Allers because he was an important person to Gibson. *Yeah, he was quite important at Gibson. Anybody that worked there would tell you that.*

Your dad seemed to work his way up in the organization. He came in early in the company history, in 1937. And you came in 1956, so you actually saw the plant grow to be pretty big. You went through all those changes, for example in 1960 when they put on that big addition. Did you have to switch jobs then? *No, I was just put in a new location. Final inspection was in the new part.*

Final inspection went from the second floor to the new part. *Yeah.*

And then in 1965, Gibson had the last huge addition. Did that affect your job? *No, I just stayed on the same job.*

You never had to go over to the other plants? You never went over to Plant 2 or Plant 3? *Yes, I went over to Plant 2 when I was a roving inspector, once in a while. If an inspector was off work, or something like that, I'd go fill in. I was inspecting everything, including the solidbodies over there. The solidbodies were built there, but finished over in Plant 1 (225 Parsons Street). They didn't do any finishing in Plant 2 at that time.. It was mostly the economy solidbody guitars over in Plant 2, for example, the Melody Maker. I never went over to Plant 3.*

What did you think about the union? Was everything fine with you concerning the union? *Yeah, everything was fine with me. I didn't go out and get too involved with it, other than what I had to.*

I heard when the amplifiers went out and the string room went out (Note: They were moved out of Kalamazoo after Ted McCarty left Gibson) there was some discontent? *Oh yeah. Yeah, there was. It didn't get involved in that.*

Did you participate in the two union strikes? *Yeah, I did. I walked the line*

Do you remember what those strikes were about? *One was money and I think the other one was pensions.*

The first strike was after Ted left? *Yeah, right. I wasn't too long after Ted left.*

Did you notice any difference in the plant after Ted left Gibson in 1966? *CMI brought in two guys from the outside to replace McCarty and Huis. There were a couple of years (1966 and 1967, before Stan Rendell became President of Gibson) when it seemed like Gibson Kalamazoo was kind of a leaderless organization. It wasn't supervised like it was when Ted was there.*

Interview 13
Huber Hill (1957–'84)

Huber Hill was interviewed using a family member as interpreter, helping out with Huber's hearing handicap. Huber was looking for work when he joined Gibson in 1957. It is believed that Larry Allers, Assistant Superintendent of the mill, hired Huber. Huber worked in the woodshop on the router, band saws and shavers. Later on, he moved to inspection because there was more pay for inspection. Huber's dad worked at Gibson. His dad started to work in the 1930s. Huber enjoyed woodworking as a hobby in the basement of his home.

After Gibson closed in 1984, Huber became one of the skilled employees that started to work for Heritage Guitar Company in Kalamazoo.

Interview 14
J. P. Moats (1957–'84)

J.P. Moats, Marv Lamb, and Jim Deurloo are the co-founders of Heritage Guitars, Kalamazoo, Michigan. Moats, Lamb, and Deurloo founded the company after Gibson pulled out of Kalamazoo in 1984. Heritage is located at 225 Parsons Street, Kalamazoo. The guitar maker continues to use some of the production equipment that was used by Gibson.

Take me from your high school days to getting into Gibson. *Okay, what happened to me, I'll just start out, when I was in high school, I was working on my dad's farm in Alabama. I went up to Michigan when I was 16 years old. My first cousin and her husband wanted me to go over to the paper mill and get a job over there. I didn't think they would hire me, but they hired me at 16 years old. I worked there for 4½ years. And I quit and went back down to Alabama.*

What was the name of that mill? *The name of the company was St. Regis Paper Mill. That was located here in Kalamazoo.*

Where was that relative to Gibson? Was it on the north end? *No, it was on the southeast side of Kalamazoo. Probably, in the paper mill, they had about 1,200 people. I started out working on a paper machine as 4th hand. They closed that machine down because they were having a lot of problems with it, and they put in a new machine. And they had me to go over to what you call the coating machine, where you coat the paper. I stayed on the coating machine until I left to go back to Alabama.*

When did you hire in, and who got you lined up with the paper mill? *I hired in about 1951. My first cousin's husband, he worked over there. I just came up to Michigan for a vacation, really. He said, while you're up here, instead of going back down working on a farm in Alabama for $2.00 a day, why don't* *you go to work at the paper mill. I can get you a job, and you can make some good money. And when you want to go back to Alabama then you can quit and go back. So I got into the paper mill and I started making such good money. I wanted to work! So they had me working seven days a week. I was working a lot of 16 hour days pulling a double shift. I figured I was going to save $100 a week, paying for my food and rent, and still make a $100 week. That's what I had my mind set on.*

Where were you living at that time in Kalamazoo? *My sister and I were living together in an apartment on Alcott Street. It was right across the street from the paper mill. That's where they had me, and if anybody got sick at night, they'd just knock on my door, and I'd go fill in for them. Sometimes I'd work my shift, and if somebody didn't come in, I'd work their shift. I'd go home and maybe sleep three hours, and then they'd come over and knock on my door, and I'd go over and work the rest of that shift, and then work my shift again, and sometimes I would work another shift after that. They had me working on all the stuff in all the departments, because they couldn't get anybody to work hardly back then. But making that kind of good money, I wanted to get every hour that I could get. I'd work 16 hours, seven days a week if they'd give it to me, so that is the way I kind of got started.*

Where you aware that Gibson even existed at that time, in 1951 and 1952? *Yeah, because I hung around with a lot of guys that played music, and they played a lot of Gibsons. And right at the tail end of my last two year working at the paper mill, my sister worked for the Gibson Guitar Company.*

Was her name Moats at the time, or was she married? *No, her name was Moats at the time.*

Why did she decide to work at Gibson? *She came up here before I came up and she started working at United Cleaners. She worked there for about three years until they closed the cleaners down. So she went over to Gibson. John Huis was the one who hired her in. Ted McCarty was there at the time. They hired her in and she told John Huis that I had come back from Alabama and I was looking for a job. He wanted me to come in, so I went to Gibson and he hired me. I went to work the next day.*

You just quit the paper mill? You just got tired of it? *Well, I was young, I wasn't married. I really wanted to go back to Moulton, Alabama. I wanted to see my friends and I had saved up some money, and bought me a car. I was getting old enough that I wanted to go back to Alabama. After I got down there I spend about half of the money that I had saved, so after about three months I figured I better go back up to Kalamazoo and get me a job. I figured otherwise I wouldn't have any money (laughing). I turned around and came back and got a job at Gibson.*

It didn't seem to be terribly difficult to get a job in Kalamazoo in the 1950s? *In the 1950s they would hire anybody that walked in. They (all the plants) couldn't get enough people to work. That's when the boom really started in about 1956. In about 1955, 1956, 1957. A lot of people from the south came up here to the paper mills and started working.*

So in the 1950s, it didn't matter whether it was Gibson or Shakespeare or the paper mill, they all needed workers? *They needed workers, yes sir.*

So your sister, did she get you an interview with John Huis? *No, she just told John Huis that I had worked at the paper mill, that I was back up here looking for a job. He said for me to come in. He had me fill out an application, and he asked me a few questions, and then he said, 'Well, can you start to work tomorrow?' I said, 'Sure.'*

The 1961 Gibson catalog

232

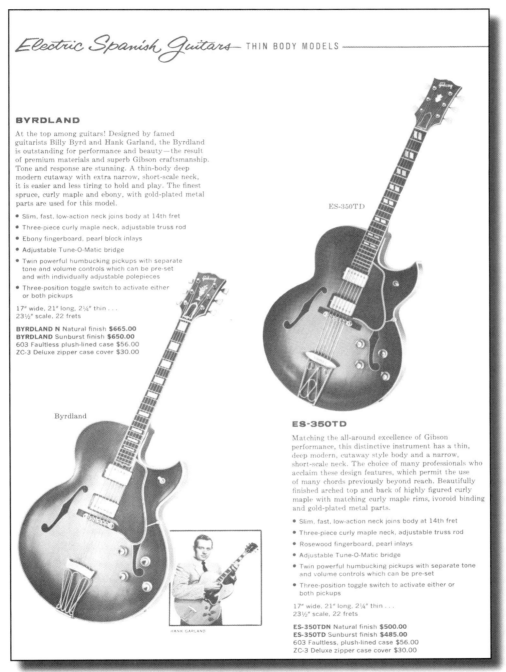

Electric Spanish Guitars — THIN BODY MODELS

BYRDLAND

At the top among guitars! Designed by famed guitarists Billy Byrd and Hank Garland, the Byrdland is outstanding for performance and beauty — the result of premium materials and superb Gibson craftsmanship. Tone and response are stunning. A thin-body deep modern cutaway with extra narrow, short-scale neck, it is easier and less tiring to hold and play. The finest spruce, curly maple and ebony, with gold-plated metal parts are used for this model.

- Slim, fast, low-action neck joins body at 14th fret
- Three-piece curly maple neck, adjustable truss rod
- Ebony fingerboard, pearl block inlays
- Adjustable Tune-O-Matic bridge
- Twin powerful humbucking pickups with separate tone and volume controls which can be pre-set and with individually adjustable polepieces
- Three-position toggle switch to activate either or both pickups

17" wide, 21" long, 2¼" thin . . .
23½" scale, 22 frets

BYRDLAND N Natural finish **$665.00**
BYRDLAND Sunburst finish **$650.00**
603 Faultless plush-lined case **$56.00**
ZC-3 Deluxe zipper case cover $30.00

Byrdland

HANK GARLAND

ES-350TD

ES-350TD

Matching the all-around excellence of Gibson performance, this distinctive instrument has a thin, deep modern, cutaway style body and a narrow, short-scale neck. The choice of many professionals who acclaim these design features, which permit the use of many chords previously beyond reach. Beautifully finished arched top and back of highly figured curly maple with matching curly maple rims, ivoroid binding and gold-plated metal parts.

- Slim, fast, low-action neck joins body at 14th fret
- Three-piece curly maple neck, adjustable truss rod
- Rosewood fingerboard, pearl inlays
- Adjustable Tune-O-Matic bridge
- Twin powerful humbucking pickups with separate tone and volume controls which can be pre-set
- Three-position toggle switch to activate either or both pickups

17" wide, 21" long, 2¼" thin . . .
23½" scale, 22 frets

ES-350TDN Natural finish **$500.00**
ES-350TD Sunburst finish **$485.00**
603 Faultless, plush-lined case $56.00
ZC-3 Deluxe zipper case cover $30.00

The 1961 Gibson catalog

ES-355TD-SV

This magnificent jazz guitar reflects all the beauty and skill of the guitar maker's art. Made with semi-solid body construction to the Gibson wonder-thin silhouette, it's easy and comfortable to hold; its feel is just right. The slim low-action neck makes strings seem feather-light and the double cutaway provides easy access down to the very last fret. With tone ranging from a clear treble to a throaty bass, with thrilling vibrato and instant response, it offers the jazz artist everything. The new Gibson cherry-red finish on curly maple with gold-plated metal parts makes it a beauty. Deluxe, padded leather strap included.

- Slim, fast, low-action neck joins body at 20th fret
- One-piece mahogany neck, adjustable truss rod
- Ebony fingerboard, pearl block inlays
- Adjustable Tune-O-Matic bridge
- Twin humbucking pickups with separate tone and volume controls which can be pre-set
- Three-position toggle switch to activate either or both pickups
- Vibrato tailpiece for added effects

16″ wide, 19″ long, 1¾″ thin . . .
24¾″ scale, 22 frets

ES-355TD Cherry finish **$595.00**
ES-355TD-SV with Stereo and Vari-Tone **$645.00**
519 Faultless plush-lined case $50.00
304 Archcraft plush-lined case $26.00
ZC-19 Deluxe zipper case cover $30.00

GIBSON STEREO

ES-355TD-SV

Barney Kessel Custom

BARNEY KESSEL GUITAR

A Gibson guitar designed by the great jazz guitarist himself, with musical capability to match his tremendous technique and vital, inventive playing. With slim, fast, low-action neck and new modern deep double cutaway, it permits fleetest fingering on every fret. It offers the purest tone over the entire range with a special magnetic field in the bridge pickup to emphasize the highs. Exquisitely fashioned with laminated spruce arched top and laminated maple back . . . cream and black royalite binding. Pickguard has black and white binding with revealed edges. Gold-plated metal parts.

- Slim, fast, low-action neck joins body at 14th fret
- Three-piece curly maple neck, adjustable truss rod
- 20-fret rosewood fingerboard with "bow-tie" pearl inlays
- Gold-plated adjustable Tune-O-Matic bridge
- Twin powerful humbucking pickups . . . separate tone and volume controls can be pre-set . . . special magnetic field in bridge pickup
- Three-position toggle switch to activate either or both pickups

17″ wide, 21″ long, 3″ thin
25½″ scale, 20 frets

Barney Kessel Custom Cherry sunburst finish **$560.00**

Barney Kessel Regular Cherry sunburst finish **$395.00**
Like the custom model with these differences: mahogany neck with pearl inlaid peghead, rosewood fingerboard with rectangular pearl inlays, rosewood bridge, nickel-plated metal parts.

600 Faultless plush-lined case $56.00
ZC-3 Deluxe zipper case cover $30.00

The 1961 Gibson catalog

Electric Spanish Guitars

SOLID BODY MODELS

LES PAUL CUSTOM

Players call it the "Fretless Wonder" for its extremely low frets and fast action. Now it's more wonderful than ever with new body design and new features. Ultra thin, hand contoured, delicately balanced, it adjusts into a natural comfortable playing position for any guitarist, with or without strap. With three humbucking adjustable pickups, Tune-O-Matic bridge, and new Vibrato* ... with increased power, greater sustain, and a clear, resonant sparkling tone, the "Custom" provides the widest range of tonal colorings and effects. Three-way toggle switch provides a unique method of tone mixing: top position selects top pickup for rhythm; center position activates center and lower pickups simultaneously for extreme highs and special effects; lower position operates lower pickup for playing lead.

Finished in gleaming white for smart contrast with gold-plated metal parts. Deluxe, padded leather strap included.

- Ultra thin, hand contoured, double cutaway body
- New extra slim, fast, low-action neck—with exclusive extra low frets—joins body at 22nd fret
- One-piece mahogany neck with adjustable truss rod
- Ebony fingerboard, deluxe pearl inlays
- Adjustable Tune-O-Matic bridge
- Three powerful, humbucking pickups with unique wiring arrangement
- Two sets of tone and volume controls
- Three-way specially wired toggle switch
- New Gibson Vibrato*—operates in direction of pick stroke; swings out of way for rhythm playing

12¾" wide, 16" long, 1⁵⁄₁₆" thin ... 24¾" scale, 22 frets

Les Paul Custom
White finish **$425.00**
0537 Faultless gold plush-lined case $47.50
ZC-CLP Deluxe zipper case cover $30.00

*patented

10

LES PAUL STANDARD

An established favorite with completely new modern styling ... with thinner, lighter weight contoured body, and deep double cutaway that provides easy access to all 22 frets. The new Gibson Vibrato* and the extremely slim, fast, low-action neck make this guitar a joy to play. Tone is clear and bell-like throughout its entire range. The perfectly balanced solid body makes playing comfortable in any position, sitting or standing. The Tune-O-Matic bridge permits adjusting string action and individual string lengths. The finish is a beautiful cherry-red with nickel-plated metal parts and individual machine heads with deluxe buttons. Deluxe padded leather strap included.

- Ultra thin, contoured, double cutaway body
- Slim, fast, low-action neck—with exclusive extra low frets—joins body at 22nd fret
- One-piece mahogany neck with adjustable truss rod
- Rosewood fingerboard, pearl inlays
- Adjustable Tune-O-Matic bridge
- Twin powerful humbucking pickups with separate tone and volume controls which can be pre-set
- New Gibson Vibrato*—operates in direction of pick stroke; swings out of way for rhythm playing
- Three-position toggle switch to activate either or both pickups

12¾" wide, 16" long, 1⁵⁄₁₆" thin ... 24¾" scale. 22 frets

Les Paul Standard
Cherry finish **$290.00**
0537 Faultless, gold plush-lined case $47.50
ZC-CLP Deluxe zipper case cover $30.00

The 1961 Gibson catalog

235

SPECIAL

Two ways new! A lovely new finish in a new shade of limed mahogany or Gibson's new cherry red . . . an ultra-modern new sculptured shape—the solid body double cutaway design that provides easy access to *all* 22 frets. Outstanding for its tone, versatility, and low fast action at a modest price. Very graceful and sturdy with beautifully finished, nickel-plated metal parts. Enclosed individual machine heads. Leather strap included.

- Slim, fast, low-action neck—with exclusive extra low frets, joins body at 22nd fret
- Rosewood fingerboard, pearl dot inlays
- One-piece mahogany neck, adjustable truss rod
- Combination metal bridge and tailpiece, adjustable horizontally and vertically
- Twin powerful pickups with separate tone and volume controls which can be pre-set
- Three-position toggle switch to activate either or both pickups

12¾" wide, 16" long, 1⅞" thin . . . 24¾" scale, 22 frets

SG-R Special Cherry-red finish **$210.00**
SGC Special Cream finish **$210.00**
0537 Faultless plush case $47.50
316 Archcraft plush-lined case $24.00
116 Durabilt case $15.00
ZC-CLP Deluxe zipper case cover $30.00

TV

An exciting guitar, handsomely modern in design and finish, the TV offers unusual quality, features, and performance at a popular price. The finish is a beautiful cream; the thin sculptured, contoured body has a deep double cutaway for easy access to all frets. Easy, low playing action, a slender neck, and clear sustaining tone make the TV a favorite with students and advanced players. Bright nickel-plated metal parts and quality machine heads. Leather strap included.

- Slim, fast, low-action neck—with exclusive extra low frets—joins body at the 22nd fret
- One-piece mahogany neck, adjustable truss rod
- Rosewood fingerboard, pearl dot inlays
- Combination bridge and tailpiece, adjustable horizontally and vertically
- Powerful pickup with individually adjustable polepieces
- Separate tone and volume controls which can be pre-set

12¾" wide, 16" long, 1⅞" thin . . . 24¾" scale, 22 frets

SG TV Cream finish **$147.50**
0537 Faultless plush case $47.50
316 Archcraft plush-lined case $24.00
116 Durabilt case $15.00

Maestro Vibrola available for Melody Maker Guitars, Les Paul Jr., SG-TV or SG Special **$27.50**

LES PAUL AND MARY FORD

11

The 1961 Gibson catalog

236

Electric Spanish Guitars

SOLID BODY MODELS

LES PAUL JUNIOR

A best seller that's now even better—with its handsome new cherry-red finish and its highly desirable new double cutaway sculptured design, and its very low popular price. You get Gibson quality and top performance. A small, thin, sturdy, solid body guitar, its beautiful cherry-red finish on the finest mahogany. Nickel-plated metal parts and quality machine heads. Leather strap included.

- Slim, fast, low-action neck—with exclusive extra low frets, joins body at the 22nd fret
- One-piece mahogany neck, adjustable truss rod
- Rosewood fingerboard, pearl dot inlays
- Combination bridge and tailpiece, adjustable horizontally and vertically
- Powerful pickup with individually adjustable polepieces
- Separate tone and volume controls which can be pre-set

12¾" wide, 16" long, 1½6" thin
. . . 24¾" scale, 22 frets

Les Paul Jr. Cherry-red finish **$147.50**
116 Durabilt case $15.00
316 Archcraft plush-lined case $24.00
0537 Faultless plush-lined case $47.50

MELODY MAKER
MELODY MAKER 3/4

Greatest value ever in a Solid Body electric with full-size neck and scale length. Acclaimed by players, teachers and students for its fine sound, big tone, sensitive pickup, feather-light touch, and beautiful sunburst finish. Expert workmanship and finest materials are used throughout to produce this top quality low-priced instrument. Nickel-plated metal parts. Leather strap included. Available also with three-quarter size neck and fingerboard that joins the body at the 12th fret.

- Slim, fast, low-action neck—with exclusive extra low frets, joins body at the 16th fret
- One-piece mahogany neck, adjustable truss rod
- Graceful, cutaway design
- Rosewood fingerboard, pearl dot inlays
- Combination bridge and tailpiece, adjustable horizontally and vertically
- Powerful pickup near bridge with individually adjustable polepieces
- Separate tone and volume controls

12⅜" wide, 17¼" long, 1⅜" thin
. . . 24¾" scale, 22 frets

Melody Maker D with two pickups **$147.50**
Melody Maker Sunburst finish **$109.50**
114 Durabilt case $12.00
Melody Maker ¾ Sunburst finish **$109.50**
114¾ Durabilt case $12.00

12

The 1961 Gibson catalog

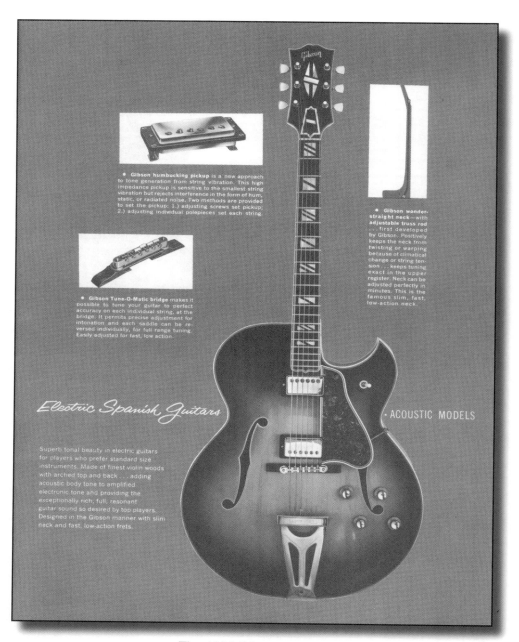

The 1961 Gibson catalog

Electric Spanish Guitars — ACOUSTIC MODELS

SUPER 400 CES

A crowning achievement! Developed through years of research, the luxurious Super 400 CES has been acclaimed by outstanding musicians everywhere as the finest electric Spanish guitar. Superior materials and superb Gibson craftsmanship produce its clear, clean-cut powerful tone and dependable performance. A modern deep cutaway design . . . hand-graduated carved top of finest spruce, arched back of highly figured curly maple with matching rims, black and white ivoroid binding, exclusive pearl-inlaid peghead, hand-bound custom pickguard, gold-plated metal parts, and deluxe individual machine heads.

- Slim, fast, low-action neck joins body at 14th fret
- Three-piece curly maple neck, adjustable truss rod
- Ebony fingerboard, pearl block inlays
- Adjustable Tune-O-Matic bridge
- Exclusive Super 400 adjustable tailpiece
- Twin, powerful humbucking pickups with separate tone and volume controls which can be pre-set
- Three-position toggle switch to activate either or both pickups

18″ wide, 21¾″ long, 3⅜″ deep . . . 25½″ scale, 20 frets

Super 400 CESN Natural finish **$850.00**
Super 400 CES Sunburst finish **$825.00**
400 Faultless plush-lined case $60.00
ZC-4 Deluxe zipper case cover $35.00

Super 400 CES

JOHNNY SMITH GUITAR

This new artist's guitar offers the most perfect combination of acoustic response and electronic amplification ever produced. An entirely new humbucking pickup and new method of mounting were designed to produce the purest tone amplification without restricting the acoustic response of the carved top. Intonation is incomparably clear. The superb speed neck responds to the lightest touch with a very wide range of highs and lows. The beautifully crafted body has a carved spruce top with bound "*f*" sound holes and matched figured maple rim, neck, and carved back . . . shell celluloid pickguard, multiple black and white binding, rich pearl inlays, gold plated metal parts, and Sealfast machine heads with keytone metal buttons.

- Slim, graduated speed neck with fast low action joins body at 14th fret
- Three-piece curly maple neck with adjustable truss rod
- Ebony fingerboard with pearl block inlays and nickel silver frets
- Special ebony bridge with slanted ebony saddle to accommodate Johnny Smith strings
- Special balanced tone humbucking pickup mounted free of body on end of fingerboard
- Volume control and instrument jack mounted on pickguard, free of body, completely shielded

17″ wide, 20½″ long, 3⅛″ deep
25″ scale, 20 frets

Johnny Smith Guitar Natural finish **$810.00**
Johnny Smith Guitar Sunburst finish **$795.00**
Complete with special Faultless gold plush-lined case and zipper case cover

14

The 1961 Gibson catalog

EB-3

Here is the ultimate in an all new, ultra thin, hand contoured solid body Gibson Electric Bass. The delicately balanced design automatically adjusts into a natural, comfortable playing position with or without a strap. Equipped with string damper, twin humbucking pickups, finger or hand brace on pickguard, and a new 4 position switch which provide versatility, fine response, and a variety of tone changes. The EB-3 offers great facility and handling ease for all string bass effects—tremendous sustain and tremolo, fast plucking and slap bass. A truly remarkable instrument for performance, plus outstanding appearance with nickel plated metal parts and cherry red finish.

- New extra thin, custom contoured, double cutaway body design
- New extra slim, fast, low action, one-piece mahogany neck with adjustable truss rod
- Rosewood fingerboard with pearl dot inlays
- Combination bridge and tailpiece adjustable horizontally and vertically
- Twin powerful humbucking pickups for greater tonal range
- New four position switch for versatile tonal response: #1 for normal bass response; #2 for a clear treble quality timbre; #3 for a combination of #1 and #2; and #4 for a baritone quality response
- New nickel plated string damper can be switched into position for muted effects
- Hand brace for plucking strings mounted on pickguard
- Heavy duty bass type individual machine heads with metal buttons

12¾″ wide, 16″ long, 1⁵⁄₁₆″ thin . . . 30½″ scale, 20 frets

EB-3 Cherry red finish **$310.00**
540 Faultless, plush-lined case $60.00
329 Archcraft plush-lined case $26.50

EB-3

EB-O

A new, economy priced bass by Gibson—it offers clear sustaining bass response, easy and fast playing action, and modern cherry-red finish. Double cutaway sculptured body brings the entire length of the fingerboard within easy reach. Expensive bass style machine heads further enhance the value of this instrument. Once your hear its throaty bass tone and feel the quick, easy response, you'll agree—the EB-O gives the professional artist the quality he wants.

- Slim, fast, low-action neck joins body beyond 17th fret
- One-piece mahogany neck, adjustable truss rod
- Rosewood fingerboard, pearl dot inlays
- Combination bridge and tailpiece, adjustable horizontally and vertically
- Hand brace for plucking strings mounted on pickguard
- Powerful humbucking pickup with separate tone and volume controls

12¾″ wide, 16″ long, 1⁵⁄₁₆″ thin . . . 30½″ scale, 20 frets

EB-O Cherry finish **$210.00**
540 Faultless plush-lined case $60.00
329 Archcraft plush-lined case $26.50   EB-O

EB-6
Electric Six-String Bass

Six-string electric bass, similar in design to the ES-335TD, giving a full octave lower guitar tuning on a regular bass scale length. Single pickup, vari-tone pushbutton switch for variable frequency resonating response. Neck joins body at the 18 fret, providing easy access to all six strings.

EB-6 Sunburst finish **$325.00**
538 Faultless plush-lined case $57.50

The 1961 Gibson catalog

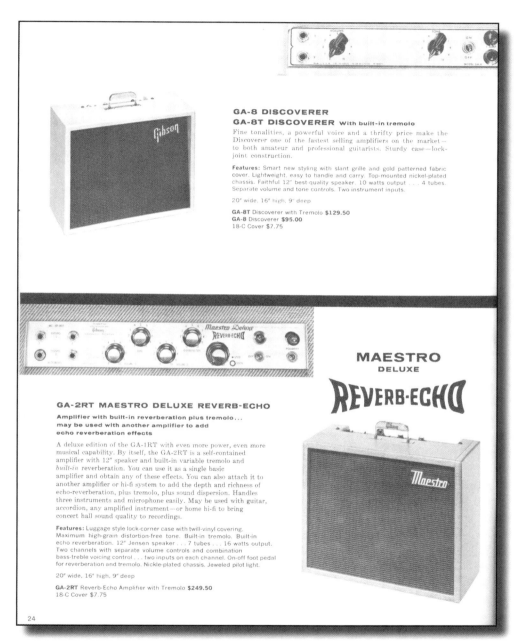

GA-8 DISCOVERER
GA-8T DISCOVERER With built-in tremolo

Fine tonalities, a powerful voice and a thrifty price make the Discoverer one of the fastest selling amplifiers on the market—to both amateur and professional guitarists. Sturdy case—lock-joint construction.

Features: Smart new styling with slant grille and gold patterned fabric cover. Lightweight, easy to handle and carry. Top-mounted nickel-plated chassis. Faithful 12″ best-quality speaker. 10 watts output . . . 4 tubes. Separate volume and tone controls. Two instrument inputs.

20″ wide, 16″ high, 9″ deep

GA-8T Discoverer with Tremolo **$129.50**
GA-8 Discoverer **$95.00**
18-C Cover $7.75

MAESTRO
DELUXE
REVERB-ECHO

GA-2RT MAESTRO DELUXE REVERB-ECHO

Amplifier with built-in reverberation plus tremolo . . .
may be used with another amplifier to add
echo reverberation effects

A deluxe edition of the GA-1RT with even more power, even more musical capability. By itself, the GA-2RT is a self-contained amplifier with 12″ speaker and built-in variable tremolo and *built-in* reverberation. You can use it as a single basic amplifier and obtain any of these effects. You can also attach it to another amplifier or hi-fi system to add the depth and richness of echo-reverberation, plus tremolo, plus sound dispersion. Handles three instruments and microphone easily. May be used with guitar, accordion, any amplified instrument—or home hi-fi to bring concert hall sound quality to recordings.

Features: Luggage style lock-corner case with twill-vinyl covering. Maximum high-grain distortion-free tone. Built-in tremolo. Built-in echo reverberation. 12″ Jensen speaker . . . 7 tubes . . . 16 watts output. Two channels with separate volume controls and combination bass-treble voicing control . . . two inputs on each channel. On-off foot pedal for reverberation and tremolo. Nickle-plated chassis. Jeweled pilot light.

20″ wide, 16″ high, 9″ deep

GA-2RT Reverb-Echo Amplifier with Tremolo **$249.50**
18-C Cover $7.75

24

The 1961 Gibson catalog

GA-100 BASS AMPLIFIER
With deep, deep sound and flat response

Designed especially for three particular musicians: the bass player, the jazz guitarist, and the classic artist who uses an electric guitar. The large bass reflex enclosure assures completely undistorted sound: bass tones whisper or roar without shattering, brash highs are banished. The jazz player will love its flat response; the classic guitarist will find settings especially for him. Separate speaker and chassis.

Features: Improved built-in compression circuit assures distortion-free sound and prevents overloading. Heavy duty imported 12-inch speaker. One channel, two inputs . . . one volume control, two tone controls. 9 tubes—panel mounted fuse. 35 watts output. Standby and polarity switches. Jeweled pilot light. Trim, durable case with vinyl-twill covering and contrasting grille. Separate control panel mounts on tripod.

22" wide, 20" high, 10" deep

GA-100 Bass Amplifier **$325.00**   100-C Cover $11.00
Tripod for chassis (control panel) $25.00

GA-1RT MAESTRO REVERB-ECHO
Amplifies...adds tremolo...converts any amplifier to reverberation

A remarkable three-in-one sound unit—lightweight, compact, and inexpensive. By itself, it is a basic amplifier with variable tremolo. But attach it to another amplifier or hi-fi system, and it supplies echo-reverberation with all its exciting richness and depth . . . plus tremolo . . . plus the sound dispersion obtained when using two amplifiers. May be used with guitar, accordion, or any amplified instrument—or home hi-fi system to bring concert hall sound quality to recordings.

Features: Luggage style lock-corner case with twill-vinyl covering. 8" Jensen speaker. Volume control and variable tremolo control. On-off foot switch for reverberation. 8 watts output . . . 3 tubes. Two instrument inputs. Nickel plated chassis. Jeweled pilot light.

18¾" wide, 13½" high, 7" deep

GA-1RT Reverb-Echo with Tremolo **$149.50**

The 1961 Gibson catalog

Amplifiers with Reverberation

With Gibson Reverb, the guitar player can get concert hall richness and depth *anywhere*, adding a "third dimension" to sound amplification. Reverb in sound deficiencies of the ordinary room and creates the optimum acoustical environment for sound reproduction. It's the exciting, new "Gibson sound for the 60's."

GA-79RV STEREO-REVERB
With stereo sound and reverberation

Here it is—Gibson's excitingly new "three dimensional sound" amplifier. One compact unit gives you stereophonic sound in all its range and brilliance . . . plus monaural sound . . . plus reverberation, adding new scope and magnitude to your music. Just right for stereo guitar, regular guitar, or record player . . . for single player or combo—four can play through it.

Features: Handsome stereo cabinet with top mounted controls . . . woven Saran grille covers. Two hi-fidelity Jensen 10" speakers (each facing at a 45° angle) give 180° of stereophonic sound. Two channels, each with separate volume and tone controls. 8 tubes . . . 30 watts output. Four instrument inputs . . . phono jack for use with stereo or monaural turntables. On-off foot pedal for reverberation. Polarity switch and ground clip eliminate interference.

25¾" wide at back (11" at front.) 18¾" high, 10½" deep at center

GA-79RV Multipurpose with Stereo-Reverb **$350.00**
GA-79RVT Multipurpose with Stereo-
Reverb and Tremolo **$395.00**
79-C Cover $11.00

GA-77RV VANGUARD
With Gibson reverberation...with high gain channel

Bell clear reproduction with brilliant highs, a wide range of tonal effects, plus the added richness and depth of reverberation for the professional guitarist. Two can play through this amp and each can achieve as much bass or treble as he wants.

Features: All new Gibson styling—slant grille, twill vinyl covering, lock-corner case. 15" best-quality speaker . . . 6 tubes. Two channels . . . separate volume and tone controls for each . . . two inputs for each. High frequency filter for brilliant highs in channel 2. Standby polarity switch and ground clip eliminate interference. 25 watts normal output, over 35 at peak.

22" wide, 21⅛" high, 10½" deep

GA-77RV Vanguard with Reverb **$365.00**
GA-77 Vanguard without Reverb **$315.00**
80-C Cover $9.50

GA-30RV INVADER
With Gibson reverberation...dual speakers

Handles three instruments and microphone with ease, *and* gives you Concert Hall sound—all the extra clarity and quality of Gibson reverberation. A big-voiced professional amp with two speakers, ample-power, and a wide range of tonal qualities.

Features: Modern styling with woven Saran grille cover . . . jeweled pilot light. 12" and 8" best-quality speakers. 6 tubes . . . 16 watts output. Combination treble and bass voicing control plus tone expanders. 4 input circuits: two for instruments or microphones, two for instruments only . . . separate volume controls for each. Combination polarity switch with off-standby-on positions.

22" wide, 20" high, 10⅛" deep

GA-30RV Invader with Reverb **$265.00**
80-C Cover $9.50

26

The 1961 Gibson catalog

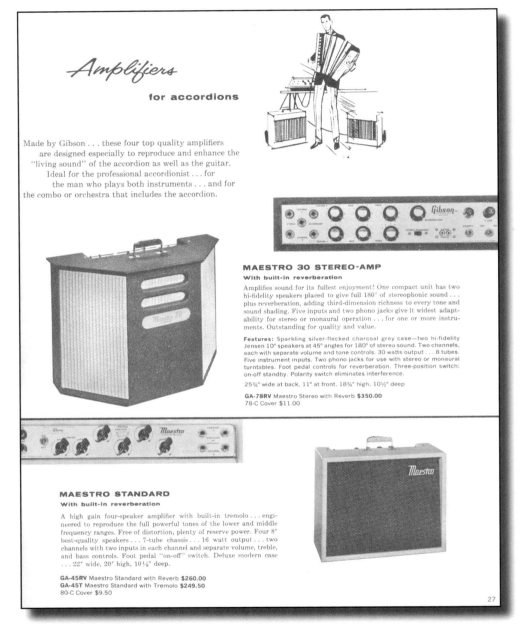

Amplifiers

for accordions

Made by Gibson . . . these four top quality amplifiers are designed especially to reproduce and enhance the "living sound" of the accordion as well as the guitar. Ideal for the professional accordionist . . . for the man who plays both instruments . . . and for the combo or orchestra that includes the accordion.

MAESTRO 30 STEREO-AMP
With built-in reverberation

Amplifies sound for its fullest enjoyment! One compact unit has two hi-fidelity speakers placed to give full 180° of stereophonic sound . . . plus reverberation, adding third-dimension richness to every tone and sound shading. Five inputs and two phono jacks give it widest adaptability for stereo or monaural operation . . . for one or more instruments. Outstanding for quality and value.

Features: Sparkling silver-flecked charcoal grey case—two hi-fidelity Jensen 10″ speakers at 45° angles for 180° of stereo sound. Two channels, each with separate volume and tone controls. 30 watts output . . . 8 tubes. Five instrument inputs. Two phono jacks for use with stereo or monaural turntables. Foot pedal controls for reverberation. Three-position switch: on-off standby. Polarity switch eliminates interference.

25¼″ wide at back, 11″ at front, 18¾″ high, 10½″ deep

GA-78RV Maestro Stereo with Reverb **$350.00**
78-C Cover $11.00

MAESTRO STANDARD
With built-in reverberation

A high gain four-speaker amplifier with built-in tremolo . . . engineered to reproduce the full powerful tones of the lower and middle frequency ranges. Free of distortion, plenty of reserve power. Four 8″ best-quality speakers . . . 7-tube chassis . . . 16 watt output . . . two channels with two inputs in each channel and separate volume, treble, and bass controls. Foot pedal "on-off" switch. Deluxe modern case . . . 22″ wide, 20″ high, 10⅛″ deep.

GA-45RV Maestro Standard with Reverb **$260.00**
GA-45T Maestro Standard with Tremolo **$249.50**
80-C Cover $9.50

27

The 1961 Gibson catalog

Amplifiers for accordions

MAESTRO 15RV AMPLIFIER

With built-in reverberation

Another superb amplifier providing all the exciting sound effects of reverberation . . . plus hi-fidelity distortion-free amplification throughout the full tone range of your instrument. Two channels have four instrument or microphone inputs with simple easy-to-use controls for easiest playability. Compact, lightweight, smartly styled.

Features: Built-in reverberation with variable control to regulate reverberation, reverberation intensity and foot pedal on-off switch. 12" Jensen speaker. Two channels four instrument or microphone inputs. Separate volume control and combination bass-treble voicing control. 14 to 16 watts output . . . 7 tubes. Jeweled pilot light. 2 amp protective fuse. On-off switch. Polarity switche liminates interference.

22" wide, 20" high, 9½" deep. Weight 35 lbs.

GA-15RV Maestro 15RV with Reverb **$230.00**
80-C Cover $9.50

MAESTRO VISCOUNT

A full-sized amplifier with powerful voice . . . quick-change controls for volume, tone, depth and frequency of tremolo . . . 10" heavy-duty concert speaker . . . 5 tubes—2 dual purpose—giving 7 tube performance . . . 3 input jacks . . . 14 watt output. Designed for perfect tone reproduction, its full sound range, wide-swing tremolo make this newest Maestro Amplifier the most desirable unit of its size to be found anywhere. Smart new slant grille—20" wide, 16½" high, 9" deep. And the low price makes it truly exceptional.

GA-16T Maestro Viscount Amplifier **$165.00**
18-C Cover $7.75

28

The 1961 Gibson catalog

Flat Top Guitars • JUMBO MODELS

THE HUMMINGBIRD

A fabulous new accoustical guitar—one of the finest ever made for voice accompaniment. The sound is big, and round, and full with the deep rumbly bass so prized by guitar players. There's plenty of showmanship for the player in its wonderful resonant tone and carrying power, and in its striking beauty, too. The finish is Gibson's incomparable cherry-red sunburst color, complimented by an exquisite pickguard, depicting hummingbirds in flight—so lovely the guitar was named for it.

Features: Fine grained spruce sound board in cherry-red sunburst finish with Honduras mahogany back and rims and beautiful hummingbird pickguard. New extra slim neck for fast, low action and more comfortable playing—one piece Honduras mahogany neck with adjustable truss rod. Bound rosewood fingerboard with large parallel pearloid inlays. Special adjustable rosewood bridge. Nickel plated enclosed individual machine heads.

16¼" wide, 20¼" long, 4⅞" deep
24¾" scale, 20 frets

Hummingbird Guitar,
Cherry-red finish **$250.00**
515 Faultless plush-lined case $50.00
318 Archcraft plush-lined case $26.00
118 Durabilt case $14.50
ZC-5 Deluxe zipper case for 515 $30.00

J-200 N

Called "King of the Flat Top Guitars" for its dramatic beauty, booming resonance, and penetrating carrying power . . . built with an extra large tone chamber and many exclusive design features. Very showy in appearance, flawless in workmanship, outstanding in performance.

Features: Finest close-grained spruce top with highly figured curly maple back and rims. Decorative black-and-white ivoroid binding, multiple inlaid purfling rings, and etched brown celluloid finger rest. Slim, fast, low-action neck—three-piece curly maple with adjustable truss rod. Bound rosewood fingerboard with large pearl inlays. Pearl-inlaid rosewood bridge. Gold-plated enclosed individual machine heads with metal tuning buttons.

17" wide, 21" long, 4⅞" deep
25½" scale, 20 frets

J-200N Natural finish **$450.00**
J-200 Sunburst finish **$435.00**
600 Faultless plush-lined case $56.00
609 Archcraft plush-lined case $22.50
ZC-6 Deluxe zipper case cover $30.00

34

The 1961 Gibson catalog

B-45-12 TWELVE STRING

Twelve strings with their special tuning and reinforced tone provide a unique guitar sound—favored by folk singers, effective in combos and solo. The first three double strings are tuned in unison; the last three in octaves. A traditional jumbo size instrument with fine resonance and response . . traditional Gibson tone, quality, and beautiful cherry-sunburst finish.

Features: Selected spruce top, Honduras mahogany back and rim with attractive ivoroid binding and purfling. Twelve-string, fast, low-action neck—one-piece mahogany with adjustable truss rod. Rosewood fingerboard with pearl dot inlays. Special adjustable twelve-string bridge. Tortoise shell finger rest. Nickel-plated enclosed machine heads. Attractive jumbo size and shape peghead.

16¼" wide, 21¼" long, 4⅞" deep
24¾" scale, 20 frets

B-45-12 Cherry sunburst finish **$239.00**
345 Archcraft case $26.50

SJN COUNTRY WESTERN

Country-Western artists have no greater favorite! They praise the SJN's traditional jumbo size and shape, its deep resonance, powerful tone and deluxe appearance, and its Gibson quality.

Features: Top of natural finish selected spruce; back, neck, and matching rims of rich red Honduras mahogany. Handsome multiple white-black-white binding and purfling rings. Slim, fast, low-action neck—one-piece mahogany with adjustable truss rod. Bound rosewood fingerboard with large parallel pearl inlays. Gibson special rosewood bridge. Large tortoise shell finish finger rest and nickel-plated enclosed individual machine heads.

16¼" wide, 20¼" long, 4⅞" deep
24¾" scale, 20 frets

SJN Natural finish top **$195.00**
515 Faultless plush-lined case $50.00
318 Archcraft plush-lined case $26.00
118 Durabilt case $14.50
ZC-5 Deluxe zipper case cover $30.00

SJ SOUTHERNER JUMBO

A special favorite with southern balladiers, but preferred by many Country-Western artists, too, especially for its dramatic appearance. The SJ has all the outstanding features, the tonal response, and quality workmanship of the SJN.

Features: Top in a glowing golden sunburst finish with rims, neck, and back in rich red Honduras mahogany. Multiple white-black-white binding and purfling rings. Slim, fast, low-action neck—one-piece mahogany with adjustable truss rod. Bound rosewood fingerboard with large parallel pearl inlays. Gibson special rosewood bridge. Large tortoise shell finish finger rest and nickel-plated enclosed individual machine heads.

16¼" wide, 20¼" long, 4⅞" deep
24¾" scale, 20 frets

SJ Sunburst finish **$180.00**
515 Faultless plush-lined case $50.00
318 Archcraft plush-lined case $26.00
118 Durabilt case $14.50
ZC-5 Deluxe zipper case cover $30.00

35

The 1961 Gibson catalog

When you went over to Gibson, do you remember, did you stop at the guard shack, and then the guard got a hold of Mr. Huis? Is that how it worked? *Yes sir. They had a guard, and they called Mr. John Huis, and they let me go into his office.*

So you didn't see Bellson (Personnel Manager)? *I didn't see Mr. Julius Bellson at that time. Not until I got hired, and probably three or four days later I got into see Mr. Bellson.*

Okay, then the next day you went in, and where did Huis have you work? *They started me on what you call the white wood cleaning line. Where you would do the sanding and everything just before it goes to finishing. That was on the first floor near the mill room. That was before the 1960 addition, so it was on the first floor right along the north side windows. That was the white wood cleaning line all set-up to handle the instruments after they were neck-fitted, drilled, and everything. Then we did what we called the hand sanding. We touched the instrument up and sanded and got the instrument ready for the finish to be put on. After the white wood line the next step would be pore filling & staining on the third floor of the old building.*

When was that? *That was somewhere around the last of January in 1957.*

Who else was on the line with you? *Marv Lamb was on the line, in fact he was the one who helped break me in on the cleaning, because he hired in a year before I did.*

Was the white wood cleaning line where most of the new workers went? *Not necessarily. If they had an opening in the mill room, or if they had an opening in finishing, or if they had an opening anywhere, they hired them in and put them on that job. It was a union shop, so they had it so that if somebody wanted to bid on that other job, then when the bids were over they'd hire somebody on the job that they didn't have a bid on.*

On your first job you were hand sanding? Where did you go from the hand sanding, what was the next move? *I went up to the third floor of the old building where they had the instrument all finished, all strung up, and ready to be shipped. I had to do what they called the final cleaning, to make sure there were no scratches or no jams. You had to use a buffing wheel to buff any kind of flaws or anything out on them that anybody put in when they put the pickups in them, or machine heads on them, and strings, and all of that stuff. You know if they scuffed them or put a little jam in them. I had to take and put touch-ups on them, or lacquer burn-in on them. Then after I got everything done and got them buffed, I had to take polish and polish them up really nice. Then they were ready to go and be packed up to be shipped.*

Why did you go up to that job, did you post for that, did you apply for that? *They asked me. They had an opening up there, and they asked me if I'd like to go up there and do that. Nobody had bid on it. I hadn't been there all that long. I was going to stick with the white wood cleaning, but they asked me to go up there and do that, and I said that I wouldn't mind learning the job. So I went up and took that job. That was around 1958.*

Do you remember who else was in the department at the time? *Fred Wilke was what you call the 'leader.' He was the one that broke people in on the final cleaning line. Rem Wall, he was the inspector there, inspecting our work. Inspecting the guitars, to play, to be sent out.*

Did he actually play them to make sure that they were okay? *Yeah, he checked every one of them. He played them, and run down through them, to make sure that they weren't, what you call 'buzzing', to make sure the fret work was done well, and to make sure it was tuned up good. And then he'd looked at them to make sure the finish was good on them. Then they were ready to ship.*

What happened to your career next? *Mr. Fred Wilke, he retired, and they wanted me to take over the 'leader' position over the final cleaning line. Which I did. That was about 1960, when the whole new building went in, and they put the new spray room in. When they moved to the new building (1960), Fred Wilke retired.*

Was a 'leader' the same as a foreman? *No, that wouldn't be a foreman. The leader was all about breaking people in, showing them how to do the job. If somebody was new, and they couldn't do the job, and it was a critical type spot on the guitar body that the new person couldn't get into, the leader would do that.*

When you originally hired in, into sanding, was Marv Lamb the leader? Was there a leader out there too? *Yeah, they had a leader out there. But, in that case, he didn't really break too many people in. Marv Lamb, he was really good on that white wood cleaning. Some of the other guys tried to show me what to do, but Marv, he helped me out more than anybody on that cleaning line.*

It doesn't sound like a lot of people really posted for jobs. When I've talked with the other employees there in the 1950s and early 1960s, it doesn't seem like people switched jobs too much. *No they didn't. There were a lot of them that wanted to stick with just what they were doing.*

I have been asking people about the union. When you hired in I believe there was a short waiting period, a probationary period, before you could join the union. *It was about 30 days. After that period you were automatically part of the union.*

In the 1950s I think the union was pretty peaceful. What do you remember about the union? *The union was really good. We didn't have any problems in the 1950s and early 1960s.*

There was a short strike around 1966 after Ted McCarty left Gibson. Do you remember walking the picket line or getting involved in that? *I had to go in to join the picket line. I just went out there on the picket line and sat down; I really didn't want to do it. If you didn't do it, you didn't get any pay. The union gave you a little bit of money if you did it. I went in more or less to just sit around and do it.*

The two small strikes in the 1960s were over wages, is that what you remember it was? *Yes, I'm sure that was what it was.*

Do you remember Ted McCarty walking through the plant when you were there in the 1950s and early 1960s? *I sure do. He was a very well dressed man, I remember his pants and everything had to be just so-so, and his shoes had to be shined like a mirror so you could see yourself in them. He was a very neat person and a very, very good guy. He never tried to be a bad guy. He just seemed to be a really good guy. Ted McCarty and Julius Bellson, the two of them were just real gentlemen, I'll tell you.*

Did Ted McCarty ever stop at your work station to talk? *Yes he did. He talked to me and asked me how I liked the job, and all of that kind of stuff. I told him that I loved my job. I'd never taken off any time, or anything. It was like when I was at the paper mill where I worked all the overtime. When I was at Gibson I used to take and work 10 hours a day, sometimes I'd work six days a week. So just like at the paper mill, I was working all the time.*

They were paying overtime at Gibson then? *Oh yes. It was overtime at time and a half. Overtime was paid on anything over 40 hours. If you worked four 10 hour days and you didn't come in on Friday to get more than 40 hours, you didn't get overtime.*

Did you see Mr. McCarty out there quite a bit then? *He would come through the shop. I'd say I'd see him come through the shop maybe a couple times a week.*

Now how about John Huis? *John Huis was out there on the floor, you'd see him probably six, seven, or eight times a day.*

Did he stop and ask you how things were going? *Oh yes, he'd stop and if you had any problem he'd be glad to talk to you about it. You could stop him even and ask him a question. Back in those days, the '50s and '60s they were very nice, very good about standing and talking to you, and asking you questions – and you'd ask them questions. (Pausing) John, he even signed me up in the TPA, the Traveler's Protection Association. He was President over that. He signed me up in TPA, and I've been in that for 48 years now (laughing). What they call Traveler's Protection Association, it's an insurance deal, that if you get hurt or anything, accidental, it's an accidental insurance type thing, but it is also a fraternal organization type thing. He signed me up in that and he had me get on the Board with him. I've been on the Board with TPA for about 40 years. (Pausing) John and I were real close. We did things together like that; go to meetings together, travel to different places when TPA was having things. He liked me and I liked John, too.*

Did Bellson come through? *Yes sir, Mr. Bellson came through, not too often, but I'd say maybe like Mr. McCarty, maybe twice a week. He was a guy that you could go in his office and talk to him anytime about any kind of problem that you had. He was the guy that would handle that part of it. If there were any union problems or anything, if you had any problems whatsoever, he'd be glad for you to come in and sit down and talk to him at anytime.*

When you came back up from Alabama and worked for Gibson, where were you living? *I was living on the north side, about 8 blocks from Gibson. That was on North Street, south of the plant. I walked to work every day. I walked to work in the winter too.*

How long did you live there? *We lived there about a year and a half. Then we bought a house over in Parchment, Michigan, which was north of the plant, about three miles. Then I started driving to work.*

Did you know Rollo Werner, the purchasing guy? *Rollo Werner was the purchasing guy. After Rollo retired they had another purchasing guy come in and he didn't know anything about wood whatsoever. When Rollo was there he had to go out to the wood suppliers and inspect all the wood, and purchase the wood right on the spot. He'd look over the wood and tell them how many semi-truck loads he would take. Rollo was the wood buyer. He purchased everything, really. He went out on the west coast and areas like that. [Note: Rollo Werner worked at Gibson from November 15, 1942 to December 31, 1974 (32 years of service). He joined Gibson as a plastics engineer and was named Director of Purchasing by Ted McCarty in 1948].*

The neighborhood around Parsons Street was getting to be 'a little rough' even in the 1950s? *Yeah, it sure was. Nothing like the neighborhood is now. Right now, there are a lot of drugs and that kind of stuff. Back in the 1950s and 1960s there wasn't any drugs in the neighborhood, but there was drinking and stuff like that, and it was kind of rough. But now it's really bad and rough down around the plant.*

Was there evidence of the minority population throwing rocks through the plant's windows in the 1950s and 1960s? *Oh yes. They threw rocks through windows. When the women would come in, they'd take their purse away from them and knock them down and run off with their purse.*

Ted was responsible for integrating the plant. Ted needed to integrate the plant. Do you remember any hard times with that in the plant? *No sir, I don't remember any problems.*

Do you remember much about Larry Allers, Gibson's chief wood working engineer when Ted McCarty was at Gibson. *Yes sir. I worked around Larry. I talked to him and saw him around. I knew him really well. His son, Ron Allers, also worked at Gibson. Larry was the Chief Engineer at one time, and Jim Deurloo used to work with him. Larry was another really fine gentleman too.*

You worked with Rem, did you ever go out and hear him play in his band? *Yes sir. And he played on television too. He had a band on television every week. His son Rendal worked at Gibson too. And Rendal works for Heritage, ever since we've been in business. All I ever remember Rem Wall doing at Gibson was being an inspector. When I hired in to Gibson he was an inspector, and when he left there he was an inspector. Rem's wife was an invalid so Rem had to stay up with her at night and sleep in a chair, and then he'd come to work, and then he'd go do the music (play in his band), and then he'd go back home, and that's the way he had to sleep, in a chair by his wife's side. He really had it rough with his wife. But he stuck right with her until she passed away.*

For the 1960 expansion, that was one of the big expansions, you were still up on the third floor on the cleaning operation, correct? *Yes sir.*

In 1960 major department relocations occurred. The third floor became the Customs / Service Department, so the finishing department and final cleaning moved off of the third floor. *I believe the final cleaning moved down to the second floor. Then when they put the final addition on in 1965 the final cleaning moved out into the back of the 1960 building, back where they put the finishing/ spraying department. In 1965 they had a conveyor back there where they'd spray the instruments, and they'd go up the conveyor into the oven, and they'd go through and dry, and they'd spray them again, and they'd go back up in the oven and dry, and they'd put on about four coats of lacquer like that. Before that change, they would do about two coats and air dry them.*

In 1960 with the new expansion there must have been a lot of people changing jobs, or did they just keep their jobs? Because of the union leveling the plant (giving everyone a chance to post for new jobs), was there a lot of people changing jobs, or did people, pretty much just keep their same job? *Really all it was, when they shifted, and got into the new facility, they just expanded the department. Gibson was running more guitars (increasing production), so in the filling & sanding area, if they had four people there, well they had to expand and maybe get six people. Most of the time, people would not want to fill & sand, so they'd just have to hire them right off the street. Buffing, a lot of times, it was a job that paid more money, sometimes you would get a person that would want to bid on that, for more money. Buffing is hard on the back, and a lot of people didn't like that job, but once you got used to it and learned the job, buffing wasn't all that bad. I used to do a little bit of buffing myself; I never did have the job as a buffer, but I used to do a lot of buffing. In the final cleaning you had to do the buffing too, and sometimes if somebody was out of buffing, and buffing really needed something, and we didn't have enough stuff coming over to my bench, then I'd go over and maybe buff ½ a day or something.*

In 1960, when they had that big expansion, I think they doubled the size of the plant. It sounds like it wasn't too disorganized because people just stayed in their department. As you said, if they needed more people, they would just add more people to each department. *Exactly, yes sir.*

That's why the quality didn't seem to drop, because I've never heard about the early 1960s models from 1960 to 1964, being of less quality. *Yes (that's right).*

When the last expansion occurred in 1965, was it the same kind of thing, there was no major disruption because the people stayed in the department? *If a person didn't bid on a new job, then they stayed right in their department.*

It doesn't sound like people bid on jobs a lot? *Not a lot, no. People back in the 1950s and early 1960s, when they got a job, they liked it, they wanted to stick with it. When someone switched jobs, most of it was for money. If it was another $0.25 an hour, they would go for that. For some people, the $0.25 an hour didn't mean that much to them, because they loved what they were doing, and they didn't want to go on something and do it and not like what they were doing.*

Which jobs paid the most? What type of jobs? *Well … buffing, that paid more. Finishing spraying … shaving …. those would pay more. The inspectors, they got paid more. Somebody that was working out on machinery that was doing an A-operators job (classification) where they would have to set up their own machine and run their own parts, they would get paid more than a B-operator (classification). A B-operator had to have somebody else like a department leader set the machine up for them. Also, most of the time, if a machine was running, the A-operator would run and feed the machine, and the B-operator would take (the parts) off. The B-operator would make $0.15 or $0.20 an hour less than the A-operator would be making.*

In this October 1, 2001 photo J.P. Moats (right) and Wilbur Fuller are standing in front of a vintage Gibson glue wheel that was used to glue the two piece tops of the famous Les Paul Standards. The men are standing in the northeast corner of the basement. In the 1950s, near this section of the basement, the model makers built the first Les Paul, the 1955 Test Guitar, the first Flying V, the first Explorer, the first ES-335, and many more.

Was the A-operator and B-operator classification used when Ted McCarty was there, or was that used later? *That was used when Ted McCarty was there and right on through.*

How about the pattern makers, did they make more? *Yes, the pattern makers made more money.*

How did a person become a pattern maker? *Most of the time, like I said (concerning other key assignments), they would try to get somebody that had been working with wood and knew about tools and things, and try to get them into that job. Gibson may have taken and hired a few off the street but I would say there were very few pattern makers that got hired off the street. Jim Deurloo hired into the mill doing band sawing and stuff like that, and then they wanted him to go down and get into the pattern shop.*

There was a kiln, an old one down in the basement, just up the ramp, next to the machine shop. There was a kiln, right at the very back. Were they using that in the 1950s and '60s? *They had that old kiln going in the 1950s. They had lumber in there when I first went there (1957). They had that kiln running, to keep the lumber. When they put on that first addition (1960), that's when they put on a new lumber yard, and then they started buying lumber that was already kiln dried. Up in Grand Rapids, and out on the west coast, we got to the point that we wanted everything kiln dried before we got it. Because in 1960 we got so big, that old kiln would not put out enough stuff to keep us going. We had to start buying stuff that was all kiln dried.*

So that's what you called the 'old kiln' and it sounds like they used that up to about 1959? *I would say so, yeah, exactly.*

So every guitar built in the '50s probably had wood that went through that kiln? *Yes, sir. It had to be because that was the only way Gibson had to dry the wood and keep it stable, until they could start getting other people (suppliers) to start kiln drying the wood. [Note: Prior to 1960, and particularly prior to 1950, Gibson also air dried wood in wood storage areas.]*

Do you ever remember that old kiln being in a backlog? Or were they pretty good about keeping the wood available? *Back then, it seemed like we had wood all the time. You could get all the wood you wanted. There was no problem with the wood.*

Then they didn't use that old kiln anymore after 1959? *No (they didn't use it as a kiln anymore). They started to just store stuff in it. They had shelving put up to store stuff in.*

When Ted McCarty left Gibson, did you hear anything, was there an announcement? How did you hear about it? *I heard that Ted and John had bought out the Bigsby Company, and they were going to go out and start running that. They did Bigsby and then what's called Flex-Lite.*

In 1959, after Gibson got Epiphone, when Epiphone came in, Gibson had a place over on Eleanor Street. They had Eleanor Street for Epiphone and some of the (Gibson) solidbodies. *Exactly.*

Did you ever go over there in 1959, or did you have anything to do with that? *No, I didn't have anything to do with that building whatsoever.*

When they say the solidbodies where made there, what does that mean? Does that mean the mill work was done, and the sanding and everything? *The mill work was done there. The way I recall it, they brought them over and finished them over in the regular plant (third floor of the Parsons*

Street old building). *Eleanor Street was for all of the white wood, yeah. That's what I recall, but like I said, I never went over there in that building. But I do remember the guitars coming over to the regular plant to be finished.*

Did you have any friends working over on Eleanor Street? *To tell you the true, the ones that worked over there, at the time, I really didn't know. When they started hiring them in, there were very few people that went from the regular plant (Parsons Street) over to (Eleanor Street). [Note: This comment agrees with what others have said. New plant departments were generally populated by new people. Sometimes an employee would post for the new plant. If the new plant was the result of a total departmental transfer then most of the existing departmental employees were transferred to the new plant. Most of those employees wanted to remain in their department even though it was in a new site. That was true with the electronics department transfer from Plant I to Plant II, the whole department transferred over. That happened again to electronics when it went from Plant II to Plant III.]*

Okay, so they just started new-hires at Eleanor Street? *They had to do a lot of new hiring there. Like I said, they might have taken a few people that wanted to go over there. I think there was very few that went over there, because they wanted to stay in the regular plant.*

How did someone become an engineer at Gibson? Like when Larry Allers (Chief Engineer in the 1950s) became an engineer, and when Jim Deurloo became an engineer. Was it like the pattern makers being selected for the job? Similar to that? *Yeah. They'd pick out a guy that seemed to be good at what he was doing, and if it seemed like he could do something like that, they would ask him to go and do it. If the person went into it, they could do the job, then good. But if they couldn't do it, then they'd have to let them go, but I don't know of anybody that they ever really let go. Because most of the ones that would get into something like that, they were pretty sharp, and Gibson knew that, and that's why Gibson asked them to get in there to start with.*

Gibson is known for quality. Gibson had been there a long time before you were there, a long time before Ted McCarty was there. It seems to me that one of the reasons Gibson did so well was that they did build quality. They had quality material, but Gibson seemed to have this good system about the 'leaders' telling the people how to do the job. And it just seemed to be passed down from person to person, generation to generation. Does that sound about right? *That is just exactly right. On every job they had a 'leader.' On every job, the 'leader" would train the people. Like I said, a new person had 30 days to get into the union. When I first went to Gibson, it was kind of tough for me to learn that job on white wood cleaning. That's when Marv Lamb came over and started helping me, because my boss came up and told me, 'Now you have 30 days to get things going, so I can approve you or let you go.' So I said, 'Okay.' So I got to working and the boss came over after about 15 days and he said, 'Really, you're not up to what you should be doing. You should be doing more than what you're doing.' I said, 'Well, I'll see if I can start doing things.' Then Marv started coming over and helping me, showing me what to do and everything, and I caught on to it. Generally, back then, on the white wood line, we were doing 12 to 15 guitars a day. I was up to around about 10, after about 15 days. That's when my boss came up to me and told me, 'Hey, you're not doing so good. You better get going good, because I only have a few more days left to either approve you or let you go, before you get in the union.' I said, 'Okay.' So I told Marv and them, and they said, 'Okay, we'll help you.' And then, all of a sudden, it wasn't but about two days, I started getting 14 or 15 guitars out. And then, just about two or three days before my boss was going to put me in, my boss called me in and he wanted to know what was going on. He* said, 'If I was only there for 20 days and I could do that many guitars, then why can't the people that'd been there for two years, why can't they do more guitars than 14 or 15 per day?' And I said, 'Well, you're the boss, you tell me why they can't do it?' I said, 'I'm doing what you told me to do, I've got it done, and as far as I'm concerned we don't need to be talking.' What he was trying to do was to pick me and say, 'Well those people out there ought to be doing 20 a day.' But I wouldn't do that (laughing). His name, the boss, was Clarence Coleman. He was the supervisor over that white wood line.*

Did Clarence Coleman turn out to be a pretty good guy? *He (pause) wasn't liked by too many people. He was something else to work for.*

Was he an old timer? *Oh yeah. He was an old timer. Another person that worked through there in that department was Gerald Bergeon. He was a nice guy. The whole time I was there he was a supervisor.*

Back in the 1950s, when Clarence Coleman asked you about your volume, that you needed to be a little higher, and you were just getting started, was there any discussion about quality? In terms of, 'This needs to be sanded a little bit better?' *Oh yes. You see they had an inspector out on the line. The boss was going over to the inspector and saying, 'How much stuff are you marking up?' And the inspector would let the boss know everyday, 'Well, we're marking up 8 or 10 things on every guitar.' So the boss would come back and say, 'Hey, you got to start getting this stuff better, you can't keep sending this stuff up to the inspector like this.'*

A mark up was like a little something here and a little something there? *Yeah, like there was a little scratch in it here, or I might not have put a little bit of wood dough in it where there was a little bitty opening between the binding and the wood. It was just little bitty things that I was missing because I wasn't trained within those 10 or 12 days, to really know that job that good. They were right on you to the point that they didn't let you get away with nothing. You had to know the quality. They were pushing you for quality and pushing you for quantity at the same time.*

When you went up to your second job, when you went up in the final cleaning, did you still have the 'leader' evaluating what you did? Was there that kind of process up there too? *Yes sir. Fred Wilkie, he was the one that was the 'leader' up there on that final cleaning line. He showed everybody that came in new, what to do, how to buff, how to do the stick-burn-in. We'd take a soldering iron and you'd take this stick lacquer, and if you had a little jam, a little hole there, you'd take and put that soldering iron and melt that and that stuff would harden within about a half a minute. You could file it, sand it, and buff it, and you'd never see where that jam, or pit, or hole was at.*

So they had the same process, and they were pretty hard, and they were on top of you? *Yes sir. It was the same way. Once I started learning what I was doing, if I sent stuff in to the inspector, and he came back and he rejected it, and it came back to me, then my supervisor wanted to know what's wrong. Then he'd get the 'leader' involved in it and say, 'Did you show this guy what to do? Are you showing him right?' They were right on top of it. You couldn't get away with nothing. It was quality and quantity. It had to be both. If you had the quantity and it went into the inspector and he rejected it, then you didn't get that instrument out. You couldn't count that guitar. The quality has got to be there with it. Back in those days, back in the 1950s, it was very tight on quality.*

Back in the 1950s, when you first started, where did you park? *There was a dirt parking lot out in the front (directly across Parsons Street at the south end of the building, where the entrance was to the 225*

Parsons Street old building). There was no fence around the parking lot. They had parking on the northwest side. I remember that parking lot, because one day a lady that lived there had just purchased a brand new Buick, and when she came out that day it was jacked up and they had taken her four brand new tires off of it. Now they also had a parking lot on the other side of the railroad tracks (east of the railroad tracks) on the southeast side, there was a parking place over there. And we parked right along down by the railroad tracks, down Pitcher Street. They had it so you could nose right up to the railroad track there. Gibson didn't own that, and they didn't own some of the other places, but you just went and parked there because nobody said anything.

Where did Ted McCarty park? *Ted parked right up in the front, where you pull into the dock, where they had the guard shack. Some people would park right in the street, right in front of the office. You could park on the street then. John Huis and Mr. Julius Bellson would park out there, and walk right into the front door.*

In the 1950s and 1960s, was Gibson one of the best factories to work at? Was it just a good place to work? *It was a very good place to work, but when I worked at the paper mill, that was a very good place to work too. When I was working at the paper mill, as long as that paper was running, you'd have to take out a roll of paper about once every hour and fifteen minutes. It would take you ten minutes to do it, and if it was running good, for the next hour you were just sitting there reading the paper, or doing what ever you wanted to do. As far as an easy job, the paper mill was probably easier to work, than for me working at Gibson. There was more labor type stuff that I had to do at Gibson. Gibson was a very classy place to work back then.*

How long did your sister work at Gibson? *I had two sisters work at Gibson. I forgot to tell you about the other one. The one sister worked there for about eight years. The other one worked there about five years. That was in the 1950s. My sister worked in the amplifier department, and my other sister worked in what they called the rim-lining, where they put lining inside of the rim.*

Which one was the one that got you to meet John Huis? *She worked in the amplifier department. She hired in to the amplifier department, and as far as I know she never changed. She got into that department and she was working for Les Bonnell. He was the supervisor in there. She liked her supervisor, she liked the people who were in there working, she liked her job, so she just stayed there. My other sister was with the rim-liners. They were right at the end of where the amplifier cabinets were. That sister loved it there.*

Why did they leave? *The one that was only there for five years, she was married, and her husband had a job up here, but something came about that he wanted to go back down to Alabama and start working on the farm with his dad. Now my other sister, her husband worked over there at the paper mill with me. He was there when I got hired into Gibson. They stayed here, and when they left Kalamazoo they went back down to Alabama. They wanted me to come down with them and start up that new paper mill down there in Alabama. I went down there and the paper mill wanted me to start out at $3.50 and hour and I was making more than that at Gibson, and the company didn't want to pay to move me down there. I thought, 'That's not for me, I didn't want to do that.' That Alabama paper mill was about $3.00 an hour cheaper than what they were paying in the Michigan paper mills.*

Interview 15
Jim Deurloo (1958–'69, 1974 - 1984)

Jim Deurloo was the last of the three Heritage Guitar co-founders to be interviewed. He was a native of Michigan, born in 1939. He joined Gibson in 1958 and moved up quickly but left in 1969 to become plant manager of Guild Guitars. He returned to Gibson in 1974 as a project engineer for the Gibson Nashville plant start-up. He was also head of engineering for Gibson, and by 1978 he was Plant Manager.

Take me from your high school days to getting into Gibson. *I started at Gibson in August of 1958. It was just a year out of high school. I worked at Valley Metal Products, a window factory were they made aluminum windows. And I did a little farming. Then I got a job at Gibson. I started out sanding, from there I went to the mill room, and from the mill room to the pattern shop, and from there I went to expediting. Then I went back and ran the pattern shop as an engineer.*

Why did you decide to go to Gibson? Was it a suggestion by somebody? *I knew a guy by the name of Ed Gilbert. He worked for Clarence Coleman, who was the foreman in white wood. So I went and talked with Clarence, and really Clarence hired me, but it had to be blessed by John Huis. John Huis was the Vice President at that time. I started in rim sanding, and I did that for a while, and then I progressed.*

Why did you move out of rim sanding? Did they recognize that you had skill and they wanted to move you over to another spot? *They needed someone to sand the necks. So I went and sanded the necks. And then a job opened up in the mill room running the band saw. I did that, really, to make more money. I really enjoyed running the band saw. I did a lot of things with the band saw, and I ran a lot of other equipment in the mill room.*

Who was your foreman in the mill room? *That was Gerald Bergeon.*

Did they ask you, or did you have to post for these jobs? *I had to post for them. When I was in the mill room, though, Larry Allers came to see me, and asked if I would bid on a pattern maker job.*

When did you become an engineer? *That would have been 1961 or so.*

Okay, you progressed very rapidly? *Yeah kind of (humble tone). I ran the pattern shop and the machine shop and worked in engineering until 1969. And in 1969 I left and went to Guild.*

Who did you work for as an engineer? Were you under Larry Allers? *Yeah.*

Was he the Chief Engineer and that was pretty much the top spot for engineering? *Yes. He was already Chief Engineer when I got to Gibson in 1958.*

Did you ever talk with Larry Allers about his contribution to the Les Paul Model? There's speculation that he was a key figure in the development of that. *He probably was, and Gar Bos (seniority date March 3, 1919), and maybe Bill Westman (seniority date September 13, 1944), who was also a pattern maker.*

So Larry came to you and wanted you to move into the basement with the pattern makers? *Yeah, he asked me if I'd bid on the job, so I did.*

What were some of the first patterns that you worked on? *I made some drill fixtures for bridges.*

I made some fixtures for the amplifiers at that time. I made some drill fixtures and machining fixtures to cut the grilles. Also to cut a frame that had a lap joint that was kind of a trapezoid. And neck fixtures and body fixtures. We did some prototype work. I remember we made prototypes for some of the amplifiers, getting ready to go to the Show.

Did Gibson make the metal chassis for the amplifiers? *No the chassis were stamped. They were purchased from a machine shop. We made a lot of parts for amplifiers; we made some of the springs and that kind of stuff. But primarily amplifier things like the chassis were purchased from the outside.*

Did you get involved with the tooling and equipment for the wood cabinets for the amplifiers? *Oh yeah.*

As an engineer what were your responsibilities? *Prototype tooling, machine process routings – to run parts through the factory, trouble shooting if there were problems with new tools or old tools.* [Note: A manufacturing tool is defined as anything that physically touches the product.] *If parts weren't coming out right, I'd do the trouble shooting for that. If there was a new method, I was primarily responsible to implement the new method – to buy equipment or whatever that would entail, or have new equipment made – to have a piece of machinery made to our specifications, kind of a custom piece of equipment.*

Did you have a lot of machine experience in high school, such that you developed these skills? *A little bit, but I've always been pretty mechanically inclined. That was something that I enjoyed doing, and I learned a lot in the pattern shop, that was kind of a natural for me too.*

Who was your leader or your mentor in the pattern shop? *Larry Allers. I also worked with a guy named R.L. Kingsley (seniority date November 15, 1943), and Garrett Bos (seniority March 3, 1919), and George Merica (seniority date August 16, 1944). Those three guys, I worked with them pretty closely in the pattern shop.* [Note: Garrett Bos is another Gibson legend. During the McCarty era Garrett Bos held the oldest seniority date, being hired into Gibson March 3, 1919. Gar Bos contributed to all of Gibson's great eras, the Lloyd Loar era of the 1920s, the Granada five-string flat head tone ring banjo era of the 1930s, and the Ted McCarty era.]

In 1961 was the pattern shop still in the basement of the 'old building?' *Yes, it was in the basement.*

And where was Larry Allers' office? Was it over near Ted's office just outside the door to the plant next to John Huis' office? *Just outside that door, yeah.*

How were the assignments made for the pattern makers and engineering? *They tried to spread the work out. Sometimes some of us pattern makers would work on the same project. But sometimes you'd get a guitar to tool and you'd tool the whole thing.*

Did they ever ask you for ideas as a pattern maker? *Well, they didn't ask for them, but they got ideas from the pattern makers. We tried to figure out the best way to do something.*

For example, the SG, the solidbody guitar that came out in 1961, replaced the single-cutaway Les Paul? *I didn't work on that. I think Larry Allers, George Mercia, and Gar Bos worked on that.*

After the pattern shop, what was your next move? *Then I went to expediting.*

Where was your office for expediting? *I was in with Larry Allers (in the engineering office next to*

John Huis). *I had a desk in Larry's office but I was an expediter. I did that for less than a year, then, Larry Allers got me to be the foreman of the pattern shop and the machine shop. That was 1962 or 1963.*

Larry Allers was a key person at Gibson. *He was a good guy. Larry came up with a lot of things that really kept Gibson coming out with new products. Larry was a bright guy; he was a good guy. He came up with a lot of new methods. He was a good toolmaker in his own right. He was a die maker. He did a lot of hand work to make self-centering fixtures and things like that. He came up with a lot of ideas. Multiple-drill machines to drill the necks – drills for the truss rods – proper curve on the truss rod – methods to make braces – machines that made the braces – multiple cutter heads to take labor out of various operations. Larry was on the ball. He'd order a bunch of cylinders and gears, some metal, and he would go down to the maintenance shop and tell them, well this is what I want you to do. He came up with a gang-saw, an arbor, a way to continually run fingerboards, cut to scale on the fingerboards. He had lots of ideas (laughing).*

Yeah, I know he has the patent for the EB-2 bass. You know, the ES-335 style bass that came out in 1958. He has the patent on that. *Yeah... but let me tell you how the patents worked. I'm not saying that Larry was not heavily involved in that, he probably was, but my name is on a patent or two that I really had nothing to do with. The company had to have someone put their name on the patent.*

Why wouldn't have Ted put his name on all of them? *He could have (laughs).*

Patent holders didn't really get the revenue from it, they were all owned by Gibson? *Oh yeah. They were an employee of the company. It's (the company) property. That's part of the deal.*

How do you compare Larry Allers (Chief Engineer) with John Huis (Vice President / Manufacturing)? Do you think Larry Allers was technically stronger? *Larry was a technician. John Huis was more of a politician. John didn't have the individual ideas on how to do things or how to make things, or even design. He was more or less the administrator that ran the plant. That's how he (Huis) spent all his time.*

Did Larry Allers report to John Huis. *Yeah.*

Do you recall Ted McCarty working with Larry Allers directly? *Very little. Ted was kind of isolated from us (Note: By the 1960s). Ted McCarty always treated me well. I liked Ted. I always got along with Ted. But Ted was a little aloof. But when you're in charge you have to maintain a little distance. That was okay, I understand that. After Ted left Gibson, he was like a buddy (laughing).*

The Flying V was already going by the time you got there? *You know a run of the Flying Vs and the Explorer, white wood instruments, sat in a rack outside the office for literally years. There were 25 instruments there. They were all made out of Korina just sitting in that rack. No one wanted them, for years.*

Reflecting back on your career during the McCarty era, 1948–'66, what was the thing you were most proud of? *I did a good job running the pattern shop. I was happy with my choosing of the people who were subsequent pattern makers.*

Who were some of those people? *Jim Hutchins (seniority date March 25, 1963) and Bob Sweitzer (seniority date December 19, 1954) were really good ones.*

Now Vi Bradford was in there making truss rods. Did you have anything to do with that department? *That was the machine shop, yes. I was over that too.*

Was that just to the west of the pattern maker benches (in about 1963)? *The machine shop was north. The pattern shop kind of had the south end of the basement. The dividing line of the basement (in the early 1960s after the 1960 expansion) was where you came down the stairs (the west wall stairwell). That was the middle of the room. South of that was mainly storage for parts and materials. Then there was a little research area run by Bill Gaut. He did the high-frequency gluing fixtures. The first couple of bays north (of the center), that would have been the pattern shop. And north of that still was the machine shop.*

That was still before you got to the north wall? *Yeah, that was still all in the basement.*

What was on the other side of the north wall of the basement? *That was maintenance.*

Then behind that was the old kiln? *Behind that (north of) was the old kiln, and in front of the old kiln was the rim sanders and the dove-tail machines. The string room was in the basement for a very short while. They were down there with the pattern makers for a short while.*

In 1963, what happened next? *I worked over the pattern makers and machine shop until about 1969.*

Did you work with Rollo Werner (in purchasing) much? *When I was an expediter I worked a lot with Rollo. Rollo was another guy that really knew his stuff. He had a lot of contacts. Rollo was just a real high quality guy.*

I put Larry Allers at the top of the list for unsung heroes. Would you put Rollo Werner as an 'unsung hero' at Gibson? *I think Rollo saved Gibson a whole lot of money. He was a good purchasing agent. He knew a lot of people. There was a lot of sourcing that needed to be done for new parts that had to be made, and he did that. He knew how to get new parts in when you needed them. Yeah, I'd say he was kind of an 'unsung hero', sure.* [Note: Rollo Werner was the purchasing agent for the entire McCarty era. Ted McCarty appointed him. Often after a prototype like the Les Paul or humbucking pickup was finished, it took a year or more to get the purchase parts lined up. Rollo's workload may explain the typical 12-to-18-month startup of new products. Engineers also ordered equipment if it was special design for the plant.]

Did you know George Comee, the finance guy, very well during the McCarty era? *Yup. Good guy, a real gentleman.*

How about Walt Fuller and Seth Lover back in those days (early to mid 1960s)? *Walt Fuller, I worked a lot with him when I was expediting. When I had the expediters, I had trucking. I had three trucks running around. We had three plants and five warehouses. Walt Fuller was a plant manager of electronics. I didn't know Seth Lover a lot.*

Where were the warehouses? Was it finished goods, or incoming material or both? *We rented space from various spaces in town. There was Shippers, Brundage, Dekreks, and two other warehouses, one was over by Plant III. A lot of the storage was instrumentation in cartons, some were amplifier cases, some were finished goods amplifiers, obsolete inventory, and some lumber.*

You were there when Gibson brought in Epiphone. *All the new models for Gibson and Epiphone were run through the pattern shop in the same way.*

In the plant, they would not keep the Epiphones and the Gibsons on the same rack, say if they were both 335 style bodies? They went through the plant on separate racks? *They would issue them at the same time, maybe, but they were kept separate. You might finish 35 Gibson necks and start on 35 Epiphone necks (laughing).*

You were there when the so-called 'non-reverse' Firebird was built? They had the original Firebird, the reverse-Firebird that looked more like a reversed Fender. That was a neck-through body. Then in 1965, they changed it to the 'non-reverse' which was a standard body with a glued-in neck. *Yes, I wrote the process for that probably. Around that time too, maybe just a little after that, they went to a 5/8s nut from an 11/16th nut. They did that for a couple of years and then they changed it back.*

Right about 1965/1966 they started making the necks thinner and shallower. *That was a hell of a thing. To change everything, you can imagine, all the fingerboards, all the necks, all the head veneers, all had to be changed?*

Why did they say they wanted to do that? *It was a directive from CMI* [Note: This was at the time Arnie Berlin was starting to be in charge. This was the type of thing that Ted McCarty said was wrong with the new management, but it was out of McCarty's control, the new thinner neck profile was a CMI directive. McCarty noticed several things that Arnold Berlin did that were not good for business. But, Ted McCarty did not have Arnold Berlin's respect. No one had Arnold Berlin's respect. That led to McCarty leaving Gibson.]

A lot of the players didn't like that change... *Yeah, well they changed it back. I'm sure you're well aware, no matter what people (CMI's new management) do to try and screw up a company, you can't do it, because people who actually do the work, keep on doing the work the way they always did. And that actually saves the company (laughing).*

That's an excellent, excellent point! It's really profound, literally. Gibson started adding all of this volume, starting in 1960 and 1961. By 1963 and 1964 the additional output was unbelievable. But still most vintage guitar collectors think the quality was still high in 1964. And in 1965 CMI ordered several goofy engineering changes. *It was the workers (who saved the company and continued to put out good quality). They'd come into work every day, and they'd work the same way every day. No matter how people (CMI's new management) tried to screw it up (laughing).*

But eventually over two, three, five, seven, ten years these so-called 'management changes' became just too much, and the workers lost out. Like you said, the workers continued to do a great job, but when they got piled on with all these changes, it ultimately took its toll. Don't you think? *There was a migration of workers. If it was exactly the same workforce doing exactly the same job then I don't think the quality really suffered. But what happens though, is you finally got some new people in doing some of these jobs.*

When do you think quality started dropping? When do you think the first year was when you felt quality dropped at Gibson? *(During my time, up to 1969) I was not aware of quality dropping at Gibson. I'm aware that some specifications were dictated that weren't too good, after I left (1969). I'm thinking of the flat tops with the thin tops and shrinking brace patterns. That was the 1970s, that kind of stuff. I was gone (to Guild). During the year, 1969, after Stan Rendell came in 1968, we changed everything. We went from a dome in the flat top to a flat top. It was all of that kind of stuff. We were just flat out, with all the new products and all the new changes. By October (of 1969) I had left.*

After Ted McCarty left in 1966 there is a great mystery period. There was a two year period before Stan Rendell came in 1968. That's a two year period! Who was running the plant? *Al someone. He was never President. He was Vice President. He ran it, and at the same time they had another guy. They brought the pair in together. The guy they brought in to run Gibson was not from Kalamazoo. He was hired by CMI. [Note: Al Stanely, a finance man, was brought in by CMI to handle Ted McCarty's job. Ed Strand, a materials management man, was brought in by CMI to handle John Huis' job. They lasted less than two years.]*

Nobody seems to know very much about this guy. *He did not do anything to help the company. He wasn't a guitar man. I think he was a financial guy. And they hired a superintendent, to replace John Huis, who did not know which end was which. His name was Ed Strand. He was brought in from the outside. He was supposed to be a materials management person. Mac McConachie worked for Ed Strand (Note: People generally think of Mac McConachie as the person who replaced John Huis. That was not true. Mac was the plant superintendent.)*

To replace Ted McCarty and John Huis, CMI brought in a finance guy and a materials management guy. And CMI lost a guitar guy (Ted McCarty), who had been around guitars since his Wurlitzer days (the 1930s)? *Yes, that was kind of a dark period (1966–'68) I would say.*

You think that when Ted left, for those two years, that was a dark period? *Yes.*

Maybe Stan Rendell did a heck of a job when he had to come in? *I think Stan Rendell saved the company. Stan did a lot of radical things, and he would throw a lot of things on the wall, and see what stuck. He was changing things just to change, just to shake it up and get it going, and he did get it going. But Stan was not really a guitar guy either. But at that time, 1969, he bailed Gibson out. He did a lot of things that were good, and a lot of things that weren't so good.*

You and Larry Allers had to live through this dark period? These CMI guys, sounded like they were not guitar men. They didn't know what they were doing? *They had nothing to bring to the party. But right around then the Japanese started having quite an influence and we started losing some of our market share.*

Do you think the 1965 expansion at Gibson was too much, that it probably should not have been done? Gibson got so big then. Gibson had a nice expansion in 1960, when you had just hired in, and they doubled the size of the plant, and volume was increasing. Then Gibson got two more plants (Plant II and Plant III) and then they put another big expansion in the 1965. Wasn't that a bit too much? *It probably was, but how do you know that? Yeah, you can say that looking back, but you have to base your decisions on what you see before you right now, and what you are hearing out of the market place. There's nobody in marketing that ever looks at the market like it might not grow. Any expansion should probably be more conservative than it actually turns out to be. But, that's what fuels the economy, you buy a lot of stuff, it creates jobs, and that's kind of the way things are done.*

Interview 16
Merrill 'Mac' McConackie (1958–'75)

What year did you start with Gibson? *1958. I was in production control. I had just gotten out of college at the Western Michigan University (located on the far west side of Kalamazoo about 10 minutes from Gibson).*

Were you a Kalamazoo native? *Yeah. I went to Kalamazoo Central High School too.*

What did you major in at Western Michigan? *Business.*

How did you get a job at Gibson? *They had an ad in the paper (laughing).*

Who did you talk to first? *Ted McCarty.*

Ted was looking for a production control man? *Yeah. After we talked a while he asked me what job I wanted. And I told him (laughing), 'I want your job.' He said (laughing), 'You're hired.'*

In 1958, where was the production control office? *It was up in the main office, near to Ted's office and Julius Bellson's office, and John Huis was down the hall. Ted's office was kitty-corner from mine and Julius Bellson's office was across the hall.*

Who was in that office before you? *I don't think there was anybody in there. When I came in Julius Bellson was the head of production control. Julius was doing it when I got there and he trained me. I was there three days and then I put out a production control schedule (laughing).*

How did you develop the schedule in 1958? *They had a sheet with all the models on it and the department listed on there. We'd go through and inventory the units each month. And we'd take off the production coming out of each department. As it moved through each department we'd add it on. When it went off the end of the line it would come off the schedule. It was a really simple thing (laughing). Back then, it was like the dark ages (laughing). I had production control for Plant I [Note: After Plants II and III were added, they had their own plant production control coordinator.]*

Did Chicago Musical Instruments tell you what to build? *In an indirect way they did, yeah. At that time (in the late 1950s) we were building against back orders, which made sense. Then, after Ted McCarty left, CMI got the bright idea that they were going to forecast sales. That's when the trouble started. CMI started that. After Ted left there was a guy from Chicago Musical Instruments that came in. Stan (someone), but he wasn't there very long. CMI's idea to forecast sales was not a very good idea.*

What did you do after production control? *I ran the Custom Instruments department.*

How did custom instruments orders come in? *They came in through the Chicago Musical Instrument Company. A custom instrument had to be ordered. What they were doing at first (in the early 1960s) they'd give the dealer the same discount on a custom instrument as they got on a regular one. I talked with Ted one day and I said, "Geeze, we're crazy, because the guy doesn't have any inventory problem with this unit, it's already sold and he gets half of his money up front. And we do the extra work on it and he gets the same discount on the extra work. That's foolish. We ought to give him (only) the discount on the basic instrument, and we'd get the money for the extra work." Ted said, "That makes sense." So that's the way we did it."*

You are the first example that I have found, of being a young man, pretty much right out of college, that had such important positions. *It didn't seem like that at the time. I was there. I did it.*

Was that because the factory was kind of small and it was manageable? *Yeah. Gibson was a good place to work when Ted was there. There were a lot of good people there. For example, we had shaper operators, a father and son that were running shapers. And old Lew Draper (seniority date April 18, 1946), he still had all his fingers. That's unusual for a shaper operator, and he'd been running the shaper for many years! His son (Loren Draper seniority date April 13, 1959) did the same job while his dad was there; he learned to do the shaper job too. Those were the kind of folks we had. We had folks that had been there for 25 to 30 years. Their kids were there. It was a good place to work; there were a lot of good folks.*

Did you work with Rollo Werner? *Rollo was in charge of purchasing. He was up in the main office. In the lobby, his office would have been to the left (west) of the lobby, but you didn't get to his office off the lobby, you went into the main office and down the west isle. Then the big main office of office workers was on the left side of Rollo's office. [Note: The office workers were west of Rollo's office; the office workers could look out the large bank of windows overlooking Parsons Street.] That's where the girls worked and Katie Harris worked.*

Where was the conference room? *Actually, when I started in 1958, the conference room was directly across from Julius Bellson's office, and that's where I sat when I started. I worked in there. Eventually I worked in the office next (north) to that, which was directly across from John Huis. [Note: It is believed that there may have been two conference rooms. One was for the office personnel and one was for Ted Mc-Carty and his staff.. Ted's conference room in the 1950s was at one time just kitty-corner to Ted's executive office. Historical pictures of Julius Bellson and Wilbur Marker playing Gibson instruments indicate that the pictures were taken in Ted's conference room.]*

Do you remember much about the amplifier business? *Very little. I wasn't that involved. Walt Fuller was involved with that. We had a special plant. We did make the cases in Plant I and then they had another plant in town where they made the amplifiers (electronics).*

When you hired into Gibson in 1958, and you walked out past John Huis' office out into the plant, past the quality control area, past the engineer's office, in that area, was that where they built amplifiers? *There was an amplifier department there, yeah. [Note: In this era other employees have confirmed that final assembly of the amp chassis, cabinet, and speakers was in this area.]*

Did you know Larry Allers? *Oh yeah, I used to play poker with Larry. He was a good fella. There was Larry and I and Ward Arbanas and Gerald Bergeon (that played poker).*

Eventually you went to Gibson Nashville? *I went to Nashville, yeah. I came to Nashville in 1975. I came down to Nashville for quality assurance. I was in charge of quality.*

Any other reflections about Ted McCarty or those days? *Oh Ted (sincere pause) he was a good fella. Working at Gibson was a lot of fun at first. After Ted left and CMI started making the sales forecast it wasn't fun. And instead of having the dealerships with mom and pop dealers in the little towns, CMI started putting the dealerships in the big malls. That's (in my opinion) what ruined it. That was a downfall for Gibson and the guitar division.*

Interview 17
Hubie Friar (1959–'84)

Even though most employees at Gibson did not play guitar, when compared to what historians have said about the 1950s and early 1960s Fender Company, Gibson had a lot of guitar players working at Gibson. Hubie Friar is one of those.

Take me from your high school days, and how you got over to Gibson? *I came to Michigan in 1955. I graduated from high school in a little town called Ewing, Virginia. My mother and step-dad migrated to Kalamazoo, and that's how I ended up here after I finished high school. I stayed with my grandparents until I finished that.*

Why did they come to Kalamazoo? *They were looking for work in a paper mill. They started out at what used to be Sutherlands Paper Company. That's how that came about.*

How did they know about the paper mills in Kalamazoo? *They ran across a guy. I grew up in Virginia, but across the mountain you were in Kentucky, where there was a bigger town. So they ran into a guy over there at a little restaurant. He was in Kentucky looking for people to come work in the paper mill. So he brought them back to Kalamazoo, and got them an apartment, and both of them started working at the Sutherland paper mill.*

What did they do there? *I think the Division where they worked made Dixie Cups and paper plates, back in those days. That was the biggest thing in the Division where they worked.*

So you went up to Kalamazoo? *Yup, I got a job. I got a job, when I first came to Kalamazoo at a service station. It was a one stall Standard Oil station. This guy kind of ran the place and they needed a little help from me so he gave me a job. I made about a buck an hour back then. That was pretty good money back then, and I could work all the hours that I wanted to. After that I worked at a company that made steel shelving and storage type metal things.*

Where were you living? *I was living where I live now, except then, my mother lived there. On McKinley in Kalamazoo. That's within 10 miles of Gibson. That was around 1957 or 1958. I started at Gibson in 1959.*

How did you get to Gibson? *Actually, it was Rem Wall, he worked at Gibson. Rem talked with then vice president John Huis. Rem talked to him about needing somebody else to tune up the guitars, and check them over, and that I would be available for that. [Note: Rem Wall, Gibson's most famous employee-musician from the McCarty era, was founder of The Green Valley Boys. Rem had a multi-year contract with Columbia Records in the early 1960s. Hubie Friar was a member of that band.]*

Were you in The Green Valley Boys at that time? *More or less, I had just started with them, maybe six months before.*

You went up to Kalamazoo and you were working, and you wanted to get into a band? *Actually another guy that played with us helped me get into the band. In The Green Valley Boys band, he was the steel guitar player that I worked with.*

Did the steel guitar man work at Gibson? *Yes he did. His name was Howie (Howard) Quibell (seniority date 7-17-59).*

Did you meet him before Rem? *Yeah, we had a little trio, along with a guy by the name of Tommy Gibson.*

How did you meet Howard? How did you get with these guys, to play music? *Well, let's see, that goes back a ways. A musician must have stopped at the service station. I must have met them that way. Howie knew Rem, and he's the one that brought my name up to Rem. The Green Valley Boys bass player was quitting, and I found out that they needed a bass player. And that's when Rem came to me and I became The Green Valley Boys bass player. Then Rem mentioned about working at Gibson to me. And I said that I'd be glad to get into Gibson working on instruments and tuning them up. Rem was the final inspector at Gibson.*

So Rem talked to John Huis? *Yeah, and John had me come in on a Friday, and I talked with him for a little bit. I got the paperwork from the guy out in the guard shack, Dale Humphrey. He's the one that gave me the stuff to sign up. They had the union card and all the stuff like that. The next Monday September 21, 1959 I started at Gibson. I quit my other job on Friday. I called them and told them I was offered a musician type job, and they were really good about it.*

Where did you start? *I started out tuning up the instruments.*

Just like you thought you would? *Yes, that was the main reason, because I could tune them by ear.*

Were you working right next to Rem? *It was the same area, kind of the same room. It was over on the east side. He had a booth where he would take the instruments in and check them over. That was the second floor (of the old building), the floor below the third floor spray room, and above the basement floor. I was right next to the railroad tracks (the east side of the building), pretty close to where Parsons Street crosses (the south east side of the second floor of the old building). It was near the parts department (the parts crib - located in the center of the second floor). There were four of us that did fret work and tuning and so forth.*

Was the electronics lab close to there? *I'm pretty sure that was down in the basement area (Experimental lab).*

Who was the 'leader' in that area. *The foreman was Jim Collins (seniority date September 19, 1941). He would take the guitars into his booth. If there was a high fret, he'd send it back to you and you'd have to make it better. After he got through with the instruments, they'd go into Rem for final inspection. Sometimes Rem would send them back. Jim Collins was the supervisor of that section. Then there was Bud Uptograff, he was one of the fret filers, like myself. There was Cliff Davis, Jim Loosier, and Jim Hanchett.*

You were fret filing and stringing? *They came to us with strings. We'd just tuned them up and set the action and the neck. You would have to see where it buzzes. Then you would raise the strings up and get a ¾ file back in there and touch it up a little until you got it right. Then you'd have to loosen the strings and polish the frets up with a piece of steel wool. It was kind of interesting.*

So you did all the different types of guitars? *Yeah, anything that came.*

So you might do a Les Paul or a Southern Jumbo, all of them? But they came through in racks, so you might have a rack of Les Pauls? *Oh, yeah. They came through in a rack of eight. Jim Hanchett, he did most of the Les Paul Customs (the fretless wonder with low slim frets), and Jim did the lap steel guitars, because he played Hawaiian music himself.*

It was enjoyable? *Yeah, that was enjoyable. I could also spot check the instruments, even after the final inspector checked them out too. I could have hands-on with something that was tuned up.*

Were all of those guys in the department guitar players, like you and Rem and Jim Hanchett? *No, they knew a couple of chords. But they knew how to file them and set them up.*

But you had to check it out all the way up to the 12th fret and above, wouldn't you? Wouldn't you have to check every fret? *Oh yeah, you had to make sure that there was 'no turn-up' down towards the end of the fret board. Everybody had to know how to tune. They had the A-440 bar, you'd hit that, and that would be the A-note. When you hit that note, you'd have to be able to tune the other five strings, once you got the A-note right.*

When Rem was all done and it was all okay, what would Rem do with that guitar? *He'd put some sort of tag on it. Then they'd put them in an 8-rack. The storage area was not a real, real big room. That was within 15 or 20 feet of where our department was.*

The guitar would go into the storeroom. When was it put into a box and shipped? *They'd take the guitars off the rack of 8 and they had shelves that they'd lay the instruments down on. I think they had a small area up there where they would pack them. And then they'd take them down (the elevator) and the shipping truck would back in there on the dock.*

How long were you in that department? *Until they moved into the new building. We thought it was really going to be something in the new building, but then we found out how much better it was in the old building. In the new building you were out in the open. In the old building it seemed like you had a little more privacy even though there were people within 10 feet of you. The new building just wasn't what we thought it was going to be.*

Then what? *Then I got into roving inspection. I'd go through all the areas and spot check the instruments. That was a little before Ted left in 1966. I was all over the building. I was out in the wood shop and out in the spray area. I got to meet Mr. McCarty a few times.*

Did he come out through the plant and say hi? *Yeah! Quite often he'd come through and say good morning to everybody. He was a real likeable person.*

Did he ever stop and talk with you about any specifics? *No, not really. I think, more or less, he wanted to know how I liked the job in the new building.*

Did he come out by himself, generally, or was he with John Huis? *Both. Ted was a likable person. I got to know him quite well. He was a nice person to be around. He'd always come through the plant wanting to know if you liked things, and if you had any suggestions or anything like that. John Huis, too, he'd come through once in a while by himself, or with Ted, or with a musician. I remember once, McCarty brought Johnny Smith through and I remember meeting him. I wasn't into jazz but I recognized the name, but I still wasn't sure who he was until afterwards. We had a special Johnny Smith model, I remember those well, the big body guitars.*

When you went out to the new expansion in 1960, did supervision change or did anything change? *No, not really, I think it was about the same. I know Jim Collins went out there with us. He had his own little booth where he would check the guitars out. Rem had a booth also.*

Had Jim Collins be around a long time? *Yeah, he'd been there about 12 years.*

There was a 30 day period when you first hired in, before you became part of the union. Do you remember anything about that? *They gave you a manual that had the 'does' and 'do nots'. It had things like how to file a grievance. I never got into any of that. It seemed like the union had a 'three year contract.' [Note: A three year contract was common for Michigan unions].*

There was a small strike around 1966, do you remember that? *Yeah, I do remember, it was awfully close to 1966. I walked the picket line. It only lasted a couple to three days. The strike was probably about a raise (laughs). The picket line was near the guard shack and another one on Edwards Street (west side middle). The strike that really did us in was later.*

Did they give you an employee manual too, giving the hours, etc. for all employees? Did you get a manual like that? *Yup. When you started, they gave you all of that type of information.*

What was your starting pay? *I really can't remember. Rem told me once that he started for $1.35 (in 1947) and it seemed like we were still under $2.00 an hour when I first started.*

So for your job at Gibson and your job within the plant, you never got the itch to change jobs? *No, not really. Once I got there, I guess I found my calling.*

I have noticed that not too many people changed jobs at Gibson. They kind of stayed on their job. *Yeah, you know at the time it was a good paying job. You had your insurance and stuff like that.*

In 1960 Gibson started adding a lot of people. 1963 and 1964 were huge years for adding people. *Oh yeah, Rock & Roll had started and the solidbody guitars were in demand.*

Did you notice if adding a lot of people affected the plant? With all these new people coming in? It seems like the quality of the 1963 and 1964 product was still pretty good. *The quality seemed to stay right up there when we added people. My wife started at Gibson during the 1960s expansion.*

How did that work, did you say to her why don't you go over there? *Actually I met her at the Gibson bowling team. She started at Gibson right out of high school working at the Gibson electronics department, where they made the amplifiers.*

Who hired her? *John Huis.*

How did she decide to go to Gibson? *I think it was her and three or four other girls that were right out of high school from Otsego, Michigan. The pay was better at Gibson. Two of her friends that came with her were Sheila Ray (hired October 19, 1960) and Kathy Harmon (hired October 18, 1960). They could all ride together to Gibson from Ostego. She stayed at Gibson for 23 years, and I had 25 years at Gibson, but we had to both start over when Gibson moved to Tennessee.*

Tell me about The Green Valley Boys (in the 1950s). Were you doing the TV Show at that time? *Yeah. That was up in the Burdick Hotel when I started. Up on the second floor, that's where WKZO-TV was located. The radio station was up there also. I started with Rem in 1956 (three years before Hubie hired into Gibson). I was on the TV in 1956. I remember they only put up one microphone, and we all had to gather around it. Later on they got to two.*

In 1956 what kind of bass, what kind of model did you have? *I'd never played bass before, and when Howie told me about it, I bought a ¾ sized Kay upright bass. I played it mostly on television, but to play out at some tavern, it was too hard on the fingers. Luckily Rem had one of the first electric basses that Gibson made. That made things a lot easier. I played through Rem's amp. We used a Gibson amp. We only had one big amp and we all played through it except the guitar player. He had his own amp.*

What model did the guitar player use? *He played a ES-295 gold cutaway with crème color pick-guard. Later on he got a ES-355. I got an EB-2 bass with the same body style and the same color. We matched with the bass and guitar the same color. Billy had his own auto parts shop and machine shop in Hartford, Michigan (40 minutes away from Kalamazoo).*

Were the Gibson workers supportive of The Green Valley Boys? *Yes, they were happy for us. They were always asking where the show was located, and things about the show. It was in black and white television in those days.*

Did Ted McCarty get involved with it? Did he come to watch the band? Did he give any moral support? *No, I can't remember him doing that. Rem was kind of close with Ted. They went to Germany (Berlin Industrial Fair). I don't believe Ted came up to the TV show.*

Rem's big hit was in the early 1960s? 'Home Is Where The Hurt Is'. *Yeah, that was mid-1960s I believe.*

Did you record that one? *No, the record company used their own Nashville musicians. But we did do quite a few things on an independent label out of Gary, IN and Chicago. That was the Glen label.*

Rem had a contract with a national label too? *He got connected with Columbia Records in Nash-ville. Rem went on the road with Ernest Tubbs, opening his show. He left me in charge of the television show. I was the MC back then.*

Getting back to the plant, in 1959, in the 'old building', was it hot in the summer and cold in the winter? Was it okay inside the plant? *It was pretty good. They had the old boiler. It was nice and cozy. A lot of times you had to open the window in the winter time, to let a little fresh air in. The radiators would really put out the heat (laughing).*

Do you happen to know if they used saw dust to run the two boilers? *Seemed like they did! They used saw dust and then some scrap wood with it.*

Is there anything else that you remember about the years that Ted was there? *Yes, there was a little restaurant at the corner of Edwards and Parsons. We'd go in there. I know Rem went in there all the time. We would get there around 6:30 a.m, because we started at 7 a.m. A black guy ran it. His name was Bill Bowden. He owned the place. They called that Bill's Restaurant; I think so. They always made the best oatmeal. Every morning I'd have oatmeal. Other people would sit down with us. We did go over there for lunch too. He always had lunch specials. He would get you in the morning and he would get you at noon. The restaurant was crowded but not too bad. He could dish that stuff up. You wouldn't believe how quickly you could get your food. You only had 30 minutes to eat and get back. He was a nice guy too. He had a lot of people coming and going (laughs).*

Interview 18
Bob Knowlton (1959–'84)

Bob was one of the first Gibson employees that I met. I talked with many of the employees that worked at Gibson in the 1950s who were still living. So many more had already passed away. I was fortunate to find people with divergent Gibson backgrounds. Bob, for example, was a night watchman.

When did you join Gibson and what did you do? *I started in 1959 as the night watchman and I took care of the furnace. I stayed at Gibson until about six months before they closed in 1984.*

I've been told that even in 1959 the neighborhood around Parsons Street was getting pretty rough. As night watchman did you have any problem with people breaking into the plant? *No, there was no problem with people breaking in.*

What did you do next at Gibson? *I went to amplifier assembly and put the speakers into the cabinets. That was the last part of the line.*

Where was that department located? *It was just inside near the (administrative) office area. [Note: On the first floor annex between the receiving dock and the mill room near the isle to the administration offices of McCarty, Huis, etc.] Then we moved to Fulford Street.*

Did you know Ted McCarty? *I talked with him a few times. He was a nice guy.*

Interview 19
Jacqueline Fergusson Friar (1961–'84)

My last interview was with Jackie Fergusson. She was the only employee that I interviewed that did not start at Gibson in the 1950s or before. I wanted to talk with Jackie because she married Hubie Friar; Hubie mentioned his wife in his interview.

From your high school days, how did you end up at Gibson? *How I ended up getting started there, I had four or five girls that I graduated with, that worked there. So they finally ended up getting me in there.*

They actually started there before you did? *Yes. I actually worked in a dirty place and they worked in a clean place, and they were making way more money than me (laughs). I thought, hey, this is not right. So that's how I ended up getting in there. I originally started out in the electronics department at Gibson's.*

Did they hire in 1961 also? *They started about a year or so before me. Mostly right after we graduated in 1960.*

How did, let's say the No. 1 girl in that group find out about Gibson, because you were all from Otsego (about ½ hour drive north-northwest of Kalamazoo)? *I'm not sure how they did it, if they knew of somebody. At that stage in your life you're out looking for a job, and you're going and putting applications into just about anywhere.*

What were the girl's names? *Sheila Ray (hired 10-19-60), Kathy Sullivan, they're all married now, so they all have married names, Diane Forney, Deann Lutes, and Sandy Burchett.*

You were all buddies from high school? *Yes, more or less. We all stuck together.*

Who did you talk to first about getting a job at Gibson? *My friends Sheila and Kathy. It was really weird. We all rode together and they'd drop me off at my job, and then they went on. I worked at Pemco. They made wheels for grocery carts. So that was right on their way, so they would drop me off. And one day, we were just getting out of Otsego, and one of them said that I was supposed to go in for an interview at Gibson that day. So they ended up taking me back home (laughs). Then I went up for the interview with John Huis and Henry Penning. Henry Penning, at that time, was over electronics.*

Where did you start at Gibson? *I started at Plant 1 (Parsons Street). Gibson had Plant 1, Plant 2, and Plant 3, and I eventually worked in all three of them.*

When you started in 1961, were you doing amplifiers in Plant 1? *Yes. In 1961 we were upstairs. We were up above the second floor cafeteria, on the third floor. I assembled the inside of the amplifiers. We put all the wiring in it. The stuff that I did was the last step before it went to the inspectors.*

That was on the third floor, on what is the south side, over by Parsons Street. *Yes, over by the railroad tracks (the south east side of the third floor of the 'old building').*

Penning was your supervisor, but did they have what they called a 'leader' in the department, or was it just the supervisor that took care of things? *No, they had what they called 'line leaders.' Each line that made a different amp, had a 'line leader' over them. If you took a break, then they'd sit in as a substitute for you. One line leader was Mary Lou Pauf (seniority date 7-14-61). On the line that I was on, there were about six of us, doing up the wiring. We didn't put the tubes or anything in it. We put the controls on it, and the knobs, and the things like that. Then it was all ready when it got to final inspection.*

When you got your parts (raw material & component parts), where had they come from (what other Gibson department)? *We had a big stock room. We were assembling those parts in the amps. Our (component) parts were all ready for us, but they were prepared for us at another station. We were on the assembly line. Other people would build the terminal boards.*

Almost everything for the electronics for the amplifiers was up on the third floor? *Yeah, everything was.*

The construction of the wood amplifier cabinets was down on the first floor, down in the newer building (the 1950 addition). *Yeah, after we got done with the amp chassis they went there [Note: Over to the third floor elevator, down to the shipping dock, across the shipping doc, down the annex ramp to the 1950 annex staging area, and over to the amp cabinet work area.]*

Was Walter Fuller around to look at the amps? *Yes, but in 1961, they didn't have Plant II yet. I don't remember where Walt Fuller was, but our supervisors all had an office on the floor we were on.*

In 1961–'62, where was the cafeteria? *That was below us on the second floor (south end of the second floor, the Parsons Street side). And the string room (by the early 1960s) was down below that, on the very bottom floor (generally called the basement).*

Where did your girl friends work? *We all worked in electronics (third floor of the old building in the early 1960s). All of us worked there. There were so many of us. [Note: In the 1950s the electronics department was located on the south end of the second floor. It was expanded there in 1950 when the former administration offices were moved out of that area on the second floor. Electronics during World War II was also done on the second floor. The general administrative offices were moved into the new administration building in 1950. With the 1960 rearrange, electronic amplifier assembly was located on the south end of the third floor. The employee cafeteria went into a portion of the south end second floor in 1960 where electronics were earlier.]*

In 1961–'62, for the third floor electronics department, were there any other bosses besides Penning? *At one time there was Clyde Flora that was a boss.*

How about Seth Lover? Do you remember that name, Seth Lover? *Boy, I don't. I'd heard the name, but I wouldn't know who he was.*

But Walt Fuller would come up every once in a while? *Yeah, yeah.*

Now did Ted McCarty come up to your area? Did he come up to see how things were going? *Yeah, all of them would get up and wander around. John Huis and McCarty. They made their presence known throughout the whole area.*

Did Ted McCarty or John Huis ever stop to talk to you? *Oh yes, they were very friendly people.*

Just to see how things were going? *Oh yes, to see how you were doing. It was a very close knit place, I think.*

In the electronics department, was it mostly women? *Yeah, mostly women and we had guys that were the inspectors.*

How long were the lines, how many people? *Probably about five or six people. Each person would do their part and hand it to the next person. I was the final one before the inspector.*

It wasn't like an assembly line with a belt? *Oh no, no. You would work on one and you would just slide it over. A lot of times there would be three or four amps between each person. If you got caught up, you just automatically went ahead and helped somebody else. Everybody looked out for one another. We worked together.*

How did the inspector do his part? Did he plug them in? Or did he just look at them with a spy-glass? How did he inspect them? *They plugged them in and made sure everything was hooked up. I'm not sure what they did to them, but it was more than just a visual. The tubes were not in them when we saw them, it was just the plain chassis when it started out, and by the time it got to the end everything was in it. The ones that I can remember working on were the bigger ones, they were wide.*

You were on that job in 1961, 1962 and 1963, and then Gibson opened up the amplifier plant in 1964? *Plant II. I went there in 1962.*

How was that transfer? Was it easily done, was everything all set for you in the new plant, or was there start-up problems or confusion? *The best that I can remember, I don't think there was that much confusion.*

Did they hire on a lot of new people for that, or was the department pretty much the same? *The department was pretty much the same. They just took everybody that was on that third floor.*

Did you like the electronics department at the old building better, or the new Plant II building better? *They were pretty much the same. But when we went to Plant III, in 1964, that was kind of out of the way. It was quite a ways from the Parson Street office. Plant III was the amplifiers and the string room.*

How was that transition from Plant II to Plant III, other than it being farther south, and more difficult to get to? *The operations went smoothly. I think what it was, that we had a lot of people that worked together, and they were determined that everything was going to work. Everybody worked together as a team. We didn't have very many people that said, 'Well, I'm not going to do this, I'm not going to do that.' We were all there for the same reason, to make money and to make a nice amp.*

In Plant II and Plant III you were still on that same assembly line? *At one time, in Plant III, I cut all the parts, for the orders, for the girls. All the parts were cut to size. And they had a machine that bent the transistors. I got the parts ready for the girls to assemble, for the girls that were on the assembly line. (Regarding supervision) Henry Penning was in Plant I and Plant II, but by the time we got to Plant III I believe Clyde Flora was the supervisor. And I remember Walt Fuller being over in Plant II more. His office was there.*

Was the electronics department a place where some of the people wanted to work because it was clean? *I think so.*

Were people trying to post (apply for a job opening) to get those jobs? *There were probably some, but I think the biggest share (of the people at Gibson) were happy with where they were at.*

That's what I keep hearing. People got their job and they pretty much stuck with it. *Yeah, they did. They (supervision) were not afraid to praise you when you did a good job, or they weren't afraid to tell you when something went wrong. I think people were content with where they were at. I don't think we had a really big turnover for the electronics department.*

Was the inspector the same in Plant II and III? *Rem Wall came over. I remember after the chassis were put into the cases (wood cabinets) in Plant II, the amps went into final inspection, because I remember Rem had a sound room. He was the one that checked the amps for any buzzes or anything else in them. Rem moved over to Plant II with us. He was the final-final inspector. He'd plug a guitar through them and played through the amp. I remember Vi Bradford worked in there with Rem.*

When Ted McCarty left Gibson in 1966, were you still in the amp plant in Plant III? *Yeah, I was still in Plant III. I was in Plant III when I got married (to Hubie Friar).*

Other Employee Histories

The idea for a book on the Gibson McCarty era , its people and its manufacturing plants, was based upon my initial interview with Ted McCarty on May 5, 1999 . Ted invited my wife and I over to Kalamazoo to meet many of the people that worked at Gibson during Ted's tenure 1948 to 1966. Ted suggested that I get supplemental information from these Gibson retirees. My goal was to contact the people in order of their seniority date.

Of course many important Gibson names died or where unavailable for interview during the book's research period. None the less, non-interviewed Gibson employees that worked for McCarty's team need to be included in this book. Although not intentional, there will be omissions, and the seniority cutoff date was the 1950s. I attempted to list everyone that had a seniority date of 1949 or prior and who was still working at Gibson in 1966. Then, a few other people were selected based upon other historical importance.

Garrett Bos (1919–'65)

Kathryn Harris (1920–'71)

John Huis (1926–'65)

Cornelius Triezenberg (1926–'73)

Ernest Kuhn (1926–'66+)

Sylvia Howard (1927–'73)

Leonard Shedore (1928–'72)

Harlan Clair (1928–'73)

Ed Rosenberger (1928–'66+)

Walter Fuller 1933–'68)

John Klien (1933–'66+)

Basil Raynes (1933–'66+)

Julius Bellson (1935–'73)

George Comee (1936–'75)

Larry Allers (1937–'70)

Wilbur Marker (1938 - 1956)

Gerald Bergeon (ca.1930s–'60s)

Gerald Woodworth (1938 - ca.1960s)

Seth Lover (1941–'67)

James Collins (1941–'66+)

Rollo Werner (1942–'73)

Irene Marble (1942–'65+)

Bernice Penhollow (1942–'66+)

Hartford Snyder (1943–'74)

Jacob Doorenbos (1943–'66+)

R. L. Kingsley (1943–'66+)

Clarence Coleman (1944–'64)

Carleton Pease (1944–'74)

George, Mercia (1944–'73)

Bertha Bushell (1944–'66+)

Mary Belle Smith (1944–'66+)

Elizabeth Ferens (1946–'75+)

Robert Powers (1946–'76+)

Paul Vallier (1948–'66+)

Rembert Wall (1948-'73+)

Ward Arbanas (1953–'69)

YOU

and **your** job

Front cover of the 1953 employee manual.

Know Your Company

Gibson, Inc. of Kalamazoo, Michigan has established and maintained an enviable reputation throughout the world as Makers of Fine Stringed Musical Instruments since 1894. Only high quality products are built, with some instruments valued at over $1,000.00.

The first Gibson Mandolins and Guitars were made by Orville Gibson in the 1890's by applying the principles of Violin making to the then popular instruments of the day. The resulting quality of performance and workmanship gained immediate favorable recognition and demand soon exceeded the possible supply.

Starting with a few craftsmen in Orville Gibson's Workshop, the building of Mandolins was expanded to a manufacturing space on Harrison Court and moved into its present site at 225 Parsons Street in 1917. Additional expansion in 1944 and again in 1950 provides Gibson with the largest known floor area devoted to the manufacture of Fretted Instruments.

From 1894 to the early 1920's Gibson specialized in the Mandolin and also made a few guitars. During the 20's, banjos led the parade in popularity. Guitars began to take over in 1927-30 and the electric guitars came in 1933-35. Since 1940 the guitar has been King with the electrics gaining ground each year to a point where they require the greater portion of our facilities to meet current demand. During these changes or popularity trends, Gibson proved flexible and supplied what was needed for the public in a quality that has become a household word — this reputation is treasured and zealously guarded by old and new employees alike.

In its quest for better products at economical costs; improved service to dealers and players; good steady jobs for its employees; and efficient operations, Gibson through the years has diversified its production to be self sufficient and manufactures instruments from high quality woods and other materials to the finished product tuned and ready to play.

We now make more than a hundred models of Guitars, Hawaiian Guitars, Mandolins, Banjos, Ukuleles,

2

Amplifiers, and the Clavioline. In addition, a good portion of our production is devoted to making strings and other accessories as well as component parts that go into each unit.

All Gibson products are distributed throughout the United States, and all parts of the world (except Canada) by the Chicago Musical Instrument Company. This outstanding firm, through its sales representatives, adequately serve over 2000 Gibson dealers — it maintains a steady demand for the goods we make. The Turner Musical Instrument Company of Canada is our distributor throughout Canada.

Gibson Products are used by leading performers in orchestras and bands; on radio and television, and by recording stars. But the greatest number of units are in the hands of the day by day players who oddly enough are enthusiasts who want and take pride in owning the best.

Gibson quality and workmanship are backed by a "Lifetime Guarantee." A tribute to the lasting qualities of our products is the countless number still in use that were manufactured 20 to 60 years ago.

A GOOD PLACE TO WORK

Gibson, Inc. is proud of its record and standing in the community; its recognition throughout the world as a standard of comparison in the manufacture of fine stringed musical instruments, amplifiers and accessories; its good relations with employees through an earnest desire to do what is fair and right; and its ability to provide steady year around employment.

You can be happy in the knowledge that each of your assignments here is important. Each job well done earns for you merited respect and each measure of sincere co-operation makes it easier for the entire Gibson team to progress through harmonious and efficient production.

WHAT YOU CAN DO

You are part of the Gibson team because your efforts are needed; come on time and man your station every day — when it is not possible, notify your Supervisor,

3

preferably in advance. Whenever you need guidance or instructions consult your Supervisor. You will find a helping hand anxious for you to make good. Take care of yourself by doing things the safe and right way, and report immediately any injury however slight. Approach each job with the will to do your best; in this way you can be proud of your work every day.

SUGGESTIONS

It takes the best thoughts of everyone to keep this the kind of Company you, and all of us, want to work for. Your suggestions are most welcome. See your departmental bulletin boards for making suggestions that will save Time, Money, or Material — it may mean extra money for you.

HOLIDAY PAY

Except for watchmen there is generally no work required on the holidays mentioned in the next paragraph.

For the six holidays (New Years day, Memorial Day, Fourth of July, Labor Day, Thanksgiving Day and Christmas) designated as paid holidays when not worked, all regular employees receive 8 hours pay at their straight time hourly rate provided they work both the last full scheduled work day before and the first full scheduled work day after the holiday.

New employees become regular employees after a 30 work day probationary period. Upon completion of this period all new employees are eligible for subsequent holiday pay immediately.

GROUP INSURANCE

Gibson, Inc. has a very complete group insurance policy. The company pays a good share of the premium for hospitalization, disability, sickness and surgical benefits available to you and your dependents. We also have group life insurance benefits for employees.

Each employee retiring at 65 or over with 15 or more years length of service will have group life insur-

4

ance of ½ the amount being carried at time of retirement continued in operation with entire premium paid by the company — provided the retirement is under favorable circumstances.

New employees become eligible for group insurance benefits (when properly applied for) on the first day of the month following completion of 30 work days. The rates for this insurance are comparatively low. The Personnel Department will be glad to discuss our insurance program with you.

WORKING HOURS

The plant work day starts at 7:00 A.M. and ends at 3:15 P.M. A guard is on duty 15 minutes before working hours to admit early arrivals and 15 minutes after quitting time. There is a 10 minute rest period at 9:30 A.M., then at 12:30 P.M. there is a 15 minute lunch period followed by a 10 minute rest period. The company pays you for the two 10 minute rest periods so your actual work day is 7 hours and 40 minutes.

Office hours which include the shipping, receiving, and stock room departments, are from 8.00 A.M. to 5:00 P.M. with one hour for lunch between 12.00 and 1:00 P.M.

If there are to be any changes in the hours outlined here, the Supervisors in charge of the departments will explain them to you.

Be at your machine or work place when the starting work bell rings at the beginning of each day and after the Rest and Lunch periods. A buzzer is sounded before each work period to give you time to reach your work place. Rest periods for which the company pays are provided for rest and relaxation and are intended to eliminate going to wash rooms during work periods.

If you find it necessary to go from one department to another during the course of your work first ask your supervisor.

Plant employees enter and leave the plant through the guard house where you record your time card IN at the beginning of the day and OUT at the end of the day. Your time card is a record of your work and attendance.

5

Keep a good record by regular and prompt attendance.

To leave the premises before normal quitting time, a gate pass signed by your Supervisor is required.

PAY DAYS

Pay day for hourly rated employees is Wednesday of each week. Office employees are paid on the 15th and last day of each month.

For your protection you will be paid by check which will be handed to you personally by the timekeeper. If a check is lost or there are any errors in your check report it immediately to your supervisor.

When it is necessary to have someone besides yourself get your check, be sure he or she has a signed authorization from you to get the check.

PROBATIONARY PERIOD

As a new employee you have a thirty day work period to adjust yourself to your work and to acquaint yourself with your supervisor and other employees. After you have completed the 30 work day probationary period your plant seniority begins as of the day you were last hired.

CHANGE OF ADDRESS

If you change your address or there are any changes in your dependents etc. let the Personnel Department know about it so your records will be up to date and accurate.

ABSENCES

Absence without cause or notification for three (3) working days automatically removes you from the payroll. Avoid shorter absences without good cause or without notification. Notify the company before 8:00 A.M. on the day you are absent whenever possible, notify your Foreman at least a day ahead if necessary, due to an emergency, for you to remain away from your job, and obtain his permission for such absence. It is your responsibility to keep us informed if you must be absent.

TARDINESS

Habitual tardiness subjects an employee to dismissal, so make it a practice to be on time. Avoid loss of pay — be prompt in your attendance. If you are late one through fifteen minutes you lose ¼ hour of pay. When you are late more than 15 minutes your hourly pay starts at the beginning of the quarter hour following recorded time on your time card.

SAFETY

We are doing everything possible to make Gibson a safe place to work. If at any time you find unsafe conditions on your job report it to your supervisor so that corrective measures can be taken.

Do everything you can to keep your work space clean and use safety equipment provided, in this way everyone will benefit.

Girls working at machinery in any department should wear slacks, coveralls, or trousers; should wear sensibly heeled shoes; and wear a covering for the hair. These are all safety precautions.

ACCIDENTS ON THE JOB

If an accident or injury occurs on the job and it is necessary to go to the doctor, you will be taken to the company doctor by a company representative. An employee will be paid for time lost on day of injury if he returns and is able to work after seeing the doctor. If it is necessary to go home directly from the doctor's office the employee will be paid for the full days work.

Lost time occupational accidents or injuries are covered by Workmans Compensation and will be paid for beginning the 8th day of lost time.

PARKING

Through the efforts of Gibson, Inc., there are now no parking restrictions on both sides of Parson Street and the West side of Edwards Street. This allows you to park close to your work.

7

The Company also owns and maintains a parking lot on Parsons Street East of the railroad tracks. Parking in this lot is limited and is assigned to employees according to their length of service.

The parking space on Scudder Court is reserved for office and supervisory employees.

TELEPHONES

All incoming calls to plant employees will be handled thru the Personnel Department. Emergency calls will be given to you immediately. Because of the location of the telephones and the size of the departments it is impossible to call employees to the telephone during work periods. You may use the telephone during work periods in urgent cases by getting an OK from your supervisor.

Telephone operators will be on duty to handle calls you may wish to make during rest and lunch periods. These calls should be limited.

RECREATION

Gibson, Inc. will support any recreational activities that are not of a professional nature and that encourage competition and sportmanship between employees and departments. Contact the Personnel Department if you are interested in recreational or cultural activity.

VENDING MACHINES

The company has placed Coca Cola, candy and ice cream vending machines in convenient places in the plant so employees can enjoy refreshments before and after working hours, during rest periods, and lunch hours.

The proceeds from these machines form an activity fund which is used for the benefit of all employees.

SOCIAL SECURITY

The company is required by law to deduct a small amount from each of your paychecks in accordance with the Federal Social Security Act. All money deducted from your pay under this law is matched by an equal amount by the company and the combined amount is ac-

8

cumulated in your own social security account with the Federal Government. This fund provides for monthly payments to eligible people 65 years of age or older, monthly payments to dependents of those receiving old-age benefits, monthly or other payments to survivors of workers who die at any age.

UNEMPLOYMENT COMPENSATION

Under the Unemployment Compensation Law, the Company makes contributions to a state fund. This money provides for weekly payments in case you are laid off or are off work for other reasons specified by this law. All payments to this fund are made by the Company; none of your deductions go for Unemployment Compensation.

BULLETIN BOARDS

Throughout the factory and offices there are bulletin boards which are used for announcements to employees. All notices which do not pertain to Company matters are to be approved by the Superintendent or Personnel Department before posting. As it is not possible to grant requests to post notices of a non company nature — the use of the bulletin boards for such purposes is restricted.

SOME SUGGESTIONS

Visits by employees off duty or by employees friends and relatives should be made only in cases of necessity.

Solicitations in the factory or offices should not be made without the approval of the Personnel Department, and the sale of merchandise or chances on punch boards or raffles is not permitted on our premises.

Employees are expected to manage their personal finances in such a manner as to avoid wage assignments and garnishments.

Good housekeeping is important and we all want to be proud of our company and cooperate in keeping our buildings and grounds clean.

A material pass authorization signed by your Supervisor, Superintendent, or Personnel Department is required to take out personal belongings, tools, or purchased

9

items. Give this pass, describing the materials, to the plant guard when you leave the premises.

EMPLOYEE DISCOUNTS

You may purchase strings, cases and accessories for your own personal use or for gifts at a substantial discount. Instruments, amplifiers, and other major items may be purchased for personal use only after you have completed six months of employment. These purchases may be paid for on a limited time basis. Ask your Supervisor for details when you want to make a purchase.

VACATIONS

Vacation pay is earned by completion of specified lengths of continuous service from last date of hire to July 1st. of any year. Vacation pay will be computed on the basis of an eight hour day or a forty hour week at the employees regular straight time hourly rate as follows:

Six months or more but less than one year — 2 days or 16 hrs. pay.

One year or more but less than five years — one week or 40 hrs. pay.

Five years or more but less than 15 years — 2 weeks or 80 hrs. pay.

Fifteen years or more—3 weeks or 120 hrs. pay.

Vacation periods will be granted during July and August and whenever possible at a time desired by employee unless the plant is closed for a vacation period for the purpose of repairs and installation of facilities, and to maintain production with the least amount of disruption; or unless employees are required to continue work and receive vacation pay in lieu of vacations.

UNION CONTRACT

Our continued interest for improvement has resulted in policies that assure good working conditions, fair wages and hours, and opportunity for advancement.

The production and maintenance employees are represented by the United Steelworkers of America CIO in behalf of Local Union 3596. Detailed practices concerning rates of pay, hours of work, and working conditions for employees in the unit have been determined or modified through collective bargaining. All new production and maintenance employees are required to join and maintain membership in the union after completion of the 30 work day probationary period.

Supervisors will answer to the best of their ability your questions about the union contract and its application to your job and will give you the names of the union officers and bargaining committee members on request.

GENERAL RULES OF CONDUCT

GIBSON, INC.

ESTABLISHED JANUARY 1, 1946

Here at Gibson, we are convinced that each employee is desirous of building a good work record — one that will be a credit to an honest effort to do what is right and best for the individual, fellow workers, and the Company.

When an individual disrupts reasonable procedures, it is fitting to discuss the problem verbally and to clearly point out a remedy. When the problem persists, written warnings and disciplinary action will be administered as follows:

GENERAL RULES OF CONDUCT

Rules with number of warnings leading to dismissal for each type of rule broken.
Each employee will start with a clean slate on January first of each year.

1. Smoking when prohibited. 3 warnings; 4th offense, dismissal. However —
   (a). Smoking in plant work area is subject to immediate dismissal.
2. Quitting before quitting signal; 3 warnings; 4th offense, dismissal.
3. Not starting work at starting signal: 3 warnings; 4th offense, dismissal.

11

4. Absence without cause or notification (for less than a three day period). 2 warnings; 3rd offense, dismissal.

5. Insubordination (refusal to follow instructions): 3 warnings; 4th offense, dismissal.

6. Poor quality and quantity of work: 3 warnings, 4th offense, dismissal.

7. Stealing: Instant dismissal.

8. Reporting under influence of, or bringing into premises intoxicating licquors. Instant dismissal.

9. Habitual tardiness (4 times in one month): 2 warnings; 3rd offense dismissal.

10. Punching in or out other than your own time card: 1 warning; 2nd offense, dismissal. However —
    (a). Punching in or out of fellow employees time card when a person is not here: Immediate dismissal.

11. Falsifying on application and other records: Instant dismissal.

12. Disorderly conduct: 1 warning; 2nd offense, dismissal.

13. Carrying out materials without authorization: Instant dismissal.

14. Quarreling, scuffling, horseplay: 3 warnings; 4th offense, dismissal.

15. Failure to wear goggles where required: 3 warnings, 4th offense, dismissal.

16. Leaving workspace, plant or premises without permission: 3 warnings; 4th offense, dismissal.

17. Failure to report for first aid when injured: 3 warnings; 4th offense, dismissal.

18. Failure to shut off power when leaving machines or for repairs: 3 warnings, 4th offense, instant dismissal.

19. Loitering in toilets, washrooms, or elsewhere: 3 warnings, 4th offense, dismissal.

20. Removing safety devices without permission: 2 warnings, 3rd offense, dismissal.

12

History 1
Garrett Bos (1919–'65)

Garrett Bos is an unsung hero at Gibson. He was still very active at Gibson during the 1950s, holding a key position in the pattern makers department. Bos is credited with significant input and hands-on design for Gibson's original Les Paul prototype built in 1951. With his lengthy service, Bos contributed to all of Gibson's finest eras. He was there with Lloyd Loar in the 1920s, he was there when the great flat head Mastertone banjos were made in the 1930s, and he was there when the legendary Advanced Jumbo flat tops were made in the 1930s. As a skilled pattern maker, machinist, and wood worker, it is likely that Gar Bos contributed as much as any single employee in Gibson's history.

History 2
Kathryn Harris (1920–'71)

Katie Harris' 51 year seniority at Gibson is legendary. She started with the Gibson Mandolin-Guitar Company on May 20, 1920, shortly after graduating from Kalamazoo Central High School. (Note: 1920 was the same year Maurice Berlin founded

(Left to right) In 1953, Dorothy Kuras, Kathryn Harris, Marian Thorpe, and Martha Junker stand in front of the attractive general office main entrance lobby. Four of Gibson's finest instruments can be seen in the lobby showcase.

Chicago Musical Instruments, CMI.] Katie started as the office switchboard operator and rotated through other assignments in the office. In 1953 some of her co-workers in the office were Dorothy Kuras, Marian Thorpe, and Martha Junker. Katie worked with many of Gibson's greatest names, including Clarence Havenga, Rodney Chittenden, G. Ferris (General Manager in 1924), Russ Stout (Superintendent in 1924), Guy Hart (General Manager in 1925), Lloyd Loar (F-5 mandolin engineer in the 1920s), and of course all of the McCarty era staff. Katie was an able mandolin & banjo player. She enjoyed playing with various musical groups and mandolin orchestras during her lifetime.

History 3
John Huis (1926–'65)

John Huis needs no introduction. He was Ted McCarty's trusted assistant who held the position as the No. 1 production man at Gibson during the McCarty era. McCarty described Huis as being a hands-on production man. According to McCarty, Huis wasn't particularly skilled at business management per se. The Huis specialty was knowledge of equipment and manufacturing processes. That was the basis of the McCarty-Huis team.

McCarty was the businessman, the skilled business man. Huis was the factory man. He was the blue collar worker who knew the factory. Huis and McCarty were friends outside of work. They enjoyed activities like duck hunting.

Huis was typical of the type of person who emerged to leadership at Gibson. During Gibson's glory years, promotion from within was typical. Men who showed exceptional skill at producing both high volume and high quality were appreciated at Gibson. These men were often asked to accept more responsibility as line leader, inspector, assistant foreman, pattern maker, production foreman, quality control foreman, engineer, general foreman, assistant superintendent, and finally the top factory job, superintendent.

Women were not ignored for promotion, but in those days many of the women working at Gibson were working as second wage earners. Many of them had families. Within a department that was populated by women, women were offered supervisory positions. That was the case, for example, with Helen Charkowski, but supervision didn't fit with Helen's goals and she did not pursue supervision at Gibson.

Huis started at Gibson in 1926 at age 17. Prior to being promoted by Ted McCarty, Huis was just one of the skilled supervisory employees that worked at Gibson. John started on the bench at Gibson but progressed to trouble shooter in the woodshop, then inspector, superintendent, and Vice President of Production. Gibson believed in promotion-from-within. Huis was a perfect example. Inspectors, pattern makers, and engineers were encouraged to advance by Gibson management because they showed skill, ability, and an interest in getting the job done. The true strength of Gibson, starting back in the early 1900s was its ability to recognize talent and to promote that talent. Any number of the employees that we've interviewed could have likely assumed the leadership post given to Huis. Huis returned to Gibson from the war, just a few months before Maurice Berlin sent Ted McCarty to tour Gibson. John Huis was there when Ted made his historic fact-finding tour of Gibson in January of 1948. It was Huis who McCarty chose to be the leader of the factory. John Huis retired from Gibson, having accumulated many years of seniority both before and after the war. He became co-owner and junior partner of Bigsby Accessories.

In a 1953 photo, Gibson Finishing Room foreman Cornelius 'Case' Triezenberg shows Sherman W. Lees of Forbes – PPG the high quality finish found on Gibson guitars.

History 4
Cornelius (Case) Triezenberg (1926–'73)

Case Triezenberg is an employee who is constantly referred to by Gibson old-timers. He worked for Gibson for 47 years. Here is Julius Bellson's proclamation at Case's retirement, "Case came to Gibson on May 1, 1926 when he was only 16 years old. He started as a dry sander then moved into spray painting which quickly became his life's work. He is considered an expert in the finishing of new instruments and he is skilled in the art of repairing older models. On February 6, 1948 he was promoted to Foreman of the Finishing Department [Note: This was done just prior to Ted McCarty joining Gibson in March, 1948, but after Ted's plant tour in January, 1948.] Case held that position for over 25 years. Case's pleasing personality, and his more than 47 years of experience has earned him the respect of his fellow co-workers."

All McCarty era instruments were finished under the leadership of Case Triezenberg. His responsibility in the Finishing Department included all of the activities on the 1950s third floor of 225 Parsons Street. The activities included pore filling and staining all the way through to final inspection.

History 5
Ernest Kuhn (1926–'66+)

Ernest Kuhn worked in the mill room during the McCarty era. He hired into Gibson on August 10, 1926, just a few months after John Huis joined Gibson. Ernest continued to work in the mill room, in department 9100, the year that McCarty left, having the highest seniority in the hourly workforce.

History 6
Sylvia Howard (1927–'73)

Kalamazoo native, Sylvia Howard, graduated from Kalamazoo Central High School and Parsons Business College, going to the Gibson Sales Department in October, 1927. In her early years, like co-worker Katie Harris of the same generation, Sylvia played guitar. She was a member of the 1930s 'Gib-

A 1953 photo of the 3rd floor spray gun booth. PPG's Forbes Finishes supplied Gibson with varnishes, lacquers, lacquer-sealers, and colored lacquers for over 30 years.

son Mandolin Girls' , a six-member mandolin orchestra which consisted of all mandolin body sizes and Sylvia's Gibson guitar. She married Don Howard in 1933 and resigned from Gibson in 1938 in order to stay home with her family. She worked in Don's family-owned corner grocery until the store was sold in 1954. She returned to Gibson that year as secretary to Julius Bellson and John Huis. As Bellson's secretary, she was in the middle of every-

The 3rd floor spray booth vents mark the spot where Case Triezenberg and Harlan Clair did so much great work in the 1950s. This is where the great 1959 Les Paul Standards and late 1950s ES-335 received there historic vintage finishes. The 1st floor annex (at the right of the photo) housed the maintenance department and the kiln in the 1950s.

thing. Her own office was directly across the hall from Mr. Bellson's and it was just a few steps from Mr. McCarty's corner office. Sylvia worked for Gibson for 29 years and retired in 1973, the same year as Mr. Bellson.

History 7
Leonard Shedore (1928–'72)

Len Shedore was hired on September 8, 1928. Len worked in the service and repair department at Gibson and he was admired nationally for his knowledge of older Gibson instruments. Len was a musician who played in bands and groups in Kalamazoo in the 1940s and 1950s. When Ted McCarty left Gibson in 1966, Len was the service-adjuster in the Parsons Street repair department 3800-1. Ted McCarty acknowledged that some of his key people could repair anything. Leonard Shedore was one of those people.

History 8
Harlan Clair (1928–'73)

Harlan Clair started at Gibson in 1928 in the finishing department. Like so many employees Harlan chose to stay in his department for most of his career. He was considered among the best if not the best master craftsman in the art of fine finishes. Harlan worked closely with Case Trieszenberg for 45 years, and their names are closely associated with the fine finishes that grace many McCarty era instruments.

History 9
Ed Rosenberger (1928–'66+)

Ed Rosenberger, who started at Gibson in 1928, was one of three mill foremen in the 1950s. Rosenberger was over the lumber yard and rough mill where Gibson's quality really started.

History 10
Walter Fuller (1933–'68)

Walter Fuller is one of the Gibson legends. His father was a janitor at Gibson and it is expected that his dad suggested that Walter come to Gibson after graduating from high school. Walter's cousin, Wilbur Fuller, also worked at Gibson, also making immeasurable contributions. Wilbur and Walter's dad were brothers. Walter was the one who suggested that Wilbur give Gibson a try in 1954.

Walt began his career in Gibson's machine shop, but within three months he was promoted to Cost Estimator & Timekeeper. In 1935 he was promoted to Electrical Engineer. In this position Walt developed Gibson's first electric instruments. In 1941 he asked Gibson legend Seth Lover to join the electronics lab as an amplifier trouble-shooter. Seth left Gibson during the war.

Walt's greatest design is considered to be Gibson's P-90 single-coil guitar pickup. After World War II Gibson became interested in manufacturing its own amplifiers, something that Ted McCarty totally supported. By 1952, Fuller needed more help in the electronics lab so Ted McCarty asked Seth Lover to return to Kalamazoo and Gibson.

Fuller and Lover did the engineering for Gibson's pickups, amps, and electronic assemblies. Walt was rewarded for his efforts by being named Chief Electronics Engineer and then Plant Manager of Gibson's new 1962 Plant II Electronics Division. In 1964 Fuller assumed leadership of Gibson's Plant III, the relocated amplifier and electronics plant. Gibson ceased amplifier production in Kalamazoo in 1968. The business was transferred to CMI and Walt followed that to Chicago. He returned to Gibson Kalamazoo in 1971 as the head of electric guitar development and testing. For more information, see the Humbucking Pickup Section of the book.

History 11 & 12
John Klien and Basil Raynes (1933–'66+)

John Klien joined Gibson on August 19, 1933. Two weeks later, on September 3 Basil Raynes hired-in. During the McCarty Era both men worked in the maintenance department, and they continued to work there, in Department 3700-1 Maintenance, Sweepers, and Millwrights, the year Ted McCarty resigned.

History 13
Julius Bellson (1935–'73)

Julius Bellson deserves to be included on any list of legendary Gibson employees. In the McCarty Golden Era, 1948–'66, Gibson employees, the people that made the great Gibson instruments, singled out Ted McCarty, John Huis, Julius Bellson, and Larry Allers. To the employees, those men were the key figures. Relative to that list, Larry Allers, the chief engineer, although almost totally overlooked by historians, was probably a key figure in the development of the Gibson Les Paul Model, and many other great woodworking designs.

Julius Bellson wore many hats at Gibson. He was listed as an Officer of the company in 1950, as Assistant Treasurer. He was listed as Treasurer in 1966 (the year Ted left). Bellson was born June 3, 1905 in Salerno, Italy. He was four years older than Ted McCarty, so the men were of the same generation. He was born into a musical family. His brother was a successful music teacher and Gibson Agent, selling Gibsons during the period prior to the development of the Gibson franchise dealership which was finalized under M. H. Berlin. After his school years Julius was also a professional music teacher and Gibson agent. Bellson performed at the Masonic Temple in Kalamazoo in 1925 and apparently caught the eyes and ears of Gibson. He was recruited by Gibson in 1935, at age 30, and moved to Kalamazoo from Minneapolis.

Bellson's first job was as the Gibson Musicologist, where he supervised writing, printing, and distribution of several Gibson guitar instruction courses. Throughout his career he also handled special assignments, such as inside sales (for example, the sale of the 1955 Test Guitar), in addition to handling sales correspondence and advertising. During World War II he became Personnel Manager, hiring dozens of replacement workers, mostly women, during the war years. It was in the position of Personnel Manager that most employees remember Julius. Up until circa 1955, the foremen/supervisors could hire directly for their own departments. Employment opportunities were abundant in Kalamazoo, and other Michigan blue collar cities like Flint. While the foreman often met with a potential candidate first, the second trip for the candidate was to Mr. Bellson's office. Bellson was an accomplished musician. Along with others such as Rem Wall and Wilbur Marker, he often demonstrated Gibson products for Gibson at Trade Shows and Exhibits. For example, Bellson, along with McCarty, unveiled the Gibson L-5CES and Super 400CES in 1951 at the Gotham Hotel, back when Trade Shows were held in hotel rooms.

History 14
George Comee (1936–'75)

George Comee was one of very, very few college graduates that worked at Gibson during the McCarty era. That wasn't uncommon for that time in Michigan industry. Even office jobs were generally filled by promotion from within. In the day, company accountants generally started in the time-office keeping track of time cards, employee hours and adjustments. Comee was different, graduating from Kalamazoo College, a small prestigious college located high on a hill in western-central Kalamazoo. Kalamazoo College was very selective and students were from upper-middle class or wealthy families. In that regard, he would have been a peer to Ted McCarty. Ted grew up in an upper-middle class household, with an Uncle that was well-known and respected.

Comee started as a bookkeeper at Gibson, taking advantage of specialized skills. McCarty himself started in the Wurlitzer accounting department in January 1936, making McCarty and Comee businessmen who were educated and lived by the same set of accounting practices and procedures. Comee was part of the Guy Hart/Neil Abrams era at Gibson, experiencing the final fall of their leadership at Gibson in 1947 when both men were ill. Comee, who knew what was in Gibson's books, was helpful to Ted McCarty during Ted's January, 1948 fact finding trip for Maurice Berlin. On that historic trip, McCarty wasn't too worried about Gibson's ability to recover. McCarty discovered that Gibson had confused top management in poor health, low manufacturing productivity that couldn't absorb factory burdens allocated in a 'profit center' system of accounting, and general post war confusion over tools – dies- fixtures, and generally poor employee morale.

George Comee was on Ted McCarty's staff, but he stayed behind the scenes. Like Comee, McCarty was also trained in accounting, as part of his Commercial Engineering degree from the University of Cincinnati. A Commercial Engineer from Cincinnati was educated in both business administration and engineering. Ted's assignments for Wurlitzer also made him aware of all aspects of business accounting, including sales accounting, pricing, cost accounting, burden control, plant accounting, payables and receivables, audit, and general ledger.

Gibson during the McCarty era was a 'profit center.' This meant that Gibson was responsible for recording profit. Sales from Gibson to CMI would be true sales. (In the post-McCarty era, Gibson was changed to a 'cost center' which meant it only showed expenses on CMI's books). McCarty era Gibson was a 'profit center' for two reasons. One, Gibson was a separate Michigan Corporation, the other CMI business entities were not. Gibson was expected to sell to CMI at a contracted price and Gibson's sales less all expenses were expected to generate a profit.

McCarty must have been a formidable boss for George Comee. McCarty understood all the nuances of corporate bookkeeping. McCarty's knowledge allowed him to give his full confidence to George Comee. Ted strongly delegated all financial and accounting responsibilities to Comee. McCarty's ability to quickly absorb all financial matters allowed him to spend a greater amount of time on personnel activities, and on his favorite niche, engineering.

George Comee was rewarded for his hard work by being named an officer of Gibson, the Secretary of Gibson, in 1962. In four years, 1966, he was named Secretary-Controller of Gibson.

History 15
Larry Allers (1937- 1970)

The No. 1 unsung hero of the Ted McCarty era has to be Larry Allers. He's not a household name among vintage Gibson enthusiasts. He isn't mentioned in the same sentence with Walter Fuller, Seth Love, John Huis, or Julius Bellson. Yet feedback and testimony from the employees validates Larry as one of the most important people at Gibson

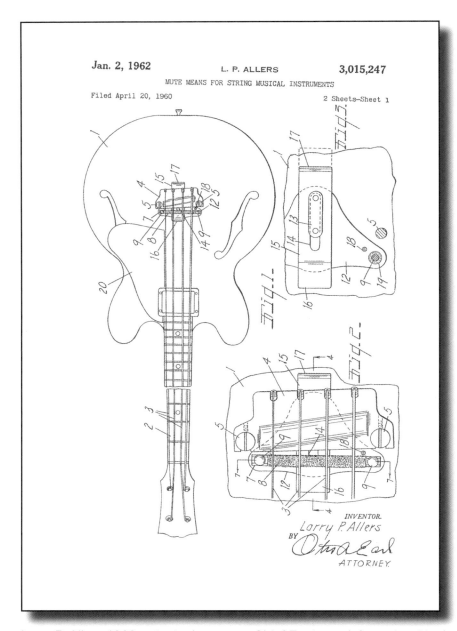

Larry P. Allers 1962 patent. Larry was Chief Engineer (of woodworking) for most of the 1950s and 1960s. He is perhaps the most important 'unknown name' that worked at Gibson during Ted McCarty's Golden Era.

A 1954 photo of Wilbur Marker (standing) playing a Les Paul goldtop, his son Curtis Marker (age 9) with a ukulele, and his father C.J. Marker with a mando cello. All three were accomplished musicians on their instrument of choice.   This photo was probably taken in the 'general office conference room.' Another well documented photo (not shown) of Marker, Fuller, and Bellson was taken in the other conference room, the 'executive conference room' located across from Ted McCarty's corner office.

during Ted McCarty's Golden Era.

All indications from employees are that Larry was the main designer and builder of the Gibson Les Paul Model. He also developed a variety of Gibson features and instruments ranging from the flat top adjustable bridge to the EB-2 bass.

Larry was born in 1908, making him one year older than Ted McCarty. He was a native of Beaver Island, out in Lake Michigan. His dad was a carpenter on Beaver Island, so wood work ran naturally in the family. After school Larry moved from Beaver Island to South Haven, Michigan. He was living in South Haven when he landed the job at Gibson. Larry was a guitar player who played in bands around South Haven, so he was probably attracted to Gibson because it was a famous guitar factory. For his first year at Gibson Larry used to hitchhike back and forth to get to work from South Haven to Kalamazoo.

Larry started at Gibson in 1937 as a sander in the mill. His wife used to say that Larry used to come home with his fingers all bloody. Larry moved to Kalamazoo in 1938 to a home at 3630 Madison that was about 5 miles from Parsons Street. After a time Larry was made foreman in the woodshop. From foreman they promoted him to assistant superintendent and Chief Engineer in the early 1950s. Chief Engineer was one of the most important positions at Gibson and it was always filled from within by men that were motivated and highly skilled. His son Ron said, "I know he's the one that designed the Les Paul guitars. And he also invented the adjustable bridge on the acoustic guitar."

After 33 years, Larry retired in 1970. He died in 1995. He was 87 years old, living a long productive life like his peer Ted McCarty.

A Gibson engineer is analyzing changes in power output. Complete modern test equipment includes oscillators, voltmeters, analyzers and oscilloscopes to check amplifier performance.

Seth Lover in a 1961 Gibson catalog.

History 16
Wilbur Marker (1938 - 1956)

Wilbur Marker was brought to Gibson in 1938 to pen Gibson's instructional material. He supported Julius Bellson in this endeavor. He also traveled for Gibson promoting Gibson instruments and teaching methods until the war effort began in 1942. During World War II he was Gibson's Chief Inspector, a position he held until 1948. When Ted McCarty replaced Guy Hart in 1948, Marker was named Service Manager & Custom Instruments Manager. Custom-made, higher-end models were made throughout the Parsons Street factory during this time. (In 1960, Gibson moved all of the Custom Instrument lutherie to the company's new Custom Department on the north end of the third floor of Parson's Street.) As manager of Custom Instruments in the early 1950s it is reasonable to assume that Marker was yet another name that should be added to the creative team that developed and designed the 1952 Les Paul Model goldtop. Because Marker was a guitar player too, and given the fact that the organization was not blessed with too many guitar players, it is logical to assume Wilbur Marker was one of the select employees, including Rem Wall and Julius Bellson, who tested the first Gibson Les Paul solidbody.

Marker went on the road for Gibson from 1953–'56 as part of Gibson's promotional 'Gibson Caravan.' Undoubtedly, in 1953, Marker was promoting the new Les Paul solidbody. During this promotion Marker visited Gibson dealers in every part of the country. Gibson employees at Parson Street were aware of his travel and often mentioned Marker as the man who would travel for Gibson. Wilbur would come back to Parsons Street often and tour the plant talking with people in a manner similar to Ted McCarty's tours of the plant.

Wilbur Marker transferred to CMI Sales in Chicago, in 1956 and traveled Gibson's Midwest territories. At the end of the McCarty era, 1965 to 1966, Wilbur Marker was named 'CMI Diplomat Salesman' and he was presented an internal CMI award that was used to honor the top sales people. In the post McCarty era at Gibson, Wilbur Marker was the CMI/Gibson General Manager of Customer Relations.

Marker came from a family of musicians. His father, C.J. Marker purchased a Gibson mandolin in 1906 and a Gibson Mando Cello in 1911. Elder Marker introduced music to his son. Wilbur Marker's musical talents were well used by Gibson. As was the case with Julius Bellson, Rem Wall, Hubie Friar, James Hanchett, and Larry Allers, Gibson was successful in maximizing the musical talent in the plant.

History 17
Gerald Bergeon (ca.1930-1960s)

Gerald Bergeon is another historic figure at Gibson and he was one of the three mill foreman in the 1950s. He is also referenced many times in the employee interviews with Wilbur Fuller, Marv Lamb, and J.P. Moats. His father Ralph Bergeon was also a foreman in the mill in earlier decades. Bergeon is one of the important Gibson family names, like Marker, Lamb, Moats, Bradford and others.

History 18
Gerald M. Woodworth (1938-1960s)

According to historian Julius Bellson, "Gerald M. Woodworth was one of the finest steel guitar players of the day. He assembled and tested amplifiers, and wrote the fine arrangements in the Mastertone System. He became Supervisor of the String Division (in the 1940s), was in charge of Quality Control, and finally headed up the Service Department where he performed with marked distinction for many years."

History 19
Seth Lover (1941–'67)

Kalamazoo's own Seth Lover was born in 1910, making him a peer of Ted McCarty. Lover and McCarty grew up in the 'radio generation' and both were fascinated and inspired by the radio. When the radio began to become popular in the early 1920s both boys wanted to know everything they could about it. Lover's knowledge of radios paved the way for a job as a tube amplifier trouble-shooter at Gibson. Lover is the 'father of the Gibson humbucking pickup.' Ted McCarty properly allowed Seth Lover's name to appear on the 1955 Gibson patent for the hum-bucking device. Ted McCarty clearly recalled that Seth not only coined the name 'humbucker', he also invented the name 'Flying V.' For more on Seth Lover, refer to the Gibson Humbucker section of the book.

McCarty looked upon Lover as both hero and goat. He was a hero for his pickup work but some what of a scapegoat for the failure of the Gibson amplifier business. The employees of Gibson unanimously agree that Seth Lover was not the type of person to be seen on the manufacturing floor. He was not the type of person that interacted with the amplifier department. In that way, it is easy to assume that Seth Lover was somewhat like Leo Fender, in that Lover preferred to stay locked up in his electronics lab to tinker with electronic designs. While most Gibson factory workers knew the Seth Lover name, none of the workers seemed to know the man. In 1967 Lover retired from his position as Senior Project Engineer at Gibson. This had something to do with Gibson canceling amplifier production in Kalamazoo. Seth and his wife Lavone moved to Garden Grove, CA where Seth began working with Fender Musical Instruments as a designer of their new amplifiers and pickups. Richard Evans, who was appointed Chief Electronics Engineer for Gibson's new Plant II and Plant III electronics plants also lost his job when amplifiers left Gibson. Evans left Gibson around the same time as Seth Lover and he too joined Fender.

History 20
James Collins (1941–'66+).

James started in 1941 before the war effort really began and before the union organized the Gibson factory. Jim worked in department 2500C Custom Assembly and Adjusting the year Ted left Gibson. He is referenced in the employee interviews.

History 21
Rollo Werner (1942–'73)

Rollo Werner is another behind-the-scenes 'big name' at Gibson. He joined Gibson on November 15, 1942 as a plastics engineer. He was one of several people promoted by

Ted McCarty in 1948 when Rollo was named Director of Purchasing for Gibson. Gibson historian Julius Bellson described Werner as, "Very valuable to the company because of his knowledge of operations, production, equipment, maintenance, engineering, quality, and the type of production and material needed and the worldwide sources of materials."

Werner was responsible for buying everything, including wood. He would be one of the main people to go to the lumber mills and select the wood. Ted McCarty, Larry Allers and others would also share that responsibility. Wood buying was a join effort, with plant personnel constantly talking about wood supplies and requirements. Werner's office during the McCarty era was next to the front lobby of the administration office. This was the normal location for a buyer, a location that provided easy access for visiting vendors.

A couple of Gibson's famous Dutchmen that worked in the plant were known to have exceptional wood working knowledge. Ted McCarty was trained by the Dutchmen prior to becoming a wood buyer for Gibson. It is assumed that Rollo Werner was also trained by the Dutchmen. It was noted in the employee interviews that when Rollo Werner retired, it left a big hole in the Gibson organization.

History 22
Irene Marble (1942–'66+)

Irene Marble was another early hire that was hired to do war work. Gibson's employment rolls increased during the war, most of the new people were women. Because of the labor shortage in Kalamazoo in the 1950s, it was relatively easy for a woman to work, and the women could often set their own work schedules to accommodate family life. Irene apparently did not leave work because she retained her early seniority data. The war work at Gibson was mostly electronics work and that department became the electronics department at the end of the war. Irene worked in the inspection department 1700E in the Plant III (the amplifier plant) when Ted left in 1966.

History 23
Bernice Penhollow (1942–'66+)

Bernice Penhollow was an early hire that did war work and stayed on at Gibson in the High Frequency and Body Assembly department that used Gibson's high speed microwave glue machine. That department was highly populated with women. Woman made up 90% of that department's workforce. Bernice worked in that department (9420) when Ted resigned in 1966.

History 24
Hartford Snider (1943–'74)

Hartford started at Gibson on September 3, 1943 in the woodshop under the supervision of Ralph Bergeon [Note: Ralph was Gerald Bergeon's father/father and son both held the important position of mill room foreman at Gibson.] Hartford moved to the Custom Department in 1964 under the supervision of Wilbur Fuller. In the Custom Department he designed and made patterns for Gibson's custom build instruments. He also designed and made a special finger rest for a variety of instruments, in addition to other custom made parts. He also performed special and intricate repair work in the service section of the

Custom / Service Department located (since 1960) on the third floor of the 'old building.' Hartford was the highest seniority person working in department 2500B Custom Instruments Finishing when Ted left Gibson in 1966.

History 25

Jacob Doorenbos (1943–'66+)

Jacob joined Gibson on October 22, 1943 and worked in the machine shop / tool room / model maker department. He was there (department 3600) when Ted left Gibson in 1966.

History 26

R. L. Kingsley (1943–'66+)

R. L. Kingsley was an important member of the Gibson team and his name is mentioned several times in the interviews. He hired into Gibson on November 15, 1943, and was active in the machine shop / tool room / model maker department. He was boss of the repair department in the 1950s. He was in the department 3600 machine shop when Ted left Gibson in 1966.

History 27

Clarence Coleman (1944 – 1964)

Clarence Coleman, a prominent employee in the 1950s, was one of the three Gibson mill foremen. He is referenced many times in the employee interviews with Wilbur Fuller, Marv Lamb, and J.P. Moats. Since many new employees went through hand sanding and cleaning in the mill Clarence had an important impact on their careers.

History 28

Carleton Pease (1944–'74)

Carleton started at Gibson in 1944 as a time study man in the Time Office. He progressed to Stockroom Supervisor, Head of Production Scheduling, Supervisor of Material Stores, and finally Supervisor of the Parcel Post Department. Starting in the time office as a time study man, Carleton's assignment was equivalent to a modern day I.E. (Industrial Engineer), someone who time studies how long it should take to completely perform a certain job, and then prepares a time routing. I.E.s (Industrial Engineers) did not begin to enter the Michigan workforce until the mid-1960s, and that was about the time that Gibson hired Art Palumbo, Gibson's first official industrial engineer.

Jobs in both the time office and administrative office were considered 'indirect' jobs. An 'indirect' employee was someone who did not touch the product. A 'direct' employee was someone who did touch the product. Production workers were 'direct' employees. Gibson had both 'direct' and 'indirect' employees. Maintaining a relatively small number of 'indirect' jobs meant lower costs. Salary employees were often called 'indirect employees' since most salaried employees did not touch the product. Gibson seemed to maintain a minimum number of 'indirect jobs.' That meant each salary employee had plenty to do and plenty of responsibility. Jobs that Carleton held were 'indirect', including supervising the stockroom, supervising production control, supervising indirect material and supervising finished goods shipping (called the parcel post department at Gibson). While woodworkers get the credit for doing a great job at Gibson, those woodworkers were supported by a small, but important cadre of 'indirect' workers.

Carleton started in the Gibson time office as a time study man. Time study during the McCarty era balanced the need for quality and quantity. This fine balance was one of a ½ dozen reasons that McCarty era factories could maintain high quality. While cost was always something that McCarty and George Comee looked at, 'cost' could be a negative metric that acted as a third party in the quality vs. quantity manufacturing formula. As Gibson's cost increased in 1965, cost became a third variable that began upsetting the quality vs. quantity equation. With rising fixed costs, such as new plant depreciation, added pressure was put on the production

Back row, from left: Jim Bailey, Walt Bodchick, Les Bonnell, Wayne Marker, Ken Powers, Dick Aukes, Ralph Slater

Front row: Paul Vallier, Bill Worth, Russ Bjorkman, Argell Paddock

The 1950 Gibson Softball Team. They ended up in second place during the 1950 season.

volume. More quantity was needed to thin out the additional fixed and semi-variable costs.

History 29
George Mercia (1944–'73)

George Mercia started at Gibson about a year before the end of World War II. He was hired on August 16, 1944. He began in the Machine Shop located in the north end of the 'old building' basement. At that time Gibson was mostly machining parts for government war work. After the machine shop, George joined the repair department (also located in the basement) and then he became a pattern maker that supported the engineers. He finished out his career as an Inspector. He was working in the Plant I inspection department 1700 when Ted left Gibson. When Ted left Gibson, the Plant I inspection department was one of the most experienced departments at Gibson.

History 30 & History 31
Bertha Bushell (1944–'67) & Mary Belle Smith (1944–'66+)

Bertha and Mary Belle Smith hired into Gibson in the late war years to do electronics work. While some women were hired as temporary workers, Bertha and Mary Belle were permanent workers who established early seniority dates. As was normal, both stayed with electronics and they were both working in department 2200A Plant III electronics, along with Jacqueline Fergusson Friar (see that interview), when Ted McCarty left Gibson.

History 32
Elizabeth Ferens (1946–'75+)

Betty Ferens joined Gibson on May 9, 1946. She met her husband John during World War II while working for Douglas Aircraft in Tulsa, OK. After the war, they moved to Kalamazoo, which was her husband's hometown. Betty applied for work and was hired at Gibson. She started out as a machine operator in the string room. Then she transferred to the amplifier department, and later she became a guitar builder in the rim lining area.

Betty was typical in that she worked in two areas that were heavily populated by female employees. Betty was in the string room and later in the electronics department.

It was not uncommon for women to post for the electronics department and move into the job that they really wanted to have. That formula for success began to fall apart for Gibson after Ted McCarty left. When plant unit volumes went down and fewer people were needed, jobs were rotated in the plant based upon seniority. Often, even though a person did not want to work in a certain department, they had to because it was either take that job or lose your job. That was not the case during the McCarty era. During McCarty's years, when employment was growing, a person could hold onto their favorite job because of their seniority. The seniority system worked well during a period of growth, but the seniority system created unwanted transfers during a period of declining production volume.

Three important product segments were removed from Gibson Kalamazoo by Arnie Berlin. The amplifier business and Epiphone product line were removed from 1968 to 1970. In 1973 the Gibson string division, which had been relocated in the basement of the 'old building' was removed from Kalamazoo. In 1968 only one hourly rate person was added by Gibson Kalamazoo, in 1969 and 1970 no hourly people were added. This was unheard of at McCarty's Gibson. With the lost of the amp business, the string room and the Epiphone business some employees were required to take jobs that they perhaps would have otherwise not wanted. This was not a positive thing and it became possible, for the first time since World War II for some employees to be unhappy about their assignments. This type of environment exposed the downside of having a union shop. When times were good, from 1944 to 1968, a union shop operated nearly unnoticed. When times were not so good, with a declining manufacturing base, unionization became a negative.

In Betty's case, she lost her job building amplifiers and she transitioned to body building, something that probably would not have happened had the amplifier business stayed in Kalamazoo, Michigan. In Betty's case, she made the transition very well, being a model employee in both the electronics department and body building.

History 33
Robert Powers (1946–'76+)

Robert Powers graduated from Kalamazoo Central High School in 1942. He spent four years in the army during World War II. He was hired by Gibson on April 8, 1946 as a machine operator in the mill room and woodshop. After four years he was promoted to inspector in the mill room. Bob followed mill room inspection protocol which stipulated that the quality of a Gibson instrument started in the mill room. The mill room woodworkers knew Gibson quality started right there. They were proud of that. Each and every piece of wood needed to be selected, cut, matched, and machined to exact specifications. A variety of gauges, samples, templates, and other 'soft tools' were used. In the mill room each new setup was fully inspected and subsequent spot checks were performed during the run. Like so many higher seniority employees, Robert stayed in the same department for most of his career, which in his case was 30+ years.

History 34

Paul Vallier (1948–'66+)

Paul joined Gibson on January 9, 1948 around the time that Ted McCarty made his historic tour of Gibson. Paul's forte was in finishing where he was line leader by the late 1950s and later worked under Wilbur Fuller in the Gibson Customs Department. Paul was still in Department 2500B Custom Instrument Finishing when Ted left Gibson in 1966.

History 35

Rem Wall (1948–'73+)

Fender historian Richard Smith has pointed to Freddie Tavares and Bill Carson as Fender Electric Instruments Company employees who were good players. Their musical skills were valuable to Fender. Gibson's equivalent employee-musician would be Rembert "Rem" Wall. Working as a Gibson inspector Rem utilized his playing skills and knowledge of instruments in final cleaning, adjustment, and inspection. Before a guitar was approved for the finished goods stockroom, it was played and approved by Rem Wall. But Rem's larger reputation was really as a guitar player, entertainer, song writer, and Michigan celebrity.

Rem's son Rendal Wall, also a Gibson employee who joined Gibson on September 9, 1960, recalls, "Rem started his country music career in Southern Illinois, where he was affectionately known as the 'Yodeling Romeo.' Rem sang all over the south for a number of years, often doing radio shows with notables in the country music business. Rem moved to Kalamazoo in 1940 and formed his own band known as the 'Green Valley Boys.'

The Kalamazoo Gazette covered Rem's life as follows: *Local Country Music Legend Rem Wall Dies : "A man who came to Kalamazoo more that 50 years ago with a bag lunch, $10, and a gunnysack wrapped guitar and found local country music stardom died Sunday. Rembert 'Rem' Wall, 75, of Parchment, died at Borgess Medical Center ….*

"Wall and his band, the Green Valley Boys, brought country music into the home of several generations through radio and television with his popular show 'The Green Valley Jamboree. After a 30-year stint of WKZO-TV, the last show aired in 1980. The radio show ended after about 40 years. Wall was known for hit songs including 'Keep On Loving You" which topped the nation's country music charts for six weeks. He recorded more than 30 records with his band and other musicians, Rendal Wall said. Wall was inducted into the Michigan Country Music Hall of Fame in 1977."

" 'I know he's going to be missed by so many people in the entire industry,' Rendal Wall said. His father counted such famous performers as Gene Autry, Hank Williams and Roy Clark among his friends, he said. Everybody remembers him.' Rendal said, 'No matter where he'd go, they'd be asking for his autograph, even right up to the last.'"

Rem Wall was born in 1918 on a farm near West Frankfort, IL. Rem's dad was a coal miner in Franklin County, IL. Rem first heard of Kalamazoo when he realized his favorite guitar, a Gibson was made there. Rem moved to Kalamazoo in 1940, and before long went to work at Gibson. Rem's official seniority date is October 26, 1948, suggesting a few quits and rehires, as he pursued his music career.

In the late 1940s, the city of Kalamazoo was interested in jumping on the music business boom by starting a music program modeled after the weekly barn dance hosted by WLS in Chicago. In 1950 Rem formed the Green Valley Boys, named after Kalamazoo's nickname, the Green Valley. [Note: Most historians believe the Kalamazoo name is based on a local Native American language. Originally the city of Kalamazoo was named Bronson, named after a local pioneer.] In 1950 The Green Valley Jamboree show broadcast began on WKZO TV. It was a local broadcast that reached southwest Michigan and northern Indiana. The show lasted 30 years. Rem took advantage of country music legends passing through Kalamazoo, and most of them appeared on The Green Valley Jamboree. In the 1950s most of Michigan, including other cities like Flint, was populated by die-hard country music fans. Many of them had relocated from the south looking for work. Jobs were plentiful in the 1950s. In Flint, Michigan many came from Kentucky. In Kalamazoo, many came from Alabama and Kentucky.

In 1959, Rem accompanied Ted McCarty and Julius Bellson to Berlin, Germany and he represented American country music and the Gibson / City of Kalamazoo at the Berlin Industrial Fair. This was part of Kalamazoo being recognized as an All-American city, a city of prospering industry, which of course it was.

In the early 1960s, national powerhouse Columbia Records signed Rem Wall to record seven records over a seven year period - one record per year. In 1963, Rem released his most successful record, a gold record, 'Home Is Where the Hurt Is' and 'Keep On Loving You.' At the time, his wife, Roberta, became very ill and Rem's focus was on helping her, which meant nearly no travel time to support his record.

History 36
Ward Arbanas (1953–'69)

Historian Julius Bellson described Ward Arbanas. "Ward Arbanas joined the Gibson Staff in April 1953. During his 16 years of service Ward made a valuable contribution as Expediter, Supervisor of Displays, Production Manager of Epiphone Products, and Manager of the Custom Service Departments." He left Gibson in 1969 the same year that the Epiphone line was sourced to Japan.

The McCarty Legacy and Second Golden Era

1985 and the Second Golden Era

Gibson CEO Henry Juszkiewicz holding an Epiphone Juszkiewicz Signature Model displayed at Winter NAMM, January 2002. Many people give Juszkiewicz credit for presiding over Gibson's second golden era of electric guitars. Juszkiewicz played guitar in bands during college and post-graduate days.

Guitar historian Walter Carter at Winter NAMM '02. In his research, Carter discovered that Gibson was three months from liquidation when the Juszkiewicz team bought Gibson in the mid 1980s.

Larry Thomas, Chairman and co-C.E.O. of Guitar Center (left), and Paul Smith of PRS Guitars at Winter NAMM '02. In the '90s, Thomas and Smith joined Juszkiewicz and Schultz as key music industry leaders, and both are accomplished guitarists.

After 1966, Gibson and Fender began a decline in quality and popularity that lasted until 1985, when Henry Juszkiewicz, David Berryman, and Gary Zebrowski showed interest in saving Gibson.

"The consensus is that Gibson was about three months from being liquidated, its equipment sold off piecemeal, and its name given to the highest bidder," said guitar historian Walter Carter. "If Juszkiewicz, Berryman, and Zebrowski hadn't purchased Gibson in January, 1986, there would probably be no new Gibson guitars today."

In March, 1985, Fender Musical Instrument's future was also bleak as it was sold to a group of investors led by William Schultz. Fender's decline began in '65, when CBS management took control of the company. Workers did all they could, but even their best work could not offset the blunders made by management.

The Juszkiewicz and Schultz teams began lengthy journeys that ultimately reinstated Gibson and Fender as leaders in the industry. Both accomplished this by returning to their roots, building on what Ted McCarty did at Gibson and Leo Fender did at Fender, and crafting quality, hand-built guitars in the 1990s and 2000s. These are considered by many to be part of a second "Golden Era" of solidbody guitar making.

It's likely no accident that Paul Reed Smith was able to launch his company in 1985, within months of the start up of the new Gibson and new Fender. Smith skillfully combined what he considered the best of Fender and Gibson solidbody guitars into a new concept. His number one mentor and advisor was McCarty, who told Smith how to build a quality guitar and how to run a company that treated people like people, not just workers. Smith worked hard, and with the help of his team, he reintroduced the high-quality, well-built, easy-to-play electric solidbody guitar.

The McCarty Legacy – Introduction

Ted McCarty's legacy was built around the guitars made by Gibson between 1948 and 1965. That legacy came to a close in 1965, when specification changes dictated by CMI Chicago – *not* Kalamazoo – led to a change in direction for Gibson. The most important were a result of new neck-carving machines placed into service during the company's 1965 expansion. The new necks had a shallower neck angle, a smaller width at the nut, and a smaller neck profile. Other spec changes included the change from nickel-silver to chrome plating and the replacement of the bar bridge by the trapeze bridge on the ES-335 series. These occurred at the end of McCarty's watch, during what he called a "change in management" at CMI. Among other things, CMI's new managers thought kids liked to play guitars with thinner necks because they made it easier to learn. They didn't know that a thin neck was not an attribute of a quality guitar.

Other things happened, as well. The

The late Bill Schultz, Fender C.E.O., at Winter NAMM '02. Many people give Schultz credit for presiding over Fender's second golden era, when the company was larger than Gibson. Its success was bolstered by its dominance in the amplifier business.

pop-music "British invasion" of 1964 was based mostly on thinline hollowbody electric guitars like the Gretsch Country Gentleman used by George Harrison of the Beatles (as well as his Rickenbacker and Epiphone guitar). By '65, solidbody guitars such as the Fender Stratocaster were less favored in the market compared to thinline hollowbodies. Solidstate amplifiers also threatened to surpass vacuum-tube-based amplifier designs, especially at Fender. Leo Fender knew very little about the solidstate technology, and it troubled him to think about old-technology tubes competing with new technology resistors. Leo Fender, with the help of Don Randall, sold Fender Musical Instruments to CBS in January, 1965. While Mr. Fender cited health issues as the reason he sold, it's reasonable to assume the main reason FMIC was sold was because it had become too large for Leo Fender. More importantly, a shift in the market suggested the bolt-neck solidbody was becoming passé. Forecasters also suggested tube-based amplifiers were a thing of the past.

Leo Fender's sale of Fender Musical Instruments certainly put McCarty on notice. He had problems with Arnie Berlin at CMI. The year Fender sold FMIC, McCarty made plans to leave Gibson and ultimately bought Bigsby. But before Bigsby became available, he was looking at opportunities in Kalamazoo. His friend, John Huis, was of age to draw a pen-

The Gibson Les Paul, Electric Guitar
featured by Les Paul and Mary Ford on Recordings,
Radio, Television, and Personal Appearances.

The back cover of the 1953 Gibson Employee Manual

sion from Gibson while he continued to work with McCarty in a new venture.

The demise of Fender and Gibson began in 1965, but it took about 20 years for the companies to collapse. Perhaps the main reason for the downfall of the icons was their size. But there were other reasons, as well. By '65, corporate management began to change. In the 1940s, '50s, and into the early '60s, college graduates in management were rare. Michigan-based companies like Gibson and General Motors promoted from within, which often meant high school graduates who went straight to work for the company were promoted through the ranks. The advantage of this was that these people knew their jobs. When McCarty ran Gibson, the only college graduates at Kalamazoo were himself, George Comee from Kalamazoo College, perhaps Rollo Werner in purchasing, perhaps Bill Gaut, and Western Michigan University graduate Mac McConackie. Almost everyone else was promoted based on their desire to advance, and their natural talents. This made for a very effective organization with a high degree of skill and institutional knowledge. But by the mid '60s, Arnold Berlin and many like him thought all a person needed to manage a guitar company was a degree from an Ivy League school. But management by degree didn't work at the Gibson Guitar Company – history had proven that.

Demand for guitars also began to drop in the mid '60s, just as major corporations upgraded facilities to handle larger production quantities. This created a conundrum, and it was rumored that even CMI thought the electric-guitar business was dying. Also, there was the impact of imported guitars, as foreign companies stole market share from established domestics.

In the 1970s, Gibson and CMI were led by Arnold Berlin and Norton Stevens, the infamous "Norlin boys." It took about 20 years for Berlin and Norlin to ruin Gibson; it held on that long only because of the tradition of excellence established by the likes of Orville Gibson, Sylvo Reams, and Ted McCarty.

Regardless of what CMI management did, Gibson employees continued to do the best they could in the post-McCarty era, building guitars using as many time-tested procedures as possible. But, under a regime of reduced quality control and inferior designs it was only a matter of time before Gibson, the one-time industry giant, was on the verge of extinction.

It's human nature to think of the McCarty legacy only in terms of the great guitars his staff created – the '59 Gibson Les Paul Standard, the '58 Flying V, '58 Explorer, and '58 ES-335 to name a few. But McCarty's legacy is so much more. It's about his being a quality person, running a quality plant, respecting people, and asking how he could help them do better work. Former employees repeatedly say that working for McCarty was like working within a friendly family. They also say that when he left, things were different. McCarty's Gibson was a friendly place where people enjoyed going to work and helping co-workers. His legacy includes his products, the people who worked for him, the manufacturing plants he designed and oversaw, and a personal style that emphasized getting things done.

When discussing the McCarty legacy, it's difficult to separate the man from the guitars. As has been pointed out several times, instruments are the stars of the McCarty "Golden Era." But so much of McCarty is inside those guitars that it's entirely appropriate to revisit McCarty, the man.

The final section of this book has four interviews, the first with guitar historian Tom Wheeler, whose contribution summarizes some of the things said in the book. After Wheeler are interviews with three people who were there during the final segments of McCarty's career. The first is with Jerry Ash, who has one of the last remaining insider memories of the 1950s. Next is Gene Kornblum, who is known for his years at St. Louis Music. Music-industry people often refer to Kornblum, and his interview centers around McCarty's transition to Bigsby. Finally, Paul Smith, founder of PRS Guitars, is the last insider who got to know McCarty. These three interviews concern more than just Ted McCarty, there is also new interesting industry historical information. And again, these interviews provide a good summary of some of the things that appear in the book.

An Interview with Tom Wheeler

Tom Wheeler was the last interview taken for the book. By intention the interview was more of a fact check than an attempt to net new information.

In your book, *American Guitars*, you said, "Theodore McCarty is an unsung giant of modern guitar manufacturing, and his story is one of talent obscured by modesty." How many times did you talk with McCarty, and is that where you discovered just how modest he was? *Tom Wheeler: I spoke to him many times. There were probably two or three major interviews. One was for* Guitar Player *which, as far as I know, was the first time that Ted had been profiled outside of the local paper in Kalamazoo. I don't think the guitar public in general knew anything about him, and most guitar players had never heard his name. I went to Kalamazoo and interviewed him for my book, and I'm sure I've interviewed him once or twice after that for something in* Guitar Player. *And all of the rest of the times, we'd have dinner together, or I'd call him on his birthday, and I've done a couple of things with Paul Smith, of PRS, that involved Ted. So we would get a chance to visit, that sort of thing. (Pause) I think the conclusion about his modesty - we could tell that even without talking to Ted. It's not that he wasn't a proud person. I think he was proud of his accomplishments, but he was not one to toot his own horn at the same time. I think we can say his career was one of talent obscured by modesty simply because of the astonishing fact the person behind the Les Paul and the SG, and the Firebird to some extent, the 335 and its sister instruments, the humbucking pickup to some extent, and a long list of other things, (this person) was unknown to typical guitar players. (Pause) I think I remember writing somewhere that had he, like Leo Fender, put his own name on his products, had it been called the McCarty Model instead of the Les Paul, or the McCarty pickup, there are many possibilities, then all of us would have known his name for decades and decades prior to his name finally coming to light.*

In your book it was the Tune-O-Matic where you referenced that point. You said had it been called the McCarty Bridge instead of the Tune-O-Matic bridge his name would have been legendary like Seth Lover's. *Well, I think so. Had Gibson elected to call that the McCarty Bridge, or the McCarty Pickup, or the McCarty wiring harness, or the McCarty model of this or that guitar, I mean any of those things would have brought his name to the public mind. But that's just not the way he operated, and was not really the way Gibson operated.*

In *American Guitars*, you called the Ted McCarty Era, "The Golden Era, even in that company's long and proud history." Could you elaborate on that? *First I should say such an opinion is somewhat subjective because Gibson has a very long tradition and one can pick all sorts of criteria for a Golden Era. One can look at the popularity of mandolins and related instruments, the popularity of banjos, various flat top guitars from the '30s and '40s, and so on. But for me, and I think for a great many of the people who grew up with Rock and Roll, the guitars that we fell in love with, and the players whose music we fell in love with are very much a part of the Ted McCarty era. If you look at the Les Paul coming out in the spring of '52 and everything that happened for the next ten years, the Firebird, SG, 335s, and all the rest, those are the Gibsons that many rock and rollers long to have,*

Tom Wheeler was the first journalist outside of Kalamazoo to interview Ted McCarty in the 1970s. Wheeler is shown here at an April '04 book signing at the Dallas Guitar Show.

and they were products of the Ted McCarty era, as were of course some of the great jazz guitars. As some of us learned more and more about jazz and we found out about the L-5 and the Johnny Smith, I mean these were by far the best known of the elegant jazz guitars, as opposed to a Stromberg. You could be a working professional musician for many years and never come across a Stromberg. Whereas a L-5 was widely considered to be the standard from its inception in the 1920s. So there are many aspects to this.

In your book, *American Guitars*, right after Ted's quote concerning the greatness of Gibson, he said, "When you pick up, say, a 1958 ES-335, or an old Les Paul, one thing you can see right away, the people who built this guitar cared about it, they cared a lot." What are your thoughts about Ted's statement that people seemed to care about what they were building and the employees of Gibson? *Ted said that they had a lot of Hollanders. They had very deep roots in woodworking traditions of the old country. Some of them were just a generation or two removed from their immigrant forbearers. They carried with them a very European sense of quality and tradition. It was very clear from talking with Ted, that he valued the traditions, and the skills, and the commitment to quality of the people who reported to him. He had an engineering background himself, as I'm sure you know. And he appreciated that level of commitment.*

That's something that has been written about, the Hollanders, and actually western Michigan is full of them, and they have a place called Holland, Michigan, which is known for its tulip festivals. For Gibson, there were several people at Gibson with Holland/Dutch names. I think the Dutchman were some of the higher-seniority people; I traced as many as I could.

What type of guitar did you learn to play on? *My first good guitar was a McCarty-era SG Special (made in) 1960 or 1961 with two P-90s. I used to leave it on the arms of a chair in its case with the case open so I could see it first thing in the morning and last thing at night when I fell asleep (laughing). I loved that guitar. I had a 335 that I played all through college. I still have it. Absolutely, and I've played that guitar on many a gig. And I have that same kind of relationship that I think a lot of players have with their guitars. It's your best friend, it's a tool of expression, it's a beautiful thing to look at, it's a work of art, its all those things and I had this relationship with various Gibson guitars for years before I ever heard the words "Ted McCarty." That's why it was such a great thrill to meet him. Like, holy cow, you're the person behind all this history that has meant so much to me throughout my life.*

The 1959 Gibson Les Paul Standard and other vintage Gibsons have really been accepted in the guitar market. What are your thoughts on that? *Simply that I don't think that it has much to do with Ted McCarty. In other words, none of these guys, I mean I spoke to the Gretsch family, Semie Moseley, Ted McCarty, Leo Fender, I mean none of them were thinking about making future classics. And all of them, to a person, without exception, were astonished that the guitars that they built in the '50s and '60s were worth $20,000, let alone $200,000. So (the relative value of a vintage instrument) has a lot to do with rarity, snob appeal, market perception, and so on, but not that much to do with what John D'Angelico, or Ted McCarty, or any of these other great folks were trying to do.*

Speaking of Leo Fender, based upon your interviews with Leo Fender and Ted McCarty, do you have any thoughts concerning a comparison of Leo Fender with Ted McCarty? Any thoughts about the two men? *Well, I think they were pretty different. I wrote somewhere that Ted McCarty really had two careers. One was being in touch with players and dealers through his marketing people and dreaming up these great ideas, and seeing them to fruition. Like the 335 for example. But the other was, he knew how to run a company. When he took over in 1948 Gibson was not in great shape, but they'd been around for a while. Whereas in Fender's case, by the time the Stratocaster was introduced in early 1954, (Fender) was really kind of a glorified shop. And Leo Fender was not going to be the person to turn that glorified shop into a modern high production manufacturing facility. Leo Fender was happiest in his lab at the workbench, working on pickups, designing a new guitar, a new bass; constantly, relentlessly experimenting with amplifiers, changing components, talking to musicians. Leo Fender was more of a hands on kind of person. And he really was perfectly content to let someone like Forrest White build that factory and run it, and a genius like Don Randall to conceive of these brilliant marketing ideas, do the ads, do the catalogs, supervise this growing network of salesmen and so on. Leo was perfectly content to have other people do that. Ted was more of hands on in the business – running the company side. Leo was more of a hands on in the tinkering with new products on the drawing board.*

Did you interview Leo Fender often? *Many times. I had major interviews on several occasions.*

The quality of the replies that you got from Ted McCarty versus the quality of replies that you got from Leo Fender, how would you compare the two? *I think in that respect (they were) similar. I was fairly early in talking with these guys. I was interviewing them in the '70s, and the whole vintage guitar business was just getting going. So early on, both of them were kind of a little surprised and a little amused and maybe even a little bit baffled to why someone would be asking them about the details of screws, or wires, or pickups, of things that they had done 10 or 20 years before. It was their first experience with that kind of thing.*

(Pausing – returning to a comparison of Leo and Ted) They were both gentlemen. They were both quiet. Leo was shy to the point of almost being, not quite a recluse, but he had few friends, and he was something of a workaholic. Ted, I think, had a more balanced life. But they were both very generous with me, they were both very forthcoming, they both gave me all the time I asked for. Neither of them ever cut me off. It was a great thrill for me to spend time in their company.

I want to ask about Maurice Berlin, I'll be happy if you talked with him. *Sorry, I didn't know him.*

In your book, *The Stratocaster Chronicles*, you indicated that Don Randall gave some credit to Gibson and indirectly to Ted because the Les Paul Model was such a nice guitar. *That's right.* You indicated that Don Randall needed something better than the plain-Jane Tele. *Well, it went back and forth. Let's start with the plain-Jane Tele in 1950. Ted told me – and Ted was very forthcoming about this – "Look, these guys out there in California, these upstarts, we could see that they were getting a part of the business with the solidbody guitar idea." Ted was aware of Fender. Now it has often been said that the folks at Gibson looked down their noses at Fender. And I think that's a fair statement, I think that's true. Don Randall and Leo, they all talked about people from the other companies referring to the Telecaster as a boat paddle, or a canoe paddle, you know, all these sorts of derogatory terms, because it was not a product of the old school Gepetto-like workmen at the bench producing these elegant things. Leo wasn't interested in that stuff. He was a manufacturing guy. These were factory products. That was the whole idea. Leo thought it was crazy to glue in the necks, for example. He thought it was impractical. He thought those Gibson guitars, and everybody's guitars, had way too many parts. He thought the processes were too complicated. He said I can do this much simpler. It will be stronger. It will be more durable. All of these sorts of things had everything to do with that Fender Telecaster. It was definitely in response to the Telecaster that*

Gibson committed to the whole solidbody project. Ted told me that Fred Gretsch called him and said please don't do this, because Gibson had such stature, and if Gibson commits to the solidbody project, it's kind of legitimizing this whole concept. But Ted, being a visionary guy could see that this was going to be part of the future. And Ted said we're going to do it and we're going to do it in a way Fender can't do it. We're going to carve the top, it's going to look like a Gibson, it's going to be very high caliber… it's going to look like a Gibson. And it did. Then, we go back to California and we have Don Randall out there telling Leo Fender, first of all, we need more than one guitar. Don Randall had to kind of grab Leo by the shoulders and say, look, we need a line of guitars. It is not enough to have one guitar that is continuously evolving. We need a bunch of guitars for beginners, for professionals to choose between, and we need a top of the line. That was very much in response to Gibson. And one of the things that Don wanted to do was to have the new top of the line Fender to have a sunburst finish. Even though the Les Pauls still had goldtops, there were many prestigious Gibsons with sunburst finishes.

The Stratocaster Chronicles pointed that out, and in my book I'm trying to give Gibson and Ted McCarty a little bit of credit for having a little something to do with what the Stratocaster ended up looking like. It was sunburst, not plain-Jane. *I think that's a fair way to say it. But there were many factors that were going into the Stratocaster. The Les Paul was one. There were a lot of things going on. But Gibson was one of the influences.*

What is the Ted McCarty legacy? Is it more than just great 1959 Gibson Les Paul Standards and 1958 Explorers? *I think the Ted McCarty legacy depends upon who you talk to. To the average guitar player walking down the street the legacy is one of great instruments that raised the bar for the entire industry. So it isn't simply a matter of Gibson. Ted had a profound influence on the entire music industry. I think if you asked somebody like Paul Reed Smith, I think the influence of Ted McCarty in some of Paul's designs is evident. I think for the people that knew him personally, such as myself, and again sighting Paul Smith, Ted was a lesson in how to be a man, and how to grow old with dignity and humor and grace.*

One of the reasons Ted McCarty was a ground breaker was that there was ground to be broken when he arrived at Gibson. He was a man of great vision and there were things to be done in the guitar industry that Ted McCarty was perfectly able to do. He had (experience) in marketing, he had an engineering background, he was a leader. He could marshal marketers, designers, engineers, and sales people, in a way that benefits Gibson to this day, and will continue to benefit Gibson as long as there is a Gibson Company.

An Interview with Jerry Ash

Jerry Ash, first son of Rose and Sam Ash, played a key role in advancing the Sam Ash Music Company, the company founded by his parents. Jerry started at Sam Ash Music in 1946, about the time Ted McCarty returned to Chicago with Wurlitzer. Jerry was working for Sam Ash Music two years before McCarty went to Gibson. The Ash store was located in Brooklyn, and Jerry was the only salesman.

"I've been active in Sam Ash Music since 1946," Ash said. "In those days, guitar was not the dominant instrument it is today. In the low price ranges – 25 percent to 75 percent of the people were buying Har-

mony and Kay guitars made in the U.S. – there were virtually no imports. Better players were buying Gibson, Gretsch, and Epiphone archtops. Cutaway-guitars were pretty much unknown. They caught on quickly, but initially there was resistance to the double-cutaway. (Pause) The real revolution came with the Fender Telecaster. I was skeptical at first, and so was the public. But when they caught on, there was no turning back. I kept bugging Gibson to get in the act, but they were so traditionally-minded."

You told me that landing the Gibson account was a big deal for Sam Ash Music. *Oh yeah, we were a very, very small company. You see we only had one store at the time. And Gibson had only one dealer in all of New York. That was somebody called Eddie Bell. Eddie Bell's main business was selling to the professional guitarist, hollowbody guitars, which were used at the time in all the big bands. So we took the Gibson line on. They gave us the line.*

About what year was that? *It must have been somewhere before the Fender Telecaster came out (in 1950). When I got to speaking with Gibson, they started respecting my opinion because we were in business together. I was urging them to come out with a solidbody. And they were hemming and hawing.*

Were you talking with your Gibson sales rep, or were you talking with Ted McCarty, or were you talking with Maurice Berlin? *Marc Carlucci (of CMI headquarters) and I spoke on a regular basis.*

Jerry Ash in a composite from 1962 at the Sam Ash Hempstead, NY location

So he would have been your main person to give ideas to? *Yes, and there was one guy above him. He died kind of young and he was the heir apparent to Mr. Berlin. Anyway, I told Marc that this solidbody instrument is starting to make waves, and you better get in with it. [Note: There are two different versions of how the Les Paul Model was created. One is that Maurice Berlin, after being told about the new Fender solidbody, issued an immediate search order for 'the guy with a broomstick with pickups.' That guy was Les Paul. That version suggests that Berlin, Carlucci, and Les Paul met in Chicago and discussed the Gibson solidbody guitar design. Jerry Ash's statement seems to indicate that CMI Chicago was certainly very active in creating the Gibson solidbody. Ted McCarty suggests that he told Maurice Berlin that Gibson needed to produce a solidbody to avoid Leo Fender from 'stealing the take.' In reality, it seems that both versions are correct and that both activities did occur simultaneously, starting at opposite poles, but meeting in the middle. In my opinion, there is no controversy about who developed the Les Paul. Everyone did, working on it at about the same time. But there is one thing that's undeniable – it's Ted McCarty's name on the Gibson solidbody guitar patent. There is also no controversy about where the first prototype was built. It was at 225 Parsons Street, Kalamazoo, Michigan, under the direction of Ted McCarty and Larry Allers.]*

At the time, in the early 1950s, what were you doing? Were you running the store? *I was in the store full time. I was the only sales person on the floor at the time.*

And you were selling all instruments? *Yeah!*

In other words, you had more than just guitars? *Oh yeah. It was a tiny business, you can't imagine how small it was.*

When you landed the Gibson account, it was probably good for Gibson because that was a laboratory for them to see how well they'd do against Epiphone and Gretsch (in the New York City market)? *Yes, that was one thing. The other thing was that we had a more diverse clientele than Eddie Bell who was in a loft in Manhattan. It wasn't a regular store. The people that went there, went there on purpose. The people in our store, sometimes they'd come in just to browse.*

You were in Brooklyn at that time. *Yes, only in Brooklyn.*

You had Fender and Gibson? *Yes. The thing was that in Manhattan where there were 15 or so stores on the block, maybe more, one guy might have Fender, somebody else might have something else, but in Brooklyn we were alone. So Gibson and Fender and the others had no qualms about giving us the stuff.*

How would you compare those early days, Fender versus Gibson sales? *Well Gibson was the prestige brand at the time. Fender started to make major inroads, which astonished me. I never thought that solidbody would come to anything. It was so radical at the time.*

Did you know Maurice Berlin very well? *I knew him. I met him several times. He was out in Chicago, I was in Brooklyn. I was out in Chicago on a number of occasions. I was invited out there, to give them feedback on things. I met him maybe four times.*

Did you meet him enough to give an opinion about the man? *We'd always meet on formal terms. I can only say that the people that worked for him really looked up to him. They really revered the guy. It was his visions that took just another jobber up to the point where he became 'the real stuff.' To a point where CMI was owning factories. Everything he did was class. He was really something.*

When you went to Chicago, what were they asking you? *They'd ask what we were selling, and what should they do (to offer new products). I remember one thing. They had the Les Paul Custom out and they were using these heavy flatwound strings. And at that time the thin strings started to become the vogue. People would buy the guitar, take it home, put on the thin strings, and the neck would bow backwards. And the strings were sitting on the neck. So I had to explain to them, 'You're doing it wrong.' I told them, 'Don't come out with these heavy strings, or at least make the neck so that when you put the thin strings on it would be okay.' They didn't even notice. They had no idea what was going on in the field. (Pause) Gibson came out once with a line of amplifiers and they brought them to our store to compare them against others. And model to model, they were demolished by the other brand.*

So the Fenders were much better amplifiers? *Gibson did a really stupid thing. Fender had what you call a "quick pot," when you get up to 4 or 5 it was very loud. So Gibson was going to do them one better. They were very loud at about 1. So you couldn't control the amp. This was inferior. This was because (the Gibson amp) people didn't know what they were doing.*

The Gibson amplifier people really didn't know what they were doing? Is that what you are saying? *Yep. That was the late 1950s. The Fender amps took over. I know that almost every studio musician was buying the little Fender amp with a 10" speaker because it recorded so well. They were taking it down to the recording sessions.*

When did you start going to the NAMM Shows, and what do you recall about the Gibson room? *In the early 1950s. NAMM was all in rooms, but Gibson was part of CMI, which was the giant of the industry. CMI and Gibson were in a different hotel in the basement. They had a huge exhibit. By those day's standards it was a huge exhibit.*

They were a much bigger exhibit than Fender, for example? *Oh, Fender was a small company at the time.*

Would you talk with Ted McCarty at these NAMM shows? *I met Ted once when I went out to the factory, and the other time was at one of the shows.*

Did you tour the Gibson Kalamazoo factory? *Yes, Gibson took us out there (assume for the 1950 plant tour covered previously in the book).*

What was your reaction to the factory? *It was the first factory I had ever seen. I had nothing to compare it with. The factory had a very industrious bunch of people. We saw people putting in frets, we saw people putting the binding on the hollowbody guitar. Everything was hand done, pretty much. But I was so impressed, never having been to any factory before.*

Do you remember when the Flying V came out in 1958? Do you remember that NAMM, when Ted was trying to shake up the industry? *At the time, it was not a big thing. I mean, every dealer felt they had to have it, but it is not the most comfortable guitar to hold. I don't know what the dealers had in mind. All I can tell you is that we bought them, but they were slow movers.*

How about the ES-335? *That took off. Finally they had a guitar that looked like a hollow guitar that didn't have the feedback. But it really wasn't a hollow guitar. That guitar took off.*

Toward the end of the '50s, Gibson had the single cutaway Les Paul Standard solidbody. And then in '61 they introduced the SG Series, which was the very thin solid guitar with a double cutaway. *Originally they called that a Les Paul (Les Paul SG Standard).*

Did you think the SG was a good idea? Were sales beginning to get slow for the single cutaway? *The SG was a nice guitar, but I don't think they should have used it as a replacement for the Les Paul. We found that for a certain number of SGs the neck would break. That was the problem with it.*

Do you remember that sideways pull vibrola that pulled sideways? *It was terrible. It was really bad.*

Were you giving your sales rep a lot of feedback at that time about Gibson? *Our sales rep was in very often.*

Did you give your feedback more to him or when you went to the NAMM shows? *I was in contact maybe once a month or so with Marc Carlucci , the Gibson sales manager. Our Gibson sales rep was Oren Sepp. Oren was a really classy guy, he had been with them almost from day one. I remember Oren had a certain amount of stock in the company. When Gibson went public, he was an automatic millionaire.*

Why do you think Ted McCarty left Gibson? *I don't know. Was he pushed out, did he leave on his own accord? I have no way of knowing.*

It seems for the 1950s era, you put Gibson at the top? *Yes. Quite honestly, we pushed Gibson above everything else.*

What do you think Ted McCarty's legacy will be? What will people remember him for? *I feel one thing. The quality of the instruments in those days was so much better than what you see around now. That may be the reason for all the (valuable) vintage Gibsons from Kalamazoo. It was the hand work that went into the guitar.*

You saw the hand work! *Yes, I did.*

So you think that Ted's legacy is the quality that his factory was putting out at the time? *I think so. When Ted was there, he got good instruments. That's what he did.*

An Interview with Gene Kornblum

Gene Kornblum met Ted McCarty after McCarty left Gibson, during the Bigsby period, and used Chicago Musical Instruments as a business model for St. Louis Music.

I started with the company in 1957. I graduated from the University of Pennsylvania, the Wharton School, and then came to work at St. Louis Music. St. Louis Music was a regional wholesaler at that point. Since then the company has been radically transformed. At the time that I came in, St. Louis Music looked at Gibson as the symbol of people that had arrived. Berlin had done great things in terms of buying Gibson (during the war), and Ted McCarty was running Gibson.

Did you know Ted McCarty? *I knew Ted, but I knew him from afar. First of all he was considerably older than I was. St. Louis Music was a fly on the wall compared to what he was. I mean, he had arrived and we were a regional wholesaler.*

When do you first recall meeting him? *I met him after he had left Gibson when Gibson became Norlin, and Ted left at that point. I think he had had enough of the new management. I met him when he was involved with Bigsby. He was selling Bigsby vibrato tailpieces through wholesalers. That's how I met him at that point. I found him to be a very, very down to earth person. He was easy to talk with. There was no pretense about him in terms of where he came from and the experience that he had. I found him to be a very approachable, knowledgeable guy. I was quite young at that time, and my perspective was more of being in awe of the guy that had done so well with Maurie Berlin's financial assistance. It was my impression that Berlin ran his company as a bunch of individual companies, and he gave the people, of which Ted McCarty was one of them, a good deal of autonomy. In effect that was really the basis of the model that I tried to do with St. Louis Music, in terms of having a bunch of separate entities that were all under the umbrella of St. Louis Music. And I also knew Ted when he was doing consulting work for Paul Reed Smith.*

Your dad, Bernard Kornblum, started the business in 1922. That was a long time ago. He must have known Ted and Leo Fender? *No, I don't think he knew Leo Fender. It was my impression that Leo Fender really stuck to himself. He was a very capable guy, but I think that he did not really go out. He was not really a highly visible corporate citizen. I think that Ted was more outgoing, but I think that Ted was not a politician type. He was clearly not a politician type from what I gathered.*

Did you know Leo Fender? *No, I never met Leo, but I knew Don Randall.*

He was the hub of the wheel I understand? *I think Randall was a good guy. He really, really was. He was an outspoken guy, I think he was very bright. He was the kind of guy that was open to talk to anybody, particularly in view of the kind of success that they (Fender) had. In the mid 1950s, Fender really got going, and in the 1960s Fender was gold. I mean they really left Gibson in the dust, latching onto the solidbody electric guitar.*

An Interview with Paul Reed Smith

Paul Smith built his first guitar at St. Mary's College (Maryland), in the spring of 1975. By mid 1977 Smith had built 17 guitars. Smith launched PRS guitars in 1985. (For in-depth information about PRS Guitars, see *The PRS Guitars Book*, by Dave Burrluck, written in 1999.)

Your first face-to-face meeting with Ted McCarty was in Kalamazoo in 1986. What can you tell me about it? *I enjoyed it. He was very honest. I don't really think of it as our first meeting because I had talked with him on the phone several times before. But he got very angry at the end of the conversation. He was kind of quietly seething. I said, "What's wrong?" He said, "No one's asked me these questions in 20 years." I said, "What do you mean?" He said, "Nobody asked me how I glued my frets, and nobody asked me how I glued the fretboards on, nobody asked me any of this stuff." He said, "This* *is what I did. This is how I made my living. Nobody is asking me that. They were asking me if I had a Moderne in my basement."*

(Smith reflecting) That's not entirely true, because there was a very large article written by Tom Wheeler, where he was talking to him about his history. But basically nobody had asked him how-to (questions) or what kind of glue to glue frets, which, by the way, was something called "fish glue." Many in our industry don't even glue frets. It was like asking Eric Clapton, "How did you do your old records?" and the only thing people wanted to know was, "Do you have a guitar in your basement?"

I would say (the first meeting) went very, very well. I found it fascinating. I had assumptions and ideas of what all the answers were before I went, but I didn't know. It verified probably two-thirds of what I already thought. A third of it I just didn't know.

At the first meeting, Ted said that he felt you had a very good understanding of guitar building. I got the impression that your first meeting concerned questions about how to best run a guitar -manufacturing business. And then, of course you had some specific questions on guitar-building minutia? *We got into everything. I said, "How did you do it?" He said, "I had 50 years of experience when I walked in." For PRS, we had no years of experience; they just had me as a teacher. So I had a lot more learning to do than Ted did. Ted took off when he walked in and made (Gibson woodworkers) the teachers.*

(Pause) Yeah, I asked him millions of questions. One time, just not too far from when he died, PRS was moving. So I called him and said, "What should I do?" He said, "You are going to get really angry... keep your cool." That was his advice. He was right – I got very (angry) because something hadn't been done right, and I kept my cool. But I thought his advice was going to be how to do the trucks, you know?

I always thought Ted was about evolution, and not revolution. His motto seemed to be "Do 1,000 different things 1% better." Do you agree? *His motto was "Improve one thing every day" when he walked around the shop. Ted and John Huis walked around that factory every morning. The idea was that they would improve something everyday. He thought his best work was the Electric Spanish stuff (ES-335, ES-345, etc.). I don't think he thought in terms of evolution or revolution. I don't think he thought in those terms at all. I think he thought in terms of... he'd seen it done wrong a whole bunch and he wanted to do it right. He wanted to improve something everyday. That was part of his goal.*

Your introduction to Ted was really through the instruments he built. When you were learning to play, did you learn on a Gibson? *Yes and no. My introduction to Ted was not through the instruments he built, but rather by seeing his name in the patent office*

Right, but subliminally? *In terms of the guitars I leaned to play on, they were a nylon-string and a solidbody Rickenbacker. I had a Gibson Les Paul Deluxe. I had a Melody Maker. I got a '53 Les Paul.*

When did you start playing? When did you play your first note? *I would say junior high, on my mother's nylon-string. I learned Beatles' tunes. So the question is, "When you were learning to play guitar, were you learning to play on Gibson instruments?" So yes, that was more of my benchmark than Fender instruments, but I've come to love both of them. (Pause) They asked me at the clinic yesterday (the April 2006 Dallas Guitar Show), "Why do I build guitars?" I said, "I love all the same stuff that you guys do." The whole room (at the Dallas Guitar Show) loved the same stuff. I would say that Gibsons were more of a benchmark in a way.*

The *PRS Guitars* book mentions that a lot of D.C. musicians, back in the day, were using Gibson Les Paul Juniors. Did you see those Les Paul Juniors at the Bayou, down in Georgetown? And what type of guitars did you use when you sat in with the bands playing at the Bayou? *There were only two guys using Les Paul Juniors — Rick Benick, who was in a band called the Cherry People and now is in a band called Roadmaster — and a guy named Russell Stone, who lived in Annapolis. Rick played a double-cutaway Junior and Russel played a single-cutaway Junior. Both were extraordinary players. When I sat in at the Bayou, I was always playing a guitar that I made. I was well into that. I remember I was playing in the band and one guy came up to me and started pointing his finger saying, "Where did you get the money for that guitar, that was made by some guy in Annapolis, you don't look like you make the money for that!" The band cracked up.*

Did you play at the Rabbits Foot or anywhere else? *Rick used to play at The Keg. I used to play at the Bayou. Mostly I was playing in Baltimore, but I learned to play in D.C. driving down to K (and M) Street. It's nice that you know all about that. I never saw the Rabbits Foot. My brother actually played in the Rocket Room (Note: Well known Washington D.C. guitar headquarters for Roy Buchanan in 1965 and 1966).*

Some people believe that the original PRS guitar was a great blend of Fender and Gibson. The PRS had a Fender style body but otherwise it was more of a nod to Gibson. Beyond that the major contribution of PRS to the guitar market was the establishment of the $2,000 guitar. That is, a guitar that is of very high quality and beauty, which costs about $2,000. There really wasn't anything on the market like that in the mid 1980s. Do you generally agree with that? *Yes. I think crossing the point where a customer would pay over $1,000 for a guitar was a huge deal. We were selling the guitars for around $1,000 when we started. $2,000 was the second milestone. The first one was $1,000. People would pay $2,000 for a drum set. They'd pay $4,000 for a P.A. They'd pay $2,000 for a bass, but don't dare ask me to pay over $950 for a guitar. I thought that was wrong. Drummers paid more than that. And it wasn't just about the money. It cost more money than that for me to make.*

Did Ted influence you when it came to producing a high-quality product? Or was that already your goal? Perhaps we've already talked about this with the $2,000 guitar. *No, this is a little bit different question. I made my living studying the old masters, and figured out what they were thinking, before I met them. If they were alive, I'd go find them. If they weren't alive, I'd figure out, what were they thinking. Not what did they do. Don't copy what they do. Understand and go back even farther. Ask, "What were they thinking?" So in my mind when I picked up an old Strat or an old Tele, long before I ever met Leo Fender, and long before I met Ted, they were benchmarks. They were real benchmarks. I was trying to not just figure out what they did or how they did it, but what were they thinking about. And then to be able to go from that point forward. I had in my mind the vintage guitars and what they were about as a benchmark a long, long, long time ago. So look, PRS guitars are in competition with a million vintage guitars. (Pausing) Let me give you an example, if Brent Rowan from Nashville, who has probably played on more hit records than anybody in the history of the world, has an old '55 Strat and a '53 Tele. And he's got this and he's got that, and they're magic instruments. And he's searched the world for them. If I send him a guitar, I've got to beat that. So I'm in competition with millions of cherry picking. So high quality, it's almost not even a term we use. People take their information 80% with their eyes, and the rest of it with their feelings, ears, smells, and all that stuff. So high quality — these people are spending their money on these guitars at the expense of their kids' college accounts. So they're not going to give you the money easily. So I don't think in terms of high quality, I think in terms of artistic lust. If a guitar takes somebody's breath away with the way it sounds and plays you might have a chance of selling it. I had already gone down that road. We were already in business before I met Ted McCarty.*

You talked about Leo Fender briefly; did you have much time to spend with Leo? *No. He used to come by and pay his respects at NAMM. So did Les Paul, Les Paul always used to come by and pay his respects at NAMM. (Pause) Nobody wants to die and not have their baton handed to somebody. So Leo would come by and tell me what a good job he thought I was doing.*

Ted and his cross-country rival, Fender, survived the late 1960s import crisis because, according to Ted, "Gibson meant quality" and the Japanese imports could not defeat Gibson's quality. Since then and continuing to this day, import guitars have not been able to defeat the great American companies because PRS, Gibson, and Fender stand for American-made quality. Is that part of the Ted McCarty legacy? Is his legacy more than just the great guitars that he built in the 1950s and early 1960s? *Yes, I would say it is part of his legacy. That room (pointing to Market Hall at the Dallas Guitar Show) is full of Leo Fender and Ted McCarty guitars. And Martin – I would say Martin, Leo Fender, and Ted McCarty guitars – yes of course – it is a part of all three of their legacies that they established the benchmark for American quality. Not just in the way they looked and they played, but how they sounded. So yeah, of course, the way you are looking at this is right on the money. If that hadn't of happened it would be completely different. The import guitars wouldn't have had anything to copy. I don't even know where it would have been. One of the nice things in this industry, if you take a Mercedes Benz and a Corvette and you cross them you get a pretty good looking car. If you cross a Fender and a Gibson and you just cross them, meld them, it doesn't look good. So there are a lot of instruments that have hit the market that were just crosses. At one point there was a guitar that was a cross between an SG and a Les Paul and Yamaha made it. You don't see them drawing high money on the floor (of the Dallas Guitar Show). It just didn't have the grace.*

There is only going to be in history one time when the solidbody electric guitar becomes commercially successful. That's only going to happen once. That was 1950 to 1952. *I wouldn't say it became commercially acceptable until around 1955. I think when the P-Bass became completely accepted the whole world had accepted electric guitars because then a musician didn't have to put his upright bass in the cab. That was a big deal. The P-Bass was a big deal. I would give it a little bit later year than that because the 1952 and 1953 bridges were moving and they wouldn't stay in tune. 1954 and 1955 I would say, is where you had a real acceptance that this was going to go on.*

"Success" has been defined as timing and talent. For Leo Fender and Ted McCarty they were successful because they had talent but their timing was just right too. For Paul Reed Smith, 30 years later, timing and talent came together again, because 1985 was probably the second most important year in the guitar industry in modern history, behind 1955, like we just mentioned, because in 1985 Fender was getting ready to become non-existent, Gibson was getting ready to become non-existent, and Paul Reed Smith was starting. What is the reaction to 'timing and talent' to the start of your company? *Well I think if Leo Fender or Ted McCarty were alive now they could have created the same thing now as then. I am not sure "timing" was so important. But it was, I mean you're right. 1985 was an important year because as Walter Cronkite said to me, "Why do I need another guitar company, I just sold one?" Fender was basically out of business,*

Kramer had filled the void, Ned Steinberger had just shown up and was going great guns, Jackson was doing really well, you couldn't give a Les Paul away, you couldn't give one away, they (Gibson) were basically out of production, again. Then Slash picked one up and that was history, and Bill Schultz bought Fender and that made that history, and things at Kramer became untenable and that made that history, Steinberger got sold to Gibson, that made that history, Grover and Joann sold to IMC and that changed that whole thing, and we (PRS) showed up. So I would say yes that was a very important year. The windows of opportunity were open, and things were living and dying left and right. And it was unnoticed as an issue because people would walk into my (NAMM) booth in 1985 and say, "What do I need with another guitar line? I don't need another guitar, go away." But I said, "Wait a minute! You need to play this before you say that." (Pause) I would say you're right about 1985. You're right on the money. 1985 was a very important year. A lot of people have been naming the last four or five years as the resurgence of the electric guitar business. The New Golden Age.

Yes, that's going to be in the book, the second golden era of electric guitars. *I didn't define that. I think we (PRS) had some impact on it.*

Every interviewee for this book expressed great loyalty toward Ted, and all recognized that by 1965, the Gibson factory was very large. Ted left in 1966. There were about 1,000 people, so most would consider it a large company. There were about 850 hourly workers according to the seniority list, and there were probably 10% more that were salary. Here's my question, in terms of size, how big are you now in terms of employees? *192 people. We have 25,000 square feet and we're putting up an additional 92,000 square feet.*

(Pause) By the way, did Ted tell you why he quit? Yes, but I'll take it from you too. *Ted found out that the son of the guy who runs Chicago Music had made a deal with his roommate to buy Gibson. And (the corporate raider) was the roommate's father's flower company. And Ted found out about this and went to Maurice Berlin and said "Your son is doing this." But he didn't believe him. Also, they had a rule that you had to retire by a certain age, which he never believed in. And basically it was a real problem. So Ted and John (Huis) quit and bought Bigsby. [Note: Part of CMI history is clouded in mystery and there is not a lot of information about M.H. Berlin, but Jerry Ash disclosed an important fact when Jerry indicated that M.H. Berlin had a successor in mind for CMI, but the man died prematurely. Perhaps that loss left M. H. Berlin with little choice but to remain the CEO past age 65.]*

Did Ted ever talk to you about Larry Allers? Larry Allers was his main engineer. *He talked about John Huis. (Pause) Did you know that they used to glue the tops on Les Pauls and the fretboards with radio glue. If you held a light bulb in your hand, not plugged in, anywhere near it, it would light up in your hand. Ted said, "I don't think OSHA would let you do that anymore."*

(Pause) Do you know how they used to spray the lacquer on? Did he ever tell you that? They had this stuff in the consistency of thick honey in a 55-gallon drum, and they put a heater coil in a drum of lacquer. Now that's a bomb. And they would heat it up really hot, so when they sprayed it on the guitar, like when you heat honey up in the micro-wave, and it would go on really easily, and when it cooled off it would get really thick. That's how they got so much lacquer on those guitars. It was actually brilliant. Hot lacquer was a common thing of the day.

Did Ted ever tell you about 'the seconds'? There was a '2' below the serial number. Did he ever talk to you about that? *No, he had very few 'seconds.' He did have an expert repairman finish them that could fix anything.*

(Smith reflecting) I spent a tremendous amount of time with Ted. He ended up being the grandfather I never had. When he started repeating stories, I knew I had them all. I spent about a week interviewing Ted in Maui. Ted sent me a thing called a Material Handbook. In his office he had accounting books, physics, and engineering books. He was raised by his uncle. His uncle built every single train trestle and tunnel up through the Appalachian Mountains from Georgia to Virginia. So engineering ran in his blood.

Ted had a library of books on wood... *Yeah. He never called korina by korina. It was limba. You can still buy it.*

Getting back to the size of a company. You said your company is about 192 people?

That, to me, having talked with Ted's employees, sounds like a very good size to be able to manage quality. The Gibson people said when it got up to be 900 people it was more difficult. Do you see that as part of your business strategy? *No. I just had a meeting with my managers and we were talking about a quality problem. That could happen with 900 people or 200 people. I do agree that Gibson had a problem at about 900 people. I think it's very difficult to keep quality up at any point. Ted's people are telling you about an experience that they had and they are kind of warning other people that at that size, it creates a problem. That I agree with.*

Do you have mostly males or females? *It used to be all male but now we have a much higher percentage of females. Ted was very clear about what it was he wanted the women doing different than the men doing. The women were very good at ironing, so he had them sanding on the stroke sanders. They were very good at needle work so he had those making pickups. He would take the natural talents that they had and he would have them doing those same movements. We don't do that. You'd get shot for that today.*

Sue (Ted's daughter) told me that you went to visit Ted in his last days. She told me you took your guitar over there and played for him. What songs did you play? *I don't remember. I remember what was said. Songs... it was either a Beatles song or "Sitting On The Dock Of The Bay." Something everybody in the room knew.*

He liked the mellow sound, didn't he? *Yeah. He used to gather all the best guitar players in the world, once a year, in New York. I'll give you an example. All the guitar players said, "When you make a vibrato, make its arm go in the same movement as the pick movement." That's where the SG sideways vibrola came from. Ted said, "Ah, that was a mistake." (Pause) Ted had no illusions about good or bad. He just called it the way he saw it.*

What else? What haven't I covered? What kind of questions? *Ted was a champion. What I mean by that – he used to bring himself to the moment, and make it happen every single time. I've seen him be asleep, wake up, do the photo shoot, do perfectly, and go back to sleep. I've seen him be exhausted, then someone sits down to do an interview, and he comes to life and he nails it and he goes back to sleep. I never saw him bring himself to a moment that he did not win. That's Ted. He's a champion. He was not a second-place guy.*

Did he ever talk to you about his feelings about Leo Fender? Did he ever talk to you about that? *Yes.*

What did he tell you? *He said that he admired Leo Fender for two reasons. First of all he admired Leo Fender's amplifiers greatly. He said that Gibson could never compete. He considered Leo Fender to be an amplifier man, not a guitar builder. His second thing that he admired about Leo Fender was when the Fender Company sold for $13 million. Ted, being a CEO, found value in wealth. I think Ted was very much impressed with that big selling price. That would be my main thoughts.*

Ted didn't like Leo Fender. I said, "Why didn't you like Leo?" He said, "Because he wouldn't join any of our clubs." He wouldn't join any of the organizations. Ted was the head of all of those organizations. GAMA, whatever they were at the time. (Pauses) I asked Ted everything. I can tell you how they glued the fretboards on, I can tell you how they glued the tops on, and I can tell you what tops they had – here – there. John Huis was a big part of that place. He was Ted's production manager.

McCarty and Huis went hunting together, too. They spent time together outside work. *He loved John. Ted was an odd duck in a really neat way. He did not love until he loved and when he did it was fierce. You did not ask for it, you did not get it. You earned his respect, you weren't given it. Did he tell you about the day he shut the Gibson amplifier company? It wasn't profitable. He just shut it down. And they were selling a lot of amps. One day he just shut it down. He just walked in and shut it down. That was it.*

I know Gibson amps were a disappointment for him. And that's why he so admired Leo Fender, because of the Fender amps. *He said Leo was an amplifier man? That's funny.*

Since this book is partly a legacy to Ted McCarty, it will probably end up that way. If you were writing a book about Ted McCarty, that's kind of a legacy to him, what would you title the book? What do you think a good title for a book would be? *I would say, "Ted McCarty – One of the Two Founding Fathers of the Electric Guitar Business." He was one of the two founding fathers. (Pausing to reflect) Ted is the founding father of the electric, semi-acoustic, and acoustic part of our business. I would say he wasn't a founding father of Gibson Guitars; he was the founding father of what is considered the "golden age" of Gibson Guitars. He was the founding father of the golden age of Gibson Guitars – that's what he was.*

Conclusion

McCarty didn't particularly like country western music. He didn't bother with rock and roll music. His favorite tune was *"Moonlight In Vermont,"* by Johnny Smith. His favorite players were Andrés Segovia and Johnny Smith. In his youth, he preferred sports, but did dabble with acting. A musical background was not the reason McCarty and his people were able to make the world's finest electric guitars.

McCarty was born to be a C.E.O. Even in elementary school he pursued positions of responsibility such as co-editor of the elementary school newspaper. Once eligible, McCarty always worked to earn money. While in high school he was a clerk at Kroger's. He selected a co-op program in college, allowing him to earn money and a degree.

In college, he excelled in leadership roles, being named president of Alpha Tau Omega and Alpha Kappa Psi. He was selected to be a member of two of the university's most prestigious organizations, The Engineering Tribunal and Omicron Delta Kappa. At the university, he followed Uncle Pop's profession – engineering. As a commercial engineer, he also received a business education. All of these things were the things that contributed to Ted's success with electric guitars.

McCarty learned the guitar business at Wurlitzer. Then at Gibson Guitars, Ted McCarty was the right man, being in the right place, at the right time. It was the beginning of rock & roll, the beginning of the solidbody electric guitar, and he was president and C.E.O. of the finest guitar factory in the world.

For the solidbody electric guitar, McCarty disregarded the thoughts of most other guitar makers. For sure, his boss, M.H. Berlin, also had something to do with that. Unlike other prominent makers, McCarty accepted the solidbody guitar. Using his skill as an engineer, he led his engineering staff in the development of Gibson's first solidbody. McCarty holds the patent for the Les Paul solidbody guitar.

As a businessman, he

Rock guitarist Slash is credited with leading a revival in the popularity of the sunburst Les Paul in the 1980s and '90s. He, along with Eric Clapton, Jimmy Page, and Duane Allman are examples of players who kept the Les Paul model in the public eye.

knew that it was his job to assure that new guitar models were available each year for the NAMM trade shows. Ted knew about trade show introductions from attending NAMM while working for Wurlitzer. At Gibson, when the most important innovations were accomplished, McCarty led the team. He was responsible for the Les Paul Model family, the ES-335 family, Korina family, and SG family.

Business and engineering skills were only a part of the McCarty story. He was a genius when dealing with people, naturally gracious, which he learned from Berlin. The charm and politeness exhibited by both men earned extraordinary loyalty and affection from their employees at CMI and Gibson.

McCarty knew of the Gibson system of building high-quality instruments, but he found that Gibson in 1948 had gotten away from it. Using his instinct for working with people, McCarty brought the plant back to the system and he knew that people – the workers – made the company.

At Gibson, McCarty promoted John Huis to the top factory job and recruited Seth Lover for electronics and the soon-to-be patent-applied-for humbucking pickup. He supported Gibson's promotion-from-within policy with key appointments like Larry Allers as Chief Engineer and Wilbur Fuller in Gibson's first custom shop.

His skills in engineering, business, and personnel management were the foundation for McCarty's "Golden Era." But his name is not famous for those reasons; it's famous because of the guitars built by the skilled workers in the world's greatest guitar factory. The guitars were so well-designed and well-built that they were universally accepted. His instruments lured virtuoso players and master songwriters like Michael Bloomfield, Eric Clapton, Jimmy Page, and Duane Allman. Their songs and performances put the instruments in front of people, and the instruments then became known as the best.

Using market value as a guide, when comparing all the great eras, Gibson guitars from McCarty's era are the finest fretted instruments ever made.

Theodore M. McCarty:
73-Year Business Career

University of Cincinnati Engineering Coop: 1928-'33 (Class of '33)
University Book Store District Manager/Cincinnati 1933-'35
Wurlitzer Accounting Dept. trainee/Cincinnati 1936
Wurlitzer Retail Store Assistant Manager/Rochester 1937-'38
Wurlitzer Rochester Store Sales Manager/Rochester 1939
Wurlitzer Retail Stores Accounting Manager/Cincinnati 1940
Wurlitzer interim General Credit Manager/Cincinnati
Wurlitzer Corporate Department Head Real Estate & Insurance/Cincinnati
Wurlitzer Corporate Department Head/Chicago
Wurlitzer Purchasing Agent/DeKalb 1942-'44
Wurlitzer Divisional Purchasing Agent/Chicago 1944-'47
Gibson Guitar Corporation General Manager/Kalamazoo 1948-'49
Gibson Guitar Corporation President/Kalamazoo 1950-'66
American Music Conference President 1960s
Bigsby Accessories & Flex-Lite President/Kalamazoo 1966-'99
American Music Conference Director/Kalamazoo 1971-'78
Paul Reed Smith Guitars consultant/Kalamazoo 1986-'01

Your Guitar

If you own a McCarty-era Gibson made between 1948 and 1966, hopefully you've looked at it, played it, and admired it during the time that you've been reading this book. Having read the book, you know the names of many of the skilled people who created your guitar. You know how they did it. You know where they did it. *Gibson Guitars: Ted McCarty's Golden Era* is dedicated to those skilled workers. They worked at Gibson during a once-only era of guitar building.

As co-author of *The Official Vintage Guitar Price Guide*, I've been a crusader for guitar "provenance," which is nothing more than a written document that describes where a guitar has been since leaving the factory. In the best-case scenario, provenance starts with the guitar's original owner and includes the original owner's name, date of the original purchase, name of the music store purchased from, city, and the reasons for purchase. Ideally, each successive owner would be documented in the provenance book, and the same type of information would be recorded. The information would be kept in a small album in the guitar's case. A single photo of each owner would be included.

How interesting would it be if every Stradivarius violin had such provenance? In fact, some Strads *do* have this. And it's not too late to document and start a book for your guitar.

I document and maintain a provenance book for each guitar. Yes, recording provenance is a bit time-consuming. But I encourage everyone to prepare a provenance book for their guitar. In fact, part of the motivation for this book was to establish the provenance of *your guitar* when your guitar was in Kalamazoo. I'm talking about when your guitar was transformed from a large plank of wood into a fine musical instrument.

The following page is a blank designed to be used to record the provenance of your favorite vintage instrument. You could dedicate this book to that instrument and hopefully you would keep this book and the guitar close together. When the instrument finally is passed along to the next owner, they would get both the guitar and the book. They would then know the complete story.

Guitar Provenance/Dedication

Year: _____

Model: _____

Serial Number: _____

Color: _____

Attributions: _____

Provenance (Ownership History): _____

_____

_____

_____

_____

_____

_____

_____

_____

_____

Photo or additional text:

ACKNOWLEDGMENTS

Allers, Ron – Gibson retiree

Andrews, Thomas B. – Kalamazoo Symphony Orchestra

Ash, Jerry – Sam Ash Music

Ash, Sammy – Sam Ash Music

Barnes, Darrah – Kalamazoo Gazette

Berfield, Laura – Alpha Tau Omega

Bradford, Linda – Gibson retiree

Bradford, Vi – Gibson retiree

Carter, Walter – Author and historian

Charkowski, Helen – Gibson retiree

Davis, Susan McCarty – McCarty family

Del Fiorentino, Dan – NAMM / AMC

Deurloo, Jim – Heritage Guitars

Duncan, Seymour W. - Foreword

Eberts, Randell – Kalamazoo Rotary Club

Eaddy, Rebecca – Paul Reed Smith Guitars

Farrell, James – Gibson retiree

Farrell, Tom – Gibson retiree

Ferraro, Sharon – City of Kalamazoo

Friar, Hubie – Gibson retiree

Friar, Jacqueline – Gibson retiree

Fuller, Wilbur – Gibson retiree

Galloway, Caroline – Gibson Guitar Corporation

Grace, Kevin – University of Cincinnati

Greenwood, Alan – Vintage Guitar magazine

Hanchett, James – Gibson retiree

Hemgesberg, Nora - Titlebond

Hill, Huber – Gibson retiree

Hembree, Jane Wait – First-draft edit

Hoogenboom, Mary Lou – Gibson retiree

Hutchins, Jim – Gibson Kalamazoo & Nashville

Johnston, Harriet – Gibson retiree

Kornblum, Gene – St. Louis Music

Kuhn, Judy McCarty – McCarty family

Lamb, Marvin – Heritage Guitars

Lommen, Dana – Guitarpatents

Majeski, Brian – The Music Trades

Majeski, John Jr. – The Music Trades

McConackie, Merrill 'Mac" – Gibson retiree

Meeker, Penny – Layout & Art

Meeker, Ward – Edit

Moats, J.P. – Heritage Guitars

BIBLIOGRAPHY

BOOKS

Bacon, Tony, and Paul Day. *The Gibson Les Paul Book*. San Francisco: GPI Books, 1993.

Bellson, Julius. *The Gibson Story*. Kalamazoo: Julius Bellson, 1973.

Burrluck, Dave. *The PRS Guitar Book*. London: Balfon Books, 1999.

Carter, Walter. *Epiphone: The Complete History*. Milwaukee: Hal Leonard Corporation, 1995.

Carter, Walter. *Gibson Guitars: 100 Years of an American Icon*. Los Angeles: General Publishing Group, 1994.

Duchossoir, Andre R., *Gibson Electrics: Volume 1*. Milwaukee: Hal Leonard Publishing Corporation, 1991.

Dunbar, Willis F., *Kalamazoo and how it grew*. Kalamazoo: Western Michigan University, 1959.

Faber, Toby. *Stradivari's Genius*. New York: Random House. 2004.

Greenwood, Alan. *The Official Vintage Guitar magazine Price Guide: Volume 1*. Bismarck: Vintage Guitar Books, 1991.

Greenwood, Alan. *The Official Vintage Guitar magazine Price Guide: 1993 Edition*. Bismarck: Vintage Guitar Books, 1993.

Greenwood, Alan. *The Official Vintage Guitar magazine Price Guide: Winter/Spring 1995 Edition*. Bismarck: Vintage Guitar Books, 1994.

Greenwood, Alan. *The Official Vintage Guitar magazine Price Guide: 5th Edition*. Bismarck: Vintage Guitar Books, 1996.

Greenwood, Alan. *The Official Vintage Guitar magazine Price Guide: 6th Edition.* Bismarck: Vintage Guitar Books, 1998.

Greenwood, Alan, and Gil Hembree. *The Official Vintage Guitar magazine Price Guide: 2001.* Bismarck: Vintage Guitar Books, 2000.

Greenwood, Alan, and Gil Hembree. *The Official Vintage Guitar magazine Price Guide: 2002.* Bismarck: Vintage Guitar Books, 2001.

Greenwood, Alan, and Gil Hembree. *The Official Vintage Guitar magazine Price Guide: 2003.* Bismarck: Vintage Guitar Books, 2002.

Greenwood, Alan, and Gil Hembree. *The Official Vintage Guitar magazine Price Guide: 2004.* Bismarck: Vintage Guitar Books, 2003.

Greenwood, Alan, and Gil Hembree. *The Official Vintage Guitar magazine Price Guide: 2005.* Bismarck: Vintage Guitar Books, 2004.

Greenwood, Alan, and Gil Hembree. *The Official Vintage Guitar magazine Price Guide: 2006.* Bismarck: Vintage Guitar Books, 2005.

Greenwood, Alan, and Gil Hembree. *The Official Vintage Guitar magazine Price Guide: 2007.* Bismarck: Vintage Guitar Books, 2006.

Gruhn, George, and Walter Carter. *Acoustic Guitars and Other Fretted Instruments: A Photographic History.* San Francisco: GPI Books, 1993.

Gruhn, George, and Walter Carter. *Electric Guitars and Basses: A Photographic History.* San Francisco: GPI Books, 1994.

Gruhn, George, and Walter Carter. *Gruhn's Guide to Vintage Guitars.* San Francisco: Miller Freeman Books, 1999.

Iwanade, Yasuhiko. *The Beauty of the 'Burst.* Tokyo: Rittor Music Inc., 1998.

J.T.G. Gibson Shipping Totals 1948 – 1979. J.T.G., 1992.

Regional History Reprints. *Early History of Kalamazoo.* L'Anse: Regional History Reprints, 2005.

Rittor Music, Inc. *The Gibson.* Tokyo: Rittor Music Inc., 1996.

Smith, Richard R. *Fender: The Sound Heard 'Round the World.* Fullerton: Garfish Publishing Co., 1995.

Teagle, John, and John Sprung. *Fender Amps: The First Fifty Years.* Milwaukee:Hal Leonard Corporation, 1995.

Massie, Larry B., and Peter J. Schmitt. *Kalamazoo: The Place Behind the Product*s. Kalamazoo: Windsor Publications, 1981.

Pittman, Aspen. *The Tube Amp Book: Volume 3.* Sylmar, GT Electronics, 1991.

Washburn, Jim, and Richard Johnston. *Martin Guitars: An Illustrated Celebration of America's Premier Guitarmaker.* Emmaus: Rodale Press, 1997.

Wheeler, Tom. *American Guitars: An Illustrated History.* New York: HarperCollins, 1992.

Wheeler, Tom. *The Stratocaster Chronicles.* Milwaukee: Hal Leonard, 2004.

Whitford, Eldon, David Vinopal, and Dan Erlewine. *Gibson's Fabulous Flat-Top Guitars: An Illustrated History & Guide.* San Francisco: Miller Freeman Books, 1994.

INTERVIEWS

Allers, Ron. Telephone interview. 11 May 2006.

Ash, Jerry. Telephone interview. 10 May 2006.

Bradford, Linda. Personal interview. 21 August 1999.

Bradford, Viola. Telephone interview. 3 August 2001.

Charkowski, Helen. Personal interview. 1 October 2001.

Charkowski, Helen. Telephone interview. 25 July 2001.

Davis, Susan McCarty. Telephone interview. 19 September 2005.

Deurloo, Jim. Telephone interview. 16 September 2005.

Farrell, James 26 September 2001.

Friar, Hubert. Telephone interview. 6 September 2005.

Friar, Jacqueline Fergusson. Telephone interview. 7 September 2005.

Fuller, Wilbur. Personal interview. 21 August 1999.

Fuller, Wilbur. Telephone interview. 28 April 2001.

Fuller, Wilbur. Personal interview. 10 May 2001.

Fuller, Wilbur. Telephone interview. 23 July 2001.

Fuller, Wilbur. Telephone interview. 1 August 2001.

Hanchett, Jim. Personal interview. 21 August 1999.

Hill, Huber. Personal interview. 30 September 2001.

Hoogenboom, Mary Lou. Personal interview. 30 September 2001.

Johnston, Harriet. Personal interview. 30 September 2001.

Knowlton, Bob. Personal interview. 21 August 1999.

Kornblum, Eugene. Telephone interview. 18 May 2006.

Lamb, Marv. Telephone interview. 30 August 2005.

McCarty, Ted. Pre-recorded interview. 6 November 1995.

McCarty, Ted. Telephone interview. 5 May 1999.

McCarty, Ted. Telephone interview. 12 August 1999.

McCarty, Ted. Personal interview. 21 August 1999.

McCarty, Ted. Personal interview. 23 October 1999.

McCarty, Ted. Personal interview. 13 November 1999.

McCarty, Ted. Personal interview. 6 May 2000.

McConacki, Merrill 'Mac'. Telephone interview. 29 July 2006.

Majeski, John Jr. Telephone interview. 14 October 2005.

Moats, JP. Personal interview, 30 September 2002

Moats, JP. Telephone interview. 24 August 2005.

Paul, Les. Personal interview. 20 June 2002.

Shelven, Joyce. Telephone interview. 24 July 2001.

Sherrill, Mable. Telephone interview. 28 July 2005.

Sherrill, Mable. Telephone interview. 15 September 2005.

Smith, Paul. Personal interview. 23 April 2006

Van Noorloos, Clara. Personal interview. 20 September, 2002.

Vette, Maxine. Personal interview. 21 August 1999.

Walton, Neal. Personal interview. 20 September 2002

Walton, Neal. Telephone interview. 24 July 2001

Walton, Neal. Telephone interview. 25 July 2001

Wheeler, Tom. Telephone interview. 30 June 2006.

Williams, Bernice. Personal interview. 21 August 1999.

[Misc. follow-up conversations are not included.]

LETTERS

Bradford, Viola. Plant Layout. 17 October 2001.

Davis, Susan McCarty. Photos. 12 July 2006.

Hill, Huber. Plant Layout. 12 October 2001.

Fuller, Wilbur. Plant Layout. 18 October 2001.

Fuller, Wilbur. The Gibson Customs Department. 22 August 2005.

Hoogenboom, Mary Lou. Plant Layout. 16 October 2001.

Johnston, Harriet. Plant Layout. 16 October 2001.

Shelven, Joyce. Plant Layout. 19 October 2001.

Shelven, Joyce. Photos. 18 July 2006.

Walton, Neal. Plant Layout. 17 October 2001.

MAGAZINES

"2005 The Guitar Market: A Look Back – Pioneer Ted McCarty And The Humbucking Pickup." The Music Trades October 2005. 120.

"Amplifier – Every Need – Gibson, Inc." International Musician Nov. 1955: 7.

Dronge, Alfred. "A Million Is Still A Lot of Guitars." PTM June 1968: 41.

"Gibson Holds Dealer Convention." The Music Trades July 1950. 22.

Hembree, Gil. "50 Years of Crunchy Clean Dirt." Vintage Guitar magazine Mar. 2005: 46.

Hembree, Gil. "Dealer News: Sam Ash Music." Vintage Guitar magazine Sep. 2003: 44.

Hembree, Gil. "Gibson's Humbucker Test Guitar: From a Kalamazoo Closet." Vintage Guitar magazine Nov. 1999: 106.

Hembree, Gil. "Les Paul: Birth of a Guitar Icon." Vintage Guitar magazine Nov. 2002. 76.

Hembree, Gil. "Ted McCarty's Electric Uke: By Request of Arthur Godfrey." Vintage Guitar magazine Apr. 2000: 54

Hembree, Gil. "Ted McCarty: Musical Pioneer, Part 1." Vintage Guitar magazine July 2001: 78.

Hembree, Gil. "Ted McCarty: Musical Pioneer, Part 2: The Gibson Years." <u>Vintage Guitar magazine</u> Aug. 2001: 80.

Hembree, Gil. "Ted McCarty: Musical Pioneer, Part 3: Bigsby and Paul Reed Smith." <u>Vintage Guitar magazine</u> Sep. 2001: 76.

Hembree, Gil. "The Gibson Kalamazoo Award." <u>Vintage Guitar magazine</u> Sep. 2002: 106.

Hembree, Gil. "The World's Greatest Guitar Factory: A Historical Primer On Gibson's Kalamazoo Factory." <u>Vintage Guitar magazine</u> July 2002: 26.

Krisher, Donald, and Claude T. Reo. "The Undergraduates / Delta Lambda / Alpha Tau Omega / Cincinnati." <u>The Palm Vol. 53</u>, Issue 4 April 1933: 183

Lover, Seth E. "Humbucking Pickups: Their History / Their Function." <u>Guitar Player Magazine</u> March 1977: 30.

Moseley, Willie G. "Ted McCarty: I'm Not a Musician." <u>Vintage Guitar magazine</u> April 1999.

"Three of a kind." <u>Down Beat</u> August 1964. 2.

Van Buren, Mike. "Guitar Town: Kalamazoo, Julius Bellson and the Gibson Heritage." <u>Michigan History</u> Sep./Oct. 1990: 24.

NEWSPAPERS

Kalsnes, Lynett A. "Local Country Music Legend Rem Wall Dies." <u>Kalamazoo Gazette</u>.

Thomas, Craig A., and Linda Mah, "Guitar Innovator Honored." <u>Kalamazoo Gazette</u>.

"McCarty Resigns From Gibson Co." <u>Kalamazoo Gazette</u> 1966.

"Performer Rem Wall, A Gibson Employee, Gives Guitar A Final Test." <u>Kalamazoo Gazette</u> 23 Feb. 1964: 2:15.

Be Inducted Into Rock Walk of Fame." <u>Kalamazoo Gazette</u>.

OTHER/CATALOGS

Departmental Seniority List (assumed late 1959) Gibson, Inc., United Steel Workers.

Departmental Seniority List June 1, 1961, Gibson, Inc., United Steel Workers, 1961.

Departmental Seniority List Nov. 15, 1965, Gibson, Inc., United Steel Workers, 1965.

Departmental Seniority List April 18, 1966, Gibson, Inc., United Steel Workers, 1966.

Epiphone. Gibson, Inc., 1963.

Epiphone. Gibson, Inc., 1965.

Gibson Electric Guitars and Amplifiers. Gibson, Inc., 1957.

Gibson Guitars and Amplifiers (Price List). Gibson, Inc., 15 July 1957.

Gibson Electric Guitars and Amplifiers. Gibson, Inc., May 1960.

Gibson Electric Guitars and Amplifiers 1962. Gibson, Inc., May 1961.

Gibson Electric Guitars. Gibson, Inc., 1964.

Gibson Suggested Retail Prices. Gibson, Inc., 1964.

Gibson Electric Guitars. Gibson, Inc., 1966.

Good Violins: Catalogue No. 1, The Rudolph Wurlitzer Company, New York, 1938.

Pittsburgh People. August 1953.

The Gibson Amplifier, Gibson, Inc., June 1970.

The Gibson Amplifier, Gibson, Inc., October 1970.

The Gibson Amplifier, Gibson, Inc., February 1971.

The Gibson Amplifier, Gibson, Inc., June 1971.

The Gibson Amplifier, Gibson, Inc., November 1971.

The Gibson Amplifier, Gibson, Inc., December 1971-January 1972.

The Gibson Amplifier, Gibson, Inc., August-September-October 1972.

The Gibson Amplifier, Gibson, Inc., January-February-March 1973.

The Gibson Amplifier, Gibson, Inc., July-August-September 1973.

The Gibson Amplifier, Gibson, Inc., October-November-December 1973.

The Gibson Amplifier, Gibson, Inc., December-January 1974-1975.

The Gibson Amplifier, Gibson, Inc., July-August-September 1974.

The Gibson Amplifier, Gibson, Inc., February-March-April 1975.

The Gibson Amplifier, Gibson, Inc., May-June 1975.

The Gibson Amplifier, Gibson, Inc., July-August 1975.

The Gibson Amplifier, Gibson, Inc., May-June 1976.

The Cincinnatian of '30, University of Cincinnati, Cincinnati, 1930

The Cincinnatian of '32, University of Cincinnati, Cincinnati, 1932

The Purchaser's Guide to the Music Industries. New York, The Music Trades, 1965

The Purchaser's Guide to the Music Industries. New York, The Music Trades, 1966

The Purchaser's Guide to the Music Industries. New York, The Music Trades, 2005

You And Your Job, Gibson, Inc., c. 1953.

NEWS CONFERENCE

Smith, Paul. Paul Reed Smith 20th Anniversary Press Conference, 21 January 2005, NAMM Anaheim, CA.

WEB SITE

American Music Conference. "AMC Thanks Honorary Lifetime Directors". 2005. www. amc-music.org/AMCNews/newsletterFa01/lifetimedir.html .

Associated Press. "Ted McCarty / Guitar Pioneer." 2001. http://starbulletin. Com/2001/04/05/news/obits.html.

Carter, Walter. "Adventures in Achieves – Gibson 1957." October 1997. www.gibson.com/ magazines/amplifier/1997/10/archives.html .

Detroit News. "McCarty: Key Figure in Development of the Electric Guitar, Dies at 91." 2001. www/detnews.com/2001/obituaries/0104/-208142.htm .

Gibson Internet Services. "Farewell Ted McCarty." 2001. www.gibson.com/whatsnew/

pressrelease/2001/apr10a.html .

"Heritage Guitars – Owners". www.heritageguitar.com/company/owners.htm .

Jeska, Eric Foster. "A History of the Shakespeare Co." 1997. www.antiquelures.com/Shake-history.html .

Larson, Catherine. "Northside Neighborhood." Local History. Kalamazoo Public Library. March 2005. www.kpl.gov/collections/LocalHistory .

Rowe, Bob. "Rem Wall: A Legend and a Friend. September 2005. www.visioncouncil. org/bobrowe.bobrem.htm. .

CREDITS

INDEX

337

NOTES

ABOUT THE AUTHOR

Gil Hembree is the co-author of the best-selling The Official Vintage Guitar Price Guide, *published by* Vintage Guitar *magazine. Hembree began collecting guitars in 1966 as a college student working at Kitt's Music in Washington, D.C. He holds a BSBA from American University and an MBA from Midwestern State University. He worked for General Motors Corporation in Flint and Detroit, Michigan for over 30 years as a Financial Administrator and Supervisor of Corporate Audit. During that time he played music semi-professionally and he has continued collecting vintage guitars and amps. Since 1992 he has written for several guitar publications and he is a contributing writer and a columnist ("401K Guitars") for* Vintage Guitar *magazine. Gil and his wife Jane live in Austin, Texas.*